David Schofield worked for leading American and European investment banks on Wall Street, in Frankfurt and in the City of London for fourteen years. He was closely involved professionally in the events which surrounded the Asian financial collapse in 1997. He lives in London with his wife and two children.

DAVID SCHOFIELD

THE PEGASUS FORUM

SIMON & SCHUSTER
A VIACOM COMPANY

for Donna

who married a banker

and ended up with an author

First published in Great Britain by Simon & Schuster UK Ltd, 2001
A Viacom company

1 3 5 7 9 10 8 6 4 2

Simon & Schuster UK Ltd
Africa House
64–78 Kingsway
London WC2B 6AH

Simon & Schuster Australia
Sydney

A CIP catalogue record for this book is available from the British Library

ISBN Hardback: 0-7432-0967-2
ISBN Trade paperback: 0-7434-1506-X

This book is a work of fiction. Names, characters, places and incidents are
either a product of the author's imagination or are used fictitiously. Any
resemblance to actual people living or dead, events or locales is entirely
coincidental.

Typeset by Palimpsest Book Production Limited,
Polmont, Stirlingshire

Printed and bound in Great Britain by
The Bath Press, Bath

Acknowledgements

I, alone, am not to blame for this.

Many others stand accountable, not the least of which is my wife Donna, who not only bolstered my efforts with patience, love and a twisted imagination, but also encouraged me to allow others to read it.

Of these, Michael Sissons and James Gill at PFD, and John Jarrold and Ian Chapman at Simon & Schuster UK Ltd, are owed a particular debt of gratitude for their enthusiasm, insight, guidance and expertise. (And a cheque or two.)

Topical thanks are especially due to my brother, Dr Roger Schofield, and his wife Dr Niki Salt, for their knowledge of all things gory and medical; to Andrew and Ellen Hauptman for putting aside politeness in favour of critical objectivity (and for lending me a laptop at a critical moment); and to James Turner, a barrister with a sense of humour who gives a fig.

More formal thanks are due to Palgrave Publishers Ltd, for their kind permission to quote from *The Collected Writings of John Maynard Keynes*; to Katheryn Ayres at the Cambridge University Faculty of Mathematics for putting me right on a thing or two; and to Mark Devereux at Olswang for guiding me through the world of publishing contracts.

More general thanks are due to my parents, Margaret and Derek Schofield, for the games of Lexicon and for not appearing *too* worried at the antics of a wayward son; to Salomon Brothers, the best firm in the world, for starting me in the crazy business of the markets in the first place; to Ed Sherman, who, with five children of his own to take care of has always found time to keep me on the straight and narrow; to Ian and Rachel Entwisle for their encouragement and for introducing me to the delights of the Oriental Club; and to my daughters Isabella and Julia, for allowing me to play with their computer. (I promise I'll write one with pictures soon.)

'Lenin was right. There is no subtler, no surer means of overturning the existing basis of society than to debauch the currency. The process engages all the hidden forces of economic law on the side of destruction, and does it in a manner which not one man in a million is able to diagnose.'

John Maynard Keynes,
The Economic Consequences of the Peace (1919)

PROLOGUE

6 January 2002

'HEY ANNIE! GREAT NEWS. KOREA'S GETTING TOTALLY trashed.'

'Have you seen my conditioner?'

'The won's off five per cent against the dollar already this morning.'

'And my razor? Where's my goddamn razor?'

'Stocks are limit down, and looks like the bonds are getting crushed too.'

'Look. I need my razor. Can't go to the Mansion House dinner with hairy legs. Can I borrow yours?'

'Sure, sure. Whatever. Are you listening to me? Come in here. It's on CNBC. Eight more Indonesian banks have gone *and* Pusan Steel. This is like a bloody dream.'

'Sell me another two hundred million of the new Korea Global will you? Where is it now?'

'I'm not sure. I think it's in the cabinet above the washbasin. But it could be in the shower.'

'Do it now Cameron. Two hundred million dollars. Korea thirty year. At market.'

Cameron Dodds was sitting naked on his bed watching TV. He picked up the nearest phone and dialled a number in New York. Thirty seconds of mumbled conversation and he was through.

'You're done, Annie. Salomon took the lot. It's out to 1500 over.'

'No, Cameron! It's *not* there. Could it be in the guest bathroom? Will you have a look for me, honey?'

'We interrupt this broadcast to take you straight over to the Bank of England in the City of London, from where the Prime Minister is about to address the nation. Julia Mathieson is at the scene. Julia, do you have a sense of what the Prime Minister is about to tell us?'

'Well, Michael, it's difficult to say at this stage. What I can tell you is that the Chancellor of the Exchequer and the Governor of the Bank of England are here too, as you can see behind me at the podium, and this is being organized along the lines of a press briefing. I have to say it really does remind me of the set-up for those status reports we used to get during the war in Kosovo.'

'There have been many rumours of late that the UK banking system is now beginning to suffer in the wake of the financial meltdown in the Far East. Could this address be related to that?'

'Well, we certainly shouldn't rule it out. We've already had that major bank failure in Germany just last week, and the US markets have been something of a roller-coaster in recent weeks. There is an awful lot of nervousness at the moment, and it wouldn't take much to tip things over the edge. Of course we all know what has happened in South East Asia over the last three months, and all eyes are on the fall-out of that over here. I wouldn't be surprised if one of the smaller merchant banks or investment banks has got itself into trouble along the lines of Barings a few years ago. They're all heavily exposed to the Far East. Of course, the impact of Barings was fairly limited, but I imagine . . .'

'Julia, I'm sorry to interrupt but we're cutting across to the Prime Minister, who has just risen.'

'Annie, quick!' he called into the bathroom next door. 'The PM's on the box, addressing the nation from the City. Looks like something big.' Annie van Aalst, dripping wet and dressed in only a small towel, ran into the room and jumped, knees first, on to the bed alongside Dodds.

'It'd better be something big if they make me cut short my shower for it,' she laughed.

'Ssh! He's starting.'

The familiar features of the Prime Minister filled the screen. He looked grim. Not 'statesman-grim', from the colour chart of expressions available to global politicians, which he reserved for responding to news of mudslides and earthquakes, but stern and exhausted. Like he'd been up all night trying to avert a crisis. In vain.

'Ladies and gentlemen, I have taken the unusual step of addressing you this evening to inform you of a situation of the utmost gravity which affects us all.

'The Governor of the Bank of England, after lengthy consultations with myself, the Chancellor of the Exchequer and other policy advisers, has tonight telephoned the chairmen of NorthWest Commercial Bank, Langley's Bank and the National Bank of Great Britain. He has ordered them to suspend all operations and to close their doors until further notice. These are the three largest high street banks in this country, and they are no longer viable. They have acted irresponsibly, invested unwisely and largely misled the regulators as to the extent of their problems, problems which arose as a direct and rapid result of the chaos which has torn apart the economies of the countries of the Pacific Rim. The losses they have incurred are enormous, so huge in fact that these banks will most likely cease to exist in their current form.

'This may seem a harsh step to take, but the decision has not been reached lightly. It is anticipated at this stage that the smaller institutions, the building societies and the insurance companies, can continue to operate, and we hope that, by dint of our prompt action in removing the weakest links in the chain, the soundness of the overall structure will be maintained. But that rather depends on the markets' reaction tomorrow and on the behaviour of you, the general public.

'This is why I address you tonight, in an attempt to promote an orderly reaction to this catastrophe. We must maintain confidence in the overall integrity of our national banking system, and any stampede to withdraw funds on a mass basis would be simply cataclysmic. I urge you all to leave your money where it is. It is safe. You have my word. Those of you who have accounts with the affected banks will be contacted in due course and the government will do its best to protect the interests of those savers. Alternative arrangements will be made. We are all in much more danger if you attempt to withdraw your money, or to hide it under the proverbial mattress. We all have our financial future to consider. Our pensions, our savings, the fundamental ability of our society to function as normal, could be endangered if we experience a disorderly conclusion to this episode.

'You may ask the question "why does the government not intervene to bail these banks out?" and it would be a valid question. After all, that is what the French and the Scandinavians, and indeed even the Americans have done in the past during lesser crises. Well, I will give you the answer. Ladies and gentlemen, we live in a free market.'

The voice of the Prime Minister droned earnestly in the background as Dodds lowered the volume slightly.

'Jesus Christ, Annie. The banking system is collapsing! I can't believe it. What is happening?'

'It's very simple, Cameron dear. The delicate house of cards we like to call our world is about to come tumbling down. That is exactly what we set out to achieve. Our job is pretty much done.'

'But I never thought it would happen so quickly! I can't believe it's reached the UK already. Can't we stop it now? What the hell should we do?'

'Well, darling, if you weren't clever enough to have done it already, I suggest you take your honey, and plenty of money, and wrap it all up in as many five-pound notes as you can lay your hands on. Then you should either go down to any bank you can find open, remembering to avoid the rioters, looters and panic-stricken hordes on the street corners, especially the shaven-headed anarchists with dogs on string, and buy gold. Or alternatively you could buy a beautiful pea-green boat and sail off looking for Bong-trees with me.'

Cameron Dodds smiled and rolled over towards her. He yanked at the damp towel which enveloped her. 'You are such a poet, Miss van Aalst, in everything you turn your hand to.' He began to dab with his finger tip at the beads of water which had traced a path from her dripping hair all the way down to her stomach. 'Now, if you will humour an illiterate, uneducated bond trader for a second, remind me of how exactly the story goes from here?'

'Well, if I'm not much mistaken, although I don't see a small guitar anywhere, the next line would sound so much better coming from you. Now, repeat after me . . .'

At around the same time, a 1965 Austin Cambridge sputtered down an Oxfordshire lane in the rain and nosed through the wrought-iron gates of a large private estate. The security guard in his painted sentry box waved it through with a nod and without the formalities required of unfamiliar visitors. The lone occupant of the car did not deviate his gaze to acknowledge the guard, nor did he slow down as he continued down the drive the further mile or so to the imposing house he could now see through the sideways rain, the Cotswold stone glowing slightly in a stray beam of low, late-afternoon sunlight.

He pulled up on the gravel approach and reversed into his usual spot next to the gardener's tool shed. He didn't have much time today – he couldn't be late for his meeting with the Americans, today of all days – but he had to come as usual. He couldn't miss it. Cap pulled down against the rain, he ran the twenty feet or so to the columned portico and up the few steps into the entrance hall, dripping water on to the polished floor as he squeaked his way to the lift. The carriage clock on the carved mantelpiece chimed five as he slid open the old brass, scissor-action lift guard and rode up to the third floor. He cursed to himself – it had taken him half an hour to get there from Oxford, which meant he could only stay for about twenty minutes if he was to get back in time.

A nurse smiled at him as he emerged from the lift.

'Hello, Professor. We're a bit late today, aren't we? She's up, but still in her room. Not a good day, I'm afraid.'

He ignored her and walked down the landing to the last doorway. He paused outside the polished oak door before slowly turning the brass knob and walking in without knocking.

The curtains were open and no lights were on. A fire burned in the hearth, catching the silver frames of a dozen or so old photographs clustered on the thick brocade cloth draped over a round table in the corner. The familiar, but tinny sounds of some well-known forties dance tunes emerged barely from an old record player next to the bed, and a solitary figure sat by the window, staring blankly into the waning twilight from her wicker-backed wheelchair. She didn't look round as her visitor walked in and approached her. He bent over and kissed her on the cheek from behind, grasping the handles of the wheelchair to turn her round to face the room.

She was a striking woman, silver hair immaculately coiffed, erect and proud of posture despite the wheelchair, and elegantly dressed. Cashmere shawl, Burberry travelling rug over her lap, her wrinkled, bony fingers fastidiously manicured to set off the outsized Victorian brilliant-cut emerald on her left hand. She stared out into the gloom of her surroundings and said nothing. Her visitor sat directly in her gaze and answered her look challengingly. The look of one who knows what to expect. Together they sat for an eternity, saying nothing, not attempting to say anything, just staring unquestioningly across the darkened room in silent communion. Her visitor leaned forward to grasp her hand, and squeezed it gently. A whisper of a smile flickered at the corner of her mouth, and she slowly turned her head to gaze at an old black and white picture on the table beside her. A vibrant young woman, a handsome older man, an ecstatic young boy about to be swung into the air on a windswept Cape Cod beach.

The reverie was finally shattered by the clattering of the drugs trolley being pushed unceremoniously into the room.

'OK darlin', time for candy,' came the jolly voice of the unwelcome intrusion, a large Jamaican orderly. 'Open wide, now – it happy hour in this bar from now on.'

Professor Wallace Bradley rose silently from his chintz armchair and turned his back on the old lady opposite without a wave or a smile before leaving abruptly and rushing off into the evening rain. He felt a tremendous sense of relief. He too had heard the news on the car radio.

He had listened to the Prime Minister's speech, but he could only imagine the rage which was about to be unleashed on the streets of Britain. That would be a regrettable side-effect, but unavoidable. Today, at the age of fifty-four, he felt he was finally beginning to put matters to rights. He was no longer helpless, as he had been all those years ago. He was about to secure his revenge, and he relished the pettiness, the simplicity of that thought. There was no other way of putting it, no intellectual, philosophical or even metaphysical justification or interpretation for the chain of events he and his colleagues were responsible for. Nor for the climax to everything which was now only a matter of days away. It was revenge, pure and simple.

PART 1

Bellerephon

'The peculiar essence of our banking system is an unprecedented trust between man and man, and when that trust is much weakened by hidden causes, a small accident may greatly hurt it, and a great accident for a moment may almost destroy it.'

Walter Bagehot, *Lombard Street:*
A Description of the Money Markets (1873)

CHAPTER 1

December 2001

CHUAN HAD WORKED FOR THE BANGKOK METROPOLITAN Postal Service all his life, but had never before delivered a bomb.

He set off in his little *tuk-tuk*, a modified version of the ubiquitous three-wheeled vehicles used by local taxi drivers, from the General Post Office on the Charoen Krung Road at five a.m. sharp. He chose to start so early to avoid the horrors of the rush hour traffic which would begin to build up around six a.m. and would continue unabated until around nine p.m. that evening. An hour's head start on the masses would get him home in time to cook lunch for his wife and to rest before the afternoon's grind of sorting tomorrow's mail. He enjoyed his mornings, and the breeze coming off the Chao Phraya river where Bangkok's main Post Office was located, blew straight into the open cab of his *tuk-tuk* – a welcome relief from the impressive humidity already building before the million or so commuters and their cars and trains began swarming into the world's hottest city. His life had been one of simple demands, responsibilities and pleasures which he accepted as his lot and never grumbled in earnest. He had graduated several years before from the pedestrian beats of suburbia to the commercial rounds, buzzing around the financial district in his van, delivering stacks of mail to the glass palaces of the new Tiger potentates.

Two hours later, Bangkok's principal business district would be an impenetrable log jam of cars, but at this hour he turned unimpeded into Surawong road, a dense mass of corporate high-rise muscle-power, oblivious to the sinister parcel he carried. It sat in his sack buried amongst the rest of that day's load, but didn't make a sound. No ticking, no suspiciously shaped lumps or bumps, just a slim, white business envelope, heavy quality, lined with tissue, bearing the corporate crest of its sender on its reverse, and the unlucky recipient's name and address on its face. No one examining this letter would guess the concealed power of its contents. If someone had told Chuan that this letter contained a bomb, he would have dismissed it with the chuckle he reserved for the foolish. How could it be possible for such a slender package to contain such a destructive payload? Surely no such technology exists, even today, to send a bomb of such a size. Was it possible to roll out Semtex so thin that one could slide it into an envelope? And what about fuses and detonators? Could it be triggered in a chemical reaction released by the envelope's adhesive? And besides, the sender's details were printed in black and white above the seal. What terrorist would commit such a folly?

He coasted up to the pavement opposite the enormous glass double doors of his first drop. A pale-blue flag fluttered outside on a horizontal pole, the red graphic of a butterfly in flight proclaiming these to be the national headquarters of Pee Seuar Land Holdings, the largest and most successful property developer in Thailand, responsible for the construction not only of around half of the countless steel and glass office towers Chuan could see from the cab of his *tuk-tuk*, but also for around 450,000 private homes scattered around the metropolitan Bangkok area. He walked up to the building's entrance carrying the bundle of mail, and the twenty-foot glass doors glided open automatically as he approached. Twenty-four-hour security was common in these times of corporate piracy, but no security guard, however vigilant, and no electronic devices, however sophisticated, could have detected the weapon Chuan carried cheerfully concealed in the stack of paper under his arm. He ambled across the polished granite floor of the enormous, airy atrium and dropped the pile on the reception desk under the nose of the waiting guard.

'More than normal today,' smiled Chuan, keen to share some camaraderie with a fellow early-riser.

'Let's hope they're all cheques and contracts of sale,' moaned the old guard, 'otherwise we'll all be out of a job if I believe the gossip around here.'

'Never you mind worrying about that, old friend. You just get on with your guarding and let Mr Chumsai worry about the business. He would never let anything happen to his people. He is an honourable man, and still remembers his humble beginnings.'

'I'm sure you're right, Chuan my friend, and I will never let anything happen to him!'

With that, the old guard sliced open the stack of mail and began sorting the letters by department. He still had two hours before the first workers would arrive, but he liked to be ready in good time. Chuan left him to it with a wave, and shuffled back to his van to continue the morning's calls.

The bomb would not go off until the next day, and Chuan would never have an inkling that he had been responsible for delivering it. Nor would anyone ever try to find out how it had managed to slip through security. But it would cause many thousands of deaths and be indirectly responsible for suffering on a scale Chuan would never have dreamed possible.

An hour later, the security guard had finished his task, and took the carefully sorted letters over to the messenger boys' room behind the reception area. They would handle the general deliveries throughout the building that morning, but he would personally see to it that Mr Chumsai's letter was on his desk when the great man arrived at the office that morning. So he took the envelope marked 'HIGHLY CONFIDENTIAL – For the Personal and Private Attention of Mr P.L. Chumsai, Chairman and Chief Executive Officer, Pee Seuar Land Holdings', and rode with it in the elevator to the thirty-seventh floor, where he bypassed the PA's ante-room and placed it with reverence in the personal in-tray of Asia's most high-profile property tycoon. As **it happened, the said tycoon had been** away whoring in Manila that weekend and wouldn't be back until the next day, but bombs of this particular design do not degrade too quickly. And the fuse had been set for a much longer time-frame than is normal in the world of high explosives.

Ten thousand miles away and at around the same time a most unusual meeting was taking place in London, just off Oxford Street. Stratford Place is an anonymous cul-de-sac opposite Bond Street tube station, but is known to cab drivers for its small collection of minor African embassies, corporate headquarters, and especially Stratford House, the imposing Regency premises of the Oriental Club. Well away from the more high-profile circuit of Gentlemen's clubs of St James's and Pall Mall, the Oriental Club was a discreet outpost of genteel civility, a disapproving uncle frowning down on the teenage Burger Kings, mega-music stores and nylon emporiums of Europe's busiest retail thoroughfare a few yards away. Most of its members, ageing clergy, minor diplomats and an assortment of semi-retired importers, all with some kind of link to the Far East, were vaguely embarrassed by its location. They would furtively scurry along Oxford Street, the fifty yards or so from Bond Street station, heads down and overcoat collars up, before ducking into Stratford Place with the relief of a bishop emerging unnoticed from an adult cinema.

But in the club's library that evening, set up for a private dinner behind closed doors, there was an altogether different group assembled. Their host had not arrived by tube, for, as a country member, he would generally lodge at the club on his frequent visits to London from Oxford, and had been there for several days in preparation for this evening. The eight guests who were converging on Stratford Place that evening had mostly travelled from rather more distant origins, however, and had arrived in taxis directly from Gatwick, Heathrow or their Park Lane hotels. One of them, the only woman present, had arrived at Biggin Hill from Grand Cayman in a private Gulfstream V, and taken a helicopter to Battersea Heliport from where a chauffeur-driven Jaguar had whisked her straight to the club.

Only three of the diners that evening were based in London. One of them had ridden his Harley-Davidson across town in the rain from the offices of his bank in Broadgate Circle. The chrome-laden machine now stood defiantly outside the grand, classical-fronted mansion under the watchful eye of the commissionaire, now a fifty-pound note richer. The owner's leathers hung incongruously in the basement cloakroom, alongside the capes and canes of the club's more conventional visitors that evening.

One of the other London residents had set off a little earlier under his own steam, preferring pedal to horse-power. The 1950s heavy-framed black boneshaker he affected to cycle around London had carried him from his chambers in Fig Tree Court, in the heart of London's legal district, in a little under thirty minutes. It now stood chained to the railings of the Botswanan Embassy, the slight split in the old cracked leather saddle allowing rain to gradually waterlog the horse-hair stuffing in time for the journey home much later that evening.

The last of the London trio had walked to meet his colleagues from his offices in St James's Square. He had made his excuses to leave work early at seven thirty p.m., carrying with him his outsized box-style briefcase favoured by travelling salesmen, airline pilots and accountants. As the youngest ever partner in the history of Sanderson, Toomey, McClintock he would be taking his work home with him that night as usual.

The book-lined walls of the club's library were a suitably solemn setting for a meeting of such importance. An enormous oil painting of Wellington, the club's first President, glowered down from over the fireplace, surrounded by endless dark mahogany panelling and ormolu. As one who had waged campaigns in the East himself, the Duke would have been interested to hear of the plotting that was about to take place that evening.

The eight guests and their host sat around an oval polished walnut table, making subdued small talk as the club's butlers removed the last of the cheese and pudding plates. A decanter of blood-red port was placed next to the head of the table, and a bottle of old Armagnac stood on the sideboard next to nine coffee cups and a large pot of steaming

Blue Mountain. The club's senior steward was the last to enter, carrying a bottle of Wild Turkey bourbon between thumb and forefinger as if it had been a used condom. He placed it with barely concealed disdain at an unoccupied place on the table. At the head of the table, a middle-aged man in a rumpled brown suit and half-framed glasses stood and spoke to the old club servant with the confident tones of one used to dealing with staff.

'Thank you Dobson, I think that will be all for this evening. We'll help ourselves from now on. Please see to it that we are not disturbed under any circumstances. I will make sure that the fire is extinguished before my guests leave.'

Dobson inclined his head almost imperceptibly and silently spun on one heel before marching serenely out of the room and closing the door.

The Private Jet, armed with a cup of coffee from the sideboard, took her seat between the Harley and the Push-Bike. She reached for the bottle of bourbon in front of her and poured herself a healthy slug. Across the table, a balding, Three-Piece Suit stared at her with open lust. 'I like a woman who does drink like a man,' came the clipped, Germanic tones as he leered over the end of his cigar.

'Well, the professor certainly thinks of everything,' she purred in her clench-teethed, Connecticut slur, and took a large gulp, closing her eyes in pleasure as the raw burn from the fluid in her tumbler traced its way down her throat. 'But don't ogle what you can't afford, H-J. I guess this season's Fräuleins aren't doing it for you.'

The Brown Suit, still standing, smiled thinly and tapped his coffee spoon gently on his still empty port glass to call the meeting to order. The Push-Bike peered at his fob-watch. It was nine thirty p.m. and the evening's real business was about to commence.

'My dear friends, how delightful it is to see you all once again around the same table. And before we proceed any further I should like to propose a toast to ourselves and to the successful revival of the Pegasus Forum. It is many years since we all first sat around a table in Oxford. Your undergraduate careers were just beginning, and I detected in every one of you an immediate affinity for the proposal I put before you that October evening. How many of you really believed, however, that today, in the year 2001, we would all still be united in our common goal? The difference is that today, with you all now well established in the chosen posts, we are now finally in a position to do something about it. But I feel we have a secondary reason, of which you are all too aware, for being doubly committed to achieving our aims – the memory of our former member Hugh.' As he gestured to an empty space at the table, complete with untouched glass of port, a Beige Tropical Suit at the opposite end of the table lowered his head sheepishly into his Armagnac. 'We must not allow Hugh Emerson's death to have been in vain. He was, after all, one of our key members, and had already achieved so much in furthering our cause during the Passive Phase. But now, as I intimated earlier, and as I am sure you will be delighted to hear, we are ready to enter the Active Phase.'

His oration was interrupted momentarily by murmurs of approval and gentle tapping on the table from those present. The Private Jet stared at her host with eyes ablaze and mouth slightly open in anticipation. She knew she would be one of those most involved in this stage of the plan, and could hardly wait to flex her muscles.

'We have all worked hard towards establishing the conditions that now present themselves to us. There has been one previous occasion when I considered calling this meeting. That was the Mexican crisis of 1994. By then our network was probably influential enough to have added to the turmoil, but we would have been joining the party late. Events had already begun, and regrettably the authorities stepped in to restore order far too quickly. But now we are in a position to act for ourselves. We will not be merely adding fuel to an already blazing inferno, we will be striking the first match and then fanning the flames from close quarters. I will admit to being a little surprised that the situation took so long to develop, but I was convinced that the time would come. My own personal researches and involvement in the field have given me absolute assurance of the fragility of the region, which we have all helped to promote, but the time has never been more propitious for us to press ahead. Indeed, the detailed information being fed to me by our colleague in Hong Kong,' eight pairs of eyes glanced down the table to a fat Dinner Jacket, 'prompted me to call this meeting this evening. Am I correct in assuming, Jonathan, that the fuse has already been lit?'

'Professor, that is absolutely right. Assuming the Bangkok Postal Service does its work, Mr Chumsai of Pee Seuar Land should be receiving his little "message" very shortly. I followed your instructions and put it together myself. It will be totally devastating. There is no way out for him personally, and the public announcement will catch the whole world off its guard.'

'One small point, Johnny,' the Private Jet spoke. 'Given my rôle in this whole deal, don't you think you should have waited till I was back in the office before you sent Chummy his little surprise? I mean, I've got to follow it up with some ordinance of my own if we really want to cause some collateral damage.'

'You needn't worry, Annie. Our timing has been carefully planned. For technical reasons I had to post the letter before I left Hong Kong to come here for this evening, but Chumsai is currently enjoying the pleasures of Manila's more dubious night spots, and will not return to Bangkok for another twenty-four hours.'

'And it will probably take him a little while to get around to opening his personal mail,' added the brown-suited professor. 'I am assuming you will be taking the Xenfin jet back to Grand Cayman tomorrow morning, which should give you ample time to finalize your arrangements before the news breaks into the public domain. And that is the most important thing. Your fire-power is impressive, my dear, but it is nothing compared to the weight of public opinion.'

'Talking of breaking news, Professor, I have something of my own to report.' The sweating Beige Tropical Suit stood and addressed the table. 'I happened to receive a phone call yesterday from a principal in the Stockholm Embassy. He and I went through CSSB together and did the Service's training course at the same time. Anyhow, it seems that during a vodka and crayfish binge with one of his Swedish opposite numbers, he picked up that you, Professor, are on the short list for this year's Nobel Prize. Knowing you were my tutor, he thought I'd be interested in hearing it first. This is tremendous news, not only for you personally, sir, but in terms of adding credence to our plan.'

Professor Wallace Bradley, of St Mary's College, Oxford, swayed for a moment as he stood, eyes closed, before the powerful group of people he now addressed. 'Credence, my friend. You used the term and it is a most appropriate and significant turn of phrase. I am indeed most gratified that the Nobel Committee should consider rewarding my efforts. I have consulted closely with many governments over the last twenty-five years, South Korea, Malaysia, Thailand, even Indonesia itself. Together we established a system, a model if you will, which enabled these nations to establish themselves as major capitalist powers. And yet what was really behind it?'

Everyone else in the room fell silent. They sat back and waited for the homily. They had heard it many times before, the first time in a similar dining room in Oxford over fourteen years previously, and it underlay everything they all, for one reason or another, passionately believed in.

'Belief, my friends. Confidence, credence, as our friend in the Foreign Office so rightly points out. All of these words have at their root, both etymologically and philosophically, the same concept. Faith. The same concept upon which our entire financial system is based. Credit. What does this mean? Nothing more than an ability to borrow, which itself depends on nothing more than the lender's *faith* that the borrower will return their money.

'The names of the world's mightiest financial institutions are littered with these words – "*Credit* Suisse", "*Fidelity*", "Bankers *Trust*". I could go on. This ability to borrow unimaginable amounts was the mechanism by which the Asian economic miracle was able to succeed. Shipbuilding, automobiles, computers, steel, telecommunications. In less than one generation Asian countries now lead the world in those industries, and it depended on nothing more than the trust, the faith, the credulity even, of those who invested, those who lent, who fuelled the expansion, the growth, the phenomenal boom of South East Asia. And every bank, every corporation, every *government* in the region is in hock up to their neck.'

Here he paused for effect, allowing his words to sink in to the minds of his audience, looking around the table at each individual before he continued. 'And it is the loss of that faith, the withdrawal of that credit, which will be the catalyst for the collapse of the system we are committed to expose. For it lies at the very heart of the house of cards upon which our world depends. Money, as the saying goes, does indeed make the world go round, but most of that money is borrowed. Everyone does it – governments, banks, the great corporations of the world, the very institutions who can afford to live without it, yet are spurred on by greed to borrow more, to become bigger, better, richer. And they have the name, the reputation, the *credit* to support it – yet who is doing the lending? Where does all this borrowed money come from?

'Well I need hardly tell you. It does not come from banks, as most people might think. The banks may facilitate loans, but they are not lending their own money, or at least, not much of it. They simply do not have enough to cover the huge amounts we are talking about, so they borrow most of it themselves. And it is this money that comes from you and from me. With all due respect, my friends, from the little people, the population, the masses. I am an economist, but what is an economy but the fruits of all our labours, the sum of all our activity, hundreds of millions of pay packets, tiny nest eggs, put in the bank, put in government bonds, put in mutual funds, all individually a drop in the ocean. Yet when the puddles and pools and lakes are merged and flood and join forces, when all the money is combined and invested, and let us not forget that investing means nothing more than lending, they have a force capable of washing away mountains.

'It is but a small part of this force which has given life to the Asian economic miracle, yet it is a much larger force which I, which we, will harness for our purposes and then turn loose. We will expose the injustice of the rich benefiting from the thrift of the poor, and we will question the very basis of the financial system, the capitalist financial system, which controls our society today. The banks, the financial intermediaries, are merely go-betweens. What does the bank do with your pay cheque every month? Why, they just lend it to someone else without your consent. And they get fat from the accumulation of tiny slivers from every transaction they arrange. But it is *our* money which oils the machinery of the capitalist system, and we lend it without even being aware of the fact.

'But soon, my friends, soon the hoof of Pegasus will smite the ground and our very own Hippocrene will well forth with unimaginable power. The world's financial system will tumble around our ears!'

Bradley looked around the table at his audience. The rapt attention, the nodding heads, the unanimous acceptance of his sermon pleased him. They still believed it. He had rehearsed and replayed his speech so many times that he almost believed it himself. The impressionable young undergraduates he had recruited years ago with his soapbox idealism and pseudo-intellectual reasoning, had kept the faith. They all had good reason to despise the system he proposed to destroy. After all, that is why he had selected them in the first place. But they still believed, years after leaving his control in Oxford and working their way into the heart of that system. Not one of the people around the table had sold out, not one had begun to doubt the cause. The bond he had formed in Oxford and nurtured ever since was stronger than ever, and he could see the desire in the eyes of his protégés. Now it was time for the Pegasus Forum to achieve what they had set out to achieve all those years ago. But above all it was time for Wallace Bradley to get the personal reward for which he so yearned.

CHAPTER 2

JAMES EMERSON WAS IN THE DIRTIEST OF TEMPERS. AT THE age of thirty-six, he had been used to turning left when he entered an aircraft for almost eleven years now. Eleven years of business- and first-class travel, huge armchairs, linen napkins and grown-up bottles of wine with corks. But today he had been obliged to cram his six feet two inches into a stall amongst the screeching plebs and their babies at the plane's rear. He hadn't even attempted to eat, something to do with his elbows being pinned to his ribs, and had only managed to avoid two hours of cheery chat with a northerner, who held his plastic knife like a pen as he excised the fat from his slabs of ductile chicken-or-beef, by the simple expedient of being extremely rude.

He hated arriving back late in the evening, and was suffering spasms from an old disc injury as he unfolded himself from the seat and massaged blood-flow back into his lower calves, but he had to be back tonight. Oh, he was used to long hours from his former career. You don't get to be the biggest-producing bond salesman at a firm like Steinman's by leaving the office at seven. The bond and stock markets are open around the clock, have been for years now, and even if the clients had gone home, there was always something to do – research to read, spreads to monitor, files to update, bosses to impress. God, he was glad to be out of it. Grateful, of course, for the money he had made, but glad. He had enough stashed away to indulge himself for a while, and there is nothing like losing a kid brother to focus the mind and provoke one of those life-decisions.

In the case of James Emerson, that decision had involved packing in his ridiculously well-paid job with the leading American Investment

Bank in the City of London, and reclaiming his life. After eleven years of being a bond salesman, and making more in three of those years than many successful men make in an entire career, he decided to indulge his fantasy and his father by becoming the third Emerson male to write 'The Emerson Bulletin' in the *Gazette*, the highest-profile column on the country's most serious newspaper.

The 'Bulletin' had been started by his father in the sixties in an attempt to seek out and expose the corruption he was appalled to find under every stone as he sashayed in his urbane way around 'respectable' English society. Drugs, sex, fraud, espionage, the whole nine yards. It had grown in a relatively short space of time from an occasional, frivolous gossip column into a regular piece of serious crusading journalism of the highest calibre. At around the same time, Emerson senior had become a *persona* a little on the *non grata* side at the social events which both provided most of his contacts and raw material, and fed his moral indignation. The gilt-edged chunks of card ceased to land on his doormat with quite the same regularity. But, as is the case with all the most vindictive bulls, this particular red rag served only to redouble his determination, and his weekly column rapidly became not only required reading around the clubs of St James's and at suburban breakfast tables, but also for keen young officers in the Special Branch, out to make a name for themselves with a high profile bit of scandal and corruption. When the old man called it a day after twenty-five glorious years and too numerous scalps to mention, with the 'Bulletin' at the height of its fame and reputation, the mantle was assumed by his younger son Hugh, freshly down from Oxford and eager to maintain the column's momentum in a new era.

Things went pretty well, although he didn't write with quite the style of his father, but he stumbled on to the Maxwell thing after a couple of years, and that helped yank him from the shadows. He carried on producing the goods, a bit of insider trading here, a touch of exploitation there, but nothing again in the Maxwell league, until the accident took him.

Big brother James, the bond salesman, had been in the States on a corporate freebie when he got the news, holed up in an Atlantic City casino resort with some clients for the weekend. It had taken his employer for ever to track him down. He was always too drunk to check for phone messages when he crashed on to his pillow after a night at the tables, and male pride dictated that it was necessary to be up and out promptly for breakfast with the clients at seven thirty the next morning, no matter how bad the hangover. Not to mention the one stroke handicap in the morning's golf for every five minutes late. Thus a couple of days elapsed before someone finally pulled his face out of a cleavage at the blackjack table at three in the morning and called him to the phone. And if it hadn't been for the inquest into Hugh's death, James would have missed the funeral altogether. It was three years ago now, and he could still remember the hand he had been dealt at the time. He could also remember, with some pain now, how annoyed he had been at being called away to the phone with two split aces on the table. The news had hit him like a bucket of ice-cold water. Instant sobriety and instant perspective. Something in his life would have to change.

And this is why James Emerson scowled his way through the arrivals hall at Heathrow today, hobbling stiffly towards the taxi rank. *Gazette* business. It was inconceivable that an Emerson would not write 'The Emerson Bulletin' and, following Hugh's death, that is what James Emerson now did. And he did it very well, with the eye of a former banker. His exposés of scandal, fraud and more lurid crimes at the highest level in the boardrooms of Europe had already made him many enemies. Once splashed across the 'Bulletin', chairmen had been forced to resign, the share prices of the companies involved had been badly mauled, and marriages had foundered. With a shrewd financier's eye, he knew where to hit to cause maximum damage and would stop at nothing to glean the information he needed to corroborate his stories.

The story he was on now, and the reason for the flying visit to Rome, was to dig out some dirt on an Italian connection for the current focus of his attentions. An enormous Swiss drug company called Panacea Pharmaceuticals had had a best-selling product for several years now which was beginning to throw up some unfortunate side-effects in children. Emerson had dug out the original human test results and found them to be falsified. Into the bargain he had also unearthed a couple of incriminating memos between the company chairman and the senior member of the European Commission team responsible for authorizing new pharmaceuticals in the European Union. And it was in an attempt to confront the crooked Eurocrat that he had been in Italy. Despite a day and a half of doorstepping and sweet-talking the secretaries, he had failed to meet his man, but he had had to return to London that evening.

As he sat in the grey leather rear seat of one of the newest London cabs his mobile phone rang.

He took pleasure in letting it ring for a few seconds. Although he had the very latest technology, he didn't go in for the irritating, tinny opening bars from 'Ode to Joy' or the overture to *William Tell*, which the phone manufacturers allow you to choose from, and which now punctuate most train journeys and theatre lobbies with nauseating regularity. It was typical of his obsessive nature, and of his desire to take his own personal stand on things like this, that he had taken the trouble to sample the ringing tone from a good old-fashioned 1960s phone and had programmed it into his own electronic marvel, so the cab was now filled with the overloud jangling bells of a 'real' phone. Old and new combined. He loved the rhythm of it – not too urgent to set the heart fluttering, but insistent enough to demand an answer. Screw Beethoven. He loved the amusement it caused in public, as people expected him to pull a Bakelite monstrosity from his inside pocket. And the fallen Luddite in this greatest of technophiles felt a little less guilty. A nod back to the good old days.

'Emerson.'

'Ah James.'

'Who's this?'

'It's Jake Samuels, James, your editor. Remember me? I employ you.'

'OK, OK, Jake. What is it? I'm in a bit of a hurry.'

'We need the full dirt on Panacea for Wednesday's edition. It seems the *Guardian* has got a sniff of the story and is close to publishing something. Can you deliver by tomorrow night? Tell me you can. I'm keeping the front page open for you.'

Emerson thought back over his fruitless time in Rome and cursed silently. He didn't have the full story yet. A couple of key documents were missing. How on earth could he get them in time? Then he had an idea.

'It's OK, Jake. You'll have the copy by the deadline.'

Emerson dialled another number, a number which, for security reasons, was not programmed into his phone, but burned into his brain and his heart. A number which, unbeknown to his former employers and the regulatory authorities, had helped him scoop a number of deals in his earlier incarnation as a banker. It was a number that Military Intelligence didn't know he had, but a number they would very much like to have themselves. Two rings and it answered.

'Yeah.'

'Emerson. I'm sorry it's a bit late. Is it OK if I come over? I need a bit of help.'

'Jamie boy. Sure thing, man. Are you calling me land or cell?'

'Cell.'

'GSM?'

'Yes.'

'OK. I guess that's secure enough. Here's the new address . . .'

Across town in the warm and comfortable surroundings of the Oriental Club's library, only about twenty miles from James Emerson's cab as it sped in the rain from Heathrow, Wallace Bradley sank into his chair, emotionally exhausted but eager to capitalize on the climax of feeling his tirade had awakened. 'So, comrades. On to business. I would appreciate a brief summation from all of you as to your state of readiness. Mr Dodds, you are our market pulse, our ear on Wall Street, maybe you would like to commence.'

The tall, Harley-driving Cameron Dodds lolled back in his chair and lifted his right foot on to his left knee, crotch splayed, hands clasped behind his head in the approved trader's posture. He would address his audience, as he did at seven fifteen a.m. every morning at his traders' meeting, without notes.

'The desk is more active than ever before in emerging markets derivatives. I've been pushing this of course, for obvious reasons, but I would say we are now the biggest house on the Street in that sector. In fact, no other investment bank comes close in terms of the size and complexity of the deals we are structuring. We've just hired a team of analysts from Goldman who come top in all the surveys, and a couple of quant guys from Solly's who are on a different planet.

'My boss, on the other hand, has no clue about derivatives or emerging markets. For him, a call option is deciding whether or not to phone his wife when he's out on the piss with his brokers, and Indonesia is part of Bali, where he likes to take her on holiday to make up for all those ruined dinners during the year. He's an ignorant dinosaur, an old-style Eurobond trader who made his name trading new issues in the early eighties, but he knows EMG is a hot sector and likes to take the credit for our success. Of course, I've let him get away with it, which has probably cost me a lot of money in terms of bonuses over the last few years, but he wants to have one of his boys in a key seat. In return I get pretty much a free hand, which, of course, was the object of the exercise.

'What all this means, needless to say, is that when Annie over there starts firing with both barrels, we can back her up and even execute some of her trades without raising any eyebrows. At least initially. And we can probably get some of our big customers to come along for the ride. The beauty of it is, nobody will mind what we'll be doing because we should actually be making money for the bank. Lots of it. That's the benefit of having the market on your side. Nothing like a self-fulfilling prophesy and, as we all know, size is everything. Isn't that right Annie?'

He glanced with a smirk at the Private Jet, Annie van Aalst. They had had a very public 'arrangement' as undergraduates, which lasted most of their respective Oxford careers, on and off. She the glamorous but intellectual American heiress, a Rhodes scholar complete with a large endowment for the college. He the disgraced public schoolboy but brilliant mathematician who had talked his way into a place at St Mary's College, Oxford without any A levels, but with a personal refinement of Monte Carlo Simulation Theory he had developed between skateboarding and Pac Man. The professor had been aware of their liaison at the time and had disapproved, as he had not wanted to provoke jealousies within the Forum. She being the only female. But it had been harmless enough, and they had not become deeply involved beyond a rather mercenary self-gratification whenever it suited them. Despite that, he didn't want a distraction of that nature to resurface now, so he quickly intervened.

'Excellent, Dodds. I never imagined for a second that you would disappoint us. The balance sheet and the reputation of Steinman, Schwartz Inc. will be one of the most potent arms in our arsenal. And it seems that you have not only the personal authority to commit significant sums yourself, but the ear of the senior management for securing additional amounts when it comes to escalating the process in the Close-Out Phase. Congratulations. Moving on to our man on the ground – Mr Lafarge, what has the Foreign Office to tell us?'

Morley Lafarge, with two large rings of perspiration spreading below the arms of his beige linen suit, placed both palms on the polished table before him and sat forward as if for an ambassadorial briefing.

'Thank you, Professor. We are all ready to go in Jakarta. My official posting began six months ago as economic attaché to the region, and as you know, only the ambassador is aware of my dual rôle for the Service. As such I have had an extraordinary amount of freedom both in my declared capacity to examine the state of the Indonesian banking system and its business connections, and unofficially to poke around and identify potential targets for Pegasus's rupiah activities. I now have two suitable candidates in place, both middle managers in the foreign exchange departments of mid-sized banks. You may not all be aware, but Indonesia is officially the most corrupt place to do business on the planet, indeed, this was one of the reasons it was chosen as our primary target.'

Bradley smiled to himself. Technically this was true, but there was a much more important reason that Bradley had chosen Indonesia to be the primary focus of the Active Phase. A reason he chose not to share with his colleagues at this stage, and never would. He allowed Lafarge to continue uninterrupted.

'In fact, the most difficult part of my task was to decide which firms out of an exceedingly long list would be the most appropriate for our purposes. I decided to steer clear of those banks with strong links to former President Suharto's family, which narrowed down the field considerably. We don't want any feelings of kinship spoiling our game, as greed must be the only motive in this instance. The gentleman I ultimately selected will be, I am sure, only too delighted at the prospect of a discreet new Swiss client for his business. Not only will he be more than capable of handling the volume of business we will be putting their way, but he won't want to know any details of its background. The accounts will be opened in the name of Sukon Trading S.A., and Chris has helped out with all the paperwork.'

'A trifle, I assure you,' oozed the Push-Bike, rising to his feet as he did so. The inch-wide pinstripes on his black double-breasted suit, and the fob-watch completed the image of the successful City barrister. Christopher Blake was more used to addressing the High Court for £400 an hour, but tonight was *pro bono*. He stopped short of grasping his lapels whilst addressing this audience, but nonetheless managed to infuriate most with his superior tone.

'We are all cognisant of the fact that the success of our major goal, to expose the largely unworthy, fraudulent and shallow basis of our financial system, is dependent upon our remaining within the confines of the statute books ourselves. We shall commit no crimes. We shall not even dilute the spirit of the law with equivocations or trickery. Our very justification lies in the fact that we are using the system to hang itself. And what better proof could there be of an unworthy system, than one which allows itself to be destroyed specifically by adhering to its own rules? Professor Bradley has enlisted my help, and that of our colleague Mr Brookes, entirely to that end. I can now happily report, and with the clearest of consciences, that our stratagem positively squeaks with cleanliness. We may abuse a system, we may even abuse human nature, but the law, for all its assishness, is most definitely on our side.'

Bradley spoke again without rising. He swirled his port glass whilst fixing the blood-red liquid as it gyrated within the crystal bowl. 'I am most reassured to hear that we are maintaining the moral high ground. We simply cannot afford to be exposed to accusations of fraud or skulduggery. We will merely make use of the rope made available to us by the system, and slowly throttle it. Am I right, Count, in thinking that Mr Blake has had a hand in your own preparations?'

The shining pate of Heinz-Josef Graf Lessing, the twenty-eighth count, drooped with aristocratic languor as he hauled his angular frame to its entire six feet six inches. The extremely expensive dark-blue three-piece suit which hung from his rather too spare frame, made him look, to Anglo-Saxon eyes, like a provincial bank manager from the 1970s. He spoke nonetheless with the great authority of one in a market-leading rôle within one of the most powerful financial institutions in Germany, and by extension the world.

'We do now have in place, Herr Professor, the necessary legal documentation to place my employers in a most embarrassing position. The mighty Deutsche Kreditbankverein is poised to launch the largest single bond issue in the history of the Asian emerging markets. My department has arranged everything down to the last detail, and the bank has agreed to be the sole lead manager for an amount of fifteen billion US dollars to be lent to the Republic of South Korea for a period of thirty years. Korea is now a member of the OECD, and the bogus respectability which this honour confers, not to mention the favourable capital treatment, has investors falling over themselves to get a piece of the action. The bank will of course syndicate some of the deal to other banks, or rather attempt to, but I imagine those other banks will be reluctant to participate once the repercussions of Mr Quaid's small explosion begin to reverberate around the market.'

The pudgy, Eurasian features of Johnny Quaid, the Dinner Jacket and architect of the Bangkok bomb, creased into a smug grin, his eyes almost completely closed, bow-tie now untied and hanging down over his starched shirt front. He was very pleased with himself for having played the rôle of catalyst in this whole affair. He would personally have loved to be there to see the momentary shock on Chumsai's face when he realized what was in the envelope he was opening.

The German aristocrat continued: 'My employers, of course, thanks to Herr Blake's skill, will not be able to withdraw from their commitment, and will remain obliged to extend the whole sum to our Asian friends, whatever the circumstances.'

Annie van Aalst leaned forward abruptly. 'The whole sum, H-J? I thought the whole point was that we were going to take someone else along for the ride, someone that *can't* afford it.'

'*Gnädiges Fräulein*, as in *most* things,' and with that he glanced down the table to the sprawling shape of the derivatives trader Dodds, 'you do have a very sharp judgement. We will indeed attempt to secure the commitment of a sacrificial lamb, just one more signature on Mr Blake's dangerously binding little contract, before Mr Chumsai goes up in smoke. For this reason, it is imperative that you do return with me tomorrow for a most important meeting with our proposed "victim" before your return to the Caribbean. Your presence will be instrumental in persuading our poor friend to place his head in the noose. For my employer, the likely losses will be immense, but probably not deadly. The Deutsche Kreditbankverein has substantial hidden reserves, which the press and all those Jewish pressure groups can only guess at. These sums should be enough to keep the head above the waves, as you say, at least for now. However, the damage to the institution whose representative I would like you to meet tomorrow, my dear, will be catastrophic. My analysis, and that of our friend Mr Brookes,' at which point Daniel Brookes began to rummage in his outsize briefcase, 'confirms this. I had thought we might share a ride on the Gulfstream to Frankfurt tomorrow, before you depart for more exotic shores.'

Van Aalst leaned back in her chair and spoke with eyes closed. 'I'll make the detour if it's absolutely necessary, but I leave tonight. And yes you can hitch a ride, but you'll be back in steerage. I couldn't bear the thought of you drooling on my shoulder all the way to Germany.'

Wallace Bradley intervened again. The patrician German was no match for van Aalst's tongue, and he didn't want him to suffer too much in public. Spending a few hours alone with her the next day would be painful enough, but at least his peers wouldn't be around to applaud the putdowns. 'Mr Brookes, you have been quiet until now. Maybe you can enlighten us a little more as to your preparations?'

Daniel Brookes rose, clutching a sheaf of papers he had extracted from the case and proceeded to distribute them around the table. 'I have outlined the key points of the analysis of Heinz-Josef's "victim" on the attached presentation. You will see he is absolutely right in saying that the capital position of the Bankhaus Gebrüder . . .'

He was cut short by an incandescent Bradley leaping to his feet and snatching the papers back from the hands of the diners. 'You ignorant fool,' he snapped with a viciousness none of them had seen before. 'We cannot afford the risk of committing such things to paper. How many copies of this do you have? Did you leave any lying around on the copier at work, maybe, or in the bin? What were you thinking of man? This is not a presentation to the board. This is the culmination of years of preparation which I will not allow to be jeopardized by one rash act of insecurity. You are a high-powered accountant. The youngest partner ever in the largest accountancy firm in Europe. If you say that our German target cannot afford to take this loss, *I believe you*. I do not need to see it in writing!' With that he turned and thrust what he thought to be the entire sheaf of papers into the fire blazing in the marble hearth behind him, taking care that every last scrap was consumed by the flames before turning, composed once more, to his protégés.

'I cannot stress enough the need for absolute security in all that we do from now on. Any communications we have from this point on must be by secure e-mail. I have sent all of you the encryption keys, which should be used from now on to encode all of our correspondence. Failure to comply will result in disaster to our quest.'

'But I thought Chris Blake said all we are doing is legitimate,' came the voice of a softly spoken White Button-Down Collar in the shadows at the opposite head of the table to Bradley. Another American accent, this one more precise, more studied than that of the heiress from the Caymans. 'Why the cloak and dagger stuff?' His first contribution to the after-dinner proceedings, typically to the point yet calm and unperturbed by his former professor's short outburst.

'Mr Turner, of course you are right, and I am grateful to you for raising the matter.

'We are setting out to manipulate a great number of markets. Huge markets, the largest in the world. The bond and currency markets. These markets react to news, my friends. Rumours, suspicions, hopes, fears. Reality, whatever that might be, is insignificant. Truth is not an absolute commodity, and fallacies can, and do, become reality for as long as people believe in them. Our special task is to control that "reality". We will release the information we have at our disposal, valid information which we have legally obtained, *when we choose to do it*, in order to ensure its maximum impact. And of course Miss van Aalst here and Mr Dodds will start the ball rolling by acting upon it on behalf of their respective employers. The greatest possible number of people in the markets must accept *our* version of reality, as we dictate it, long enough for us to achieve our goals. This is absolutely key to our success. None of our sequences of events must come out of order, and were any documents or details of our plans to fall into the wrong hands, it would sterilize their impact immediately. Perception is reality as far as the markets are concerned, and we will steer opinion in the way we want it. I trust that is all I need to say on the matter. Now tell me, Mr Turner. I need know only one piece of information from you this evening. Did you get the job?'

A slow smile crossed his face as Scott Turner of the Federal Reserve Bank of New York gently nodded his head and straightened his tie. The charcoal-grey suit and deep black African-American skin made him almost invisible from the other end of the table. He leant back into the shadows of his chair and didn't speak again for the rest of the evening.

Daniel Brookes had remained standing, startled by the reaction his over-zealous Xeroxing had engendered. He was released from his daze by the conciliatory tone of his mentor, gently urging him to continue with the rest of his update.

'I am truly sorry, Professor, for my indiscretion. I can only assure you and the rest of my colleagues that no further copies of this documentation exist. As for my own particular situation, I am now just about ready to jump. I have all the proof we need from Sanderson's files, and I even managed to get copies of some taped phone calls, which are more than incriminating. In one of them, McClintock himself is advising a client as to exactly what should be disclosed, and I have no doubt the Fraud Squad will be most interested. We are the biggest accountancy firm in Europe, as you mentioned earlier, but our reputation has been built on our expertise in Asia. When the extent of the systematic dissimulation is revealed, no one will trust an Asian balance sheet ever again. I need no more than half an hour's notice, and I will walk into Toomey's office to resign with the greatest of pleasure.'

'How will you get the evidence out of the building?'

'The information is all safely in my deposit box at the bank. They can frogmarch me naked off the premises for all I care. My only question is, now that Hugh is no longer a part of our gang, what will we do about the press angle? Because I'll need maximum coverage when I start to blow the whistle, you know. Publicity is everything.'

'I have considered this aspect most carefully,' returned Bradley smoothly, 'and there is only one possible alternative. Hugh's death has left a big hole in many ways, and our access to press publicity has been severely curtailed. As I have just intimated, the way in which our orchestration of the events to come is reported in the press will help our cause, and the *Gazette* is an influential mouthpiece. But the Emerson tradition lives on at the *Gazette*, and we can use it to our advantage. We will give some exclusive scoops to Hugh's successor, his dull-witted brother, James Emerson.'

Bradley called the meeting to a close with those words. He was extremely pleased with the progress made by everybody, and Turner getting his promotion was an added bonus. It was incredible to consider the influence now in the hands of the nine people who sat around that table in those splendidly ornate surroundings. The conversation around the table subsided into murmured discussions between neighbours as the fire dwindled in the hearth, and slowly the company began to make their way out. Bradley was the last to leave. He ensured the fire was extinguished and stood for a few moments in the darkened room, gazing around at the history which surrounded him in the paintings and books which lined the walls. In the 175 years of the Oriental Club's history,

many plans had been devised in these rooms as to how to best exploit the
riches of the East. The spice traders, the gold miners, the silk merchants,
the military commanders of the East India Company, all had devised
ways in which to use the Orient to further their own interests and that
of their nation. Now it was the turn of Wallace Bradley and the Pegasus
Forum. They too would use the Orient to their advantage, but in this
case the goals were far more destructive, and liable to be much more
swiftly achieved, than those of their colonizing forebears.

Finally Bradley too left, for the last time, with the stern visage of
Wellington burned on to his mind.

When the meeting at the Oriental Club dissolved, Cameron Dodds was
not yet ready for bed. His mind buzzing with the expectation of what
they were about to attempt, he pulled on his biker's leathers, mounted
the shiny Harley, and took it for a cruise. It was something he did often,
revelling in the freedom of the London roads at night, no longer clogged
with traffic, and tonight he began by touring the deserted streets of the
City, the capital's financial district.

The massive engine of his motorcycle was barely idling as it growled
down the ancient thoroughfares, Moorgate, Bishopsgate, London Wall,
and Dodds stared around at the floodlit columns and porticoes and
statues of some of the globe's mightiest financial institutions, institutions
which he and his colleagues were about to set upon with a ferocity
those behemoths could never envisage. He stopped at Bank junction,
the confluence of Cornhill, Lombard Street and Poultry, and looked
around. To one side was the Bank of England. The massive, fortress-like
walls of the country's central bank and defender of the currency, glowered
darkly over all it controlled, a stone's throw from the Stock Exchange and
the Royal Exchange, with its Capitoline facade, and Dodds felt himself in
the heart of the nation's vital functions. He could almost see the billions of
dollars and pounds and euros which flowed through the system every day,
converging at this spot, before being channelled into building projects in
Pakistan, power stations in Siberia and transport networks in Nigeria, in

fact anywhere with a need to borrow and a semblance of creditworthiness to ensnare the hungry, greedy currency looking for a temporary home. The gigantic proportions of the edifices which surrounded him, the granite solidity of the portals and atria, inspired the confidence of the investors who lubricated the system; yet he and the other members of the Pegasus Forum were about to rake out the cracks in that structure and then stuff them with dynamite.

A lone policeman on foot patrol approached him as he sat on his bike staring up and around at the buildings. He must seem a sinister figure, Dodds realized, in his black leathers, on a black motorcycle in a sensitive area in the middle of the night.

'Evening, sir,' the policeman opened, as Dodds removed his helmet. 'Couldn't sleep?'

'Just taking a look around the neighbourhood, Officer. Don't seem to get a chance during the day. I work for one of the banks in the City.'

'Oh, I know that, sir. Checked the index number on your bike. We've got you logged as a regular visitor. Every day around six thirty in the morning on the way to work.'

'I didn't know you monitored specific vehicles.'

'We have to, sir, these days. Not too hard, mind you, cameras everywhere. And the IRA threat is not to be sneezed at, now, is it, sir? Bloody terrorists. Why would anyone want to destroy a bank? I just don't get it myself.'

'Well I'm glad to hear you're vigilant, Officer, but I hope you don't just rely on the cameras. Terrorism can take many forms.'

And with that, Dodds replaced his helmet and fired up the bike, leaving his last remark hanging in the air over a puzzled City of London policeman. The bike roared off down Cornhill, echoing with a throaty resonance between the tall buildings which edged the narrow road, and on towards Leadenhall Market and the route back home.

When he got home it was almost three in the morning. He knew his alarm would be going off at five thirty so he abandoned all thoughts of bed, put on some music and went hunting in the fridge. There was nothing but a jar of Gentleman's Relish, a box of crackers and an inch-deep pile of takeaway menus, none of which he fancied, so he went to the ornately carved box on the mantelpiece and took out a small, carefully folded envelope of paper. There was just enough left of the stuff he'd bought the day before from his dealer on Brick Lane for a couple of lines now, and another couple before he went into work. That should keep him going, he thought, without looking too wasted the next morning. How else could he keep up the pace of life he led, working from six thirty to eight almost every day, and still be able to sustain some sort of social life?

He divided the fine powder expertly on the glass coffee table and inhaled half an hour's salary in ten seconds of shuddering satisfaction. Within five minutes the jar of Gentleman's Relish seemed strangely attractive and he spread a couple of crackers thickly with the strong-smelling paste, and settled down with a tumblerful of neat, chilled vodka, to sit out the rest of the night with his thoughts and his habit.

It had been good to see Annie again. He was annoyed she had left for the airport directly after the dinner, especially with the German, but she had made up for that by following him to the bathrooms in the basement of the Oriental Club and surprising him with five minutes of slavering attention before coffee and port. He had never got around to doing the line he had wanted to then, she had stopped him, and given him a telling off. She could be so prudish! Anyhow, she had her own habits and he, Cameron Dodds, was glad to be one of them. It was just a shame that her own fixes were a little less frequent than his own.

Why couldn't Xenfin be in Jersey or somewhere closer to home? He only got to see her a couple of times a year now she was in the Caymans. Lucky they were in the same business and at least got invited to the same conferences and presentations, so he got to see her then. That was something. And he reckoned that worked out just fine for her, at any rate. But he needed more. He was an altogether needier character.

At around four, the phone rang.

'Cam. It's Annie. Sorry for waking you.'

'You didn't darling. I've got some Colombian and Russian friends over, and you know how they like to party . . .'

'You idiot, Cameron. Grow up, won't you? I thought you'd packed all that in! I couldn't believe it when I found you in the bathroom earlier tonight.'

'It didn't stop you . . .'

'Well, no. But I stopped *you*! You have to pack in it, Cam. This is it now. We're going to need all our wits to pull this thing off. And you and I are in the spotlight for this phase. We can't afford for you to be found stoned at work and get fired, or start making trading errors or something!'

'Leave it Annie. I know what I'm doing. Now, where are you calling from?'

'I'm at H-J's pad in Frankfurt. He's snoring next door and I was bored. Crossed my mind to go and join him.'

'For fuck's sake, Annie!'

'Just kidding, little jealous boy. But I have my needs too, you know. And you didn't seem too interested in those this evening. Been spending too much time with those Colombian friends of yours, I guess.'

'OK, OK. I'll cut back, I promise. Now. When can I see you again?'

'After Frankfurt I'm flying straight back to Cayman. I need to be there and will need you in London when Chumsai goes up in smoke. I guess it all depends how quickly things get going after that. Once Xenfin's history, though, I'll need to be somewhere else. I guess London is as good a place as any. Do you have a spare room?'

'Very funny.'

'But Cam?'

'Yes?'

'I'm only coming to stay if you clean up your act. I mean, you have to make it worth my while you know.'

'Don't worry about me. You won't be disappointed. Now, did you make the call you wanted?'

'Yes. He was very grateful. Brookes was pretty dumb to put it all in writing. Gave us a whole day's lead – I'd never have got the chance tomorrow with that crazy German slobbering around me. I faxed him a copy from the plane.'

'Are you sure it'll work out? After all this I mean?'

'Trust me, Cameron. Trust me.'

CHAPTER 3

THERE IS A WORLD OF WHICH THE PUBLIC AT LARGE KNOWS very little, a world which receives very little publicity but which wields enormous power and attracts the concern and attention of law enforcement agencies throughout the free and not-so-free parts of the globe. It was to the nerve centre of this world that James Emerson had just directed his cab driver to take him.

It is a world in which the principal players are not known, certainly not to the authorities and in some cases not even to each other. Their secrecy and privacy is the result of the most elaborate and intellectually sophisticated defence procedures known to mankind, and their identities are some of the most sought after secrets of the developed world's intelligence agencies. This is the world of the cypherpunk.

We live in an age in which our lives have gone on-line. We shop by computer, we send e-mails to our lovers and our credit-card numbers to anybody who wants them. Computers control our aircraft, our warheads and our bank balances. We annihilate, speculate and fornicate in digitally encoded binary notation, and the world could be watching and listening. To the committed cypherpunk, however, our Compaq should be our castle. The lives which we choose to lead via our computers should be as secure and private as the lives we lead behind our front doors. The government may not listen in, which means 'we' must have better security than 'them'. To that end, these disembodied creatures of the ether, the social outcasts who find their identity through anonymity, devote their lives to the creation of privacy, of data protection, of secure communication by means of unbreakable ciphers. They are the anarchist codebreakers and codemakers of the internet. Forget the juvenile hackers of the eighties. These are the PhD crackers of the nineties. And James Emerson was on his way to visit their unofficial but globally acknowledged leader.

In the netherworld of the internet he was known simply as Cubit, and Emerson was one of the few people in the world to know his true identity. Cubit's output on the internet was vast. He spent much of his time waging a one-man war for freedom of information on the one hand, and personal privacy from government interference on the other.

At best, he was viewed as a dangerous and irresponsible anarchist by all companies involved in the digital age. He amused himself by breaking the codes that were built into computer games to prevent copying, and posting them for free on the world wide web; he gave anybody who wanted it a step-by-step guide to unscrambling encrypted video signals to watch cable TV for free; he unnerved credit card companies by occasionally e-mailing them thousands of names and card numbers, complete with addresses, post codes and credit limits which he had trawled from the increasing number of transactions executed by home-shoppers over supposedly secure lines.

At worst he was viewed by the American National Security Agency, and the British GCHQ, (where, unbeknown to them, he used to work), as the single most dangerous threat to the exposure of military secrets and classified communications on the planet. He was by far the most technically advanced and brilliant civilian mind in the once arcane world of cryptography, and his rise to prominence and notoriety had accompanied the exponential rise in the use of personal computers and digital communication for both financial and military purposes. All attempts to trace him by the world's security services had failed, as all of his activities on the internet were meshed in an impenetrable cocoon of relays, false starts, firewalls and unbreakable codes. Attempts to hack in to the servers through which he accessed and posted on the web had met with universal failure.

Cubit's protective measures varied enormously, depending upon the level of sophistication or apparent malevolence of the attack.

If his systems detected a relatively low-level of sophistication in the attack, such as might be expected from a commercial enterprise or the police, the potential intruder would encounter a lurid graphic of a brick wall, bearing in graffiti-style spray-paint the phrase 'Squeamish Ossifrage', taken from a well-known code-breaking challenge set in the seventies which had taken the world's finest cryptographic and computer brains seventeen years to crack.

The more subtle and complex methods of approach employed by the American National Security Agency, the British equivalent at GCHQ, or the Israeli military computer training institute, Mamram, meet with a much more virulent defence. In fact the last time that the NSA tried to bring him down from the web, Cubit's systems covertly slipped a rather nasty little virus back down the line which, a few weeks later, resulted not only in the loss of data but in actual physical damage to a large amount of the American agency's hardware, by both inducing overheating and causing shock-damage to their delicate hard-drives.

The Chelsea townhouse in which he lived looked unremarkable to both the casual and trained observer alike, and as Emerson paid off the cab from the airport and approached the address which his friend had given him over the phone ten minutes before, he was not prepared for what he was about to find behind the glossy black front door.

As he reached the top step of the short flight leading up to the door, he heard a slight hiss as the door opened inwards before he had even announced his presence by knocking. He walked inside and the door promptly closed behind him again. There was no one else present. He found himself standing in an ordinary hallway, thickly carpeted and brightly lit, with sailing and hunting prints hanging on the walls. Conventional enough for Chelsea. Yet there was another closed door not eight feet ahead of him at the other end of the corridor, and no other means of exit. The second door immediately burst open and a familiar face walked towards him, beaming.

'Jamie my man, great to see you again, dude. Come in, come in, tell me what's goin' down.'

'Do I use your real name or should I stick to the web-alias? Could anyone be listening?'

'You can call me whatever the fuck you like in this house, man. If anyone has figured out a way to listen in here then we're all seriously screwed. And I don't mean just you and me. This is the only TEMPEST-protected private pad in the *world*.'

'As usual, you've lost me before we even shake hands, you old hippy. It's great to see you again, Max.'

The two men embraced, and Max Collins, aka Cubit, led the way into the house.

'TEMPEST, Jamie, TEMPEST. Surely you've heard of that. It's a way the spooks have dreamed up of eavesdropping on computers, or anything else electric for that matter, without even being on-line.'

'How the hell do they do that?'

'Sit down and I'll tell you.' Collins, a diminutive figure dressed in black silk from his Chinese-style house-coat down to the embroidered slippers, poured both of them a glass of wine from an already open bottle. He flopped into a low, broad grey leather armchair and Emerson sat opposite him on a deep red chinoiserie sofa.

'All electrical equipment gives off a form of electro-magnetic radiation when it's working. Anything. You know, the way an electric drill can screw up the picture on your TV? Well computers do the same sort of thing but on different frequencies. The keyboard, the cables, the monitor, they're all at it. And they all act like mini-transmitters. I could be typing away at my keyboard, and somebody with a truck-load of antennae and listening equipment parked in a road half a mile away could be picking up the tiniest of signals every time I hit a key. Doesn't matter a fuck if the computer's encoding what I write, they just pick it up from the keyboard before it even gets encrypted. That little bit of cable which joins your keyboard to the box, that could hang you. It's a bit like those evil guys in the TV licence detector vans who can tell if you've been watching "The Teletubbies" or the Playboy channel, but a bit more sophisticated.'

'So how do you protect against it? Sounds impossible.'

'You know me Jamie, never heard of the word. It is possible, and very expensive. It's also a bit risky. The technology is classified, and all those freaks at the NSA keep close tabs on anyone who might be trying to buy protection. You need to shield your computer, or the room in which the computer is located, against the emissions. In my case, I've shielded the whole fucking house. Who knows, I might want to use the laptop in the john, and if I have a good idea I don't want to have to wait till I get back to a secure room.'

'So . . .'

'So this entire pad, man, is encased in an outer shell of copper sheeting. The roof, the floors, the walls. Even the windows have special glass, impregnated with copper filaments. The doors and windows have gaskets sealing the air, so I have to generate my own air supply. Hence that little air-lock arrangement at the front door you just saw. If you listen carefully, you can hear the compressor in the basement. There can be no weak links, no outlets to the outside. No pipes, no cables, no phone lines. They can all act like mini-antennae of their own and broadcast the signals to the outside world. I have my own generator for electricity, no mains, and I only use encrypted mobile phones, no permanent land lines. As for water, I bathe, crap and brush my teeth in Evian. I must be the only guy in Chelsea to have a septic tank in the garden. And before you ask, that's protected too.'

'You're getting more paranoid by the day, Max. It must have cost you a fortune to do all this.'

'Peanuts, dude, peanuts for a man of my talents. The main expense was the copper sheeting. About fifty quid a square metre. And the special glass. More difficult was buying the stuff and getting it put in without warning the spooks. There aren't many suppliers of this sort of kit and they keep a close eye on them. Why else would anyone want to buy 10,000 square metres of copper? I had to spread my purchases around dozens of suppliers, and stagger them over a couple of years before I had enough to go ahead. Anyway, as I mentioned, we are fully insulated against any sort of eavesdropping, and any messages I *choose* to broadcast into the outside world, on to the web or whatever, are fully encrypted. Expensive, yes. Paranoid, no. These guys want to find me more than ever. Right now, they have no idea where I live so the TEMPEST-proofing gear is kind of superfluous. But you never know when they might luck into finding me. Every day some idiot tries to hack in here via my web pages, and sometimes it's the serious dudes in the dark glasses. They think I'm on to something, and I'm just about to drive them a little more crazy.'

'What do you mean, Max? Sounds like you're trying to pull the lion's tail a little too much for your own good.'

'Don't you believe it, man. These evil bastards in the US and British governments want to read all our private stuff, but don't want anyone to read theirs. They spend hundreds of millions a year on coming up with new methods to encrypt information, and by definition that means new methods to *de*-crypt information. Our information. Sure, they want to be able to tap into drug-dealers and the Mafia and all those dudes, but who's to say they won't just read *everybody's* e-mails *all* the time? Theoretically, they could read every message sent, every day, by every individual in the world. And it wouldn't take much manpower. All they have to do is get some centralized computer to trawl for key words or phrases, like "assassinate" or "tax evasion" or "communist", and send the boys in black and blue round whenever anything dodgy crops up. That is dark, man, really dark, and unless we all encrypt our communications to the max, they can do it right now. And believe me, they do. People like me are a major pain in the ass because we are making the strongest codes known to man available to the man in the street. You can't even legally export the encryption software out of the US above a certain, rudimentary level. The Feds claim the likes of me are helping the illegals, and they even classify strong codes in the same way as they do arms and munitions. But that's like blaming Porsche for making a faster getaway car. And I'm working on stuff here that will blow them away. It'll make a 911 look like a Trabant.'

'Do they know that?'

'They worry about it, man, they worry. My web-alias, Cubit, is a play on the word *Qubit*, which is an expression from the holy grail of computing right now – quantum computers. It is the computer equivalent of cold-fusion in the energy industry, a solution for just about everything which a lot of people would not want to see happen.

Too many vested interests. Right now, the strongest codes we use would take the strongest, most powerful computers thousands, if not millions of years to brute-force.'

'To *what*?'

'To check every possible combination until the code is broken. That's because even the most powerful computers can still only perform a relatively limited number of calculations per second compared to the number of possible permutations in the strongest codes. A quantum computer could theoretically perform an infinite number of calculations at one time, and crack any code in a matter of milliseconds. We know it's theoretically feasible, but nobody's managed to build one yet. The guys at the NSA and GCHQ are worried I'm on to something, and would like very much to have a word with me.'

'And are you, Max?'

'Let's just say, I'm doing nothing to dissuade them of the fact. My main website is currently carrying a couple of major hints. Call me a pricktease if you like, but I love teasing pricks like the NSA, and I love to see them squirm. And I have so much fun beating off their shitty little attacks on my systems. But enough of Cubit Castle, what brings you here Jamie boy? You want to plant a little virus in Branson's PC? Frag the Goldman web-server?'

'No Max, not quite. I need to read somebody's private e-mails and dig some documents out of his database.'

'Holy shit, man, you disappoint me. I thought this was going to be some real darkside action. You ask Cubit to do a straight hack?'

'Max, I promise I won't tell anyone. Your reputation is safe with me. I realize that most twelve-year-olds could probably do it, but you happen to be the only computer geek I know. I suppose it's a bit like getting Rembrandt to paint your front door, but can you please help me out? I need to sort it as quickly as possible.'

'Follow me, man, but put your coat on. We're going into the inner sanctum.'

The inner sanctum, as Collins had called it, was his nerve centre.

A sterile, freezing cold room where a dozen computers whirred almost silently night and day.

'Why so cold, Max? It's like an ice box in here.'

'Well, man, you might say I like to put my computers to work. All the chips inside these little babies have been specially tweaked to squeeze as much performance from them as I possibly can. I'll spare you the details, but that tends to make them run a little hot. They all have extra cooling systems built into them to stop them from actually melting, but it does help if I keep the ambient temperature of the room as low as possible.'

'Why the need for the extra performance?'

'Jamie, if you were listening just now, I told you that the strongest codes would take the best computers thousands of years to crack if they had to go through every combination. It's called brute-forcing, or exhaustive-searching. Well, the problem with those sorts of codes is that they are a little cumbersome to use in the first place. Takes ages to encrypt a long message, and even longer to decrypt it even when you have the key. Most companies go for a compromise between security and practicality, depending on the sensitivity and value of the data they're trying to protect. It all depends on the length of the key to the code. A fifty-six-bit key is breakable, but for most normal people it would take several years of computing time and a lot of money to do it. For regular businesses, protecting client lists and names and addresses and shit like that, who would spend ten million dollars and five years trying to do it? Fifty-six-bit security is pretty widely used in low-profile industry and private stuff, it's really only the military and financials who go in for the million year stuff.'

'But damn it, Max. I don't have five years. I hope you can do better than that.'

'Cool it, dude, cool it. I have a couple of machines here which should have your answer pretty quickly. All those times to crack codes I mentioned are dependent on the average sort of computing power available now. If someone were to come up with a machine that could function, say, a touch more rapidly, we'd all be laughing. No need to tell anyone, of course, otherwise they'd start using stronger, longer keys and we'd back in the hole. But "Sheila" here, can crack a fifty-six-bit key in a little under seven minutes. You see, I *have* invested the ten million in hardware which the accountants and computer security people don't reckon with when deciding on the level of protection for low-level classified data. You know, names and addresses, stuff like that. But I don't give a flying monkey's for the financial consequences, which makes me one of those wild cards or loose cannons or whatever that is very hard to protect against. My motives don't fit into the financial effort/risk-reward equation which seems to dominate this globe, you see. I'm the modern day kamikaze if you like. The suicide bomber you can't defend against.'

'But what about your own security set-up? You seem to value your own life pretty highly.'

'Don't misunderstand me, James. When I say kamikaze, I use it in the sense that I am prepared to sacrifice not my neck, but what is most valuable to most people in the current environment. Pure, hard cash. In the financial world, I am a fundamentalist freedom fighter with no concern for money, although I happen to have lots of it. That is hard for the opposition to understand, and lets me move around pretty much at will. Now give me the guy's name, his company name and e-mail address if you have it.'

'Here, what do you make of it?'

'Yeah, should be pretty straightforward.'

Collins spent a few minutes checking a few sites before he settled on one and pushed some more keys on a computer keyboard.

'"Sheila" is now calling their web server and attempting to identify a database file. Once she's located the door she'll give it a good strong knock to see what kind of ironmongery, what sort of protection they have. If it's what I suspect, we're in. If they're sophisticated, it'll take a little longer.'

Within three minutes, Collins had access to the private e-mail files of the chairman of Panacea Pharmaceuticals. They spent the next thirty minutes reading them through and printing out the incriminating ones.

'Now, you said you wanted some documents.' Collins was cracking his fingers and preparing to access another file. Within ten minutes

Emerson had everything he needed for the *Gazette* story the next day.

'Thanks, Max. You've got me out of a hole, yet again. I owe you.'

'No worries. You should ask me more often. It'd save you a lot of legwork.'

'Well I do try to be reasonably legit these days, Max.'

'I guess you're really not a banker any more.'

'Very funny. I'm supposed to be exposing the crooks, not joining their ranks. I do like to try conventional means first, but it's nice to have the option in an emergency.'

Emerson left Max Collins, aka Cubit, playing with his computers.

CHAPTER 4

I T WAS NOT UNTIL LATE THE NEXT EVENING THAT ANNIE van Aalst boarded the gleaming Gulfstream V, property of the Xenfin Partnership, at Frankfurt airport for the overnight flight back to Grand Cayman. She sank into one of the enormous leather armchairs in the opulent cabin, reclined the seat to its full, almost horizontal extent, and lay back as the executive jet soared into the air over the twinkling lights and skyscrapers of the continent's principal financial centre.

Once airborne she kicked off her corporate heels and unbuttoned the closely fitting jacket of her Chanel suit to the waist, revealing to the steward who brought her the first Martini of the trip a tantalizing glimpse of bronzed Caribbean flesh. She reflected on her day with the German Count, and smiled to herself at the ease with which they had snared their first prey.

Heinz-Josef von Lessing, pain-in-the-ass, lecherous creep that he was, had been the epitome of professionalism. They had arrived in Frankfurt, after the momentous dinner in London, at around three a.m., and she had spent the night at his urban pied-à-terre in the city's fashionable *Westend* district. Lessing's frivolous antecedents may well have frittered away the family fortune over the last couple of hundred years, but the twenty-eighth count was clearly well on the way to assembling a considerable fortune of his own by the twentieth-century expedient of a successful banking career. Over breakfast that morning she had been able to admire the considerable collection of nineteenth- and twentieth-century art that hung in the newly modernized, high-ceilinged, *altbau* duplex. A Schiele adorned the open-plan living room, whilst Ackermann was the theme in the dining area. A good bust of Goethe stood prominently in one corner, old mixing happily with new amongst the low modular furniture and sleek audio-visual equipment.

'We will meet our lamb for the slaughter for lunch today in my offices,' Lessing had begun, as he helped himself to the rye bread, cheese and cold-cuts he had set out on the table in the kitchen area. 'You need do nothing more than be yourself, represent your company in the way you are more than used to, and I will do the rest. Herr Lichtblau will probably be a little curious as to why the mighty Deutsche Kreditbankverein should be introducing him to such an illustrious client as yourself, but the reasons we have rehearsed should more than satisfy him. Besides, who could resist the proposition which we will be putting to him?'

'You're right H-J, it is kind of free money for him in exchange for renting his name and balance sheet for a while. My only concern is if he's up for the size. I mean, we are talking about an awful lot of bonds here.'

'Make no worries, *Schätzchen*. If he doesn't take the full amount we have some latitude. Danny Brookes assures me that even half the amount we are proposing will be enough to push them over the edge, coupled with the exposure we know they already have to the region. I had one of my associates perform a rudimentary inquiry, and they seem to have been quite active already in trade-financing in China for some of their wealthier clients.'

As they sat in Lessing's office later that morning on the forty-second floor of the silver-mirrored needle that was the flagship headquarters of Germany's financial powerhouse, a secretary knocked and entered to inform them of the arrival of their guest from Munich. She ushered in a short, round man in his early sixties, thinning, crinkly hair oiled back in a vain attempt to prevent the powdering of dandruff on the shoulders of his dark, almost black, fine wool suit. Unusually for German banking circles, he wore a yarmulke.

'*Herr Lichtblau, bitte kommen Sie herein. Es ist mir ein großes Vergnügen, endlich Ihre Bekanntschaft machen zu dürfen!*' Lessing sprang to his feet to shake the hand of their guest, who extended a short arm which barely reached beyond his considerable girth.

'Herr von Lessing, the pleasure is mine. Many thanks for the invitation.'

'May we continue in English? Permit me to introduce Fräulein van Aalst from the United States. She represents the Xenfin Partnership. Maybe you are familiar with them?'

'I am afraid my knowledge extends only to what I occasionally read in the newspapers about that organization.' He swivelled to greet the other guest with a smile and a proffered, pudgy hand. 'Fräulein, a pleasure.' He quickly appraised the elegant, slim female who stood before him in a dark-green Chanel suit, short but not immodest skirt, with the slightest dusting of cool make-up to complement her sun-enhanced colouring. One brief smile and a momentary contact with the hazel eyes, and he was instantly charmed.

'Herr Lichtblau, I look forward to telling you more about Xenfin at the first opportunity. I feel sure our acquaintance will prove mutually beneficial in the very near future.'

Lessing continued: 'You must be hungry after your journey, *mein Herr*, let us continue over lunch without further delay.' With that, he led the way out of his office and to the lifts, where they rode whisper-fast up to the top floor dining rooms on the sixty-third floor, constructed at great expense for the entertainment of important clients. The view over Frankfurt's high-rise skyline and the surrounding countryside was breathtaking, and the board of the Deutsche Kreditbankverein were able to have a comprehensive panorama of all that they owned and controlled. This lunch was a little different to that offered to most guests of the DKBV, however, and several pairs of eyebrows had been raised earlier in the week when Lessing had reserved a room and put in a request for a kosher lunch.

As they settled at the table in one of the smaller dining rooms, Lessing discreetly pressed a button on a device resembling the remote control of a television set, which indicated silently to the kitchen and waiting staff that service could begin. Almost immediately, liveried staff entered with serving dishes, and poured the chilled bottles of German spring water which stood in ice pails around the table. Their elderly guest's eyes widened in pleasure as he saw the familiar and much-loved contents of the tureens, and he tucked in with gusto. Lessing began his pitch.

'Fräulein, Herr Lichtblau is the *Geschäftsführer*, the chairman, of the Bankhaus Löwen-Krugmann, the largest private bank in Bavaria and the oldest in Germany. The term "private bank" should not deceive you into thinking that the Löwen-Krugmann Bank is insignificant. Indeed, even though the bank is privately held, its balance sheet places it in tenth spot in the German rankings.'

'That is quite an achievement for the partners, Herr Lichtblau. My congratulations. Can I pass you some gefilte fish?'

Lichtblau acknowledged the compliment with a gentle nod. 'Thank you, Fräulein. We have always been a family business, and our reputation extends back many years. We have grown to achieve the status we have today by means of conservative management, absolute discretion, and priding ourselves on a close relationship with every one of our clients on whose behalf we act. We have, however, not remained buried in our history, and I believe much of our success over the years is attributable to the flexibility of the partners in recognizing new opportunities, moving with the times, and offering our clients the most up-to-date services available.'

'Herr Lichtblau is modest,' said Lessing. 'To have a Löwen-Krugmann chequebook is the ultimate status-symbol in Germany today, something *I* could never aspire to. It is a sign of the utmost financial standing, and would be accepted everywhere in Germany, for just about whatever amount, without question. Why, I believe I read recently about one of your clients who purchased an estate in the *Schwarzwald* by writing a cheque on the spot for ten million marks.'

'A true story, Graf, and I am sure were you personally to open an account with us we would be delighted to issue you with one of our chequebooks. But the story to which you refer was a most regrettable incident and something we try to discourage. Of course, the cheque was valid and covered, but the curious real-estate agent was over eager to talk to the press. Our client's confidentiality was compromised, and that sort of sensationalism is exactly what we try to avoid at all times.'

'I completely sympathize, Mr Lichtblau,' added van Aalst. 'My own employer is similarly protective of its clients' privacy. We too are a partnership, and it is our goal to run our business with the minimum of publicity. As a hedge fund, perhaps you are familiar with the term, we could be subject to guilt by association with some of our less scrupulous or professional competitors. We are the largest in the world, not even Soros is bigger, but like them, we prefer to keep our activities quiet. That is why you will only see occasional references to us in the press, and most of those are unsubstantiated speculation by nosy journalists.'

'I have heard the term "hedge fund", of course, but I fear I do not completely grasp its significance.'

'Permit me to explain. Horseradish? The name is, of course, a mis-nomer. The word "hedging" implies mitigating the risks of investments, protecting against the risks of losing money, a kind of insurance policy, if you like. The best hedge funds, including ourselves at Xenfin, do indeed engage in risk-reduced strategies. We will, for example, attempt to identify a market we believe to be overvalued, and another we believe to be undervalued, and speculate on the *difference* between the two. This is a much lower-risk strategy than, say, speculating on whether one particular market, or one particular stock, is going to go up or down in the next month. Try tossing a coin, that's probably the best analytical tool there is for *those* sort of guesses. Unfortunately, that sort of outright speculation is what most hedge funds do nowadays, and it's got the respectable, top-end of the business a bad name.'

'So if most of these hedge funds don't actually hedge so much, what do they do, and how do they achieve such extraordinary performance? I read about returns for investors in these funds of thirty to forty per cent per year, when most conventional funds are getting between eight and ten.'

'It is perfectly straightforward. You see, the term "hedge fund" has come to be a blanket phrase to describe those investment companies which *borrow* most of the money they invest. We attract our money from sophisticated, high-net-worth individuals. They entrust their money to us to manage on an entirely discretionary basis. That simply means we can do whatever the hell we like with it within reason, and because we're all based offshore, we don't have to answer to the authorities, like the SEC or the Stock Exchange or the Fed. Minimum investment is one million US dollars, and we have many investors in our fund who have staked significantly more. What we do is to take that money, which at the last count amounted to over thirty *billion* US dollars, and we effectively use it as collateral, security, if you like, for bank loans. Typically, we will borrow four to five dollars for every one dollar of our client's money we have under management, and the banks are happy to lend to us on that basis. We then turn around and invest the five dollars in the markets. The banks we borrowed the money from then get to look after the five dollars' worth of bonds or stocks or whatever we've bought, as a further security for the loan.'

'So what you are saying, Fräulein van Aalst, is that for the thirty billion dollars of your clients' money you have, you can actually make investments up to *one hundred and fifty billions*? This is quite incredible! Such amounts are unimaginable.' His voice dropped to an almost admonishing tone. 'It is more than the Gross National Product of many countries in this world, Fräulein.'

'That is correct. But, in fact, our philosophy on borrowing to invest is relatively conservative. We only borrow four to five times our capital, but there are other funds, not much smaller than ourselves, who in fact regularly borrow twenty to thirty times the money they actually have to invest. It is called "leverage".'

'Excuse me, I have not understood this word.'

'"Leverage", from the word lever. When Archimedes invented the lever it proved to be a most useful device. By applying the laws of physics, he showed how it was possible for one person to exert a force vastly disproportionate to his own strength by judicious use of a long lever, correctly positioned. It made building all those Greek temples a lot easier once they figured out how to lift the stones into place. He even claimed he would be able to move the entire Earth if only he could find some place to stand. Well, financial leverage is the same thing. It enables in this case the investor in the hedge fund to have investments of vastly greater amounts than they actually have in cold, hard cash. It's not really anything new. People have been borrowing to invest on a small scale for years – they're called margin accounts – but we just do it on a bigger scale. We sort of run lots of people's margin accounts all at the same time. If we do well, and make shrewd investments, the return is of course magnified. We earn the profits made on the five dollars' worth of stock we bought, even though we originally only had one dollar and borrowed the other four. Of course, from that we have to subtract the cost of borrowing those four dollars, and we take our management fees and any performance bonuses, but that is how the high returns you mentioned are ultimately generated.'

'And do you hope to move the Earth, Fräulein van Aalst? I hope you realize that our bank is most conservative in outlook. We could not possibly consider getting involved in schemes to . . .'

Lessing could see his Bavarian guest was getting the wrong end of the stick and interjected swiftly. 'Herr Lichtblau, forgive me for interrupting, but I believe you misunderstand our intentions in inviting you here today. We are not, *um Gottes Willen*, proposing that the Bankhaus Löwen-Krugmann invests in one of Xenfin's funds. Even though Xenfin is amongst the more "restrained" of hedge funds, that would be a most inappropriate transaction for an institution of your philosophy.'

'I see. Please continue Herr von Lessing.'

'The matter is, *ja*, somewhat delicate, and I would prefer it if maybe Fräulein van Aalst continued to explain her employer's wishes.'

'Mr Lichtblau, as I have just described, my employer is a major investor in the world's capital markets. Given our size, we feel very strongly that we have a moral obligation to behave in a responsible manner when we choose to invest in a certain market or company. Because of our philosophy, you will not find our fund managers, of which I am one, speaking in the press about what we have done, or are about to do, because this may cause undesirable dislocations in the markets in which we wish to invest. Our influence is considerable, but we do not wish to leave ourselves vulnerable to accusations of manipulating markets.' Van Aalst could not help but remember the comments made in London the previous day by her lover, Cameron Dodds, about 'size' and 'self-fulfilling prophesies'. She hoped she was not blushing.

'We are based in the Cayman Islands, well away from the mainstream investment community in New York, Boston and London, and we keep ourselves very much to ourselves. Many other hedge funds, although registered offshore do not actually base their operations in offshore locations. It is an arrangement of convenience exclusively designed for the avoidance of tax and regulation. In our view it is a blatant deception. They sit in New York and Boston and Connecticut, and freely talk to the press about what they are doing in the hope that others will jump on the bandwagon, and drive the markets the way they want them to go. We at Xenfin have never engaged in any such public statements.'

'Fräulein, I well understand your position. Now may we get to the point? What is the proposal you have for Löwen-Krugmann?'

'Certainly, sir. I was coming to that. Xenfin has an extremely large portfolio dedicated to investing in the emerging markets, the markets in those countries which are currently bursting on to the world stage. Brazil, China, Poland, Indonesia, the list goes on and on. Our own clients like risk, which is why they invest with us in the first place. The emerging markets fund is our most volatile, our riskiest fund, but also the most popular with the breed of investors we tend to attract. I am the principal fund manager for the emerging markets fund, Mr Lichtblau, and frankly, we would like you to help us with one of our proposed investments.'

'Continue. How may we help, and what we can we do for you that the mighty Deutsche Kreditbankverein cannot?'

'The DKBV is arranging the single largest transaction in the history of the emerging markets next week. In brief, it will be a fifteen billion US dollar, thirty-year bond transaction for the Republic of South Korea, and Herr von Lessing here has been single-handedly responsible for putting the transaction together. It dwarfs any previous transactions that have been done.'

'That is correct, Herr Lichtblau,' added Lessing. 'The DKBV has already signed a firm commitment with the Korean Government to that effect. Everything is fixed, the amount, the price, the term. This is a very large amount, clearly too large an amount for one bank to underwrite alone, but we have taken the calculated risk that we will be able to syndicate the deal to a consortium of other banks ourselves. It was this willingness to commit a fixed price in advance which won us the deal in the face of stiff competition. I have no doubt that the market will snap off our hands when we offer it to them next week.'

'Count, I'm afraid you have wasted my time. As I am sure you are aware, Löwen-Krugmann is not in the emerging markets bond business at all. As attractive as the deal may appear, I will not be able to underwrite any of your bonds.'

'Mr Lichtblau, if I might say something.' Annie van Aalst rose from her chair, and began to pace the room, the way she would in the office when pondering a big trade. Lichtblau could see her better now, and admired what he saw. A purposeful walk, confident posture, great legs. Her tone now was different, sharper, less oiled. 'Listen. Xenfin wants to buy into this deal. In a very big way. It will be the single largest holding we have in any bond, but we want to take two billion dollars' worth of this deal, and we want to buy it from *you*.'

'But . . .'

'I know what you're thinking. Lessing here put the deal together, DKBV have all the bonds, I seem to know him, right? Why don't I just buy the fucking bonds from him?' She used the word deliberately to shock. The older man would be angry at her language. She wanted him angry because she was both about to flatter him, and redirect his anger somewhere else.

'Well let me tell you, sir, Xenfin does not deal with Nazis, OK? Our founder and senior partner is a guy by the name of Saul Krantz. You may not have heard of him, but he is probably the most prominent proponent of getting the Swiss, the Germans, the Austrians and anyone else for that matter, to hand over the money they ripped off from the Jews during the holocaust. The DKBV, for your information, was pretty much Hitler's personal banker during the war, and I cannot deal with them. But I want to buy their bonds so I need an intermediary. I would like you to fulfil that role. Your bank, sir, is a one off. A Jewish bank in Germany?

Who ever heard of such a crazy idea? How could it survive? Who would deal with you? Well, as you have so eloquently and modestly pointed out, not only have you survived, you have thrived. You have proved, in the most difficult circumstances imaginable, that integrity and sound judgement and principles are much more important than whether or not you happen to believe that Jesus H. Christ was the great Redeemer. Saul Krantz thinks you guys are the greatest. If your stock was listed, he'd have probably bought the bank by now. As it is he has to content himself with having a large personal account with you guys. Check it out. He's probably one of your biggest savers!' The account had been secretly opened, unknown to Krantz but in his name, a year previously with some surplus Xenfin funds. They used it to make strategic investments, via Löwen-Krugmann, in Israeli ventures. It had actually performed pretty well and was testament to the thoroughness and foresight of Wallace Bradley's planning.

'I hardly know what to say, Fräulein. I am of course most flattered that Mr Krantz is such a strong advocate, but . . .'

'There are no buts, sir. I wish to buy two billion dollars' worth of bonds from your bank, which you in turn will buy from the DKBV. You will have no risk. You will never need to hold the bonds, they will merely pass through your books. You have my word on that. If you wish, the bank's name need never even appear on any publicity surrounding the issue, but there is one condition. As part of our corporate indenture, if Xenfin invests in a new bond issue when it is first brought to the market, we must buy it from one of the original syndicate. It's a kind of insurance for us. The underwriters have a sort of moral responsibility to continue to trade the bond during its life. If ever we need to get out of our investment, we need to know that the bank we bought the bonds from is obliged to give us a good price. Of course, we would never expect that of you, Herr Lichtblau, but Löwen-Krugmann has to be in the official underwriting syndicate otherwise we will not be able to go ahead.'

'And in that case, Herr Lichtblau,' came the hammer blow from Lessing, 'we would not be able to pay you your fee.'

'Ah yes, our fee. I see. Just exactly, er, how much would be normal in this sort of transaction? Please excuse my ignorance but I am not too experienced in . . .'

'Think nothing of it, I entirely understand. Normal in the case of a Korean bond issue would be around one per cent for underwriting plus a further half a per cent for sales. That would amount to one and a half per cent of two billion US dollars, which is exactly thirty million.'

Lichtblau paled visibly. Beads of sweat broke out on his top lip at the prospect of such an amount, so easily earned. And without risking one pfennig of the bank's capital. He dabbed his mouth with a napkin and prepared to swallow the bait.

'Well Herr von Lessing, in the light of that I feel I have to say that . . .'

'I understand your reservations, sir. That fee structure is for a normal bond issue, and the deal we have in mind is anything but normal. It will be ten times the size of a normal deal and have a maturity of thirty years. Much longer than normal. In these circumstances we have been able to negotiate a much more advantageous fee structure with the Korean Government. Two and a half per cent for underwriting, plus a further point for sales. In your case this would amount to a sum of seventy million US dollars, to be paid into your account on the value date, Wednesday of next week.'

Lichtblau could scarcely believe his ears. This amounted to almost half of the bank's entire profit in the previous year, and in one deal! He would be a hero with the other partners. Not to mention the fact that, as senior partner himself, his share of the profit would be almost half a million dollars. Of course, he needn't mention it to them until the money came in. It would be a nice surprise to announce at the board meeting next Friday. And his wife. They'd be able to buy the place in Florida they'd been dreaming about for years. Deep breath. He swallowed and cleared his throat in preparation to talk.

'In the circumstances, er, Fräulein, Graf, on behalf of the partners of Bankhaus Löwen-Krugmann, I would be delighted to accept your most interesting proposition. Normal circumstances would, of course, require me to refer such a matter to the other partners, but, as you so rightly point out Herr von Lessing, these are anything but normal circumstances.'

'Hey that's great news. I know Saul is going to be delighted to have dealt with you guys,' added van Aalst, with a broad grin. 'He sees it as a way of transferring some of those Holocaust funds back where they belong. And it's much quicker than going through the courts.' She had switched back from battle to charm mode, and the effect was complete. Lichtblau slumped back in his chair and loosened his tie, an event which normally had to wait until sitting in his favourite armchair at home with a large pre-dinner schnapps. But here he felt amongst friends, relaxed, delighted to hear of his powerful new influential, Jewish admirer, Mr Saul Krantz, who had, in fact, never heard of Bankhaus Löwen-Krugmann.

'Mazel Tov, sir,' beamed van Aalst again, as Lessing pushed across the table Christopher Blake's poisonous underwriting agreement and handed him an enormous Mont Blanc *Meisterstück* fountain pen to sign. The barrel of the pen was already engraved with the details of the bond issue: *The Republic of South Korea 7% 20-April-2031. US$ 15,000,000,000. Senior Co-Lead Underwriter: Bankhaus Löwen-Krugmann, München.* 'You may keep the pen as a small memento of today's agreement.'

Lichtblau signed with a flourish. When had anybody, in the history of the bank, made so much in the space of one lunch, he thought? He was amused to note that the contract he had just signed was already printed with his name and title. But, alas, in his zeal he neglected to read anything else, specifically one short clause buried in the middle of the fourth page. The work of Christopher Blake, it read as follows:

'This commitment is totally binding. It may not be rescinded for any reason other than the withdrawal of the planned issue from the market. There are no other extenuating circumstances, such as volatile market conditions or a reduction in the credit-standing of the issuer, which might take precedence.'

As far as the law was concerned, unless Korea decided they didn't need to borrow the money, which in the circumstances that were about to ensue would be most unlikely, Jakob Lichtblau had just signed a cheque for two billion US dollars. And this was one cheque that the Bankhaus Löwen-Krugmann would not be able to cash.

In the Xenfin jet, high over the German landscape, Annie van Aalst picked the olive out of her Martini and sucked it with immense pleasure. Everything was falling into place. She could scarcely wait to return to Grand Cayman for the next stage of the operation in which she would play such an important and active rôle. Her own preparation was now almost complete, she just needed to do a little more work on a certain Mr Saul Krantz. She placed the empty cocktail glass on the table beside her sumptuous chair, closed her eyes and drifted into contented oblivion.

The only other occupant of the Gulfstream's cabin that evening, the steward in his white linen Xenfin uniform, noticed the regular breathing patterns which indicated his charge was sleeping, and moved up the cabin to remove the cocktail glass and dim the lights. As he stood next to the sleeping executive in the half-light, he lingered a while to admire her supine form. The unbuttoned jacket of her suit was gaping a little more now to reveal the soft curves of her seamless black silk bra and the deep brown skin and fine golden down of her concave stomach. After a few minutes he returned in some consternation to the fold-down crew seat in the rear galley, where he settled down for the eight-hour flight to read his magazine by the night-light. After he had gone, Annie van Aalst opened her eyes momentarily and smiled contentedly to herself. She thrived on the power she had over men.

Back in his London apartment, James Emerson put the finishing touches to his exposé on Panacea Pharmaceuticals and e-mailed the copy to his editor at the *Gazette*. Content that he had struck another blow against corporate crime and political corruption, he changed into a pair of shorts and a T-shirt and wandered over to the heavy punchbag which hung from a beam in the corner of his loft-style living room. As he laced up his gloves and began an energetic work-out on the bag, the tensions of the day and the pressure of his deadline slipped from his body.

As a student at Cambridge, Emerson had already been a keen boxer, anxious to build on the skills he had learned from an old-fashioned gym-master at an even more old-fashioned boarding school in Scotland. He had been desperate to win his blue for boxing, and had even begun attending a gym in London near to the bakery where he worked the night-shift to earn some extra money during the long university vacation. Back then, and with the Oxford-Cambridge 'varsity' match approaching in the winter term, he had not wanted to get out of shape during the summer away from Cambridge, so he had joined the gym and worked out hard in the late afternoons, every day, before going back to the bakery at night.

At first it had been tough. The East End of London is a rough place, and a boxing gym attracts the roughest types. Of course, there were plenty of serious boxers there and the proprietor had the reputation of attracting the best youngsters around and turning them into stars. A few national champions had passed through his hands, and in the sixties one of his protégés had fought a world title fight and lost. But there was also a fair collection of street-fighters, the sort who used the gym to sharpen their skills for the real-world fights in the back streets of Peckham on a Saturday night when the gloves were off and the Marquess of Queensberry was more likely to be a pub than a set of rules by which to fight.

In that sort of environment, nobody had spoken to the long-haired skinny student from Cambridge, or 'Toff', as everyone called him, for at least a month. He had just turned up, worked alone on the heavy bag and the rope and the free weights, and then left for the bakery.

He was an oddity. His clothes and hair always smelt vaguely of yeast and flour, and he used to read books sitting on the floor against the wall whilst taking a rest or waiting for a piece of equipment to become free. Thick books with small print and no pictures. But of course, a boxing gym is geared towards fighting and it was not until James Emerson was approached for his first sparring bout by a thick-set youth with home-made tattoos, that he earned the respect he still carried with him today.

The kid was twice Emerson's size, a bouncer in a local pub on Saturday nights, and had made his intentions clear from the outset. This was no sparring bout. More an initiation. For the 'friendly' three rounds they had agreed to dispense with the protective headgear, and Emerson soon realized, after a couple of low blows and 'accidental' clashes of heads, what was in store for him. But it was no contest. The thug was more used to dealing with drunks whose sense of timing after eight pints of lager bore no relation to the classic style and technique of a razor-sharp Emerson, who skipped and wove his way around the ring, jabbing with clinical precision, humiliating and hurting at the same time with lightning quick combinations. A small crowd had gathered around the ring as word had spread throughout the large gym that the 'Toff' was in for a beating, but scorn soon turned to respect when they saw the local bruiser systematically taken apart by the young academic. There was no spectacular *coup de grâce*, no triumphalist final upper-cut to leave his opponent bleeding in a heap on the floor, just a workmanlike, efficient workout which spared the thug some of his pride but left the spectators in no doubt as to the immense quality of Emerson's talent.

In the years since he had graduated from Cambridge and started work, his boxing workouts had become less frequent. More an eccentric sideline than a serious hobby, but he loved it.

When he had still worked for Steinman's, he had revelled in the image of the 'Boxing Banker', and it had been a good talking point with his clients, especially when he met them for lunch with a black eye or a thick lip. But despite the demands of his work, both then and now, he still managed at least one visit a month, and he loved to escape the world of designer suits and vacuous lunches in which he reluctantly still had to move. This was no self-imposed social experiment, it was a pleasure. He looked forward to his workout with the lads from the East End, and always stayed to drink with them in the bar afterwards.

He loved the raw openness of the discussions they had, but his enjoyment was not derived from some bizarre kind of 'noble-savage' idealism. There was nothing noble at all about his boxing friends. They were mostly criminals, petty burglars, car thieves or much worse, and any acts of savagery they might commit were usually entirely premeditated and brutal. He despised that side of them as much as he loved their unaffectedness. When he stood at the makeshift bar in his chalk-striped double-breasted suit and flamboyant silk tie after his shower, he epitomized the establishment cliché most of them loathed and came across more usually in the form of the prosecuting counsel at the Old Bailey.

Emerson finished his session with a final flurry of blows at bewildering speed and trooped off to shower before collapsing into bed. Despite his exhaustion his mind had become active again. The respite he had gained from delivering his last story and the hour's exercise was quickly being replaced by a fresh anxiety over what the next story was to be. Where would he begin looking? What would the angle be? What was the next cause to be taken up on behalf of the readers of 'The Emerson Bulletin'? Although he did not yet know it, he would not have to wait long to find out.

CHAPTER 5

THE XENFIN GULFSTREAM TOUCHED DOWN A LITTLE UNDER eight hours after it had left Frankfurt, at Owens Roberts International Airport, Grand Cayman. It was shortly after two a.m. local time, seven a.m. in London, and the air temperature was still pushing eighty-five. Van Aalst had changed into a more appropriate outfit for her arrival, black, raw silk T-shirt and wrap-around ankle-length batik skirt, and she quickly descended the steps from the plane carrying her slim, light-weight suit-carrier over one shoulder. She walked across the tarmac amongst the multitude of other, smaller private jets which crowded the apron like the Bentleys and Mercedes in the car park of a South Hampton golf club. Grand Cayman's status as an offshore, tax-free haven ensured there was always a healthy collection of state-of-the-art aeronautical hardware on show, and she amused herself by identifying them and figuring out who was in town to visit their money this week. Although the middle of the night, the customs and immigration desks were manned, as the privilege of wealth and private air-travel tolerates no schedules. The guards on duty recognized her immediately – she was a frequent traveller, especially to the Far East, and was always coming in at anti-social times – and waved her through with a smile and a cursory glance at her rear as she strode through and out into the car park.

Despite the lateness of the hour, she immediately lowered the roof of the powder-blue Ferrari 355 Spyder she had parked there two days before, and scorched out of the car park with tyres and Clapton squealing an accompaniment to the highly-tuned engine. She skirted the outer suburbs of the capital, Georgetown, and was soon turning on to Red

Bay Road which, in one guise or another, would wind along the southern coast of the island the twenty miles or so to her destination.

Once on the open coast road she was thrilled by both the warm night air and sea-breeze in her hair, and drove fast but sure-footedly along the darkened route, headlamps on full-beam, picking out the gates of the occasional secluded beach resort as she flashed by, beyond the tourist areas, past the famous Lighthouse Club, and on into the less-populated eastern side of the island. Finally, after around twenty minutes, she slowed, coaxed the Ferrari around an almost invisible left turn, and struck up north away from the coast road and into the heart of the island. This was a minor road, even by Cayman standards, and untarred, but van Aalst barely slowed. She could travel this route in her sleep, and she used the gears with skill and pleasure as she wound her way along what was now barely more than an overgrown track rising steadily up the side of a modest promontory. She passed her favourite tree, an enormous casuarina and handy landmark, and as she rounded the next bend, pushed a button on the remote control fixed to the top of the dashboard. The box of electronics hidden in the undergrowth at the side of the road recognized her signal, and identified her on a computer screen in a booth half a mile away as 'van Aalst, A.L. Blue Ferrari. Registration 355 EMG.' Two iron gates, fifteen feet high, and as yet unseen by her, began to swing open slowly and noiselessly so that, as she raced up the last stretch of her journey to the peak of the knoll, she was able to drive between them without braking and on into the compound. Once inside, the road was much better and flanked by low lanterns which illuminated small round pools of manicured lawns. Two hundred yards ahead, several lights still burned in the windows of a large colonial-style mansion, and she finally slowed down to pull the car up in front of the great old house, between the broad veranda and free-form swimming pool directly opposite the double entrance doors.

She resisted the temptation of a midnight swim, and hopped out of the car, exhilarated after her drive. She bounded up the wooden steps to the house and pulled out of her purse a plastic key-card, which she swiped through a reader mounted to one side of the massive, teak doors.

A slight click told her the way was now open and she pushed through into the entrance hall. As the doors swung closed behind her, the discreet brass plate screwed to the outside, reflected in the moonlight. It bore the legend 'XENFIN PARTNERSHIP'. In Grand Cayman the local time was now a little after two forty-five a.m., and Annie van Aalst had just arrived at the office.

The house from the outside was a beautifully preserved monument to British colonial tropical architecture. Principally wooden in construction and raised from the ground by stilts to allow the circulation of air, it was surrounded on all sides by shady verandas and deep, shuttered windows. The interior was a different story entirely, and the Xenfin designers had done a brilliant job in equipping the old house with all the facilities and amenities to be expected of a modern office building, without losing the impression that this had once been a private residence of some distinction.

The entrance hall betrayed nothing of the current commercial function of the house, and was preserved almost as it originally had been. The broad, highly polished wooden floorboards were the same ones which had been laid in 1907, dark oak shipped from England by an equally indulgent owner in an age of equally outrageous excess. The architects had been careful to re-lay them exactly in place and in order when they had installed the miles of fibre-optic communications cabling which now lay hidden beneath the feet, and which supplied the house with its life-blood: information. An observant visitor might also have noticed that the coolness of the air in the house owed less to the languidly spinning, purely ornamental ceiling fans which graced every room, than to the cleverly concealed air-conditioning ducts and vents which enabled the founder and owner, a rather fussy Mr Saul Krantz, to regulate the temperature of the five main zones in the house to within half a degree.

Various 'appropriate' antiques had been flown in from around the world to complete the picture. Victorian umbrella stands, Indian rugs, an aspidistra or two, all contributed to the illusion. The magnificent dining-room table and chairs, twenty feet long, could comfortably seat thirty and had been found in an old Ceylonese tea planter's mansion. The dining room itself doubled as the conference and presentation room, but the obscenely expensive audio-visual and teleconferencing equipment, including four forty-two-inch flat plasma TV screens with satellite-links, hidden cameras and digital projection hardware, all lay behind the cream-painted oak panelling. This had also been preserved from the old house, but modified to incorporate virtually silent hydraulic mechanisms which Mr Krantz liked to slide open unnoticed and surprise his guests whilst they slurped the lobster bisque. He would then, at a click of his cordless mouse while sitting at the dining table, glass of Cheval Blanc in the other hand, call up graphs and charts on the massive screens, which would display in three dimensions and 256 colours just how wonderful the performance of his clients' funds had been since their previous meeting. It never failed to amaze and impress. Most of his clients thought Saul Krantz was a genius.

Only two rooms in the house made no attempt to conceal the modern nature of their fittings, and neither was accessible by guests. One was the enormous kitchen, where the latest materials and appliances, yards of granite and steel and an entire wall of refrigeration equipment had brazenly ousted the ceramic butler's sinks and wood blocks of a bygone age. Five full-time chefs catered not only for the entertainment of visiting clients, which was lavish in scale, but also for the daily nourishment of the twenty-five professionals and twenty clerical and support staff who worked in the building. Saul Krantz was a connoisseur of epicurean proportions, and firmly believed that his employees should eat as well as he did.

To this end every member of staff, from the highest-flying fund-manager, to the most junior secretary, could choose from the daily-changing menu what they would like to eat that day, and it would be delivered to them, at their desks, concocted from the finest fresh produce and entirely free of charge. Poultry, fish, fruit and vegetables were no problem, the best being available locally, but beef was bought in from Argentina, smoked salmon from Scotland, and, if it was the right season and the postroom clerk fancied a dozen West

Cork oysters for lunch, he could put in an order and have them later that week.

The Xenfin staff were treated exceptionally well, and in return Krantz expected not only great loyalty, but Herculean performance in all that they did. The thoroughness of his recruitment process was renowned, and he would routinely take several months in identifying, interviewing, testing and researching the background of a single candidate, even a chauffeur, before hiring him. He was exceptionally proud of the fact that no one to whom he had offered a contract of employment had ever declined. Thus, once he had invested considerable time and effort, and was finally satisfied that a prospective employee was not only capable of doing that job as well as he was (and he could turn his hand to most things besides managing money, including cooking), but was also of the highest moral standards and integrity, then he was reluctant to risk losing them. He preferred to nurture and encourage, feed and water, pamper and cosset. And if somebody failed to perform, and had to be let go, he would apologize to them, pay them off handsomely and view it as a personal failing of his own making, probably down to inadequate research at the interview stage. He felt he couldn't possibly blame somebody for not being up to his standards. Few people were. He could only blame himself for not having noticed it before he hired them. It had only happened twice.

A job at Xenfin was the pinnacle of the financial world, and nobody had ever been known to leave voluntarily. It was a passport to riches for all involved, even for the support staff, all of whom participated in the firm's success. Their job was simply to make sure that the fund-managers, the demi-gods whose well-being they maintained and on whose performance the success of the firm depended, were able to function smoothly with the minimum of interruption or hassle. Thus the computer technicians knew that the slightest glitch in the systems could cost millions, and they worked around the clock, testing and re-testing, to ensure there was no break in service. If one of the external data providers, Bloomberg or Reuters, Telerate or Knight-Ridder, went down, they made sure that the fund-managers knew immediately of an alternative source to find the required information until regular service was resumed.

Similarly, the chefs knew that an overcooked steak or a frozen pastry could put some of the egos they nourished in a bad mood for the afternoon which, on a bad day, might seriously affect his or her trading judgement and the profits of the firm. So they made sure they knew the personal tastes of all the staff, who liked their steak rare, who liked their tomatoes at room temperature, who hated green peppers, and prepared each dish individually accordingly. Every foible, every whim, every complaint was recorded on computer file in the kitchens, and the records were updated after every meal. Who ate what, what came back untouched, who asked for more, and so on.

For all the pampering of his staff, Saul Krantz was as hard as nails when it came to winning business. If a potentially large account was up for grabs, he would do all in his power to see that it came to Xenfin. He would wine and dine, fight the competition tooth and claw, and fly anywhere in the world for a meeting at the drop of a hat. The Gulfstream was his favourite weapon. He had once been known to walk right out of his office in a pair of Bermudas, T-shirt and sandals, drive straight to the airport, and turn up in the office of an astonished prospective client in Montreal who had told him three hours before that he was giving his business to Moore Capital. He got the deal back.

He was, in brief, a legend in financial circles, but nobody really knew very much about his background and he deliberately eschewed the press.

At three a.m. in the Cayman Islands, following her return from Frankfurt and the deal with Löwen-Krugmann in the bag, the first person she bumped into as she strode across the cool entrance hall of Colliers Landings on her way up to the dealing room, was Saul Krantz himself, as he emerged from the men's room.

'Saul, don't you ever sleep?' she joked, as they climbed the stairs together.

'Only when there's no money to be made, ma'am,' he replied, which they both knew in his case meant never. He was in his mid fifties but had the physique and energy level of a much younger man. 'So, tell me. How was the conference in London?'

Annie's pretext for taking the company plane to London was CSFB's annual emerging markets conference. They normally held it in more exotic locations, like Monaco or Hong Kong, but it had been a tough year.

'Oh, pretty good. The usual stuff, you know. Analysts flogging a dead horse, charts and graphs to justify just about any statistic you could imagine, and forecasts of growth to the moon. You know, the more I hear of all these stellar predictions, the thinner the arguments seem. I'm beginning to get a little worried, to be honest.' She hadn't counted on having her crucial meeting with Krantz on the stairs, but what the hell, she might as well start laying the groundwork straight away. It hurt her to deceive him, but she knew she had been building towards this moment for some time. Pegasus had to come first, and the time for action was right now.

'You know Saul, we need to talk this over in more detail, but I've been running some numbers recently, and everything points towards the fact that the emerging markets, especially in Asia, are getting totally overvalued. *Everyone* is bullish and that makes me worried. When things turn around it could get really ugly, and we don't want to be the ones left holding the baby when everyone else is out and partying.'

As they arrived at the upstairs landing, Krantz held his hand over an electronic finger-print reader which gave access into *his* inner sanctum, the holy of holies, the Xenfin dealing room. They both entered the room, where the light from a handful of computer screens, work stations and telephone banks cast an eerie glow over the darkened room. As they entered, the motion sensors registered their arrival and the lights cranked up to full power. It might have been three in the afternoon, rather than three in the morning. Unusually, there was no one else in the room at that hour, it being a holiday over most of Europe and Asia. Normally, the night crew, of which Annie was the principal, were in every night covering all points east of the US during their own daylight trading hours. The markets were indeed truly global, and there was no point in the human day when some market, some exchange, some currency was not being traded for something else. Annie's speciality was Asia, and this demanded she spend most of her nights at Xenfin if she was going to exploit the opportunities as they arose. It actually suited her pretty well, as she would get in around five p.m., when Tokyo was just getting going, and leave around four a.m. by which time Asia was closed and she'd seen the first couple of hours' reaction in the London markets. That meant she could sleep till midday and enjoy the Cayman afternoon sunshine, snorkelling, diving, or just chilling in the hammock on her Georgetown balcony before she was back in at Xenfin to do it all over again. She sat at her desk, fired up her systems, and Krantz pulled up a chair.

'I hear what you're saying, Annie. What do you think we should do? Take the emerging markets weighting in the funds down a little?'

'No, Saul. I don't think that. We must go further than that. I think that Xenfin should seriously consider getting the hell out of there completely.'

Krantz was momentarily stunned at her proposal, but his expression betrayed nothing. 'You think things are that bad? Why the sudden doom and gloom?'

'Believe me, Saul, it's not sudden. I've been worried about it for a while. The Asian markets have been on a major bull run now for several years. But it's not so much the stock markets which have me worried, as the bond markets and the currencies.'

'But look at the foreign investment! It's been pouring into the region non-stop for years!'

'Exactly, and that's what has me worried. When a foreign corporation wants to invest in, say, Indonesia, what is the first thing they have to do? They have to take their dollars, or pounds or yen and buy the local currency, the rupiah, right?'

'Well, they wouldn't get very far buying some local clove-cigarette company with French francs.'

'Exactly. Except this has been going on for years.'

'So the rupiah's a little overbought. Everyone knows that. Even me, and I'm no emerging markets specialist.'

'Saul, it's much worse than that. The rupiah has come so far it's way beyond all known measures of value right now. And still people continue to buy it. It's riding for a fall. A heavy one.'

'OK, so you think the currency has gone too far, but we can hedge that risk. Now you mentioned the bond markets too. What's the problem there?'

'Well, all this foreign investment has caused the locals to want to expand their business to take advantage, to make as much as they possibly can.'

'So they've borrowed a lot. Big deal. Everyone's at it. Look at the US Government.'

'You're right, but these Indonesians aren't as sophisticated. They're massively exposed, you see. They could have borrowed from the local banks, and lots of them have done that, but the interest rates in most of these countries we're talking about are way higher than in Europe or Japan.'

'So they've borrowed overseas. I still don't see that your concern is justified, Annie.'

'The foreign banks are falling over themselves to lend to them, in yen, euros, dollars, you name it. And they've arranged bond issues in the same currencies, which amounts to the same thing. The Indonesians get to pay much lower interest rates that way, because they haven't hedged the currency risk. As long as the rupiah keeps on rising, they don't have to worry about making the interest payments. They simply take the local currency which they are earning from, say, their paper mills, and exchange it month by month for whatever currency they need to pay the bank loans or bond interest.'

'So what's the problem? It's worked out pretty well so far, and we've all gotten pretty rich on the back of it, haven't we?'

'Of course we have, Saul. But it can't go on for ever. Those guys have all borrowed *so* much, and have so much currency risk, that if the music suddenly stops there will be no place to sit for *anybody*. For me the worst sign is that the smaller companies are borrowing abroad now too, not just the big industries. Some local taxi company in Jakarta did a bond issue last week for God's sake. It's very scary, Saul.'

'What about the governments of these countries? Surely they're monitoring the situation?'

'They're worse than everybody else put together. There is so much nepotism, so much mutual back-scratching, so much self-interest at stake, that most officials just want to ride it while they can. Cronyism, they call it. The government basically tells the banks and the companies what to do, and they do it. Half of them are run by cousins, nephews and children of the politicians anyway. In Malaysia they call it "Guided Democracy"!'

'Well some people would say that has worked out pretty well. A good dose of government intervention can be a lot healthier than leaving everything to the freedom of the marketplace, don't you think?'

'No, Saul, I don't. And don't forget that the people doing the lending are foreigners. Japs, Germans, Americans. They don't give a shit what the Asian governments say. They *are* free to do whatever they want, and at the first smell of trouble, they'll be the first out. It's hot money, speculative money, not long-term investment in the infrastructure of a foreign nation out of the goodness of their hearts.'

'But if the private sector starts to hurt, won't these interventionist governments step in and help them? We've seen it before. Look at Latin America. They'll bail out the local banks, slap on some currency controls to stop the hot money leaving the country and tough it out.'

'They can't afford to. Not on the scale I think we're looking at. When it comes to borrowing, the governments have been hard at it too. The national debt of these countries is getting out of control. They can only just about service the debt they have now, with a following wind and a strong domestic currency, and yet they continue to borrow. I just found out at the conference in London that Korea is planning to issue fifteen *billion* dollars in thirty-year bonds next week. It will be the biggest issue ever out of South East Asia, and in my opinion you would have to be insane to buy it. It's going to yield around seven per cent, which is only about a point and a half over Treasuries. It won't take much, Saul, to tip the balance. I would say we're at the most critical stage in the emerging markets since the Latin American debt crisis in the eighties. It could be much worse.'

'Do you have the numbers to back this up, Annie?'

'Of course I do, you know me better than that.' She turned to her computer and punched a few keys. It had taken her hours to transfer the data from the Excel spreadsheets which Wallace Bradley had e-mailed to her the previous week, into a hard hitting Powerpoint presentation she knew Krantz would be unable to resist. He was not an Asian specialist. His own background was in mainstream finance – commercial real estate and project financing – and he was a brilliant strategist. He was master of the big picture, identifying trends, sniffing out opportunities on a global scale, but when it came down to the details he knew that the markets were too complex these days to do everything himself. He couldn't know *everything*, and he had trained himself to delegate. It hadn't been easy at first for an entrepreneur of his stature, but necessity was a strict taskmaster. In fact, over the last few years he had become reliant on the specialist, local knowledge of a few key lieutenants to handle the minutiae of his grand outlook. And today Annie van Aalst had supplied him with more details than he could feasibly question. There were graphs, piecharts, and tables by the dozen, showing the current account deficits, balance of payments data, currency analysis, everything he could possibly wish to know about the economies of Korea, Indonesia, Malaysia and Thailand. She printed it all out for him and he took the stack of paper with a frown before disappearing back into his office.

After he had gone, she punched up a few news screens about Thailand on the Bloomberg system. Good, nothing yet about Pee Seuar Land, and her friend Mr Chumsai. But she was ready now, and she was sure Saul Krantz would not take long in giving her the go ahead to proceed whenever she wanted. He just didn't know that it was all going to start tomorrow.

CHAPTER 6

P.L. CHUMSAI, MR P & L TO HIS ADMIRERS WHO MARVELLED at his rags to riches story of phenomenal success over the last ten years, arrived at the office in Bangkok early the next day as Annie van Aalst sat at her desk in her office in the Caribbean ten thousand miles away. His chauffeur opened the rear passenger door of the black Cadillac stretch limousine and he stepped from the frigidity of the air-conditioned cocoon on to the sweaty pavement outside his headquarters.

He was an impressive figure, tall for a Thai at around six feet, solidly built, and his presence was immediate as he walked slowly through the same airy atrium to which Chuan had delivered his mail forty-eight hours previously. He waved cheerily to the old security guard who hurried forward to summon the lift for the great man, pausing briefly for a slight bow, palms pressed together in the traditional Thai greeting. Chumsai indulged the old faithful guard and responded in the same manner. He winced at a slight twinge in his back as he did so, a small reminder of the athleticism of the seventeen-year-old girl, around the same age as his own daughter, whom he had left the night before in his suite at the Manila hotel. He smiled to himself at the memory and resolved to lose a few pounds before his next trip to the fleshpots. He preferred the Côte d'Azur and the European women. They were at least more his size, somebody he could really have a good grapple with, unlike the tiny young things one was served in the Orient who seemed they might break if one got too carried away.

The lift arrived, and he spent the twenty seconds or so it took to ride to his office on the thirty-seventh floor adjusting his appearance in the mirrored interior. His thick black hair was greased back flat to his head, which served to accentuate the round solidity of his head. He was extremely well-groomed. A dark-blue Italian-made suit, the ultimate status symbol in this land where a hundred dollars would buy you a passable imitation, concealed his opulent frame. Shiny black crocodile shoes and a heavy gold bracelet hovering below his crisp white shirt-cuff completed the image of the successful, if slightly tacky Asian businessman. Despite the back pain he managed his best swagger as he passed the desk of his personal assistant, a young girl he had found in his home town and had brought to the City of Angels to administer to his every need. She had been a good find, and most discreet in covering up for his jaunts away at weekends. Indeed, he would sometimes take her with him to avoid having to send out for the local fare after a particularly difficult week, say. Sometimes the comfort of the familiar was preferable to trying to impress some young foreign delicacy.

And he had had some difficult weeks lately. The Thai property market, in which he was the clear market leader, had been in a slump for almost three years now. A couple of the largest office developments had lost their principal tenants recently, and prices were falling inexorably. In the residential market, he had seven major projects in construction to provide fifteen thousand homes, but nobody seemed to want to rent them, much less buy them. Land prices were at a six-year low, and he had borrowed heavily to try to take advantage of the situation. A land bank was always a good thing to own, he reasoned, and at these prices, how could he go wrong when things began to improve a little?

At least he had powerful backers, he consoled himself. The Japanese had always invested in Thailand and seemed happy to go on lending to him despite the downturn in prices. They had faith, they knew a good investment when they saw one, even if it ended up turning into a rather longer-term investment than they had originally intended.

He walked into his office and motioned to his assistant to follow him. She sprang to her feet and trotted in behind him, closing the door as she did so.

'I'm a little stiff, Suzi, do you think you can do something for me?' he said, handing her his jacket which she dutifully hung on a hanger in the concealed wardrobe.

'You mean you didn't get enough while you were in Manila?' she giggled, coming round to his side of the desk before preparing to kneel in front of him.

'No you silly whore, not that. My back, my back is stiff. Do me one of your specials.'

He proceeded to lie flat on his stomach in the middle of his office floor, while his personal assistant and sometime companion knelt on his buttocks, twisted his shoulders and pummelled his back into submission.

'God, that's good,' he screamed as the offending vertebra jumped back into position. 'Are you sure you're not blind? You could earn a fortune downtown, you know, if you were.'

'And I'm sure you could arrange it for me too,' she laughed. 'Anyway, half of those blind masseuses the tourists pay so much for aren't really blind at all. It's not only the orgasms that are fake in Patpong.'

'You're right, the Gucci bags are too,' he added. 'That's much better, now I feel I can face the day. What do we have in store?'

'You have lunch with a director of Somprasong Land,' she replied. 'I think it's quite urgent.'

'Oh, that old misery. He sees doom and gloom at every corner. He probably wants to trick me into selling something to him on the cheap. What else?'

'Nothing much, but there is quite a stack of mail.' She pointed to the pile in his in-tray. 'That's just the stuff marked "personal". I have a ton more things for you to sign on my desk.'

'Bills, mainly, I suppose,' he grumbled. 'Any word from Mrs Chumsai?'

'Don't forget it is your anniversary tomorrow. She will be coming into town this afternoon to do some shopping, and may call in to the office.'

'God forbid. She probably just wants me to sign the credit card bills again. Oh well, I suppose you'd better book a table at the Oriental tonight for dinner. Make it about nine.'

'Very well, sir. Is that all? I'll leave you to your mail now if that's OK.'

P.L. Chumsai sat at his desk, eyeing the mail warily as his secretary left. He spread the pile over his desk and amused himself by closing his eyes, circling his fist in the air and choosing one at random with a stab of the finger. As it happened, the one he chose first was not the bomb. That lay partially concealed under the keyboard of his PC and he wouldn't find it till later. In fact, it would be the last letter he would open.

He worked his way through the stack of correspondence. Nothing significant really. A few requests for extensions of rent deadlines, all of which he stamped 'Request Declined', and a couple of proposals for development from eager young builders. He wished he had a stamp which said 'Optimistic Fools', but he never forgot his own beginnings only ten years before, and he dictated a couple of kind, encouraging refusals. These people were, after all, the future of Thailand and he didn't want to be too harsh. Their time would come, as had his.

Then he spotted the last letter of all, the heavy white envelope under his keyboard. He picked it up and noticed the Hong Kong postmark. Turning it over to open it with his silver knife he recognized the crest of the Osakumi Bank, Tokyo, on the reverse. 'Ah, my friend Mr Jonathan Quaid,' he murmured to himself. He thought it a little odd that his old friend Johnnie should be writing to him like this, all formal, but he supposed the Japanese demanded it from time to time. After all, they couldn't do all their business on the golf course or in the brothels of Tokyo, now could they? He had hoped Johnnie might be coming to Bangkok soon, so he could lay on another of their big nights. The Osakumi Bank was Chumsai's biggest lender, in fact currently their only lender. They didn't know it, of course, but they currently held mortgages on about 175 per cent of the current value of Pee Seuar Land Holdings' portfolio of property. Chumsai made sure that the periodic valuations demanded by the bank showed that ratio to be closer to 65 per cent, by greasing the appropriate palms in the valuers' offices. Nothing wrong with that, of course. Everybody did it, after all. Anyhow, he needed to keep Johnnie and Osakumi sweet, and hoped he would have the opportunity soon.

The razor sharp point of the knife found a chink in the envelope and sliced cleanly along the fold without disturbing what lay inside.

Chumsai's large fingers rubbed apart the two sides of the envelope, which gaped open to reveal the contents. He plunged in a sticky thumb and forefinger to extract the piece of paper, admiring as he did so the lining of tissue-paper which cosseted the letter. 'Paying too damn much interest if they can afford stationery like this,' he thought. He lay the folded letter on his leather desk-top and took a deep breath before opening it up.

When the bomb went off nobody in the immediate vicinity was aware of what had happened. Nobody in fact heard it at all. Only Chumsai himself heard the explosion going off as he opened up that letter, for the explosion was in his brain. As he sat at his desk and read what lay in black and white before his eyes, he could picture in his mind's eye the complete destruction of all that he had achieved over the last ten years, office buildings falling like dominoes to the ground around Bangkok, endless detonations and dust as his property empire crumbled to nothing before his very eyes.

The letter was very short, but to the point. It read as follows:

Dear Sir,

On the occasion of the annual review of our loan facility to Pee Seuar Land Holdings, it has come to our attention that the value of the outstanding loans greatly exceeds the value of the property upon which this credit is secured.

We therefore have no alternative but to demand, under the terms of our agreement, the immediate repayment of all sums owing to the Osakumi Bank.

In the event of non-payment by the 31st of this month, we will instruct our lawyers to begin proceedings to gain control of the relevant properties.

For and on behalf of the Board of Directors
J.L. Quaid.

The silence in Chumsai's office was deafening. The words rang in his head as he read the letter over and over again. He turned the letter over to see if there was any handwritten note from his old friend, proclaiming it all to be a nasty practical joke. There was nothing. In the room outside his office he heard muffled sounds of phones ringing, printers clattering, the normal signs of life in a busy concern going about its daily chores. They had no idea, no inkling of what was happening in the chairman's office at that moment. He was suddenly very afraid. He didn't dare leave his office. Maybe he could keep it quiet, smooth things over. He ran to the door of his office and locked it. No disturbances. He buzzed through to his secretary and told her to hold all calls. What next?

Some hours later and many thousands of miles away at her desk in the Cayman islands, Annie van Aalst picked up the phone and pushed one of the speed dials on the console before her. It was two a.m. local time, seven in the morning in London, and she knew Cameron Dodds would already be at his desk in the cavernous trading room of Steinman, Schwartz.

'Cameron, it's Annie. I'll be brief. Chumsai has read his letter. He's been trying to contact Johnnie Quaid all day, but he's not returning the calls. Johnnie's going to fax a copy of the letter to Reuters any time now, anonymously of course, so the news will hit the tapes soon. Start spreading some rumours now, and I'll come in with some big trades in about an hour. We want the market to be spooked before I start to put the volume through.'

'OK, Annie. I'll speak to a couple of brokers. They're always good for starting the bandwagon rolling.'

'I'll begin with the Thai baht, but it's Indonesia which is really vulnerable. We'll go for the rupiah soon after. Lafarge has set up the accounts in Jakarta, and I'll put those trades through in the name of Sukon. Have fun.'

She hung up, and Dodds sat looking around the dealing room. It was an enormous space, the size of a football pitch, and the four hundred or so dealing turrets were beginning to fill up as the highly paid minions of Mammon began drifting in to the office to prepare for the hustle of the day's activity. This day, however, was going to be slightly different. This would be the start of the Asian Crisis.

Cameron Dodds was going to enjoy this as he enjoyed most things –
teetering on the edge of disaster. He rode his motorcycle to the limits of
its capabilities, he subjected his body to a régime of work, alcohol and
hard drugs which flirted with collapse, and he tormented his friends and
colleagues by demanding the same of them:

'Mate, it's Cameron.'

'Cam, you maniac! Do you know what time it is?'

'Oh shit, sorry. Thought it was earlier than that. Anyhow, I'm taking the
bike down to Brighton. Right now. Scored some great gear from Sunil in
settlements and thought it'd be cool to sit on the beach in the moonlight
and throw pebbles into the sea while we did it. You coming? You can
ride on the back.'

'Cam, it's three in the morning!'

'We'll be back by seven. Straight into the office. Come on, man!'

And mostly they came, for his personality was as infectious as it was
addictive. He did not know how else to live, but his extremism had served
him well as a trader. And he always had been a trader.

Even whilst supplying his schoolfriends, at first with football cards
and then with a gramme here, an ounce there, he had made money from
trading, taking risk, gambling with his health and his liberty. The rush he
derived from this risk erased all sense of the consequences of his actions.
It had never occurred to him he might not come through, in some shape
or form, and that was all that mattered to him – physical survival to live
to enjoy the next experience.

His parents had been largely absent during his teenage years, trek-
king in India, playing at being missionaries in China, and generally
perpetuating their hippy pleasures well beyond a respectable age. They
had thought nothing of rolling up joints in front of a seven-year-old
Cameron and his schoolfriends at the dinner table, and there was always
a lump of something or other in a bowl on the sideboard. And Cameron
had always played along. In fact, besides mathematics, acting was his
other great talent. He had been the leading light at the various schools
he had been passed around, and when he had talked his way into Oxford
he had continued to shine on the stage whilst at the same time supplying

the cast parties with whatever was necessary to ensure they went with a swing. The career at Steinman, Schwartz was in reality nothing more than his latest rôle, an extended cameo appearance by a performer glad of the regular income from the financial 'soap', which enabled him to indulge his other personal projects.

And of course he had played along to Wallace Bradley's tune. For him, being part of the Pegasus Forum was an opportunity for one almighty thrill, a chance to play the greatest part of his life and to be close to Annie van Aalst. Bradley had thought he had known what he was getting when he had invited Cameron Dodds, the spiky-haired rebel, into the heart of his conspiracy – a mathematical prodigy with a healthy disrespect for the system, any system, who could be moulded and directed. As a living actor, Dodds was not about to disabuse him of this illusion just yet.

He picked up his phone again and punched the direct line to his favourite broker, a curious breed of intermediary used by the big trading firms for anonymously executing trades directly with other big firms. In the increasingly high-tech world of PhDs and sophisticated trading in exotic instruments, the inter-dealer broker was a refreshing anachronism. The accent was generally cockney, and the level of conversation was generally zero.

'Cam, my son. How goes it this morning? Anything cooking?'

'Woody, hi. I'm hearing some stories about a big potential bankruptcy in Thailand. You heard anything?'

'Let me do some digging, mate. I'll be back.'

Another line. 'Barnesy, it's Cameron. Anything I should know about a big failure in the Thai property sector? I'm hearing some ugly rumours.'

'Doddsy, leave it to me. I'll get on to the lads in Hong Kong.'

Within five minutes, Cameron Dodds's phone board was lit up with all incoming lights flashing.

'Cam, Woody. You were right mate. Sounds like one of the big property companies is goin' under.'

'Hello, is that Cameron? This is Jim Wilson in real estate finance at Steinman Hong Kong. Just thought you should know, we're hearing that one of the property developers here is in some trouble. You heard anything?'

'I'm hearing it's Pee Seuar Land Holdings.'

'Jesus Christ, that would be a bloody catastrophe. I hope we're not exposed.'

'Not yet, Jim. But I might try to get short. Gotta go.'

'Cameron, this is Alex in risk control. I want you to be careful with Thailand today. Real estate finance in Hong Kong just called to let me know about some potential trouble out there. Just be aware . . .'

The buzz in the office gradually rose as screens were powered up and conversation began to revolve around the crisis taking shape in Thailand. A crisis Cameron Dodds had started with two phone calls to the biggest mouths in the market. Suddenly, a cry went up from the other side of his desk.

'It's on the tapes! Reuters has it. Pee Seuar Land has gone bust with fifteen billion dollars' worth of debt! Holy shit!'

Dodds glanced at his screens. It was the last hour of trading on the Bangkok stock exchange, and the market had dropped five per cent in the last five minutes. He smiled to himself and phoned the foreign exchange desk in Hong Kong.

'It's Dodds here. I don't like this Thai thing right now. I want to sell some baht. What's the quote?'

'24.65–95.'

'Five hundred at 95.' Cameron Dodds had just sold five hundred million Thai baht, or around fifteen million pounds, at a rate of 24.95 to the dollar. 'How's it left?'

'85–15.'

'I've got another five to go at market.'

'Filled at twenty. Sorry Cameron, it's crapping out here. A bit of a fast market. 25.20–55 on the follow.'

In total, Dodds had sold one billion Thai baht, or around thirty million pounds, in thirty seconds. This was an outright speculation on the currency, in fact on currency that he did not own, but he was sure it would go down. In fact, he knew for a fact it would, as he knew what the Xenfin Partnership would be doing very shortly, and by comparison to that, his own trade in a billion would be very small fry indeed.

*   *   *

Annie van Aalst sat in conference with Saul Krantz in his office. He had spent the previous day going over the reports she had prepared for him, and he looked concerned and tired. It was two thirty a.m. and he had been in the office for eighteen hours.

'It's started already Annie, hasn't it? What we discussed last night.'

'You're right Saul. But I have an inkling Pee Suar Land is only the tip of the iceberg. If they're going under, and they're the biggest, others can't be far behind.'

'I'm sorry to say it looks like you're right, Annie. The baht has been pegged to the US dollar for too long and at too high a rate. Judging by the numbers you gave me, the stability the dollar link gave it has encouraged foreigners to invest in the country, but it's killed the economy. Seems to me that the local exporters can't survive with their own currency at such levels, and on top of that, land and property values have been falling for a year. Do whatever you have to get us out of there. And don't stop at Thailand. If these numbers are right, Indonesia and Korea can't be too healthy either. We have our investors to consider, and our performance.'

'How long have I got to get us out?'

'We've got a total of thirty billion in the region.' He used the figure without blinking. 'I figure you could do that in a week, without creating too much mayhem, but we need to do more than get out of what we own. We need to get short. Heavily short. If this thing goes where I think it's going, it could be the biggest meltdown in the emerging markets the world has ever seen. We don't need just to avoid losing money. We can *make* money out of that. Do whatever you have to, Annie, you have absolute discretion. Crank the leverage up as you see fit, we've got plenty of room for that, and don't even think about going home until we're short.'

Short. Get short. The phrase was music to her ears. She knew about the thirty billion dollars they had invested in the region, she'd done most of it after all, apart from a couple of billion the equity guys had done, but she'd not reckoned on Krantz being aggressive enough to get short. For what he was suggesting was not merely a question of disinvesting the money they had already put in, which was huge in itself, but actually selling bonds and currency that they *did not own*, with a view to buying it back more cheaply at some later date. This was tantamount to pumping not only their own money out of the region but other people's as well, at a time when it would hurt most. And she would be controlling the tap. 'Without creating too much mayhem', he had said. You wish, Saul, you wish.

She left his office and padded barefoot back to her desk. The night session in Xenfin's small dealing room was normally an eerily convivial affair, with the dozen or so traders and support staff enjoying the relative quiet and special ambience conveyed by the darkness outside. But today there was tension. The crickets chirping outside were ignored as the feeling spread that something significant was in the air. The screens on the desks were filled with numbers changing from blue to red, as the markets turned down and the momentum began to build. Annie van Aalst picked up the phone again and called her old boss at Salomon in London.

'Annie, to what do I owe the pleasure? You want to come back and work for us?'

'Cut the chat-up please. I have some business for you.' She was in serious mode, and didn't need the customary guilt trip from her former colleague. 'I want to sell some bonds. Korea globals, Indonesia 06s, Thai 07s. Good size.'

'What's going on Annie?'

'We're just making some room for the big new Korea deal next week. Need to raise a bit of cash, that's all. With the Thai news this morning, I guess the market's headed a little lower in the short term.' She didn't want him to know she was selling out of everything she owned, not yet anyway. Panic would be good, but at the time when she chose to provoke it. When she had got short.

'Just a sec.' He put her on hold while he went to speak to the trader to get the prices. She could imagine the conversation. By this stage all the Asian stock markets were between five and seven per cent lower across the board, and the currencies were beginning to come under pressure. A run on the bonds was all they needed before eight o'clock in the morning London time. How many does she want to sell? She just said 'good size'. What does that mean for her? She's at Xenfin. That could mean anything. Assume twenty at least.

'Annie. You still there? Sorry it took a while, but the trader's pissing his pants. The bids are 100.50, 98.65 and 98.70 respectively.'

'I'll do a hundred of each thanks. And thank the trader for me, will you? Who was it? Steve? Those were great prices — not like the guy at Merrill. He'd only do fifty.' Click. She hung up before the salesman could object. She knew she was chancing her arm and had behaved poorly. The Salomon trader was under no obligation to hold the prices for a hundred million dollars' worth of each bond, when normal market size was probably ten million. But she had taken a calculated gamble. She was the biggest player in the market and they'd been trying to get her business ever since she had quit to work for Saul Krantz. She guessed they would not want to risk annoying her by calling back to weasel out of the trade. And the stuff about Merrill was not true. She had not sold any more bonds that morning, yet, but she wanted to give the salesman a hard few hours. He certainly wouldn't pass the information on to his trader, who would be furious to know his client had sold more of the same bonds to another dealer before coming on to them, but she had never liked him particularly and enjoyed the thought of him sweating, worried that the trader might find it out from the market. Pleased with her first operation, she called Cameron Dodds.

'Cam, I've done some bonds with Solly's. Three hundred. Should get those spreads widening a bit. I want to have a go at the rupiah now. Anything I should know?'

'Yes Annie, there is. I don't think the rupiah will need much encouragement to go. Our mate Chumsai just splashed himself all over the Bangkok pavements from the thirty-seventh floor. Some guy from the Thai Central Bank has just come out with a statement on the currency weakness this morning, and the Finance Minister is calling into question the whole philosophy of tying the baht to the dollar. Seems like they might let the currency float, Annie. Can you believe it? On the first day? I never thought they'd go that quickly.'

'You mean Chumsai is dead? My God, that wasn't meant to happen. Is there any tie-in to us? I mean, could we be held liable?'

'Forget it. The guy was a fraudulent son of a bitch who had been misvaluing his properties for years to borrow more money. Sure, they'll probably find Quaid's letter on his desk, but it's all true. The timing might not have been the most considerate, but that was the whole point for Pegasus, wasn't it? It's great for us. The publicity of the suicide will give the whole story much more coverage than we might have hoped for at this stage. Should move things along nicely. Don't lose any sleep over Chumsai, Annie. Be happy for his wife.'

Annie van Aalst sat at her desk in silence for a while. Now they had blood on their hands. Indirectly at least. But Dodds was right. This was the point of Pegasus. The whole system stank, and they had to expose it. Chumsai was small fry, but symptomatic of the whole stinking mess. The banks were in it up to their necks, and how many lives had *they* ruined with their greedy and callous practices? As the daughter of just such a man, she knew of at least one.

CHAPTER 7

ICHAEL VAN AALST III WAS THE LATEST IN A LONG LINE
of van Aalst bankers. Word had it, his word largely, that he
could trace his financier's roots back to one René van Aalst
in Holland, one of the prime movers in that country's notorious 'Tulip
Bubble' in the sixteenth century, when the price of tulip bulbs reached
preposterous levels and fortunes were made and lost. Old Uncle René,
as Michael liked to refer to him, had made his then.

That branch of the van Aalst family had allegedly come to America in
the nineteenth century, when the residue of the floral patrimony was in
need of a boost after three hundred of years of neglect, and they had
set about building a new dynasty. They had done very well too, with
a knack for attaching themselves to the right bandwagon at the right
time, and stakes in gold mines were exchanged for others in railroads
and then more in steel before Annie van Aalst's great grandfather, a
man whose white beard and stern brow she could still remember and
who was referred to as 'Michael the First', turned the family eye back
to banking and the stock market.

That there is no 'van Aalst Centre' or 'van Aalst Hall' is most likely
testimony to the fact that, unlike the Rockefellers and Carnegies with
whom they partied, holidayed and, according to one gossip rag, occasionally interbred, they were not innovators. No van Aalst ever had an original
idea, no van Aalst ever started a trend. But they were always there or
thereabouts when there was an idea to buy into or a trend to follow. They
hovered in the background of the photographs in the society pages, and
networked and entertained insatiably, managing to accumulate enough

wealth and prestige by association that they might well have been thought
to have had the original ideas in the first place. It was Michael the First
who had known J. Pierpoint Morgan and followed him into banking, and
it was his son, another Michael in the long family tradition of sticking
with a trend, who had built the Connecticut mansion in which the
family, including Annie, had lived ever since. When he had got most
of the family funds out of the stock market in 1928, more by good luck
than good management in the manner of Old Uncle René and his tulips,
he had added the stud farm in South Carolina and the beach front lot
in Palm Beach to the family's property portfolio.

Annie had spent most of her young life flitting between these locations,
but her own father, Michael the Third, had not been around to notice her
growing up, nor to arrest his wife's slow descent into alcoholism. For he
had taken the van Aalst knack for swallowing pride and following leaders
to a level as yet unknown in the family history. They were rich by most
people's standards, a couple of hundred million salted away in various
investments and trusts, but it was never enough for Michael van Aalst
III. The people with whom he mixed and liked to call his friends all had
much more. They *owned* the banks and brokerage companies for which
he continued to work; they *built* the buildings in which he invested; they
bought and *developed* the islands in the Caribbean on which he liked to
holiday. He felt he was always the poor relation, the aspirant, the parvenu
who could emulate but never quite match. And he became a sycophantic,
toadying yes-man to the whims of all these people at the expense of his
family. The privately owned bank in which he spent most of his career
and his life ate up all of his energies. He was the one lobbying politicians
in Washington until the early hours, he was the one they sent to Europe
and the Far East on three-month foraging trips for new clients, and he
was the one who gratefully accepted the rôle if it could ingratiate him
some more into their circle. Yes, he signed the cheques for the string
of clinics a teenage Annie had tried for her mother, but all the money
in the world could not help where Betty Ford had failed.

On the rare occasions that he had shown up at one of the family homes
during Annie's childhood, he had invariably had clients in tow, clients to

schmooze, wine and dine and let ogle his pre-pubescent daughter around the pool. He had once come down from New York for the day to the South Carolina stud with an Arab client he wanted to impress with his horses. He had thought it odd, and was in fact fairly irked, that his family did not appear to be around, as he had thought he had remembered his wife telling him they would be there when he had last spoken to her the previous week. And he had spent the entire flight telling his Arab client how his daughter liked to sunbathe topless on the lawns. In fact, for all of the seven hours he had spent there that day, he had failed to notice that his daughter had actually been sobbing in her bedroom whilst his wife had been lying naked and unconscious in the bathtub, nursing an empty bottle of vodka, where she had been since eleven that morning. Neither his wife nor daughter knew that he had been in the house.

And Annie van Aalst had developed a profound hatred for him. For his mediocrity, for his selfishness, for his endless social climbing, and above all for the object of all his desires. Money. God knows, they had enough, they were wallowing in the stuff, but she hated it. She hated the museum-like atmosphere of their houses, the furniture she couldn't sit on and the paintings too expensive to hang on the walls. It was all too much, obscenely extravagant, and it symbolized everything that was rotten about her childhood, because for her father nothing was enough. He wanted more, and then more again, and his obsession with money had ruined everything *she* valued. Her mother, her happiness, her own childhood.

But Wallace Bradley and Pegasus had offered her an opportunity. For the first time in the history of the family, a van Aalst was going to be a leader. She was going to *start* a trend, not follow one, and although it meant working for a while within a system she despised, she was now going to attack the one thing her father craved. She was going to take it away from him. She was going to destroy the value of money itself.

And, sitting at her computer terminal in the Cayman Islands, she picked up the phone and followed up the carnage they had begun to cause with wave after wave of massive selling. She was just one voice on a phone, working for one firm on a Caribbean hideaway, but the name of that firm was Xenfin, and in Annie van Aalst, Wallace Bradley had chosen his disciple extremely well.

On the other side of the Atlantic a very different girl, a twenty-year-old Irish girl called Patsy O'Connor, hovered on the landing outside Wallace Bradley's rooms. It was the middle of the night but she had spent the last five hours in the college library, mustering the courage to confront once more the man who had ruined her life. She had to do it. It had taken her six months to get this far, and she could not face returning to her freezing digs in north Oxford, and all that lay in store for her, without one last try. Timidly she raised her hand and tapped twice, feebly, at his door.

'Professor. It's me, Patsy. Patsy O'Connor. I must speak to you. Please!' The words rang in her head at great volume, but in reality she had managed no more than a hoarse whisper. There was no reply. She was familiar with his sleeping habits and knew that it would take more force than she then felt capable of summoning to rouse him. She knew then that her trip had been wasted and that she would never be able to manage it again. She looked at the pitted oak door and the nameplate above it, *his* name, and thought back to June, the last time she had left that room and closed the door behind her, the last time she had set eyes on professor Wallace Bradley.

Then too it had been the middle of the night, when she had tiptoed out of his bedroom into the sitting room of his college lodgings and huddled naked in the dark on the sagging sofa. The first tears rolled down her cheek as Bradley's ejaculate seeped from her into the loose weave of the threadbare cushion.

It was three a.m. and the rest of the college was sleeping, including her economics tutor in the adjoining room who, five minutes before, had grunted in climax and rolled from his position atop her before falling into a deep and contented sleep. She had been visiting him at night once a week for over a term then, and it was an ordeal that she dreaded. It had been difficult the first time, and it had not become any easier to make love to the flabby fifty-year-old who held her future as well as her young body in his greedy hands.

It had started innocently enough. Although she wasn't a St Mary's student, her own college had an arrangement which allowed students to receive tutorial supervision from dons in other colleges when an undergraduate required specialist teaching. As she intended to write a paper in her final examinations on the economies of the Far East, Bradley was an obvious choice, and he had agreed to a weekly tutorial for one term. The Oxford tutorial system was an indulgent, privileged process. Students got to have weekly, one-on-one discussions for an hour with often world-renowned experts in their field, and this would generally take the form of the students' reading out the essay they had spent the previous week researching and writing. Patsy had been recommended to Bradley by a colleague, who at the same time suggested that she try for a five p.m. slot with Bradley, as that was the hour when he would open up the drinks cabinet. This would tend to make the potentially daunting hour's post-mortem of the week's work run a little more comfortably.

When she had timidly knocked on the old oak door to Bradley's rooms at St Mary's for her first tutorial, she had entered to find the room apparently empty. As she moved further into the room, she discovered her tutor behind the old sofa, prone and absentmindedly kicking his shoeless and sockless feet in the air as he sifted through the piles of papers which surrounded him. She stood there watching, unacknowledged, for a good minute before her gaze seemed to penetrate the haze of cigarette smoke which wreathed his head, and he glanced up, seemingly surprised to see her standing there. The fact that somebody had knocked at his door and that he had uttered the words 'Come in' barely a minute earlier seemed to have escaped him. He sprang up in consternation and hurriedly put on his shoes and socks before proffering a smelly hand, cigarette clamped between middle and forefingers.

'My dear, how rude of me not to see you there. Wallace Bradley. Do come in, come in. Have a seat. Now what can I do for you?'

'Professor Bradley, my name is Patsy O'Connor. We have our first tutorial scheduled for now. I'm from Balliol.'

'Of course, Patsy. How rude of me. I got a little side-tracked. I was just preparing something for the Malaysian Government. Now what are we talking about today?'

'You set me the title "The Monetary Tools of the South Korean Government". I have written an essay.'

'Good, good. We'll get to that. Now, I hear St Mary's church chiming five, which means only one thing. Drinkies! Can I offer you something? I normally have a gin and French around now. Would that do?'

'Well thank you, Professor, maybe a small one.'

'You will notice, Patsy, that during the course of the tutorial I will most likely have several of these, but I will not offer you any more. This is because I am working on becoming an alcoholic and wouldn't like you to embark on that journey just yet.'

She didn't know whether to laugh or commiserate, so instead took the proffered glass in silence and sat in the corner of the sofa to begin shyly reading out her first essay. The same sofa on which she had later sat, shivering and sobbing in the night.

She was not the most gifted of students. In fact, her first two years at Oxford had been something of a struggle for survival. The County Mayo comprehensive, from which she had been the first ever pupil to win a place at Oxford, had not really prepared her for being one of many able students in a high-powered university. She was used to being top of her class, and hadn't taken well to being below average in her new peer group. She couldn't share this with her parents of course. They wouldn't have understood. They had wanted her to stay at home and do something less demanding – a comfy job in the local department store, close to the family support system, marry a nice local boy and have babies. The financial privations of sending her away to college on the mainland, and Oxford on top of that with all the social pressures of mixing with the privileged and moneyed classes of the English establishment, had been a constant source of friction.

Her mother had taken in extra clerical work at home on top of her dayjob as a cleaner at the town hall, and her father had opted to work the nightshift as a security guard for a local removals and storage company, all to give her the financial support she needed. The guilt was enormous. It was built into her Catholic upbringing, of course, but no more bearable for that. It was unthinkable for her to be kicked out. She had to graduate and land a high-powered job to show her parents the value of her education. A City job in banking or stockbroking, so she could send them home some money, repay her debts, clear her name as the prodigal daughter swanning around in Oxford, sipping sherry and mixing with fancy folk. She needed all the help she could get, and Bradley had offered it to her. At a price.

She could remember exactly the first time they had had sex, and it had happened naturally enough. Bradley had dissected the first two essays she had written with all the dispassionate and analytical prowess of one at the peak of his profession discarding the juvenile, plagiarist ramblings of an intellectual naïve. He had even threatened to wind up his tutorials with her if she didn't get her act together. Why should he waste his time with her? She was using up time he could have been spending with a more able student. Didn't she know who he was?

The tears had come fairly soon after this outburst and he had taken his chance. He had moved from his desk to sit next to her on the sofa, and had wrapped a comforting arm around her shoulder. All very paternal, pastoral, protective. He had apologized for his tirade, offered help, extra tutorials. Back to basics with an individual, tailor-made crammer course to get her through her exams. Three evenings a week after hall she had tripped eagerly round to his rooms, and he had guided her gently through the academic discipline necessary to turn in a competent performance in her finals. Occasionally he would open a bottle of wine, and the sessions sometimes continued into the early hours. She was happy, gaining in confidence and grateful for the assistance. She even liked him for all his arrogance and pomposity, and excused the occasional lapse of patience. She sometimes lost patience with herself after all, for a silly mistake or elementary miscalculation. She marvelled at his erudition and felt safe under his tutelage. She imagined him sitting at her shoulder in classes and lectures, she could hear his gentle, guiding tones prompting her when she struggled for an answer, and her results improved dramatically.

So she had not demurred, in fact she had been relieved to accede, when, in his donnish and awkward way he had enquired if he might kiss her. The wine had flowed that evening; he had regaled her with anecdotes of Keynes and of Smith; they had shared jokes at the expense of Bradley's colleagues in the Senior Common Room; for the first time she had felt herself an insider, part of that academic in-crowd to which she aspired and to which Bradley had helped open the door a crack. She was not in the slightest attracted to him physically. Who could be? But she admired and pitied and felt grateful to him. What she could offer in return was her companionship, and her body.

She was not an experienced lover, and had been caught off guard by the force of his advance. Following his awkward and formal request for permission to kiss, she had expected the hesitant and delicate attentions of a shy adolescent on a first date from this famously anti-social and lonely man. Instead he had grasped her fairly roughly and immediately and hungrily tried to prise apart her lips with his tongue. His drool dribbled down her chin and he began to paw clumsily at her breasts and thighs without modesty or tenderness. She had initially shrunk further back into the depths of the sofa in an attempt to escape his advances, but he had merely interpreted this as acquiescence and proceeded to climb on top of her.

'Forgive my ardour, Patsy, but it has been so long,' he lied as he came up for air, 'and I have admired you ever since we began our tutorials. You will go far, my dear, and I can help you.' She could do little else but give in. She was so grateful for his help, and felt it would be churlish to push him away. His rough approach made her a little uncomfortable, but she put it down to inexperience and passion from a man long deprived of the pleasures of the flesh, not to the inconsiderate practices of one used to frequenting the brothels of Bangkok. Their relationship was consummated less than five minutes after their first kiss, as he knelt before her, hiked up her skirt, and folded her over the pudgy arm of that sofa. The same sofa on which she had later sat, cheeks smudged with dripping mascara, leaking semen.

Things had deteriorated since then. She had continued to visit for her after-hours tutorials, and for the first two or three evenings he had gone through the motions of teaching her and correcting her work before gravitating towards the sofa. But the study time had become shorter and shorter, and the sex had begun earlier and earlier. Within a week he had dispensed with the tuition entirely, and their relationship had become merely carnal. But there was no question of a public relationship. Bradley insisted the college authorities would disapprove, and so there was no courtship, no dinners out, no trips to museums or theatres.

Had theirs been a normal relationship she would have terminated it sooner. She had even tried to once, but there was a problem. The same problem which had continued to bring her to Bradley's rooms at night for some time but which always left her in tears.

At his suggestion, and at the height of their evening collaborations, they had hatched a plot whereby he would guarantee her a top grade in one of her final exam papers. He was to be the university's examiner for students choosing to write a paper on the economies of South East Asia, and although examination papers were submitted anonymously for grading to avoid favouritism towards candidates known to the examiner, they had agreed on one fairly unusual phrase which she would incorporate into whatever question she chose to answer, and which would alert Bradley to the fact that it was her work. She had come up with the specific wording of the phrase herself and e-mailed it to him so he had it in writing. But she was now trapped. As he had pointed out when she had first attempted to bring their meetings to an end, there was no going back. Without his help she would still struggle to pass (it was understood that he could see to that) and wouldn't it be awful if the authorities suspected that she had attempted to bribe her tutor with sex, and even suggested a means whereby he could identify her paper from the hundreds of others so that he might give her preferential treatment? Once, when she had been left alone in his study for a while, she had tried to get into his computer to retrieve her e-mail, but to no avail. It was password-protected and impossible to access. She could have gone to the university authorities to expose him, but it would be her word against his. He the Nobel-nominated economist, she the struggling student making scurrilous accusations of sexual blackmail in an attempt to get her revenge for a series of bad grades. Who would believe the truth?

Shivering in the hallway outside his door she drew her shapeless overcoat around her and started back down the creaking staircase. She felt incredibly alone, for she knew deep down that no one, not Wallace Bradley nor her mother or father, could help her through the next ordeal she faced. She resolved to save what remaining courage she had for that, and left Wallace Bradley to his own nightmares.

Bradley heard the floorboards creak and opened his eyes. Thank goodness, she'd left already. He had some important calls to make. It was the middle of the night, but that meant it was the middle of the trading day in Asia, and he needed to know what progress was being made. Was everything proceeding according to plan, or did they need to implement any of their supplementary strategies? He pulled an old flannel bathrobe about his spreading middle and walked to his desk in the adjoining study, flicking on the electric kettle on the sideboard for the obligatory coffee. Two spoonfuls of Gold Blend should do the trick. He'd have to be up for most of the night. A quick sniff of the milk before he sloshed it into the chipped mug. He picked up the telephone, and dialled a number in the Cayman Islands.

'Van Aalst.'

'Annie, this is Jason at Lehman.' It was standard practice for financial institutions to tape all the conversations of their traders and fund managers. Hundreds of millions of dollars were transacted by telephone every day, and the tapes were a back-up confirmation of the deals agreed verbally, in case of disagreements later. Bradley knew this and didn't want to leave any tracks. The alias had been agreed several months ago and they had to assume someone would be listening. If not now, then later, when things really started to get ugly and scapegoats were sought.

'Hey, how's it going? I suppose you want an update on the markets in Asia.'

'That would be great.'

'Well it's not pretty. We've had a major bankruptcy in the Thai property sector, totally out of the blue. Complete panic in the Thai bond markets. Spreads are out by about two hundred basis points and counting.'

'Wow. That's incredible. What's the knock-on effect elsewhere?'

'Well, all the Asian currencies have taken a battering, but especially Indonesia. The rupiah has seen some massive selling, mainly out of London, but we're beginning to see the hedge funds moving in. They can sense a wounded animal when they see one, and this will be no mercy killing.'

'Any reaction from the authorities?'

'Oh yeah. Just what we expected. The currency's getting killed so what do they do? Jam up interest rates to support it. Exactly what they shouldn't be doing. They forget. The weakness in the currency is just a symptom of a bigger goddamn problem. Their economy is shot to pieces, along with the rest of Asia, and they should be *cutting* rates, devaluing the currency, and giving the economy some breathing space.'

'But they're worried about the foreign debt, aren't they? They know all their banks are up to their neck in foreign debt, and if their own currency weakens it makes that debt more expensive to service.'

'True, but you know the one thing the markets like is a weak government trying to defend a weak currency. It's pretty much a one-way bet. The Indonesian Government would like to think it can support its own currency, but it only has two weapons. Hiking interest rates or buying the rupiah itself in the open market. If they hike rates too far, they kill off the economy anyway. If they try to buy rupiah, they'll find the market has way more to sell than they can buy. They're totally screwed.'

'And elsewhere?'

'Korea, Philippines, Malaysia. Same story, not so severe. Yet.'

'And Japan?' Bradley struggled to keep his voice from wavering.

'Well. The jury's still out on the Nips for now. Everybody knows they've bankrolled the whole region for years. If it goes on like this, the Japs could start to have some serious problems of their own, especially if the Indonesians and the Koreans stop paying back the loans. Don't forget, Japan has been in a recession of their own for the last ten years. They were hurting already. If the Tigers start to turn sour they could be screwed. After all, it was a Japanese bank pulling the plug on Pee Seuar Land that started the whole thing in the first place.'

'Was it now? Well that is most interesting.' Bradley smirked to himself. 'Do let me know, Annie, of any further developments in that direction.'

'Will do. By the way, the chairman of Pee Seuar topped himself. Thirty-something floors.' Bradley flinched slightly. That had not been expected. Had not been desired. It would involve police. An investigation. Accountability. They would see Johnnie Quaid's letter. He would have to justify, explain. Still, it was a commercial decision to cut Chumsai's lines. Perfectly justifiable. The man was a crook. Pegasus was isolated. No traces. Ultimate deniability.

'Really? That *is* awful. I must call Hong Kong to see how things are moving there. Goodnight, Annie.'

Johnnie Quaid in Hong Kong had been the catalyst. The trigger. He liked that. He had spent five years getting himself into a position of sufficient authority within the Osakumi Bank to be able to direct his employer's lending strategy for real estate projects within the whole South East Asian region. He was very bright, and a quick learner. And his language skills, total fluency in English and Japanese, not to mention his mother tongues of Mandarin and Cantonese, had guaranteed his rapid promotion. From shopping malls in Singapore to office buildings in downtown Kuala Lumpur, any property loans advanced by the Osakumi Bank now had to pass over his desk for final approval. Or disapproval.

For Pee Seuar Land, Osakumi had been the life-support machine on which he had personally just pulled the plug. One man, with the power of life or death over a major corporation, and he had given the thumbs down. He had had to sell the decision to his superiors, of course, for an account of that magnitude, but the case was compelling, and it fitted well into the bank's strategy of writing off the worst of its bad loans in an attempt to strengthen the balance sheet. Take a big loss today in order to prevent bigger ones in the future. The rating agencies liked it, and without a good credit rating,

Osakumi themselves wouldn't be able to borrow the money they lent to everybody else.

But nobody in the Osaka head office was really aware of the extent of the difficulties. Property values were the biggest single problem in the whole of the Asian region, and the withdrawal of credit to the biggest developer would have dire implications for the rest of the sector. And all the banks had massively overextended themselves. The amount of debt that the biggest Asian companies had taken on was mind-boggling.

He remembered in his early days out of college when he had struggled to get a mortgage which amounted to three times his annual salary. Furthermore, he had had to come up with a ten per cent deposit and the loan was to be secured on the property. In business in Asia things were different. The Korean Government, for example, pretty much told the Korean banks who to lend to, and they just lent and lent, more and more, with little regard for the economic consequences. It had got to the stage now when the *interest alone* on that debt was more than those companies earned in a year. For an individual like Johnnie Quaid, that was the equivalent of his monthly mortgage payments being more than his monthly take home pay. Nothing left over for beans on toast. In fact, less than nothing, as underpayment of interest merely led to yet more debt, which led to more interest . . .

It couldn't go on. The Japanese banks couldn't support it any more. It was only a matter of time before the whole structure collapsed. And he, Jonathan Quaid, had set off the detonating charge. Bradley had always likened it to the demolition of a huge skyscraper. It is sufficient, he would say, to place some relatively small explosive charge around the base, at key structural points, and the weight of the edifice does the rest of the work for you. His counterparts in the other banks would be scrambling already to reassess their own loan portfolios. They wouldn't want to be the last to get out. The herd mentality would kick in and the banks would unwittingly crush themselves as they scrambled to be the next to deny further aid to their moribund clients. Not appropriate for resuscitation.

Quaid had become quite a specialist in real estate in a short period, but the downturn in property values over the last couple of years had made his job a lot more difficult. He knew the bank was hurting back in Osaka, and the value of the domestic mortgage loans they had outstanding exceeded the value of the properties on which they were secured by around one hundred per cent. For the time being this was OK, as the default rates by Japanese homeowners was very low and there was no need to repossess. But if the recession deteriorated, if people lost their jobs and couldn't service their mortgages any more, that default rate would increase. The banks would suddenly find themselves in possession of thousands of properties, worth half the amount they had lent to the original buyers. And if they wanted to recoup any of their money they would have to sell them into a falling market that nobody wanted to buy into in the first place. It would be devastating. A classic vicious circle. In Bradley's language, an auto-perpetuating trend.

Markets were like that. It happened all the time. People had opinions about the future and made decisions based on that opinion. To buy or to sell? To lend or not to lend? To invest or to abandon ship? If enough people were of the same opinion, then their collective decisions actually influenced the outcome of those decisions. In Cameron Dodds's crude expression, 'size really did matter'. Markets were social animals peopled by living, thinking, breathing human beings, motivated largely by greed. There were no physical laws which applied here, no absolute facts. Bradley had instilled this into them from the very beginning. It was incredible to him that the accepted wisdom was still a blind faith in the fact that markets and economies were inherently stable, that they tended towards equilibrium, some long-term average. The history of the world was testimony to the opposite. It was full of booms and busts, great crashes followed by huge growth. It was more like a spinning top, *capable* of balance if pumped up with vast amounts of credit, but remove that steadying and energizing hand and it would either career off wildly or heel over one way or the other. *Dis*-equilibrium was inherent in the system, and it was this that Bradley and Pegasus were to exploit, to expose. And he, Johnnie Quaid of Hong Kong, was responsible for tipping the balance. For he had begun the process whereby the supply of credit would be withdrawn on a massive scale. He was very proud of himself.

As the only one of the Pegasus Forum to be a card-carrying member of the Communist Party, he was particularly proud of himself.

He had been born and brought up in Hong Kong, that glittering beacon of capitalism on the doorstep of Red China. He was the only child of one of many mixed marriages in the colony, his father a British entrepreneur who had made his fortune in shipping and haulage, his mother an illegal Chinese immigrant who had fled the régime back home during the cultural revolution. But unlike many of his ethnic origin and generation, as a sensitive child he had despised the excesses and superficiality of life in Hong Kong. The endless circuit of social events, the boats, the racetrack, the expat community. He saw every day the exploitation of the Chinese, the huge divide between the majority of them and the few, mainly Westerners, who were the repository for most of the wealth. There were many rich Chinese in Hong Kong also, of course, but he despised them equally for selling out their countrymen. He despised his mother for abandoning her own family, his family, and he despised his father for symbolizing the worst of Hong Kong society.

They had sent him, of course, to the best schools, and it was they who had insisted he go to Oxford. This, for once, he had gratefully agreed to, because for the first time since the age of thirteen, he had been able to come out of the closet. On his CV, next to interests in Chinese history and art, and his presidency of the school debating society, he had proudly written the words: Communist Party member. Several thousand miles away, this had not gone unnoticed by St Mary's College tutor for admissions, Professor Wallace Bradley.

Quaid had secretly joined the Communist Party at the age of thirteen. He attended meetings and rallies, organized the odd protest, occasionally sent information of his father's business dealings, via the youth leader, back to Beijing. He had longed for the day that Hong Kong would return to Chinese control, and dreamed of the columns of troops and military hardware he imagined would roll into town on the big day. But he had been disappointed. The hand-over had come and gone, and life had continued pretty much as it had before. The government in Beijing must have gone soft. The lure of the profits to be made out of their new territory must have been too much. They too had sold out. He had remained in touch with his communist youth groups, and they maintained contacts with the old hard-liners in Beijing. There was pressure on the new government to show more muscle in Hong Kong, to clip the wings of the profiteers who flew in and out of the markets at will, to rein in the profligate child, but to no avail. It would take more than political pressure to oust the new moderates from power in Beijing and return to the old days. It would take some harsh medicine. Jonathan Quaid knew what it would take. The demise of the Hong Kong dollar as a respected currency, including the dissolution of the links to its big brother, the US dollar; the collapse of the corrupt and nepotistic banking system in the old colony; and an embarrassing, face-losing, costly devaluation of the Chinese currency itself, the yuan. For example.

It goes without saying that Johnnie Quaid had been delighted to be invited to join the Pegasus Forum. In his case also, Wallace Bradley had chosen his candidate most wisely. He remembered very clearly that first day at Oxford. It was October 1987, cold for the time of year and, just to make life that bit more difficult for the new arrivals as they heaved their belongings from parental car to undergraduate room, pouring with rain. A number of people had strong memories of that day.

CHAPTER 8

Oxford, 1987

LORD ELLIOT OF RAVENSLEA, MASTER OF ST MARY'S COLLEGE, Oxford, stood in the third-storey window of his lodge and looked down on the activity in the main quadrangle below. It was six fifteen p.m., dark already and still raining, on the Thursday of the week before the official start of the new academic year. Thursday of noughth week in the varsity vernacular, the day in early October prior to the start of the Michaelmas term, on which all new freshmen of the university were required to present themselves at their respective colleges to embark upon their Oxford careers.

The scene which met his eyes had been repeated many times, and had changed little in the fifty years of his involvement with college, both as undergraduate and Fellow. It never failed to excite him. The sixteenth-century Cotswold stone of the ancient quadrangle glistened wet and yellow under the lamps above the entrance to each staircase, and echoed with the footsteps and resonant voices of the newly arrived, excitedly making acquaintances and exploring their historic surroundings once the proud but anxious parents had begun their journeys back to the provinces. As the hour of the first grand college dinner, Freshers' Dinner, approached, activity in the quadrangle subsided slowly and the newest members of college returned nervously to the privacy of their own rooms to change into *subfusc*, the formal academic dress of the university.

Elliot waited at his window, staring now at an empty quadrangle. What new discoveries, what talent lay within the brains of those who entered St Mary's today? What mark would those young minds make on the intellectual and political world that lay beyond the cloistered existence in which he himself had spent much of his own adult life? Maybe a Nobel Prize? A great poet? Maybe even another Prime Minister? It had been a while since St Mary's had produced one of those, he reflected, with a smile. In his own day as an undergraduate, the college had developed something of a reputation as a left-wing intellectual breeding ground, which had seemed to stick. Even today, the college's political affiliations tended to attract applications from the more 'well-thinking' and 'involved' sections of England's youthful academic cream. Lord Elliot of Ravenslea himself, in 1947 merely Anthony Elliot, had pursued a career as philosopher and generally dangerous Marxist thinker, which sat particularly well in the post-war era at St Mary's. Over the years, as his academic stature grew, his radical stance had been somewhat thinned down, in no small measure by the vintage port at high table every night, to the point that he recently felt able to accept his elevation to the Lords with good grace, whilst some of his more committed contemporaries sent clenched-teeth letters of congratulation from Moscow and Bush House.

His reverie was interrupted by the re-emergence into the gloom below of the first gowned and bow-tied teenagers, edging self-consciously at first into the slanting rain of the quadrangle and then scurrying across to hall, gown tails flying, in time for the welcoming dinner. He pulled on his own gown with a nostalgic gleam in the eye and processed alone down the uncarpeted polished wooden staircase of his lodge to the studded oak door, and out into the same dripping quadrangle to walk among his new recruits in the muted throng towards dinner.

At the same moment, a much younger Wallace Bradley flew through the porter's lodge in a panic, having abandoned his car, still steaming from the demands made on his regular return journey from Aldate's Grange, to the mercy of the parking attendants in the square outside. He did not want to be late for dinner that evening. Unlike Lord Elliot, Bradley knew rather more about the undergraduates who had arrived at

St Mary's college that day. In fact, there was a small group of them about whom he knew a very great deal.

In his capacity as tutor for admissions, alongside his academic duties as a Fellow in economics, he was responsible for sifting and shortlisting the thousands of applications received each year from final-year high-school hopefuls, eager to gain a place at St Mary's College, Oxford. He had the power to ensure that a prospective candidate was interviewed by the tutors in the respective disciplines, and his recommendation went some way to securing an offer of one of the hundred or so sought-after places. Tutor for admissions was an arduous but vital rôle in the ongoing academic well-being of the college, as he guided the selection of the raw material by which the college's academic standing in the future would live or die. It was a post studiously avoided by most Fellows of the college, but Bradley had actively pursued it, and had been the incumbent for four years. This was not, however, out of any selfless devotion to the college's future. Wallace Bradley was looking for something else, and this year, in 1987, he felt he had finally found it. Of the one hundred new college members that year, nine of them had been singled out by him for rather special attention.

He had spotted the signs of potential suitability for his purpose initially in their CVs. He had looked closely for signs of rebellion, problems with authority, frequent changes of schools. He had looked at interests, involvement with charities and the underprivileged, and he had scoured the papers they had submitted from the entrance examination, especially the general essays they were obliged to write outside the chosen academic disciplines they were applying to study. He had initially drawn up a shortlist of twenty, and had then taken a most unusual step for an admissions tutor. He had hired a private detective. For he needed more information, details of a highly personal nature which most students would be loath to include on an application form. He had been delighted with the results which had emerged, and from the twenty he had selected fifteen potentials. Nine of them had succeeded in winning a place at the college. Eight males, one female, who that evening after the Freshers' Dinner, would be joining him for port as invitees to join the newly resurrected Pegasus Forum. This would be quite an evening in the life of all of them, but for none more so than Professor Wallace Bradley.

He was the last of the Fellows to take his place at high table in the grand dining hall of the college. Lord Elliot shot him a quizzical look from the end of the table and he mumbled his apologies. The new undergraduates sat below the Fellows' raised platform on benches at rows of dark-oak refectory tables, and there was an excited hum of chatter as they introduced themselves to their new neighbours, exchanging details of schools, subject and room numbers. Nine of them, scattered throughout the seventeenth-century great hall, clutched thick card invitations, gilt-edged and printed in ornate script with the following words:

The President of the Pegasus Forum
invites you to join him for port and cigars
immediately following Freshmen's Dinner
in the Talbot Room, St Mary's College,
October 4th 1987

At the top of each invitation was a thick red wax seal, bearing the motif of Pegasus, the winged horse of mythology, which Bradley had individually applied using the signet ring he had had specially made and which he had taken to wearing on the little finger of his left hand. None of the invitees had heard of the Pegasus Forum, and assumed it was yet another of the innumerable college societies vying for their membership at the start of the academic year. The quality and mystery of the invitation, however, and the fact that very few of them appeared to have been invited, ensured that they would all attend.

The chatter was silenced by a sharp rap on a gavel from high table, and everyone rose, led by the Fellows. The college chaplain intoned a brief Latin grace, and the massed ranks of be-gowned and bow-tied students repeated a nervous 'Amen' before taking their seats again. The college servants, or scouts as they were known, mostly middle-aged men in their fifties and sixties earning extra money in semi-retirement, and all dressed in short white jackets, began moving amongst the tables to begin serving dinner to the young academic élite of 1980s Britain. As they did so, there was another rap from the gavel and Lord Elliot rose to address the students.

'Ladies and gentleman, welcome to St Mary's College. I am the Master of the college and it is my particular pleasure to see the newest talent joining the college this evening.

'I will be brief, as I am sure you are all eager to continue making acquaintance with your new colleagues and to sample the delights of a grand college dinner. I should warn you, however, that we do not dine in this style every evening!' Mumbled laughter from the students followed, as plates of game and fish, and glasses of the finest red and white Burgundies from the college's remarkable cellars were placed on the table in front of them. The trappings of academic privilege, to which they would rapidly become accustomed, had begun.

'The college has a fine tradition of academic excellence, and something of a reputation for challenging, shall we say, the conventional wisdoms of the day. Wisdom is certainly something we like to encourage at St Mary's, but convention to my mind is tantamount to banality. We look for originality within these walls, ladies and gentlemen, a freshness of thought, a new point of view. It is a pioneering spirit which sets this college apart from the rest, and I trust, on behalf of all my colleagues at high table, that you will not let us down. The motto of the college is "*Volare aude*", which I am sure I have no need to inform you, means "Dare to Fly". I thus encourage every one of you to grasp this opportunity with all your courage. Fly free from the shackles of "conventional wisdom" and seek new ways of looking at the world in which we live. This applies equally to the physicists as to the classicists, to the scientists as to the historians, to the sportsmen as to the artists. Make good use of your time here, ladies and gentlemen, exploit all the opportunities this college, this ancient university, this city have to offer you, and go out to look at the world in a new light.'

Polite applause ensued, followed by the serious business of eating the splendid dinner before them. Wallace Bradley gazed down at the students, trying to catch a glimpse of one or other of his selected nine. He had pictures, both the passport-type submitted when applying to the college, and the more candid ones taken by his private detective. But he couldn't spot them. He would have to wait until after dinner to finally meet his chosen ones, although he felt as if he knew them all so well already.

Two hours later, nine nervous undergraduates stood in a panelled hallway outside the Talbot Room. The door was wide open but the room was unoccupied. It was a fine room, again panelled, with ten armchairs arranged in a wide semi-circle around the fireplace in which a coalfire burned sedately. A small, low table stood precisely in the middle of the circle of chairs. There was nothing on it. Two crystal decanters of port, a cork tied with a thin red ribbon to the neck of each, stood on a Victorian sideboard against one wall. The lighting was low, two table lamps providing the only assistance to the glow from the fire.

'Hey guys, let's go and wait inside,' said the only girl amongst the nine, with a strong American accent. 'We're not at high school now you know, we're adults. We don't need to wait for the teacher to ask us in.' She strolled into the room and looked around curiously at the pictures and books which lined the walls before settling herself in one of the chairs, in the middle of the arc, exactly opposite the fireplace. The others slowly followed her in and also sat down, all of them still wearing the formal academic dress of dark suit, white bow-tie and gown. They all wore long, calf-length gowns, which identified them as holders of scholarships. This was an academic rather than a financial distinction, but one which set them apart even on this first day of their university experience, from the lesser mortals, or commoners, who were condemned to the indignity of the faintly ludicrous waist-length model.

'I'm Annie, by the way,' said the American. 'Anybody have a clue what all this is about?' The boys shook their heads.

'No idea,' said a tall but flabby figure in a pin-stripe suit to her left. He wore shiny, ancient black brogues which looked as if they might have belonged to his grandfather. They had. 'I'm Morley Lafarge, Winchester.'

He belonged to that group of English males who feel that identifying their school is the only introduction necessary. 'My grandfather was a Mary's man, and I put in a quick call to him before dinner this evening. He had never heard of the Pegasus Forum.'

Their conversation was cut short by the sound of footsteps outside the room. The door swung slowly open to reveal a short man in his early forties, a creased brown suit under his own, rather threadbare gown. He was struggling to carry a large silver sculpture which he proceeded to place on the small table in the middle of the semi-circle of chairs.

'Marvellous, marvellous, you are all here I see. I thank you so much for coming and may I welcome you all to this first meeting of the re-establishment of the Pegasus Forum. And this, my friends, is Pegasus himself.' He gestured to the magnificent silver figure he had placed on the table before them. It was an exquisite piece of eighteenth-century silverware, the winged horse about to take flight, front hooves rearing majestically, as the muscles and sinews visible in the hindquarters flexed to propel the beast aloft. The enormous wings, seemingly out of proportion to the body, curled upwards in aerodynamic perfection in readiness for the first, mighty downward flap which would free the stallion from its earthly encumbrance.

'A wonderful piece, is it not? Look at the detail, look at the sense of movement. Look at the sheer power of the animal and yet marvel at its seeming weightlessness. Many people would say this is the finest example of the silversmith's work to come out of the eighteenth century. Anyone have an idea of the maker?'

'Is it a Vesperini? My folks have a couple, and the work seems similar.'

'No Miss van Aalst, it is not, but a good attempt. It is the work of Maître de Larosière, a contemporary of the Italian and in the same school, but infinitely superior. The college is most fortunate to own it, or should I say, the Pegasus Forum is fortunate, as it does belong to the society. The product of an age when Oxford was populated almost exclusively by the privileged classes, and the founder of the Pegasus Forum was in a position financially to commission the work from de Larosière himself.'

'It is very beautiful, but maybe you could tell us a little more about why we are all here tonight, sir.' The request came from a round, oriental face.

'Mr Quaid, all in good time. You are perhaps surprised that I appear to know you all by name, and yet most of you do not know me. Allow me to put matters straight. My name is Bradley, Professor Wallace Bradley, and I hold the Kuniyoshi Chair in Economics at this university.' Most of the students nodded in surprise, impressed at Bradley's seniority. He didn't look more than about forty, but had already attained the status of professor. A rare feat indeed at his age.

'Three of you know me already, for I interviewed you earlier in the year. Mr Turner here, and Miss van Aalst, both from the United States, will be studying philosophy, politics and economics and I will be their tutor in economics. And then there is Mr Dodds.' He gestured to a tall, handsome boy, whose short, spiky dyed blond hair contrasted sharply with his formal dress. 'Mr Dodds and I became acquainted when he chose to pursue a rather unconventional route into St Mary's, which I, as admissions tutor for the college, was able to facilitate.'

'And what, might I ask, was that?' asked van Aalst, whose curiosity, amongst other things, was the first to be aroused.

'I didn't finish school,' said Cameron Dodds, in a surly sort of way. 'Never got those A levels everyone seems to think you ought to have.'

'Let me put it another way,' Bradley cut in. 'Mr Dodds was expelled from his school for dealing in drugs when he was fourteen. He . . .'

'Hey, what the hell do you think you are doing?' snapped Dodds. 'I don't think that's anybody else's business but mine!'

'Mr Dodds, you will soon discover that, within the confines of the Pegasus Forum, we will have no secrets from each other.' Bradley was already beginning to sow the seeds of exclusivity, of brotherhood, which would form the basis of his strategy. He neglected to mention that he alone would have one or two secrets of his own that no one would be privy to. 'Now, please allow me to continue. Dodds has since had no formal education but is a naturally brilliant mathematician. He applied to the college to be able to work with Professor Jenkins, whose work on financial modelling is renowned, and Dodds's own work, which he submitted in lieu of those A levels he mentioned, was sufficiently interesting to catch the selector's eye, so to speak. As for the rest of you, you came to my attention when I was searching for suitable candidates for the Pegasus Forum, whose rebirth we are all privileged to witness this evening.'

'So what is the Pegasus Forum?' The question came from a bookish-looking short English boy, who stared inquisitively at the professor with penetrating green eyes, distorted by the inordinately thick round frameless glasses he was obliged to wear.

'Ah Mr Emerson. I sense the family genes already coursing through your veins. The direct question, the challenging look, nowhere to hide from the newshound's gaze. Allow me to introduce Hugh Emerson, son of Charles Emerson the eminent columnist on the *Gazette*, the man who has single-handedly set about exposing the scandals which beset the upper slopes of our society. I am sure you are all familiar with the famous "Emerson Bulletin". I am sure that Hugh here will be following in his father's footsteps before too long.'

'So we still don't know, Professor. What exactly *is* the Pegasus Forum?'

'The Pegasus Forum, my inquisitive friend, is one of the oldest societies in this ancient university. It was founded in 1740 by Piers Bellefoy, our benefactor and patron, to whom we owe thanks for this magnificent piece of silverware, but more importantly for a magnificent tradition which we are all privileged to be resurrecting this evening.'

'Who was Bellefoy?' Lafarge cut in again. He had the habit of immediately referring to people by their surname. He felt it implied familiarity and superiority at the same time.

'*Piers* Bellefoy was a typical member of the English intelligentsia at the time. Very wealthy, astonishingly bright, and above all excited at being in Oxford amongst many like minds at a time of intellectual discovery. This was the Enlightenment, after all, a time when it was believed that human knowledge could achieve and understand everything. Metaphysics was dismissed in favour of physics, superstition in favour of facts, and the whole world was put under a microscope to see how it worked. Science, it was believed, could conquer all.'

'What did Bellefoy hope to achieve with the Pegasus Forum, then?'

'Piers Bellefoy was a radical. He was concerned that the Royal Society, probably the most important scientific society of the day, was becoming too institutionalized. It too had been formed at Oxford around a hundred years before, in Wadham College actually, as a forum for the leading thinkers of its time. Learned papers were submitted by leading mathematicians and other scientists, and published in their review, called *Philosophical Transactions*. Bellefoy despised the members of the Royal Society for their respectability, they represented for him the intellectual establishment of the day and he felt they had lost their pioneering spirit. They had become *too* cautious, *too* mainstream, and he set up the Pegasus Forum in direct challenge to their authority.'

'Where did the name come from?' Van Aalst's curiosity was insatiable.

'Pegasus was the ideal symbol for Bellefoy's crusade. The horse is an animal of many qualities, it represents power and beauty, speed and strength. But it is earthbound. The winged horse represented Bellefoy's desire to harness the strength of the horse and set it free from the shackles of the Earth, to have it soar high in the ether above the lesser creatures of the Royal Society, and above all to challenge the accepted thinking of the day. It is this tradition which I wish to resurrect by re-forming the Pegasus Forum this evening, my friends. In every one of your backgrounds I have perceived a spark, a desire to challenge the status quo, to take on the establishment and all that it represents. You all have the intellectual capacity and energy to continue Bellefoy's ideals, and I very much hope you will all agree to join me in my endeavours.'

'What will it cost?' asked Cameron Dodds, conscious that he was probably the only one present, judging by the appearance of the others, who needed to count the pennies.

'The cost to all of you will be nothing more than your time and your brains. We are lucky that, in addition to the silver Pegasus we see before us, Bellefoy's legacy was a fund set up to finance the Forum in perpetuity.

At 1987 prices, this will provide for a rather fine dinner once a term, and a couple of port evenings such as this, where we will drink from the cellars maintained by the college on behalf of Pegasus. Alas, the Victorian era saw the Forum come to a rather undignified demise. Material colonialism took the place of philosophical debate, and many of the young Oxford brains of nineteenth-century England were more interested in feathering their own nests than challenging the rigid strictures of Victorian morality. We lost out a lot to Cambridge at that time, as it was about then that the famous Apostles began to rise to prominence. But now we have a unique opportunity in the 1980s to reignite the earlier challenging flame of intellect and apply it to the bonds that tie the hands of society in the late twentieth century. Are you with me, my friends? Will Pegasus fly again from the ramparts of St Mary's College?'

'I'm not so sure, Professor.' Annie van Aalst was the first to voice her doubts. 'Sounds to me like a load of pretentious bullshit. You know, a bunch of students sitting around, trying to change the world from some intellectual ivory tower. Nice idea but a bit unlikely, don't you think?'

'Ah, but Miss van Aalst, you are mistaken. Certainly we will discuss our objectives within these walls, but my intention is for action in the *real* world. This is no academic exercise; we will, for want of a better word, be activists, not pamphlet writers.'

'So what *is* our direction? Where do you intend us to go with all this? Will it be a different cause every week? Sounds more like extra tutorials to me.' The questions came from Scott Turner, the other American in the group and the only black man to be starting at St Mary's that year.

'Far from it Scott, far from it. We shall be focused. We shall espouse a cause, a single cause which I believe to be close to all of your hearts, and we will pursue it to the very end. As long as we are all committed, and as long as we all play the roles we decide upon, we *will* be able to change the world. Between you, between *us*, we have the ability to do that.'

'And that cause is . . . ?' Turner's tone was highly sceptical. He had had enough of the generalities.

'As I mentioned at the beginning, Scott, I am a professor of economics. I hold a chair sponsored by a major Japanese foundation, and I specialize in research into the economies of the developing Asian world. I even act as adviser to many of the governments in that region. It is my firm conviction, however, that the world of economics, the world of money if you like, is taking on much too great a significance in today's society.'

'Amen to that!' came a low mutter from Annie van Aalst, fingering the long, black Armani skirt she had chosen for her own *subfusc* outfit.

'Above all, I view with horror the growth of the cult of the market, to which all else is becoming secondary. In the free market economy, the evolutionary concept of the survival of the fittest is applied to everybody's day-to-day life with breathtaking callousness. If someone starves, or loses their job, or becomes bankrupt, then it is simply too bad.' Danny Brookes was listening wide-eyed, and Bradley was only too aware of his gaze. 'It was probably their own fault, and just down to the laws of supply and demand acting without the interference of government.'

'But the laws of supply and demand aren't about to be repealed, Professor, are they? I mean, they're a given.' Cameron Dodds had held back until now. He still had not forgotten Bradley's revelations of his drug-peddling background, and was not coming quietly. The sneer in his tone was unmistakable.

'Cameron, you are so right in many respects. But let us not forget that the laws of which you speak are not laws as such. At least not natural laws such as those concerning gravity or motion. These are *social* phenomena, "laws" which describe, and not prescribe, human behaviour, human psychology if you will. And very useful they are too, for it is exactly that human psychology which I intend to exploit.'

'Just greed, right, Professor? Human selfishness?'

'Indeed, Mr Quaid. Most perspicacious. Distilled to its first principles, it is certainly legitimate to look at the free market in that way. It both promotes and exploits the cult of the self. Some geneticists would have us believe that all of human behaviour is dictated by a fundamental survival instinct, an inbuilt need to perpetuate our own genes. In my opinion this is rather too convenient. It may explain, but it most certainly does not excuse the behaviour we observe around us. We are all individuals, but we live in a society, ladies and gentlemen, and in order for that society to function adequately there must be limits placed upon our selfishness. The law prevents us from killing and stealing, but the authorities tell us that economic demise is down to forces beyond their control: market forces, and they are apparently sacrosanct. I note with concern the attitude of our Prime Minister Mrs Thatcher and her friend Mr Reagan in this respect, both worshippers at the altar of market fundamentalism, and I wish to do something about it. This, I propose, should be the thrust of our efforts. We will show the *world* just what can happen when those market forces are truly free. We will take their market mantra to its logical conclusion and show them how undesirable it really is.'

'It all sounds pretty Marxist to me, Professor. Are you some sort of commie?'

'Far from it Scott. My work in Asia is geared towards helping those people accumulate wealth and prosperity, but in a different way. I am developing a system with those governments which will enable them to grow by *guiding* their banks, their corporations, their individuals to success rather than throwing them to the mercy of the free market. It is more of a Confucian approach to society, a helping hand to friends and family, than the centralized, all-powerful approach of the Soviets. Benign intervention, if you will, a middle ground between the Western extreme of the cult of the self, and the Soviet extreme of the supremacy of state and subjugation of the individual.

'We could scarcely be taking on a more daunting task, as the attitudes we aim to change pervade all layers of our society. But they are an accepted wisdom, and you heard Lord Elliot's words this evening when he implored us all to challenge these so-called truths. The Pegasus Forum is just the vehicle for achieving something really significant, and if I am not mistaken, I believe you all have some reason to sympathize with my view of this material world in which we live. Now, I ask you all again: are you with me? Do you wish to make a difference? Do you wish to make your time at Oxford *really* worthwhile?'

Nine heads around the room slowly nodded their agreement as Bradley finished his pitch. He felt a pang of triumph as he saw their acceptance of his proposal. He had planned everything meticulously, and was happy with what he saw of his recruits. It had been vital to get at them early, their first day in Oxford, before they could be ensnared by the myriad cloying hands of alcohol, sport, sex and a thousand other distractions on offer to the students. He had to make them feel special, impress them with the history, both of Oxford and of the Pegasus Forum, before they became subsumed by the overwhelming apathy towards their surroundings which seemed to overcome most Oxford students after the first week or so of living in sixteenth-century cloisters. He had achieved everything he wanted so far, and now he had to maintain it. He had to nurture that feeling of being special, apart from the masses, and create a group that would do anything to further their cause.

And so it had begun. The nine impressionable but idealistic young recruits had swallowed the bait. The port began to flow and the conversations began in earnest. Who would do what, how they would achieve their goals. They had all been amazed at the extent to which Bradley had planned everything in advance, even down to the subjects they were studying and the various careers he anticipated them adopting. For this was to be a scheme long in the making. It required them not to write letters to newspapers as angry young students, but to work their way slowly into the heart of the system they would eventually expose.

Over the months and years that followed, they met and discussed and planned. Their individual rôles became more clearly defined, and their careers chosen. One of them, Christopher Blake, had even been persuaded to change his course of study after his first year from history to law, as it had become increasingly apparent that they would need someone in that field. Bradley groomed and encouraged them, constantly monitoring their progress at the same time as he followed the developments in the Asian countries that had become his life's work.

When it became time for them to leave Oxford and embark on their careers, he helped them with interview techniques, wrote glowing references and drew upon all his knowledge and contacts in the various fields to help secure them the quickest possible path to success and, above all, the influence they would need to secure the goals of Pegasus.

For some this had been easy. For Annie van Aalst and Scott Turner, both economics students, a reference from the renowned Wallace Bradley had been more than enough to get them the jobs they wanted. She joined the new emerging markets desk at Salomon Brothers as an analyst for Asia without any trouble whatsoever, and Turner walked into a job in the US Government's Treasury Department once he had finished his doctoral thesis on the 'Tiger Economies of South East Asia'. A job at the Federal Reserve, America's central bank, would be only three years away.

Morley Lafarge was destined for the Foreign Office, where his grand-father and father had both been before him, but a word from Bradley into the ear of the college's designated recruiter for the Intelligence Service was enough to have him vetted and interviewed for one of those jobs which, in the wording of the mysterious letter he received, 'occasionally arise in the field of foreign affairs alongside those traditional, diplomatic posts more usually associated with the Foreign and Commonwealth Office.' Lafarge's family experience, not to mention his own prodigious intelligence got him the job.

Hugh Emerson, English student and son of the famous Charles Emerson of the *Gazette*, was never going to have trouble joining his father on 'The Emerson Bulletin'. His literary talents were good enough, and he made sure that he had accumulated enough journalistic experience during his time at Oxford to insulate him from too many accusations of nepotism. A couple of years after Hugh joined the paper, Emerson senior retired, and Jake Samuels, the editor, was only too pleased to have another Emerson on the books to assume the mantle. Hugh would be the public voice of the Pegasus Forum for several years to come.

Heinz-Josef von Lessing was a little more difficult. His task was ultimately to penetrate German banking circles, which for an art his-torian might have been a little problematic. He was finally able to secure a position as a trainee in a small private bank in northern Germany where the family name carried considerable weight. Once his apprenticeship was finished, and his expertise in the field of cor-porate finance established, it was not long before he was poached by the expanding Deutsche Kreditbankverein in Frankfurt and he quietly applied himself to the task of rising up the ranks in their foreign division.

Christopher Blake, the historian-turned-lawyer, left Oxford to finish his legal training at the Bar School in London. He graduated top of his year and was able to pick his chambers with the minimum of fuss. He chose a set which specialized in commercial law, and was soon entrusted with some of the larger clients where his litigious skills were in great demand. He became a Q.C. at the age of thirty-one, almost unprecedented in a world ruled by octogenarian amnesiacs, and was soon able to pick and choose his briefs at will.

Daniel Brookes drew the short straw. He had no particular relevant academic experience, as a geographer, that might have qualified him for a higher-profile role, but Bradley was adamant that they needed to have the skills of an accountant amongst their number and Brookes was chosen by default. There was no shortage of demand for trainee bean-counters from the large accountancy firms in the early nineties, indeed they were the largest employers of graduates from all English universities, and Brookes landed himself a job with one of the big three. Probably the most thorough of all the nine Pegasus members, he applied himself to the task in hand with remarkable tenacity, all the time making sure he gravitated towards the department of the firm where he would be of most use to the Forum.

Jonathan Quaid, the Eurasian language student from Hong Kong, turned down four job offers before he finally got the one he wanted. Having been brought up in the British Crown Colony, son of English and Chinese parents, he spoke both languages fluently. At St Mary's he had taken on the Japanese language with a fervour his tutor had never met before in all of his years of teaching. His knowledge of Chinese characters gave him a head start, but within two years he was able to read a Japanese newspaper before breakfast, and by the time he graduated he could use a Japanese typewriter at the rate of forty words per minute – a prodigious feat matched only by the most highly paid secretaries. The foreign banks in Hong Kong scrambled to hire him. China and Japan were the places to do business in the region at the time, and he was a rare commodity as he could speak both languages. He finally surprised everybody by ignoring the Americans and taking a job with one of the top Japanese banks in Tokyo, at Bradley's insistence, and he began to specialize in real estate finance. He was transferred shortly after to Hong Kong, the hub for banking activities in the South East Asian region, and within three years had overall responsibility for all property loans made by his Japanese employers to companies in the Pacific rim region.

The most problematic creature of the nine was Cameron Dodds. His dislike for structured education was the source of constant irritation for his tutors, and for Bradley. He preferred to do things in his own way, which mostly involved smoking drugs and sleeping with Annie van Aalst, who viewed him as an attractive curiosity, and doing his course work in a flurry of activity in a few intense hours before it was due. Almost sent down from the university on two occasions for loud parties involving large-scale nudity and illegal substances, he survived only on the intervention of Wallace Bradley with the college authorities, whom he was able to convince of his protégé's brilliance and need for guidance. Bradley assumed the official role of pastoral tutor for Dodds, and nursed him through the period of final examinations, where he obtained one of the top firsts in mathematics in the university.

But when it came to securing employment, Dodds embraced the rôle in which he had been cast with great enthusiasm and skill. Acting was his passion still, and he treated the interviews as he would an audition. A hair-cut and a smart suit later, his skills in maths, not to mention his method acting skills and the script fed to him by Bradley, persuaded the powers that be at Steinman, Schwartz Inc., one of the highest-profile and most aggressive US investment banks in the City of London, to overlook his social inadequacies and hire him into the interest-rate derivative analysis group.

His transformation was spectacular. He loved the idea of being paid large amounts of money to play with computers, which is what he would have been doing anyway, and the real world application of his theoretical models intrigued him. They actually worked, and began to earn money for the traders he supported, which gave him a certain amount of gratification, but it irked him that the traders would get the credit, and the large bonuses, for the money they made using his programs. All he got was mostly pats on the back and a small rise each year. Besides that, all the other people in IRDA were computer nerds, a breed with which he had little in common, and so he was more than excited to be approached, via a head-hunter, by Merrill Lynch who offered him a job actually trading interest-rate derivatives. He walked into his boss's office at Steinman, Schwartz to resign. The man was horrified and ultimately persuaded Dodds to stay with the offer of a similar job, and twice the money. He had broken through into the ranks of money-makers, and as such was viewed in an entirely different light. This new-found respect altered his personality dramatically, and he adopted an arrogant, dismissive attitude to most of his colleagues, which sat well with the corporate style at Steinman, Schwartz. As long as he continued to make money, he could be as rude as he liked. It was not long before he was put in charge of the hot new area in the firm, emerging markets derivatives, and Wallace Bradley was delighted. The anarchic young rebel had been fully assimilated into the powerful ranks of America's most awesome money-making machine.

In late 2001, within ten years of the nine original Pegasus members leaving Oxford, Bradley considered that the second stage of his scheme was completed. His 'children' had been placed in position and were awaiting his further instructions. More importantly, they collectively had enough influence to begin to consider the possibility of activating stage three of the plan: the Active Phase of destabilization.

CHAPTER 9

CHRISTOPHER BLAKE WAS ENJOYING HIS FIRST CIGARETTE OF the day at his desk in chambers when his secretary put the call through.

'Jake Samuels on line one.' His pulse quickened, and the machinery of one of the most highly regarded legal brains in the City whirred up to working speed. He took a last quick drag on his cigarette and wasted the rest before taking the call.

'Blake.'

'Chris, it's Jake. And we need your help quickly, so please cut the usual crap about correct procedures and listen to what I have to say.'

Blake was constantly castigating Samuels for his habit of calling him directly when he needed him, instead of going through the normal legal channels and getting his solicitor to do the briefing. Still, as the most blunt and outspoken newspaper editor in London, in all that he did Samuels was used to direct access to whomever he chose.

'My dear Jake, how delightful to hear your soothing tones at such an early hour. I would not dream of even suggesting that you should not call me directly whenever you choose.'

'I should bloody well think not. Are you aware how much we have paid you this year already?'

'£237,429.71. And what good value for money you have had, my friend. Think what you have saved yourself in nasty libel payments, and smile on the fact that the crust I am earning is but a shadow of your potential costs were I not to do my job for you.'

'Well if you want to talk about costs – what's all this on your latest bill about sandwiches at the Savoy, £89.71?'

'Jake, Jake, Jake. You above all should appreciate the value of entertainment. The delicious sandwiches in question, not to mention the amusing little Sancerre, were to fuel a discreet meeting between myself and the chairman of Vital Foods. I thought a cosy fireside chat would be the best way of pointing out all the interesting surprises that would undoubtedly crop up in court should he persist in his quaint action against your revered organ. I was rather proud of achieving both lunch at the Savoy with the chairman of a FTSE 100 company and having him drop the case, all for the princely sum you mentioned. Your Mr Emerson could have cost you an awful lot more, had his talents for snooping not been so well-honed. I am so grateful for his thoroughness; makes my job just a little less arduous. Now, let us no longer sully our minds with matters so mundane as sandwiches. Let us press on to business. Which member of the Emerson clan has got you in trouble this time? Has Daddy Emerson grasped the gold-plated quill from over his desk and taken up again in pursuit of corruption and scandal? Does Hugh's legacy haunt you from Lethe's shores, or is it that heavy-handed oaf of a son, James?'

'Very droll, Chris, very droll. You know damn well who it is. Hugh never caused us any trouble, and the old man long since gave up his moral crusades. He remains firmly ensconced in retirement. Trout and pheasants are his only targets these days.'

'More's the pity. So elegant, so understated, so urbane in his damnation. Mr Profumo could hardly have been more stylishly ruined . . . so who has Jimmy boy been beating up this time? Or is it breaking and entering? My dear, you really will have to keep him on a tighter leash. One of these days he'll either kill someone or be killed himself. These boardroom types haven't got where they are today by behaving like boy scouts, you know.'

'He can look after himself.'

'Indeed so, but in the cut-and-thrust of today's global markets, and all that tiresome competition, pretty much anything goes. Young James should watch himself. His last version of the "Bulletin" wiped nearly three billion pounds from the market value of that Swiss pharmaceutical company on the first day. And if my reading of your financial pages does not deceive me, the share price has since halved. I don't think he'll be getting a Christmas card from them this year. And their list of major shareholders reads like a Who's Who of Sicilian society.'

'Panacea had been falsifying test results for years, for Christ's sake! Those bastards had been selling drugs to you and me without doing accurate research! They deserve all that comes to them. "The Emerson Bulletin" has been one of the mainstays of this newspaper's success over the last thirty years and its style must adapt to the times. It was all very well in the sixties to rely on society to condemn scandal, and you're right, old Emerson knew just where to find it and how to present it. These days, political and corporate crime is a lot more sophisticated and I need people with special skills to understand it and expose it. Nowadays it is the markets that will punish these crooks in the way that hurts them most – the bottom line. James Emerson has got those skills and he has the Emerson name to maintain. When the old man retired and Hugh joined us, we made that transition.'

'Ah yes, poor little old Hugh. But he was just a number-cruncher, wasn't he, a bean-counter. Nothing more than a forensic accountant who liked spending his time poking around balance sheets and looking for holes. I grant you, he didn't have the nose for a story and the, shall we say, tenacity of his brother. He was just a little more refined. Like the father, a little more legitimate.'

'Well let's not talk ill of the dead, Chris. He didn't do too badly you know, he was just a bit too turned on by figures for our readership. Look how well he did with the Maxwell story; that has to be the scoop of the decade!'

'So why take him off "The Emerson Bulletin"? Surely it was unimaginable for the *Gazette* not to have an Emerson writing the "Bulletin" after all these years.' Blake was a master of feigned innocence, a skill perfected over ten years of addressing the bench.

'Well I understand the surprise, but it was the damnedest thing. Hugh came to me a couple of years before he died and requested a transfer.

You remember the story back then about the abuse of child-labour in Third-World countries by large clothing manufacturers? You know the sort of thing, paying some twelve-year-old in Havana or Jakarta five pence an hour to sew jeans and selling them for seventy-five quid a pair in some high-rent space on Regent Street.'

'I remember. And if I'm not mistaken didn't the naughty chairman have a penchant for making use of his youthful workforce for "other purposes" on his many and frequent trips to the region?'

'Correct. Paedophile scumbag. Well, that had been Hugh's story, and he got all interested in the economic background in South East Asia while he was researching it. Especially Indonesia. Wanted to follow that region full-time so I transferred him to the financial pages. Ended up doing rather well, as I recall. Even managed to predict all this mess that part of the world has got itself into now. Tragic, really, that he didn't live to see his prediction come true.'

'How terribly perspicacious of the lad,' oozed Blake. 'I wonder what put him on to that . . . Anyhow, you must have been terribly pleased to get a real Emerson back on the "Bulletin", carrying the family torch, so to speak.'

'Yes. James came to talk to me at Hugh's funeral, and it was his idea to leave the world of banking and continue the family tradition on the paper. He'd had enough of wheeler-dealing, especially all that client schmoozing he'd been doing. You know, it took them two days to find him in Atlantic City before they could pull him out to tell him about Hugh. If it hadn't been for the inquest, he would've missed the damned funeral.'

'Well, Jake, I hope you'll have him house-trained soon, for his own sake. Those Machiavellian methods of his are going to put him in the morgue alongside his brother if he's not careful. And then what would I do for a living? Somebody should explain to him the difference between investigative journalism and undercover operations. He simply must not continue threatening people for information, bugging their bedrooms and hacking into their computers, however much it boosts your circulation. This is the newspaper world, old chap, and your man is behaving like some kind of self-appointed vigilante on a personal crusade. That legal advice, by the way, is free.'

'OK, OK. Point taken. But you try telling him. Anyhow, I told you I needed your help, so listen. James is about to go public on a big story about a major arms manufacturer. It seems they have been breaking the UN arms embargo to Iraq and supplying Mr Hussein with some toys that will allow him to shoot down our missiles. Very high-tech, very expensive. Worth millions to the company. Well apparently the Foreign Office and the DTI have known about it for some time and kept schtum. James is about to blow the whistle. More than that, it seems he has mentioned the fact to one of his former college chums, now in the upper ranks of the Saudi Air Force, who have since cancelled an order with British Aerospace worth four and a half billion. Should cost a few thousand jobs. Now the government is trying to put pressure on us, national security and all that sort of thing, to stop us going to press. I need advice and fast. We want to run the story in Monday's early editions before the government beats us to it and slaps an injunction on us. What do you say?'

'I shall advise you in the same way I always have, my friend. If you are sure of your facts then go ahead; they won't be able to issue an injunction in time for Monday's papers, it being Christmas and everything. They'll never find a judge sober enough to sign it. And I'm assuming you have complete faith as always in dangerous James and his thorough, if far from impeccable, methods. I would advise, however, that it might be sensible for Mr Emerson to go to ground for a while, keep a low profile, and wait for the dust to settle on this one. Those arms manufacturers play dirty and it is a filthy business to start with. Tell him to go and visit Daddy in Dorset for a while, do some fishing or something.'

'I can do better than that. I'm thinking of sending him away after Christmas. Putting him on the financial crisis in Indonesia for a bit of a change. Let him try to find out what's really behind it, eh? A real Emerson investigation into the who-did-what-to-whom-and-for-how-much, rather than the boring old economists cranking out the usual crap. Should make a juicy story and keep him busy for a while, out of harm's way don't you think? Anyway, must hop. Got a story to print.'

The podgy fingers of Christopher Blake shook ever so slightly as they fumbled with the cigarette packet on his desk. His caffe latte had gone cold during his conversation with Samuels, and he sipped at it with an irritated grimace. He hesitantly took up the phone, glanced at his fob-watch and dialled a number from memory.

'Oxford 244318' said a voice, slightly irritated. 'Senior Dean speaking.'

'Professor Bradley, this is Christopher Blake speaking. I'm most terribly sorry to disturb you during a tutorial,' he knew the rules, 'but something rather important has come up of which I felt you should be informed immediately.'

'What is it?' The question was terse and impatient.

'Sir, I have just been informed by Jake Samuels, editor of the *Gazette*, that he is going to assign James Emerson, Hugh's brother, to investigate the deep background to the current Indonesian situation. It might be nothing, but I wanted to . . .'

The phone went dead. In his private study in college, Professor Wallace Bradley, Senior Dean of St Mary's College Oxford stood up and zipped up his trousers. His face was flushed and stern as he walked silently over to his desk and unlocked the bottom drawer, taking out a manila file marked 'Pegasus' in large black script. The final year undergraduate he had left without a word on the red velvet Empire chaise-longue took her cue and left, buttoning her blouse and leaving her essay strewn unread across the floor to be corrected later. Bradley picked up his telephone and spoke to the porter's lodge at his college.

'Yes, good morning, John. Professor Bradley here. I'd like to place a long-distance call please, to Jakarta, Indonesia. Please charge it to my personal account.'

It was Christmas Eve, and Emerson was sitting in his Docklands penthouse in a silk bathrobe watching the television. He was seeing live pictures on CNN from the streets of Jakarta. Thousands of angry civilians in running battles with riot police and troops; petrol bombs and stones being hurled across army barricades, and troops clubbing, sometimes shooting, anyone who tried to loot goods from shattered shop windows. The reporter on the scene described events:

'. . . violence is reaching a crescendo here in Jakarta tonight as the President has finally mobilized the army in an attempt to restore order to the chaos of the last several weeks. As the Indonesian currency continues its nosedive on the foreign exchange markets, local companies can no longer afford to buy in the foreign raw materials they need to maintain their businesses. Thousands of jobs have already been lost and inflation is approaching two per cent per day. Food is scarce and, where available, unaffordable for the masses. With inflation rampant, those with savings see the value of their thrift decreasing every day, and to make matters worse, four major high street banks today announced they were closing their doors due to lack of funds. Armed guards protect their offices, but thousands wait outside in a desperate attempt to retrieve their lives' savings. The death toll today alone is approaching thirty as the government's line hardens and fires break out in looted buildings. The question remains as to what can be done to restore the economy of the world's fourth most populous nation before it falls to its knees in submission? The international community appears powerless to help, as the twenty-four billion dollars already pledged by the IMF seems in danger of being diverted into influential private hands, and international investors are voting with their feet as they attempt to ditch all their investments in the Indonesian stock market. The danger to the entire Asian region is considerable, and the economic shock waves are already being felt around the globe. Today on Wall Street the Dow Jones fell more than six percentage points in early trading as nervousness mounts . . .'

Emerson was disturbed from his viewing by a ring at the door. Irritated to receive a caller at this time on Christmas Eve, just as he was about to leave for Dorset, he walked across the large open plan living space to his desk and sat down at his computer. He started up the file named 'Security' and typed in the password. Scrolling through the menu on the screen, past 'Roof access' and 'Fire Escape' he stopped at 'Main Entrance' and double-clicked. Almost instantaneously a colour video image appeared on the screen, showing the area on the street outside the door to his building.

He clicked on 'Zoom' and a face filled the screen. He was surprised to see the puffy, sweating features of his editor standing outside in the slanting rain, the droplets of rain, or was it sweat, dripping down his expansive brow. The harsh lighting cast by the unflattering angle of the video light above the door illuminated an ugly image, dark shadows in the eye sockets and an angry scowl about the jowly cheeks of Jake Samuels as he squinted up at the camera and was blinded by the spotlight. Another impatient ring on the buzzer interrupted Emerson's perusal, and he flicked a switch on the desk microphone.

'Mr Samuels, what a pleasant surprise. Please type in the code 48736 and take the lift to the top floor. I'll open the sherry.'

Thirty seconds later a muted hydraulic hiss accompanied the opening of the lift doors directly into Emerson's apartment and the stocky figure of Jake Samuels stomped inside, peeling off his standard issue Burberry as he did so, dripping water on to the polished maple floor. 'Jesus Christ James, what a performance to get into a bloody building! You paranoid or something? This is London, you know, not New York.'

'Sorry Jake. Can't be too careful these days. I've accumulated a few enemies over the last couple of years. If one of the subjects of my "Bulletin" stories found out where I was . . .'

'More likely an angry husband,' growled Samuels, glancing around the ultra-modern apartment. 'And we're obviously paying you far too much.'

'Jake, you well know how little you pay me. You also know very well that I am fortunate enough to have some other friends who value my services rather more than you do. That was part of the deal for agreeing to write for you, in case you had forgotten. I get to do my own thing, and you get a real live Emerson back on the "Bulletin".'

'Oh how could I forget. That's why you're always missing the deadlines for your stories, too busy moonlighting for your corporate pimps.'

'Industrial security, I like to call it, thank you. A real growth industry. You would be amazed at the sort of dirty tricks people get up to in business these days. And the responsible chairman has an obligation to protect his business secrets, not to mention the shareholders' profits. You wouldn't be too happy if you'd spent three years designing a better mousetrap only to have it nicked from under your nose before you'd got the right patent in place, now would you? And my services don't come cheap.'

'Sounds like you've got a white-collar protection racket going, if you ask me,' grumbled Samuels, perching himself uninvited and uncomfortably on the edge of the modular chrome and leather armchair. 'Talk about poacher turned gamekeeper. I reckon these boys just pay you to protect them so you won't give them a mauling in the "Bulletin"! You have us to thank for your name, and don't you forget it.'

'And on that basis you probably think the paper deserves a cut of my private income. Am I right, Jake? Let's forget about my little sideline. That is my affair. You don't even want to know what I get up to. You should be glad to have me on your payroll for the peanuts you pay me. I only put up with this hackwork for Hugh, you know that. And I rather think it is my father who should be thanked for my name.'

He poured Lagavulin into two large tumblers and handed one to his boss with a grin. Jousting over. Emerson was always amused at the way Samuels found it necessary to complain about something whenever they met. This was actually relatively seldom, as 'fieldwork' kept him out of the office most of the time, but Samuels always had to re-establish his status as the senior of the two. Then they could both relax and talk on more equal terms.

'Merry Christmas, James. Glad to see you're not losing your bite. But I'm afraid I'm going to be cutting your holiday a little short this year.'

'Oh I see. Is this why you finally deign to visit my humble garret, Mr Scrooge? To soften the blow with your delightful company and witty repartee at this festive time of the year?'

'I have something a little different for you. And I'm glad to see,' he gestured at the television set strung on its steel gantry high above them, still showing images from Jakarta, 'that you've been putting in a bit of research already.'

'You mean Indonesia? Isn't that a story for the economists? Put some-body from the pink pages on to it, Jake, one of your markets-monkeys, and leave me the juicy stuff!'

'James, listen to me.' Samuels squeezed his frame back into the narrow armchair. 'You saw the pictures on the news. Those are live bullets they're firing at civilians, and this is fast turning into a crisis of global proportions. OK, it started as a bit of a run on the currency in Indonesia, which half the people in this country wouldn't be able to identify on a map, but it is now spreading around the world like a forest fire. It affects you, me, and most people in this country. As we speak it is undermining the value of that pension we rashly provide for you. You saw what happened to the American market today, and when America sneezes, as they say, the rest of the world catches a cold. I have had just about enough from our learned friends the economists about overvalued currencies and "market" forces and all that sort of bollocks. I see civilians being shot by *government* forces and charred bodies being thrown from ten-storey buildings. I see tanks, for Christ's sake, on the streets of Jakarta. *People* do things like that, Emerson. Not markets.

'I want a different angle. I want to know *who*, not what, is behind all this. All we get told by the economists is that the whole thing started when "the currency was sold". Well I want to know *who* sold the fucking currency, when they sold it, and how much. Then maybe we can ask the question "why", although I suspect I know the answer to that already. We hear so much about these mythical "market speculators" who drive markets. Well, I want to know who these bastards are, where they live, what cars they drive, and what they eat for breakfast. Because these boys only do things for one reason, and that is to make more money than they already have. And they are making that money at the expense of kids starving to death in Indo-fucking-nesia. I want printouts of bank accounts; I want details of transactions; I want candid pictures of their billionaire bellies hanging over their swimming trunks in the Bahamas, and I'm going to print them next to pictures of the bloated bellies on the starving kids whose parents can't afford to buy the rice they grow.

'We are going to cause a major rumpus with this one, James. We are going to call into question the morality of the financial markets in a way no one has done it before. I've had enough of reading silly articles in the Sunday supplements about twenty-two-year-olds making hundreds of thousands on Wall Street and driving Porsches. They are just stupid little pricks. Pawns. Minor players. I want to go after the institutions and the people that run them, and you, my friend, are the best I have for nailing down a story like this.'

'Well I'm not sure, I mean . . .'

'You say you want the juicy stuff, well this is the biggest fucking crime of the decade, and we are going to nail the system. I can see the headline already: "From Bonds to Bullets – the money men who kill children at the click of a mouse!" There, speech over.' Samuels wriggled forward in his chair, temples pulsing, breathless from the exertion of his tirade, and drained his glass.

Emerson had listened closely. He was sitting cross-legged on the floor, staring up at the ceiling fan. Now he spoke. Very calmly. 'I'll have a look into it when I'm finished with the Omega story.'

Samuels stood abruptly. 'No – we're running that one Boxing Day, James. Already gone to press. You have enough evidence already for me to be comfortable, and I've run it past Blake already. He's happy. I want you to drop everything else and pull out all the stops on this one. Do you understand? You will have all the resources you need, and I will personally be your direct liaison in London. I figured you would probably want to start straight away, so I've had you booked on the next KLM flight to Jakarta. Leaves on Sunday, so you'd better get packing. This is going to be an "Emerson Bulletin" to beat all others.'

When Samuels was adamant, even James Emerson was in no position to object.

His boss had left as suddenly as he had arrived. Cursing quietly to himself, Emerson pulled on a black rollneck and beige chinos and picked up his overnight bag for the trip down to Dorset. He took the lift down to the basement car park. It was eleven p.m. on Christmas Eve and the building seemed deserted. He reflected on the fact that most 'normal' people were already tightly ensconced in the clutches of their families for the holiday. Children would be tucked up in bed, sherries sipped around the tree where stacks of unopened gifts awaited tiny frenetic fingers the next morning. That all seemed an age away from his own existence.

The last two Christmases had been spent mourning the death of his brother, and never again would this time of the year hold the same unbounded, time-stopping joy of his childhood memories. There would always be one notable absentee. How could he ever forget that seemingly endless drive to Oxford for the inquest and the Coroner's verdict of 'accidental death'. That bloody 'dining' society. *Pegasus*. Pretentious claptrap. What on earth was Hugh thinking? He just wasn't used to drinking so much, he supposed, and these society dinners were expected to get a bit out of hand. In fact, it was almost a requirement. Endless food and booze followed by a high-spirited rampage through the darkened quadrangles of the college at two in the morning, terrifying the pale-faced gnomes returning to their rooms from the library after yet another essay crisis. It had been a reunion of past Pegasus members, ten years on. Lots of mutual back-slapping and catching up on careers, and the inevitable excesses of thirty-somethings trying to recapture their undergraduate spontaneity. They should all really have known better. One of the dons had even attended the dinner as senior member. Bloody idiot. Why had he let it get out of hand? And how stupid to take that drunken crowd up to the top of the gate tower, just to see the private Fellows' Library. They were more likely to have thrown up on a valuable early manuscript than appreciate the famous collection.

James Emerson covered the hundred or so miles to his father's house in a little under two hours at the wheel of his new Jaguar XK8, a bonus from one of his grateful corporate clients. The roads were empty all the way and he drove skilfully, yet almost on auto-pilot, as his head rang with thoughts of that evening in Oxford and the morose Christmas to come, alone with his father. As the car nosed along the gravel driveway approaching the house, the headlights picked out a lone figure standing in the porch, awaiting his arrival.

Emerson jumped out quickly.

'Father, what on earth are you doing up? It's gone one in the morning. How long have you been standing there?'

'Oh not long, my boy. Saw the car coming along the lane. Couldn't sleep, you see. Christmas always gets me that way now, you know. All a bit rum.'

Father and son embraced awkwardly, something the old man clearly found a modern embarrassment between two fully grown men, and he was equally surprised, but touched, to feel a kiss on his cheek from the ex-banker-turned-hatchet-man of the *Gazette*.

'Well we will have some fun, the two of us,' James assured his father, 'and speaking of rum, here's a little fuel for the Christmas pud.'

Out of his bag he pulled an ornate cut glass bottle of XO cognac with a red ribbon tied around the neck and handed it to his father.

'Well, James, you do me well. And on no account will this come within igniting distance of any seasonal confectionery you may care to mention! Come, it is late but I feel we should celebrate your visit before turning in. Care to join in me in the library for a nightcap?'

James Emerson walked with his father across the stone-flagged entrance hall of the Old Vicarage, one arm around the old man's shoulders, and looked up at the ten foot tall Christmas tree in its usual spot at the foot of the impressive staircase. It was laden with decorations of painted wood figures and glass and topped by a childish, home-made tinsel star.

'He made that, you know, James. Age seven. Very proud he was too, and he always insisted on climbing the ladder to place it himself.'

'I know, Dad. But he would hate us to mope. Christmas was always his favourite time of the year and he would have hated to think he was spoiling it for everybody. Come on, where's that brandy?'

He followed his father into the book-lined room and looked around. It was little changed from his recollection. Dark-oak shelving laden with books from floor to ceiling on two walls, French doors overlooking the lawns which swept down to a great old weeping willow tree still visible in the frosty moonlight, and facing the windows a magnificent, deep green-veined marble fireplace, from which the dying embers of that evening's fire provided the only illumination in the room. An oil painting of a distant, grand relative hung over the chimney piece, and two comfortably cracked chestnut leather armchairs were arranged either side, facing the fire. James sat down, and was soon joined by his father bearing two crystal balloons to which he added healthy measures from the new bottle.

'Merry Christmas, my boy, merry Christmas,' declared Charles Seymour Emerson, and they drank and talked further into the early hours. As the cognac did its work, the melancholy lifted and hearty laughter rose up the chimney into the night, as each entertained the other with war stories from the paper and scandalous details from tales even the *Gazette* would have balked at publishing. When James told his father of his latest assignment and imminent departure, all notions of going to bed were abandoned and hours later, as the watery dawn began to seep into the room, the two men pulled on overcoats and boots and crunched through the frost for a long walk before breakfast.

'Never underestimate Jake Samuels, James,' said his father, his chilled breath shrouding his head as they stopped to rest at a stile. 'He's an extremely shrewd character and a newspaper man through and through. I knew him as a three-bob hack when he started out, but it wasn't long before he was coming up with bright ideas and pretty soon he was running the editorial meetings. If he's on your side, you'll have nothing to worry about.'

'Well, that's a big "if". I can't imagine what he's like to his enemies if he sends his friends off to bloody Jakarta on Boxing Day.'

'Don't read anything into that, lad. Christmas isn't his bag. He's not trying to get you out of the way. And even if he is it's probably for your own good. Be happy with this assignment. It sounds to me rather as if this could be a really big one. Your Profumo. Your Maxwell. Do us proud, boy! "The Emerson Bulletin" needs its third pillar to finally bring home the bacon. You have a reputation to maintain, you know.'

The remark was designed to give a friendly needle, and the senior Emerson was delighted to see he could still get a rise from his son.

'And what do you think I've been doing these last two years? Why do you think I'm working on that bloody paper in the first place? It's not for the money, you know! God, you think my stuff isn't worthwhile, do you? I suppose it's not good enough for you that I go after the corporations, is it? Has to be somebody famous. Got to think about the circulation haven't we. My Profumo! My Maxwell! You want a high-profile scandal? OK. You just wait . . .'

'My dear boy, you do reassure me. I'm so glad to see that the passion is still in the veins. I don't give a damn about circulation, let Samuels worry about that. Fame? Poppycock. What I care about is dishonesty and hypocrisy and injustice. That more than anything else is what drove me, and that is what Hugh cared about more passionately than either of us. In my day one could expose the scoundrels in the nicest possible way and they would happily fall on their swords, quietly disappear from society. Nowadays one must chase them with a sword, plunge it into their backs and then twist it for the final *coup de grâce* before the bastards will give in. You are just the chap for "The Emerson Bulletin" of today, and it is the scale of the potential scandals involved in this case which may earn you a prize. By the way, do let me know before you go to press, won't you? I'll have to have a quick word with my broker. Just think of it. The whole financial system! It all sounds so delightfully Marxist! Elliot would be so proud!'

'Good Evening, British Embassy.'

'I should like to speak to Mr Morley Lafarge. The financial attaché. Is he still there?'

'Yes, sir. Who shall I say is calling?'

'Professor Bradley.' There was a pause and a series of clicks before Lafarge came on the line.

'Professor, good morning. An unexpected pleasure.'

'Morley, we have a slight potential problem. I need you to keep an eye on things. Can we talk on this line?'

'Let me call you back.' Lafarge walked across his office to the old fax machine in the corner, lifted the handset and dialled Bradley's private number. It was a simple security procedure, but he knew for a fact that the embassy fax lines were not routinely tapped by the listeners. Bradley answered on the second ring.

'We are secure now, Professor.'

'Have you heard of James Emerson?'

'Of course I have. Hugh's brother. Nosy bugger. Writes that column for the *Gazette*. Why do you ask?'

'Well, he's on his way to Jakarta as we speak. He's been asked to investigate the background to the Asian crisis by that Jew, Samuels. Look out for him. We don't want him making too much progress now, do we?'

'Well I don't know what I . . .'

'Look. He's a British journalist, coming to Indonesia, to investigate a financial crisis. You are the financial attaché at the British Embassy. He's bound to come to see you. I'm surprised he hasn't contacted you already. If he doesn't, make sure you get to see him. Tell him you've heard he's been asking around. And give him some background. Throw him a bone or two. But just make sure he's off in the wrong direction.'

'I hear you, Professor, but . . .'

'Listen to me. I have evidently not made myself clear. You above all have a certain interest in keeping Emerson off the scent. If he gets on to Pegasus, he'll get on to Hugh. And I'm sure you wouldn't want that particular episode reopened by a grieving brother, now would you? I am confident you will take whatever action you deem necessary to keep Mr Emerson out of our hair.'

Bradley ended the call. Lafarge was a problem. He had more or less served his purpose for Pegasus, and was no real match for the intellect and investigative talents of James Emerson. He hoped he had hinted strongly enough at what he really thought Lafarge should do to solve the latest Emerson problem.

Annie van Aalst was right, they did indeed have blood on their hands, but not in the way she thought, not Chumsai's. Things had gone too far to get squeamish now. They were close, very close, to achieving their aims. The markets were reacting more swiftly and more dramatically, even at this early stage, than Bradley had ever dreamed. And every fall in the currencies, every point in the bond market, took him closer to achieving his own personal goal. He had confided in none of the other Pegasus members as to the reality of his own motives. They still believed that he was a crusader, an idealist on a mission to shock the capitalist world.

The clock on the mantel struck ten a.m., but he ignored its reproach. He remained sitting at his desk in contemplation, although in effect he was by now far away in space and time, lost in memory. His forefinger traced the patterns of the tooling around the edges of the leather desktop, and he remembered the first time he had sat at that desk. The start of it all.

CHAPTER 10

London, 1962

C LEARING OUT DEAD PEOPLE'S STUFF IS A NASTY JOB. WHEN the corpse in question is your father's, it becomes almost unbearable. When you are faced with this responsibility at the age of sixteen, suddenly alone in the world and master of the house, the deafening enormity of the task paralyses the soul. The voices and images of the past leap from the most unlikely objects, infesting the brain, crushing the heart, searing the nerves.

A teenage Wallace Bradley sat at that same desk in his father's study. The desk, a massive, mahogany piece with that top of green tooled leather and a set of pedestal drawers left and right, was the most vocal reminder he had of his father. It was not an antique, probably a thirties' reproduction, but it was the most valuable thing he had left, ingrained as it was with his father's memory. And with the memory of one day in particular, the day when Wallace Bradley inherited that desk and its contents. He would often think of that day.

At that stage it had been only two weeks since a sixteen-year-old Wallace Bradley had been in school, sitting in a Latin class on a scorching June afternoon, dreamily gazing out of the window at the hazy sunlight filtering through the foliage of the massive oak tree on the boundary of the cricket pitch. Droning in the background the classics master intoned the mantra of scansion, of metrical feet, of iambs and trochees, dactyls and spondees, 'Dac-tyls-and Spon-dees, Mitch-ell-and Ed-wards, John-son-and Brad-ley . . . Brad-ley . . . Bradley . . . BRADLEY!'

The young Wallace Bradley's daydream was interrupted by the sound of his name being yelled and the collective scraping of twenty-five chairs on the wood-block flooring. He turned to see his classmates all standing at their desks and the headmaster of the school standing in the classroom doorway. Bradley too jumped to his feet, heart pounding with the rest of them. When the head visited a class during a lesson, it meant only one thing: trouble for somebody and most likely a flogging. This was 1962 and the practice was widespread still, especially in the minor boarding schools of which Bradley's was a typical example. A word was whispered in the ear of the teacher, and he turned to the class.

'Bradley, would you please go with Dr Mason? You can leave your books where they are, boy. Johnson will bring them to you later.'

Twenty-five pairs of eyes followed him as he made his way to the door in pursuit of the begowned headmaster, and twenty-five pairs of lungs exhaled in relief. Bradley's for it this time. Must be really bad if he's not coming back for the rest of the class. Expelled maybe?

The head led the teenager down the stone-flagged corridor and Bradley struggled to keep up without running. In the many disturbed nights that followed, it was to be this image of the fearsome man, four paces ahead, gown billowing in his wake, which remained his overwhelming memory of that day. Not the words, which he barely heard, nor the unexpected but ominous sight of his uncle standing twenty feet away, grim-faced and incongruous as he lurked in the shadows of the school's entrance hall. They came to a halt outside the head's office, but they didn't go in. The news was broken whilst they stood in a draughty corridor. Bradley remembered flinching as the headmaster raised his hand, and then feeling relieved but embarrassed to sense a comforting hand on his shoulder, before he began to process the words which seemed to be coming from the headmaster's mouth, somehow muffled and curiously out of sync. '. . . father . . . crash . . . instantaneous . . . mother . . . shock . . . breakdown . . . uncle, so sorry.' Silence.

He was aware out of the corner of his eye that his uncle, who had been edging nearer while the news was being broken, was now hovering at his shoulder ready to step in as the headmaster bolted from the embarrassment of the real world back into the leather-bound sanctuary of his office. Wallace was led out of the school's main entrance a minute later, and never set foot in the place again. From daydream to nightmare in less than three minutes.

The two weeks following that day had passed in even more of a blur, as he was handed from uncle to cousin to police to social services and back to uncle. Not really an uncle in fact, but his godfather and the oldest family friend, always known as Uncle Bill. He lived around the corner, and it had been convenient for the young Wallace to stay with him whilst dealing with the personal effects. Every morning the teenager would go back to the family house alone, let himself in and work his way through, room by room, bagging up his father's clothes for charity, sorting through photographs and bills, packing up his mother's belongings for her room at the clinic. Just trying to keep busy without thinking too much. Every afternoon Uncle Bill, who was by now Wallace's court-appointed guardian until he came of age, would take the rapidly maturing youngster out to the clinc where he would sit with his mother in her room, or wheel her out into the sunshine, and attempt to provoke some sort of response. There was never any.

They told him she had not been in the car when the accident happened. She had been ten feet away, returning from the baker's shop with a paperbag full of iced buns. He did not really believe that. He'd seen the broken nose, the black eyes, the missing teeth. But the emotional trauma had had just as devastating an effect on her mind as the juggernaut had had on their car and on her husband's body who sat waiting at the wheel. The doctors called it severe shock followed by a nervous breakdown in those days, as they wouldn't identify post traumatic stress disorder for another twenty years or so. Nor were they aware of the demons from her past that were being released. But the effect was the same.

His childhood home was already on the market, courtesy of the trustees, by the time he finally steeled himself to face up to dealing with the last room, the one he had been putting off during those two weeks since his father's death. As a child he was never allowed into his father's study. It was the room to which he retired to read, to work over his notes, his patients' cases, and he was never to be disturbed. And if the study was the holy of holies, the desk at which he now perched was the Ark of the Covenant. It sat in the middle of the room, crammed full of papers, correspondence, notes. Wallace had never even touched it before, but now it had become the closest he could get to hearing his father's voice for one last time. It was the one object, apart from a few photographs and documents, Wallace decided to salvage from the clutches of the house-clearers, the vultures who hovered, waiting to pick over the carcass of his family home.

He tried to set about clearing it as methodically as he could, sorting things into piles by subject matter – personal, professional, family – and then chronologically. The obsessive orderliness, he believed, was a legacy of his father's genes, but it was also a convenient substitute for thought. It occupied his mind and left no excess capacity for memories and melancholy. He tried to avoid looking at anything in too much detail, as he wanted to do that in his own time. Any blubbing would be done in private without the possibility of disturbance by estate agents and scavengers. Yet, as he leaned across the desk to reach a stack of old photographs, his left knee pressed against a small panel concealed on the inner face of the pedestal drawers. There was a slight click as a cubby-hole on the underside of the desktop dropped down, banging his other knee in the process. For a second he thought he had broken the desk and that the bottom of the old drawer had chosen that very moment to give way. But when there was no cascade of paper clips and drawing pins all over the carpet, he quickly realized he had activated some kind of mechanism, a secret compartment. He reached inside and felt a thick document, which he pulled out. An old file, faded beige, with a couple of coffee-cup rings in the middle.

There was a stamp in red ink in the top right-hand corner of the cover:

United States Army: Psychological Warfare Unit. G-2

Below that, and scrawled roughly in his father's unmistakable script were the words:

Patient Notes – Palembang origin

1945

A to F

Below that was another, larger stamp in black ink:

Personal Medical Records – Highly Confidential.
Property of US Army

He was about to add it to the pile of his father's professional records, but the provenance of the document, and the fact that it had been deliberately hidden, aroused his curiosity. His father, Dr Jason Bradley, had always been extremely reticent about his contribution to the war effort, and Wallace had an hour or two before the estate agent would arrive with the next lot of people interested in buying his childhood memories. And besides, this was related to his father's work. Shouldn't be too upsetting. Nothing too personal, to him at any rate, and it would at least give him an idea of what his father had really done during the war without provoking too many distressing memories. He sat back in his father's chair and began to leaf through the contents of the file. What he read would change his life for ever.

The file was very bulky and lumpy, with a multitude of paper-clipped attachments including photographs and notes from other physicians and military departments. The folder fell open at an entry related to a Miss C, a young woman in her early twenties. But he ignored that one, and turned back to the beginning of the folder. The first patient's notes seemed particularly extensive. There was even a grainy, black and white photograph, a head-and-shoulders shot, loosely glued to a box in the top right-hand corner. It looked like a blow-up from a larger group picture, as the shoulders of two neighbouring, similarly-dressed subjects, could be seen on either side. The face was indistinct, but a nurse's uniform was clearly discernible. The blonde hair, drawn back beneath a starched white cap, and the oval features, flashing a broad grin, reminded the young Wallace of somebody. One of the movie stars from the period? Those forties women all looked the same. Who was it? Betty Grable or Lana Turner? Somebody like that, vaguely familiar despite the fuzziness of the image.

The rest of the first page was closely written in his father's handwriting. There were a few basic details: Date of birth – 3/7/22. The third of July. Amazing coincidence. It was exactly forty years to the day that this woman had been born. Wallace wondered if she was still alive, and if so, what she was doing on her fortieth birthday; sex – female; ethnic origin – Caucasian. Nationality – Australian. In the section for name there were only initials: *C.E.D.* A note scribbled in the margin added the comment responds to 'Saki'. Wallace's grief didn't prevent him from noticing that this particular record was out of alphabetical order. Miss D coming before Miss C. Most unlike his father, he thought, who had been fastidious about his record-keeping. Maybe this was the last file he had looked at before he put it away. Or maybe he had been planning to come back to it soon. There were details of height and weight, but Wallace Bradley had been educated in the UK with stones and pounds, so he didn't initially compute that a weight of sixty-eight pounds, as it was always expressed in the US system, was awfully low for a woman of five feet ten inches. Not until he turned the page at least.

He was physically nauseated by what he saw. It was another photograph, a photograph of a woman. He only realized this when he looked a little more closely, as there were very few obvious clues as to the sex. It was the lack of a penis which gave it away. The woman had been photographed naked, full length, standing face on in front of a white wall on which a series of black, parallel horizontal lines had been crudely painted by hand, indicating two inch intervals in height, beginning at four feet six inches and continuing up to six feet six inches. A bit like a criminal mug shot or an individual in an identity parade, but in this case showing the whole, naked body. This particular subject stood at five feet ten inches. He flicked back a page to check the height from the patient details on the first page, and realized that this must indeed be the same woman whose glamorous, radiant face beamed from the other photograph. Other than sharing the same height, there were no other obviously matching characteristics.

The hair had been crudely cropped short, uneven and tufty in spots, bald in others. The face was a death's head, bulging brow, collapsed cheeks and dark recesses for eye sockets. There was no smile this time, merely an expressionless gaze. The slightly hunched shoulders gave the impression that it was an extreme effort for her to hold up her head to meet the camera, but there was no hint of embarrassment at being photographed naked. A creature in this condition was beyond shame.

The rest of the physique was worse. The skin of the torso was stretched tight across the ribcage, which was sickeningly prominent, and there were no apparent breasts. Indeed there was no fat on the body whatsoever. The arms were bony rods fixed all too obviously into shoulders by joints more normally unseen. The legs were just as spare, and of uniform thinness except for the bony bulge of the knee which was the widest point. Her pose was slightly knock-kneed, almost as if the legs had been deliberately turned in by the photographer to prevent the subject from toppling over, as one might balance a child's doll. The sinews of the hands, hanging limply at the side, and those of the feet, which were tensed, grasping at the ground for purchase, looked as if they might burst through the translucent webbing of the skin at any moment.

There was no humanity in this image. Not in the poor creature which stared out from the page like a barely animated anatomical diagram, and certainly not in the unseen tormentors who had done such a thing to her and who, in Wallace's eyes, were just as present in the image as the subject herself. He read on, disgusted by the subject matter but fascinated at his father's professionalism.

United States Army Psychological Warfare Group. Date of Examination and Interview – May 9, 1945.

The patient was examined in the Palembang Comfort Station, Sumatra, Dutch East Indies, by myself, Dr Jason Bradley, in the presence of Nurse Audrey Thomas and Dr Dwight C. Jamieson of the US Army Medical Corps.

ON EXAMINATION:
– Generalized signs of gross neglect and systematic and chronic abuse. The patient presented in a manner that was listless and apathetic, but also frightened and profoundly withdrawn. Though conscious at all times, she did not communicate with us throughout the entire physical examination, but was entirely cooperative to the point of complete passivity. Though unresponsive to the use of her real name, as obtained from her camp records, [here the name had been erroneously included by his father and blanked out by the censor] she does react to the name 'Saki', found crudely tattooed on her right shoulder-blade. We believe this to be a diminutive of the Japanese word 'Sakura' or 'cherry blossom'.
– Generalized, brown, maculopapular scaly rash covering eighty per cent of skin's surface area. Extensive bruising and superficial open lacerations around wrists, ankles and neck consistent with (recent) restraint. Pattern of wounds suggestive of heavy twine or similar. Loose fibres of same picked out of deeper lacerations.
– Hair brittle and traumatized. Gross lice infestation with boggy, secondary scalp infection. (Worst areas clipped/shaved on examination to facilitate access and to remove eggs).
– Swollen, spongy, bleeding gums. Loose teeth, widespread decay. Evidence of crude extractions. Possibly self-inflicted. Oral ulceration. Broad, uniform bruising to R. cheek-bone suggestive of recent heavy blow with solid flat surface. Rifle butt?
—Anaemia, widespread tender lymphadenopathy. Discharging lymph node abscess L. groin.
– Moderate dehydration. Pyrexial (102.2°F). We could find no evidence of adequate drinking water supplies in the camp. Although this is the rainy season, there were minimal collection facilities and preference was given to officers and soldiers, who show little sign of dehydration. Fever likely

due to infectious disease from contaminated water supply (cholera/amoebic dysentery). Little bowel and bladder control. Clothes and bedding stained with dried urine/ diarrhoea/semen.

– Moist, crusted yeast infection of groins and axillae. Snail-track ulcers on oral and genital mucosa; scabes burrows on hands and genitals. The scratching of these inflamed and irritated areas has clearly become an unconscious reflex action, aggravating the problem. Nails overlong, but brittle and chipped. One missing entirely (L. thumb).

– Yellow discharge from eyes, early corneal ulcers and lice amongst eyelashes. Tenderness and apparent aversion to bright lights prevented prolonged tests. In fact, the patient kept her eyes closed throughout much of our examination, unless prompted.

– Cough, mucoid sputum. Chest – L. lower lobe consolidation. The examination was interrupted several times to allow for the patient's coughing fits to subside. One resulted in vomiting, with blood.

– Abdomen: tender with guarding L. iliac fossa. Multiple traumatic anal fissures with secondary bacterial overgrowth. Purulent anal discharge. Active proctitis.

– Vaginal examination (at this point Nurse Thomas felt compelled to leave the room): foul smelling, mucoid cervical discharge. Extreme tenderness L. fornix with cervical excitation. Numerous vulval lacerations and contusions, consistent with vaginal insertion of abrasive foreign objects. (Removed several short, black prickly spines. Cf. large cactus plant from camp commandant's desk? Punishment?) Suppurating R. vulval abscess. Multiple vaginal and anal warts.

– Gross cachexy. This level of malnutrition and emaciation (cf body weight 68 lbs/height 5'10") is consistent with that seen in the most extreme POW and civilian internment camps liberated thus far (eg Bangka Island, Truk and especially Santo Tomas Camp in Manila visited in 2/1945- cf US FET Board Study #243). No apparent preferential treatment for women/ forced prostitutes.

It was only at this point that Wallace realized what his father's task had been during the war and just what this poor woman was. He had previously glossed over the phrase 'comfort station' in the report, as that phrase was not yet widely in the public domain as a euphemism for the brothels of the Japanese military. Yet he knew what a prostitute was, and a forced prostitute was a concept he could barely conceive of. His father had been travelling with the liberating forces, examining, treating and interviewing women who had been forced to provide sexual services to the Japanese soldiers on the front line. The file he held was packed with records of these women. Many Chinese and Korean women, but also Westerners. The names had been erased, but the details were there. No wonder that it was locked away and that his father never talked about his war-time experiences. What a bombshell it must have been at the time to have had hard evidence of this sort of treatment of civilian prisoners of war. He read on.

DIAGNOSIS
1. Dehydration, malnutrition, scurvy.
2. Secondary syphilis.
3. Gonorrhea – pelvic, rectal, pharyngeal.
4. Vaginal and peri-anal warts.
5. Yaws.
6. Lice and scabes infestations.
7. Widespread secondary bacterial and fungal infection.
8. Amoebic Dysentery and/or Cholera.
9. Shock resulting from gross neglect with physical and sexual abuse.
10. Opium dependency.

CONCLUSION
It is clear to the examiner that this woman has suffered the most severe form of physical, sexual and probably mental abuse that one human being is capable of inflicting on another. The neglect in evidence in her overall physical condition, in conjunction with the specific injuries from which she was suffering at the time of examination, is appalling, even in the context of the treatment of male, military prisoners already encountered in other camps.

The extreme trauma to the genital and anal region leaves me in no doubt that this patient has been subjected to prolonged and forcible sexual abuse of a particularly abhorrent nature. The abnormally high level of sodomitical activity in this case, unusual for Japanese males generally, even in brothels, is indicative that this woman was given no respite from her abuse, even during times of menstruation or vaginal infection. The widespread administration of herbal 'contraceptive' preparations by the 'mama-san' and prolonged use of permanganic acid solution as an attempt to avoid infection, have most likely added to the likelihood of the patient's being sterile. In addition, regular injections of Salvarsan were administered, a toxic arsenic compound more properly referred to as arsphenamine. This has been ineffective in this case in preventing the development of syphilis, and will likely lead to further long-term complications.

It is most unlikely that a fertile girl of twenty–twenty-two years, forced to have sexual intercourse between fifteen and twenty times a day, could avoid pregnancy. Prophylactic birth control was used, but condoms are in short supply and ineffective as they were invariably re-used after rudimentary washing. Thus, during her time here (three years), there is a good chance that she has also undergone at least three, if not more, abortions, undertaken by unqualified military staff. This to be confirmed by further examination.

These figures are estimated from the appointments book, which shows Miss D [again the name had been erased by an unknown censor] to have had an average of twelve, thirty-minute appointments per day with the regular soldiers, plus three all-night sessions per week with a particular officer. This makes her the most popular girl in the camp. Given her outrageous condition I can only imagine that the reason for this popularity over the other inmates was that she was Caucasian. In support of this is a picture of a white horse crudely daubed on the outside door to her cubicle. We have encountered this previously in Batavia in a comfort station staffed by a contingent including several Dutch women, where the 'mama-san' explained it to be a sign that there was a white woman within, ready to be ridden. Our patient also has, of course, the dubious attraction of being one of the few remaining alive. When the camp was liberated we found only thirty-five women left in the comfort station, which had been built to house 150, for a total garrison of 1350 troops. Those women that survived until the latter years were clearly overworked. I assume the others to be dead, although exhumation for the purposes of gathering evidence for war-crimes trials will take time.

In recent weeks several platoons of kamikaze have passed through this region, and it is traditional for them to be offered sex (for free in their case) prior to giving up their lives. Such men, on the threshold of certain death, are unlikely to be too considerate to their partners, especially Western women.

The prognosis for her physical recovery is good if given immediate treatment to address issues of malnutrition and dehydration. Syphilitic and gonorrheal infections are most likely containable. Rectal surgery recommended as a matter of some urgency. Localized treatment of bacterial and fungal infections already instigated. The patient is, however, likely to be sterile. Course of detoxification for opium addiction most urgent.

Her psychological condition causes more long-term concern. As previously noted, she is withdrawn, frightened and apathetic, and makes no attempt to communicate. Although she appears to understand English instructions, she responds more readily to Japanese. When first confined by US Army medical staff, she uttered a string of lewd Japanese phrases referring to sexual practices, and attempted to grasp one of the orderlies by the testicles. She has been transformed into what I can only describe as a sexual automaton, and her reflex reaction to all men is to try to initiate some form of sexual contact. This apparent willingness to comply with what she perceives to be male desires is no doubt the result of long experience of punishment beatings and more perverse brutalities meted out to the non-acquiescent. The corpse of one pregnant woman was found with a bayonet wound to the vagina.

Furthermore, we have learned in other comfort stations, notably the kempetai-run Magelang Club in Java, that those women who could attract the attentions of officers were likely to be treated more humanely than those left to the more primal instincts of the front-line fighting men. Hence the rather pathetic attempts to beautify with home-made cosmetics and to titillate with suggestive or even downright explicit language. It seems that Miss D was successful in this regard, as she regularly spent entire nights with one particular officer, thus saving her from the rigours of the half-hourly appointment schedule with the lower ranks during the night. Long-term, expert and caring psychiatric treatment will be necessary to break this behavioural conditioning and to return this patient to civilized society.

PERSONAL BACKGROUND

The amount of information is scarce but the camp record shows that Miss D arrived here in March 1942 following her successful survival of the sinking of the *Vyner Brooke*, which had attempted to evacuate sixty-five Australian nurses from Singapore. Thirty-three nurses made it to Palembang, they being the lucky ones of the shipwrecked who had not landed on Bangka Island, where we know of twenty-one who were slaughtered in cold blood on the beach by Japanese machine-gun fire.

Of the thirty-two surviving Australians moved here, we have thus far seen living evidence of only fourteen. The other surviving comfort women are either Indonesian or Chinese.

We know from the Singapore hospital records that she enrolled as a nurse in Brisbane in August 1941, and was moved to Singapore in February 1942. According to a letter to her from the Australian Ministry of Defence (q.v.) found, partially destroyed by seawater but still legible for the most part and buried with her money in her cubicle, her mother, also a nurse, was killed in the fighting for Corregidor in January 1942. This was just prior to the attempted evacuation of Miss D on board the *Vyner Brooke*.

Following emergency treatment for the immediate physical conditions, I recommend prompt repatriation with the father, who the letter informs us to be living in the United States.

This was the end of the formal medical and intelligence-gathering report destined for use by physicians and war crimes investigators alike, but Wallace's father had continued to write in the lower margin of the official form, and had added an extra sheet, obviously torn from a notebook of some kind. True, the handwriting deteriorated and the spelling and punctuation wavered from his father's punctilious ideals. But Wallace Bradley proudly imagined his father adding his own furious *post scriptum* to the clinical facts as he wrote up his notes from that day's horrific findings, in the small hours of the morning, tumbler of Scotch at his elbow, seated at his desk in a hut in the sweltering heat and stultifying humidity of Sumatra in May 1945. As Wallace sat reading the report for the first time, this was not yet twenty years ago, but it might have been another world. He had never heard his father express such passion, never sensed such subjectivity in the man he thought to be so objective, never sensed the love for his fellow human beings which must have driven the man to his vocation yet which had, until now, always remained cloaked in the antiseptic shroud of science. And locked away in that damned desk of his. He continued reading.

This woman is a twenty-two-year-old human being of extreme sensitivity. She has not yet communicated with us directly, but an unfinished letter (q.v., Appendix 2a) to her mother, probably interrupted by the receipt of the news of her death and thus unsent, displays a refinement and cultivation of rare quality.

Wallace, his curiosity aroused, flicked quickly forward through the file, looking for the letter. It was not to be found. He continued his reading.

We see through the meagre flesh and bone to a human soul. A daughter, herself in mortal danger in Singapore, concerned for the well-being of a mother in another war zone. She shrugs off her own plight in an attempt to comfort, to reassure. She speaks of home life, of her father, her friends. She conjures images, images which even now calm my spirit when I think of them and allow myself to escape into them; images of a peacetime which will see the family reunited, barefoot on a beach, huddled around her beloved piano, sleeping the untroubled sleep of the secure and the loved in the childhood bed. She speaks of her favourite piece of music in a way which leaves the notes hanging in the air such that I hear them still, and she quotes poetry with such a fluency and familiarity that I am certain her pen never once left the page to ponder the precision of a line or verse.

I can picture that pen even now, in the grace of her slender fingers, floating across the page, and wish she were writing that letter to me. I only hope that, in her current wretched condition, she can still recall the sentiments with which she expressed the strength of her spirit:

Naught broken save this body, lost but breath;

Nothing to shake the laughing heart's long peace there

But only agony, and that has ending;

And the worst friend and enemy is but Death.

I beg forgiveness for my comments, as they are well beyond the remit of my duties as medical examiner, but the scientific facts do not begin to approach a description of the enormity of the crimes that have been perpetrated here. I feel I must use this opportunity to express my personal outrage. In all my experience as a physician and psychiatrist, I have never endured such a wretched case. What extremes of depravity, what pleasure at human suffering, what perverted inhumanity are these damned people capable of? Every camp I go to, every case I see, I say to myself 'it can't get any worse than this,' and every time I am wrong. Every new case throws up some element which goes beyond the worst I have yet seen, some new twist on Man's inhumanity to Man, some added cruelty.

I implore whichever Judge might read this report to read Charlotte's letter, [the censor had missed this use of the name] which I have attached to this file. I have made a copy of it which I will carry with me always as a reminder of the beauty, the wit, the love which these barbarians have tried to expunge from her soul, and that of thousands like her, but which we will restore.

Please God, let this war be over soon, that I might begin rebuilding those souls. And my own.

Wallace put down the file for a moment to gather himself. He had deliberately avoided looking at anything too personal to his father as he had not yet felt himself ready for that, but here, in this medical file of all places, he had happened upon probably the most emotional outburst he had ever experienced from this man. He felt an immediate sense of shame that he had not known his father well enough to have suspected him capable of such depth of feeling. And at the same time an immense frustration that his father had never overtly shown him such love, nor he in return. His father had written of 'Man's inhumanity to Man', well maybe that phrase should have been written about the relationship between father and son. Why are tears only shed and love expressed when it is too late?

In his confused and grieving state, the adolescent Bradley found himself in the absurd position of feeling somehow jealous of the miserable wretch of a woman whose most intimate details he had just seen laid out before him as if she had been lying there naked on the sofa in the corner. He envied the letter from daughter to mother which his father had admired so, and promised to carry with him always. Why had he, Wallace, not written such letters from school, so that his own father might be moved to feel about him in the same way? How dare this disease-ridden whore usurp his father's affections? Typical bloody doctor. Too busy caring for all and sundry to bother with his own flesh and blood.

He looked back at the photographs. Charlotte. An incongruously pretty name for one in such an abominable state. He had to find that letter. See what sort of stuff people wrote in circumstances like that. Maybe the copy was still in his father's wallet or briefcase? He did say he would always carry it with him. Or maybe he had taken the original now that the file was back in his possession. Just so he could see that bloody woman's beautiful handwriting again, probably. Why did his father have the file, anyhow? Surely it should have been held by the authorities for the war crimes tribunals, or, when that was done with, at least by the doctor who cared for her in her convalescence?

He reached down and began searching through his father's briefcase. It must be in here somewhere. In one wallet he found a stack of letters tied up with red ribbon. All envelopes in his mother's hand, addressed to his father. Postmarks between 1949 and 1958.

There was only one other letter, which he found in a separate compartment of the briefcase, one with a zip-fastener. He pulled it out excitedly but realized immediately this was not it. It was again addressed in his mother's hand, but this time to his grandmother. He was about to place it with the rest of the correspondence on the 'personal' pile, when he noticed something unusual about it. There was no stamp and no postmark. This letter had never been sent. He pulled the letter out of the envelope where it had been slit. The date as it was written at the top of the letter was January 1942. It began:

'Dear Mama, I hope this letter finds you well, wherever you may be. Singapore is stifling . . .' He shuffled quickly through the three pages and saw that it ended: '. . . your ever-loving daughter, Lottie'.

Lottie. The word screamed at him from the page. He flipped back to the first page of the report. **Name – C.E.D.** Charlotte. He held the paper up to the light and mentally filled in the blanks as he squinted through the inadequate black blocks of the censor's pen. Charlotte Eleanor Drabble. **Date of birth – 3/7/22.** Not, of course, today's date, the third of July, but the seventh of March, as his American father would have written it. Today was not her fortieth birthday. They had celebrated that nearly four months ago. The inescapable logic of it all now bludgeoned his brain into submission and he felt an immediate sense of unbearable guilt at his thoughts of jealousy a few moments before.

This *was* the letter from Miss D. The wretched, miserable, violated, 'disease-ridden whore' his father had so admired. He looked again at the grainy, smiling photograph and compared it to that of the naked, skeletal zombie on the following page. Not Lana Turner. His mother.

PART 2

Brize

'First, a great Want of Money in any Trading Country, occasions Interest to be at a very high Rate. And here it may be observed, that it is impossible by any Laws to restrain men from giving and receiving exorbitant Interest, where Money is suitably scarce: For he that wants Money will find out ways to give 10 per cent when he cannot have it for less, altho' the Law forbids to take more than 6 per cent.'

Benjamin Franklin, *A modest inquiry into the Nature and Necessity of Paper Currency* (1729)

CHAPTER 1

JAKOB LICHTBLAU WAS NOT AN EARLY RISER AS A RULE. AS THE oldest and most senior partner at Bankhaus Löwen-Krugmann in Munich he felt he had earned the right to breakfast with his wife. He would water his ulcer with the prescribed two cups of camomile tea, and walk the kilometre or so from his townhouse in the Schwabing district, through the Englischer Garten and cross the Isar before arriving at the large pre-war villa that was the headquarters of one of Germany's largest private banks, at about nine thirty. But not this morning.

To his wife's consternation he had slept poorly and risen finally at six. He had gulped down three large cups of bitter coffee, and had barely finishing knotting his tie when the doorbell rang at seven, and a car and driver whisked him off on the short journey to the office. By eight minutes past seven he was at his desk, the only person in the building. For today was Wednesday, the launch day of the new thirty-year bond issue for the Republic of South Korea, the day on which Jakob Lichtblau would earn seventy million United States dollars for the bank.

Since he had met Annie van Aalst and Heinz-Josef von Lessing a few days before, he had found the daily routine difficult to bear. After a heavy lunch, the three-hour journey back from Frankfurt to Munich in the first class cocoon of the lightning quick Inter-City-Express had passed in a contented doze. Since then he had been wishing the days away until launch day, feeling an excitement he had not experienced since he was a boy in the run up to the family holidays every year in Sylt.

He had found numerous ways to busy himself – reading up a little bit on Korea, so as to impress his colleagues with some background knowledge when the time came to reveal the surprise, practising his speech to the board meeting, scheduled for Friday, and deciding what they should do to celebrate. He had secretly already booked a private room for twenty at Aubergine in the Maximiliansplatz, probably the finest restaurant in Germany. OK, so it would cost him at least three hundred marks per head, but that worked out at a hundred marks per Michelin star, which seemed like a good deal for such a celebration.

Of course, he had also looked into the account details of a certain Mr Saul Krantz, and found his credentials to be better than impeccable. He was not by any means their largest private client, but with deposits and investments of over thirty-five million marks, he was in the top twenty. The same thirty-five million marks had not even been noticed by the accountants at Xenfin when they had prepared their monthly reports. And as for Xenfin. Well, there was no need to check into them. They were legendary.

Bankhaus Löwen-Krugmann always accounted for everything in marks internally. It was Lichtblau's eccentricity perhaps, but the arrival of the euro had not been fêted within their walls on the Haidhausen side of the river with quite the same fanfare of trumpets as their more famous competitors on the Kardinal-Faulhaberstrasse or Briennerstrasse. Of course they published accounts in euros, and transacted in euros when necessary for their clients, but Jakob Lichtblau still liked to think in old money. And besides, it always sounded more.

But Lichtblau was worried. Since he had signed the deal, things in Asia had started to go badly wrong. Some property company in Thailand had gone bankrupt, and the currencies and bond markets in that part of the world had started to haemorrhage. He was worried for some of the bank's project finance deals in China, he was worried by stories he had heard of civil unrest in Jakarta. People had actually been killed already by government troops trying to stop looters and preventing a run on the banks there. But most of all he was worried for that charming lady who had chosen his bank to be an intermediary for their purchase of two billion dollars' worth of Korean bonds. As he sat alone in his office and read the latest Reuters reports of what was already being labelled

'The Asian Debt Crisis', he hoped that Annie van Aalst was not in over her head.

'Annie, it's Cameron.'

'God, you get in early. It's only six thirty your time.'

'Well, I actually didn't quite get around to going to bed last night. Entertaining those South Americans again. And you may have forgotten, but we have another big day before us. The Korea Global is being launched in half an hour into the weakest Asian market in living memory.' Again, they were obliged to speak for the benefit of any listening tape machines.

'Oh, I know that. I think they're crazy to go ahead with it in these conditions. We're not touching it.'

'Well the lead manager is DKBV, and they're trying to be all macho about it. They say all this Asia trouble is just a blip, a shake-out. They reckon it's a good opportunity to get in.'

'Well they would, wouldn't they? Rumour has it that they're totally committed to the deal anyway. Couldn't pull it even if they wanted to, so they have to put on a brave face. And they effectively own it at a fixed price – *pre*-crisis levels. They're gonna have a hell of a job getting a syndicate together, let alone finding any clients to invest in it. It's gonna cost them a lot.'

'I thought you were thinking of taking a big chunk.'

'Yes we were. We had an arrangement with one of the syndicate members, but we've had a change of heart given what's happened over there. That reminds me, I really should call him and let him know we won't be participating after all.' Annie van Aalst replaced the handset, but before calling Jakob Lichtblau, she used her cell phone to call a private number in the Georgetown area of Washington.

'Today?'

'Yes.'

'How much?'

'About a yard should be enough.'

'I'll put in the call to Berlin right now. Let 'em know where we stand and what we expect. Jews or no Jews.'

'Miss van Aalst. What a pleasure to hear from you. Today is the big day, is it not?'

'Today is a very big day, Herr Lichtblau, in many respects. But not a big day for us.'

'Well, I understand you are accustomed to making frequent large investments in the bond market, Fräulein, but nevertheless, I would have thought that two billion dollars would be something special.'

'Oh you're absolutely right. It would have been, but . . .'

'I understand your concerns. You are worried about the Asian situation. It is understandable. But I have spoken to the Graf at DKBV. He says the deal will go ahead as planned, and that the, er, *Unruhe* we are currently seeing in the market is a temporary phenomenon. Do not worry, Fräulein, I feel sure your investment will be safe.'

'Well it's kind of you to suggest it, sir. But I'm afraid that, given current market sentiment, it is not the kind of risk that we at Xenfin feel we can countenance. Saul, that is Mr Krantz, is quite against it. In fact, we're beginning to wind up our exposure to the area.'

Lichtblau's heart began to pound. He was still alone in the office, but he dropped his voice to a whisper, as if he couldn't bear to hear his own words. 'But we shook hands on a deal. I have signed a paper . . .'

'I'm sorry Herr Lichtblau, but I'm afraid that's the way things go. We had a verbal understanding that, should we buy into this issue, then we would buy the bonds from you, but I am sure you appreciate our misgivings about the situation. Xenfin will not be buying any bonds. Not from you, nor from anyone else. I can give you *that* in writing if you like.'

'But *our* commitment? We, Fräulein van Aalst, *are* committed.'

'As you said, sir. You have signed a paper. You are in a very prestigious deal, well up in the syndicate, and think of your fee. You'll still be getting that.'

'But we had relied on your money to pay for these bonds. Now we have to find the money ourselves. Two *billion* dollars. Tomorrow. And the bonds will be on our books! We will have, *um Gottes Willen*, market risk! On a thirty-year bond! How will I explain it to the board?'

'Well I'm sure you'll be able to sell them, sir. As Lessing said, Asia's probably OK. Just a blip. Anyhow, I really must go. I have some currency hedging to get done before the market closes in Jakarta. I do hope we will get the opportunity to collaborate again, sir. Goodbye.'

Jakob Lichtblau winced with pain. He opened the top drawer of his desk and took out a small bottle of milky antacid liquid and swigged half of it down. How would he raise two billion dollars financing by tomorrow? He would have to call on all of his committed loan facilities, and then find some more. Maybe he could pledge the bonds as collateral? What did they call that? A repo? My God, he had to sell the bonds before the board meeting on Friday. At least he had the fees as a cushion. He could afford to take some loss on the bonds if he gave up some of the fees he would earn. He hoped it wouldn't be too much.

'Danny Brookes.'

'Danny, it's Cameron. I need confirmation of a few numbers from you, pal. We can talk. I'm on my mobile in one of our conference rooms.'

'Fire away. None of my calls are taped here. I take it Lichtblau swallowed the bait and is beginning to suffer this morning. Where did the bonds open up?'

'First bid was at ninety-five.'

'Where were they issued?'

'Par. That's a hundred to you Danny.'

'Very funny. Just 'cause I'm not a bond maven doesn't mean I don't know the jargon, you silly arse.'

'Well anyway, Lichtblau is down five points on two billion already. That makes a nice round hunny bear. One hundred million dollars.'

'But don't forget the fees. He effectively owns the bonds at ninety-six and a half. So he's only down a point and a half so far. Thirty million.'

'True. But the lead is not supporting the issue. Typical DKBV. That bid of ninety-five I mentioned is really only good for about half a bar.'

'A what?'

'Half a mill. Try to sell ten million and the bid's more likely to be at ninety-two or three. If you're lucky. Try to unload two yards, and, well forget it. Not a hope in hell. What I would like to know from you is, where does this bond have to trade for Lichtblau to be having some *really* serious problems. You know what I'm talking about?'

'Oh yes, Cameron. I know. For the sacrificial lamb to be brought to the offering table. Well, I'm ready for you. I have all the numbers here. Bankhaus Löwen-Krugmann has paid-up share capital of . . .'

'Danny, don't give me all six volumes. The *Reader's Digest* version will do me. What's the bottom line.'

'Well of course, it's not as clear cut as all that. It depends on the extent to which they can put new lines in place quickly, and with what speed their existing credit lines are cut once news gets out that they're in trouble.'

'Yeeesss, Danny, come on . . .'

'But all in all, and taking everything into consideration, and assuming that the Bundesbank doesn't step in to bail them out, I would say that a paper loss of around seven hundred and fifty million of your dollars would be sufficient to close the doors.'

'OK, so seven-fifty on two billion, that's thirty-eight points, to be on the safe side. Thirty-eight points off their cost price of ninety-six and a half gets us down to a bond price of fifty-eight and a half. That's where you reckon we need it to be before Krugmann goes tits.'

'Well it does sound very low, but that is my professional judgement. You know, they have a large balance sheet, but they're not very well capitalized. The ratios are right at the limit of acceptability.'

'OK, Daniel. Thanks. I'll get on to Annie. Between us we've got some selling to do if we're to make Krugmann our first Western victim. Let's just see what sort of stomach DKBV has to buy some bonds back.'

'Really, Cameron? Did you buy some for Steinman, Schwartz's book? I thought you weren't going to touch it.'

'Oh I didn't buy any, Danny. But I sure as hell am going to sell some. This little issue is going to bond hell if Annie and I have got anything to do with it.'

Jakob Lichtblau was in serious pain. His stomach was protesting at the sixth cup of overbrewed, acrid coffee that morning, and he sat watching the price of the new Korea global bond sink like a stone. The flickering screen on his desk read a price of eighty-four already, and it was only nine o'clock. He hadn't told anybody what he had done, and the loneliness of his situation was almost as unbearable as the losses he was racking up for the bank. Two hundred and fifty million dollars in a little under two hours. And it was not going to be easy even to come up with the two billion he needed to pay for the bonds the next day. His credit lines with other banks, it seemed, were pretty full. He had only been able to draw on about another six hundred million. He was going to have to start selling some of these bonds soon if he couldn't come up with the money. To fail settlement on a transaction of this size would be financial suicide. He simply couldn't allow the bank to do it. The bank he had nurtured and built up to a reputation of such probity, such professionalism, such acumen. Forty years' work to be wiped out in one morning. But to take those losses? How could he do that? Surely Lessing at DKBV was right. They had issued the bond, after all. Korea couldn't be in such a bad way, could it? They belonged to the OECD, *verdammt noch mal*! The world's eleventh largest economy. It was Thailand and Indonesia that had the problems. Surely not Korea. Reason would prevail, the market would bounce. The price would recover. No, he couldn't sell out of the position now. He couldn't take such a loss. He would wait, wait for another few hours.

'Barnesy, Cameron.'
    'Hey mate, what gives this morning? You get your fingers burned in the Korea Global yet?'

'No – we declined the deal. They've got to be crazy bringing a deal like that into this market.'

'Well I reckon DKBV must own the whole deal. I haven't found anyone who took any yet.'

'Well I only know of one other taker. Another Kraut bank, but not one of the typical players. Smaller shop. Hope they know what they're doing. They're in for two yards.'

'Holy shit. Serious mullah. Are they good for it?'

'We'll see. Just keep that to yourself, Barnesy, though please. Don't want that sort of stuff getting round the market.' Dodds knew that within two minutes of putting the phone down, the broker would be on to his eight closest friends with the latest rumour. That was probably good for another five points off the price. 'Now, listen to me. Steinman has decided to dip a toe in the water here. Nothing like a bit of volatility to raise the old pulse, eh? I want you to stick in an offer for a hundred of these pups on your screen.'

'A hundred? Are you sure, Cam? Is this the time to go short? I mean, we're trading at eighty-two – that's the low of the day.'

'Just do it you little schmuck and leave the trading decisions to me. Otherwise the line's out, do you hear?'

'OK, OK. What level do you want to show?'

'For that size, make it seventy-nine, all or nothing. But you've only got it for ten minutes. Then I move on to Cedef.'

Dodds watched as the price he had just given his broker appeared on the screen in front of him. There was a brief pause, and the size indicator '100mm' appeared next to it. Within seconds all the other prices on the screen disappeared, one by one, as dealers in other banks phoned up their brokers to remove their prices while they considered their own next step in light of this highly aggressive move by Dodds. Of course, all they saw was an anonymous price on the screen. They didn't know who it was who was offering, at least not yet. The phone line from his broker started to flash.

'Cam, it's me, Barnesy. Look, there's a bid coming against your offer.'

'Why isn't it on the screen?'

'The guy doesn't want to show it to the market. Only to you. And it's a bit away from your level.'

'Where?'

'Seventy-two'

'Hit him. He's done. And while you're on to that cheap tosser, ask him how he'd take another two hundred on the follow!'

'Jesus Christ, Cam. What's got into you today? You sound like you've got it in for someone.'

'Nah, not really. Just didn't get laid last night. Now get off the fuckin' line and see if this pussy will take some more bonds. I have more to go!'

Saul Krantz wandered into the dealing room of their Cayman Islands office and pulled up a chair at the desk of Annie van Aalst. It was four thirty a.m. local time, nine thirty in London and six thirty p.m in Seoul, South Korea.

'Annie, how are we doing? I've been watching the screens for the last two hours straight and I can't believe what's going on.'

'We're doing great Saul. I've closed out a lot of our outright currency positions in the baht and the rupiah. The won is a bit more tricky this morning, with that bond deal hitting the market in London, but we're on track. We'll be out by the end of the week, and then we'll start to get short.'

'How's performance?'

'Well, it was never going to be easy to maintain at that level, but we're not doing too badly given the state of the Asian markets. We've gone from about up seventy-three per cent to around up sixty.'

'OK. Just be aware we're likely to see some withdrawls from the funds if this keeps going on. Keep some cash handy, we might need it.'

'Sure thing, Saul. Keep the faith. I called it right, eh?'

'You are a marvel Annie. You got it right down to the friggin' day. I don't know how you do it.'

'Just call it feminine intuition. I hope you remember me at the end of the year.'

'You keep this up and you can write your own cheque, sweetheart. Keep me informed.' With that the billionaire financier and guru of the world of fund management, tense and focused, wandered out of the door to practise his swing on the floodlit driving range he had just had built in the grounds of Colliers Landings. He found it an excellent way to concentrate the mind.

Annie van Aalst saw the Bloomberg screen flashing with a message from Dodds. She frowned, as it was a bit unsubtle of him, especially as Bradley had issued them all with encryption keys and passwords for secure e-mails. You never knew who was going to read your Bloomberg messages. She called up the message and smiled as she read:

'Tyger! Tyger! Crapping out,
Dragging with it foolish Kraut;
One immoral, handsome Thai
Has set in swing OUR strategy!'
With apologies etc. etc. to William Blake. Not bad for a maths geek, eh babe?'

She discreetly erased the message, making sure it was also gone from the temporary files and recycle bin, and settled back in her chair to watch the gradual but inexorable destruction of Bankhaus Löwen-Krugmann, played out in phosphorescent pixels and sixteen-bit colour on the screen in front of her.

CHAPTER 2

JAMES EMERSON WALKED INTO THE AIR-CONDITIONED, CALM AND dust-free chill of Café Batavia in Jakarta's old Dutch quarter and breathed an enormous sigh of relief. For the first time since he arrived he had managed a trip across town without an emergency stop to squat over a putrid hole in the ground with very little privacy and evacuate his bowels. It was around eight p.m. on December the twenty-ninth, only five days since Jake Samuels had arrived unannounced at his apartment to spoil his Christmas, and he had been in Indonesia a little over forty-eight hours.

He had already decided he loathed Jakarta, and was going to make sure he stayed there as short a time as possible if he was to escape with his health and a reasonable quantity of his own bodily fluids, which seemed to be doing their best to escape at an alarming rate. He had learned far more about the various types and standards of lavatorial facilities in Jakarta in his first couple of days than he had about the raging financial crisis, which threatened to purge Indonesia of thirty years of progress with the same efficacy that the goat's leg soup he had unwittingly eaten on his first night was managing on his own constitution. He had still been doubled up in a spasm of dry retching when the embassy official had called him in his hotel room early that morning to make a date for the evening. At first, the prospect of straying too far from the reassuring porcelain fixtures of his hotel's bathroom had been too much to contemplate but, as the day progressed, and when it became apparent that the fruit he had ventured to eat for lunch was staying put, he decided to keep his date and made his way by taxi across the stinking, unbearably humid and chaotic capital of the world's fourth most populous nation.

Café Batavia was one of Jakarta's best restaurants, and Emerson was relieved to see a selection of Western dishes on the menu, which he perused with mounting confidence as the intestinal pyrotechnics of the last two days appeared to be fizzling out. The walls were hung thick with framed (and sometimes signed) photographs of Hollywood stars, old and new, in bizarre juxtaposition. So James Dean glowered moodily alongside Sharon Stone, and Lana Turner simpered back at Johnny Depp. The place itself was still relatively empty at that hour, with most of the tables still unoccupied, but it was filling up. A handful of suited expats, mainly Scots and Australians, were holding court at the bar, and Emerson caught snatches of their conversation as he waited for his host.

'So we shorted half a yard of roops and ended up getting a call from the frigging central bank . . .'

'And you wouldn't believe the receptionist. We went in to make a presentation to their board for a new bond issue, and she was begging for it. An hour later and I'd got the mandate for the issue and her telephone number . . . Now I'll really be able to fuck the company in every sense of the word!'

'I heard Soros is getting involved. The President of Malaysia has already blamed the whole crisis on a Jewish conspiracy . . .'

'Who wants to make me a price on the first bank to go tits? I say Bank Bali . . .'

'I'll give you threes. My money's on Bank Danamon.'

'You're both wrong guys. The first bank to go has already gone.'

'Not Bumi Daya?'

'Wrong country, mate. There's a major Thai bank gone under this evening. Saw it on Reuters just before I left the office. Eight hundred million dollars in losses on various property deals. I suppose it's all down to that Pee Seuar Land business a couple of days ago . . .'

'Holy shit! Well, I guess they won't be the last if things carry on at this rate . . .'

*   *   *

In his office in Hong Kong, two thousand miles away across the South China Sea, Johnnie Quaid was grinning broadly as he read the same Reuters report referred to by the drunken trader in Jakarta. In fact he read it over and over. This was his work, he said to himself. He had caused it. If he had not written the letter to Chumsai, pulling the rug from under his feet, none of this would have happened. He was very proud of himself. The butterfly had flapped its wings and the shock waves were rapidly gaining amplitude.

He hadn't created the problem of course. He couldn't lay claim to that. No member of the Pegasus Forum, not even the great Professor Wallace Bradley, could do that. Bradley had helped, of course, with his advice to governments and their agencies. He knew the Asian model was deeply flawed and he continued to advocate it. He knew property prices were way overdone. But what was really causing the problems in the markets now was the *exposure* of the problems, the laying bare of the seething mass of worms. And it was human psychology again. The problems existed before Chumsai's suicide, they were there for all to see but nobody wanted to believe what they saw. It was much more convenient to believe in the miracle, and as long as enough people believed, that made it true. Pegasus was the dissenting voice, the little boy who pointed out the emperor's lack of clothes. But in this case, the emperor was the global banking system, and his blushes would be a breakdown in the world's capital markets. Johnnie Quaid's edifice had started to crumble, the first bank had gone bust, and he was fairly sure another bank, a Western one this time, would be hard on its heels.

In one corner of the dining room at the Café Batavia, nearest the bar, a jazz trio finished setting up and began playing. A small blackboard propped on a chair next to the tiny double-bass player, who was dwarfed by his instrument, proclaimed them to be the Batak Stompers and for the first time since he arrived in Indonesia, Emerson found himself smiling at the curious combination of 'Eez You Eez or Eez You Eyen't Ma Bebbi?'

sung in a tremulous Indonesian accent by a tiny, wiry sixty-year-old in an evening suit three sizes too large. Maybe life wouldn't be so bad in Jakarta after all.

More noise from the crowd at the bar alerted Emerson's attention to the arrival of his host. He was making his way across the room accompanied by their jeers, wolf whistles, and much mock bowing and forelock-tugging, and the band segued seamlessly into a syncopated version of the British national anthem as the senior official of Her Majesty's mission in Jakarta approached Emerson's table and proffered a hand in greeting.

'I appear to have been recognized. So tiresome. I suppose I must be something of a regular here. Awfully pleased to meet you Mr Emerson. Lafarge. Morley Lafarge. Economic attaché.'

He sat down and a waiter appeared at his shoulder immediately.

'Ah, good to see you again, *Bapak* Sutan. My usual please.'

'*Selamat*. Always a pleasure, *Bapak* Morley. And for your friend?'

'Mr Emerson?'

'I'll risk a beer, if I may. What can you recommend?'

'The local muck is as good as any, wouldn't you say so, *Bapak* Sutan? Try a Bintang, James, a large one. Chinese drink it by the gallon. It is OK if I call you James, isn't it? So much bloody easier than *Bapak* this and *Bapak* that all bloody day long.'

'Of course, of course.'

'Now, I detect from your demeanour and your,' he wrinkled his nose, 'shall we say, aura, to be polite, that you have not had the happiest time with the local cuisine since your arrival. Am I right?'

'Well, yes. Since you ask. I've been sick as a dog for the last forty-eight hours. But how do you know? And what do you mean by aura?'

'Mothballs, James. Unmistakable pong of camphor about you. Sure sign of one who has spent too much time in the indigenous washrooms. They're always full of mothballs. Keeps the 'roaches at bay, and masks the stench somewhat. Although to be frank, I'm not sure which stench is preferable.'

'Well, I seem to be on the mend now, although this dinner will be kill or cure, I fear. So let's get it out of the way and order.'

'Good man. Steer clear of the local coconut sludge for a couple of days and you'll be fine. They do a damn good steak here, no elephant brains or goat's todger involved. I'll have the same.'

Lafarge signalled to the waiter, and ordered for both of them.

'Three showers a day, that's what I recommend, James. Everybody else down here is at it all the time. Bathing is pretty much the national sport. Nothing like a regular sluicing. Only way to keep fresh. Especially if you fancy attracting some of the young local talent a little later on. See them lined up over there by the bar? Not tarts, mind you, but the next best thing. Great white hunters, looking for Western husbands, and this is the place to come. Can't be much over seventeen, any one of them.'

'Now, Morley, steady on. I've already picked up one local illness, and if you don't mind I'll leave it at that for now. It is extremely kind of you to invite me here, but tell me one thing before we continue. How did you know I was in Jakarta?'

'Ah, well.' He'd been expecting the question. 'One of our little tricks in diplomatic circles. We have an arrangement with the airlines. Garuda and BA both fly here from London, and they always fax us a passenger list in the morning, just so we're on top of who is coming to visit us, so to speak. BA is no problem, HMG and all that. Garuda just requires the occasional bit of *sogok*, you know, *baksheesh*, *Schmiergeld*. No word for it in English of course because we're all so bloody proper, but you get my drift. Wonga. Brown envelopes. A bung, to use the solar vernacular.'

'Solar?'

'The *Sun*, old boy, the *Sun*. Most sought after daily in these cursed islands, amongst the expats, of course. High premium for today's edition. Didn't bring a copy with you by any chance?'

''Fraid not. Still, it's nice to be recognized and welcomed like this. Particularly at this time of year.'

'Not too many Christmas trees in these parts, I'm afraid, James. Ninety per cent Muslim you see. Still, we do our best. Had a damn good turkey at the Lafarge residence this year. Even managed to find some plum duff. And I must say, Mrs Lafarge roasts an excellent sweet potato. Now. Talking of family, I do have another interest to declare. And the moment I saw your name on the passenger log, I thought, Morley, you simply have to get together with Mr James Emerson. You see, I was at college with your wonderful brother Hugh.'

'You were at Oxford?'

'Of course I was at Oxford, dear boy. But I mean we were together at St Mary's. Same college. Same year. He read English of course, and I was a greats man, but we were friends. An awful loss to us all. I'm so glad to see you are continuing the family tradition on the *Gazette*.'

'Well, it seemed like the right thing to do, and the banking thing was getting to me. I needed something a little more satisfying, a way to make a difference.'

'So what brings you to the City of Victory? You're more of an investigative type these days, or am I wrong? Wouldn't have thought the financial pages were your bag, really.'

'You're right of course, Morley, but we want to have a look at this story from a different angle. The analysts can write all they like about the big-picture reasons for the crisis, but my brief is to dig into the actual mechanics of what causes these markets to crash on any one particular day. Find out how it actually started and who was in there at the beginning. You know, name names and expose the winners instead of just the losers.'

'I don't envy you, my friend. The locals are notoriously reluctant to talk. Especially to outsiders. They take their nationalism very seriously, you know, and the currency, the rupiah itself, is one of the most high-profile symbols of national worth. Any attack on their currency is almost an act of war, an attack on the national pride.'

'It certainly seems like a war zone in some parts of town. What the hell has happened?'

'Fear, James, mixed with a touch of panic and good old-fashioned greed.'

'Fear? Of what?'

'Total ruin, for starters. The people in Jakarta are the best off in the whole of Indonesia. That's not saying much, of course, but the people who live here have come from all over the country to find their fortune.

The population of Jakarta is growing at around two hundred thousand a year, we're over ten million now, and that's all urban migration from within Indonesia. No foreign immigrants allowed in since seventy-one. They work hard, save, send money home to the folks in the jungle and make babies. Except that now, within a few short weeks, they are worried that they might lose everything. Many of them have already. It's only a matter of time before more banks start to close. We've had troops guarding the doors and fights at the cash-machines. There are over three hundred banks in this country, James, and they're all held together by string and chewing gum. They lend to their friends, or to whoever they're told to lend to by the government, and most of the money ends up in the pockets of government officials or business-leaders. The companies they've lent to are up to their necks in debt, a lot of it in foreign currency, and if the rupiah devalues as it has, that makes the debt a lot more expensive to service. We've already had one major corporate bankruptcy this week, one of the grand old *Pribumi* conglomerates, and countless small manufacturers have gone belly up. The banks can't write off too many more failures like that. Something has to give and the people know it. They just want to get their money the hell out of the banks and stash it under their smelly mattresses.'

'But why the violence? Why burnt-out buildings?'

'Well, I mentioned fear and greed going hand in hand. We've seen a lot of looting, especially of the Chinese-owned businesses. The Chinks have been here for centuries, and have always done well. That entrepreneurial streak, you see. Hard work and business acumen. The Jews of Indonesia if you like. But that tends to inspire a lot of jealousy, and whenever things begin to get a bit iffy economically, the Indos tend to vent their spleen in that direction. We've seen it all before, but not quite on this scale. Take a walk around Glodok, that's the slope ghetto, and you'll see a lot of smoking ruins. Of course the government sends in the troops to restore order, but that just tends to make things worse. We're not far from there now actually. You could stroll back that way after dinner and take a look for yourself. Just head for the columns of smoke.' Lafarge knew this would be dangerous, but James

Emerson's welfare was not high on his personal list of goals for that evening.

'And what about the government itself? Do you think they would be willing to help me find out a little more?'

'Of course, of course. I was coming to that. In fact, I've already had a chat with my contact at the Finance Ministry. Took the liberty, hope you don't mind. They monitor all the activities of the banks, especially in the foreign exchange and bond markets. Hand in hand with the central bank, naturally. But I told my guy to expect a call from you. His name is Andi Sartono, terribly helpful, but fiercely patriotic. Be careful with him. Ethnically he's a Bugi, originally a ferocious race of pirates and brigands, and it's fairly unusual to find one of them in high government office in Java. Most of them are still in Kalimantan and Sulawesi. Still, he's your man, and if you're lucky he'll give you access to the financial records. Good luck, James. You'll need it.'

The rest of the evening had passed in a pleasant haze of alcohol, spicy smells and sweet cigarette smoke. Emerson stuck to a couple of beers and his steak for the sake of gastric peace, but Lafarge imbibed a steady series of premium *arak*, a potent rice wine which induced him to monopolize the conversation even more than was his normally garrulous wont. Yet he gave nothing away, no hint of his purpose in sending Emerson into the bowels of a blind bureaucracy, no clue as to his own involvement in the conspiracy. The two traders he had 'recruited' as conduits for Pegasus's rupiah activities were, or so he believed, well concealed. Low-profile banks, minor executives. The mass of foreign exchange activity that had been flowing through Jakarta in the last few days would tie Emerson up for weeks if he tried to trace it all through the Finance Ministry. And Andi Sartono was a mate. He'd have no interest in letting some snooping foreign hack have access to the right data. No. Pegasus was safe.

'Well thanks for a marvellous evening, Morley. You've been a tremendous help. Good background information, a quick cultural tour and a couple of concrete leads. What more could I want? I'll call Sartono tomorrow and send your best. Hope we can do this again before I leave. In the meantime, I think I'll follow your suggestion and take a wander down to Chinatown. Get a feel for just how bad things are out here.' And James Emerson left his host who went to join the expat group of traders still sitting at the bar, ready to continue the session well into the night.

Emerson walked out of the air-conditioned, colonial haven to be met at the door with the dark cloak of humidity and dust which immediately wrapped itself around every square inch of his frame as he set off to find the area known as Glodok. As he walked, he pondered the one overwhelming impression left by Morley Lafarge. Not that he was an overstuffed, pompous and racist arse; not that he drank too much and undoubtedly preferred the taste of the local, barely ripe forbidden fruit to that of his wife's sweet potatoes; not even the cold brutality he hadn't managed to suppress in his eye as he cheerfully sent an unarmed new arrival to walk at night around the most dangerous part of town at a time of lawlessness and civil unrest; more than that, Morley Lafarge was a liar. For Emerson had not arrived by BA or Garuda. The flights were full and Samuels's secretary had only managed to get him on the KLM flight via Amsterdam. Somebody else had tipped Lafarge off that he was on his way, and he wanted to know who and why.

It was twelve hours earlier in the Cayman Islands, a little after eleven thirty in the morning. Saul Krantz was still at his desk after an all night session watching the meltdown in the markets during Asia's trading day as James Emerson wandered into the dangers of the night in downtown Jakarta some twelve thousand miles away. The intercom on his desk beeped gently, and his secretary's voice was piped through in crystal clear digital stereo sound.

'Saul, there's a call for you from Berlin, Germany. A Mr Brunner.'

'Who is he? What does he want?'

'Sounded official. Something to do with bank supervision. Unpronounceable.'

'OK I'll take him.' He pushed a button on the phone console and the spools on one of the call recorders in the belly of the building two floors below began to turn silently. Unlike the traders' calls, his own phone was not routinely taped. He didn't do much actual dealing himself these days so there wasn't really a need for it, but if it was something important he liked to have the option.

'Saul Krantz here, Herr Brunner. What can I do for you?'

'Mr Krantz, it is indeed an honour. And thank you so much for taking my call. I am the director of the Bundesaufsichtsamt für Kreditwesen, the supervisory body for all credit institutions, er, banks, in my country, and we are having a problem with one of our member institutions in the context of which your name, or should I say the name of Xenfin, has cropped up.'

'Well, that is very interesting. How can I help?'

'It seems that one of your employees had a verbal agreement with the chairman of this bank, a Mr Lichtblau of Bankhaus Löwen-Krugmann, to buy some bonds from him. A very significant amount. Two billion dollars to be precise. The name of your employee was a Miss van Aalst. On the strength of this commitment, Mr Lichtblau committed to buy the same amount of this bond, a thirty-year bond recently issued by the Republic of South Korea, from the lead manager of the issue, and signed a binding underwriting agreement to that effect. Unfortunately, Miss van Aalst reneged on her commitment to buy, given the dreadful events in the Asian markets over the last few days, but by this time it was too late for Mr Lichtblau to pull out from his own commitment.'

'Herr Brunner, you use words such as "renege" and "commitment" which are very emotive in this business. Are you suggesting that Annie van Aalst broke a contract with this bank?'

'Alas, there was no written contract. As you know, Mr Krantz, in the world of the capital markets there are very few written agreements, even in transactions of this magnitude. Billions can be committed by telephone in a second, and the only safeguard is the ability of both counterparties to recognize each other's voices down a crackly long-distance telephone line. Traders do not use video phones or require password authentication of identity before dealing. "My word is my bond", Mr Krantz, is the moral foundation, and "know your customer" is the watchword.'

'Allow me a minute to speak with Annie, Herr Brunner.' He put the German on hold.

Van Aalst was in his office thirty seconds later. Krantz filled her in quickly on the situation. Her reaction was immediate and to the point.

'Bullshit!'

'That's all I wanted to hear, Annie. I have implicit faith in you. Now, you speak to Brunner and tell him what happened.'

'Mr Brunner, Annie van Aalst here. It appears there has been some sort of misunderstanding. I did indeed meet with Lichtblau, at DKBV's offices in Frankfurt last week. DKBV wanted him in the syndicate. I said we were looking at the Korea issue, and if we decided to take some, I'd give him a call. No more than that. He seemed happy enough with the deal, and signed the underwriting agreement on the spot. Now if the old man has got a little carried away, and thought I was giving him an order or something, well, I'm afraid that's not my problem. I even called him on the day of issue to let him know that we wouldn't be taking any. Not after that business in Thailand and all the rest since. Anyhow, what's the problem?'

'Well, Miss van Aalst, I thank you for your explanation. We will, of course, investigate further and speak to the other party to the meeting, but it does indeed seem that Mr Lichtblau was a little too exuberant with his fountain pen. I suspected as much. He is not really used to market dealings, you see. He is more of an old-fashioned banker. Regrettably, the problem is this: Bankhaus Löwen-Krugmann has a paper loss of close to one billion dollars on this transaction, which takes it below the standards of capital adequacy required by the banking authorities. I am afraid, if the situation persists, we will have no alternative in this case but to close down the bank and order them to stop trading. Most regrettable, but it is not our policy to bail out a bank that has acted irresponsibly in this way. Especially when the person principally involved is the chairman. We will be making a statement shortly, but in the meantime, please consider yourself insiders to this information and take no action upon it.' He chuckled. 'At least until it is in the public domain.'

Annie smiled to herself. Her lies had been smooth and natural. She knew there was no way of checking what she had said to Lichtblau over their lunch. That was one of the advantages of the face to face meeting. No tape recordings, no comebacks. The word of a senior professional at probably the best-known fund management company in the world, against the word of an old man on the verge of retirement. There was a witness, of course, but there was no doubt whose side Heinz-Josef von Lessing would take if the dispute were taken further. And he worked for the DKBV, the largest bank in Germany. Bradley had planned it so well, she pondered. This business *was* all about belief and trust, and why would anyone think two senior officers of DKBV and Xenfin would deliberately conspire to ruin an old man and his bank? What could their motivation possibly be?

Morley Lafarge had been truthful about one thing. It didn't take Emerson long to reach Glodok, and the columns of rising smoke had pointed him in the right direction. What he had not been ready for were the scenes that met his eyes as he approached the district.

Although it was almost midnight, no matter which way he turned there were hundreds of people on every one of the narrow streets. They grouped in gangs of twenty and thirty on every corner, belligerent, jumpy, very cocky, looking for something. An excuse, he presumed, or trouble in general. A fight, preferably. They chanted a variety of incomprehensible slogans, many of them swigging from unlabelled bottles of, he assumed, some rough, home-made distillate, and although he was now deep in the Chinese ghetto, not one of the crazed, stoned pairs of eyes darting around, scanning the windows and rooftops, was Chinese. They were mostly male, and young, but he did spot an occasional female face. One of them he saw hurling a lighted petrol bomb through the window of a Chinese chemist's shop. She couldn't have been more than nine years old. He remembered Lafarge's explanation of the troubles and immediately felt threatened. Would their wrath towards the Chinese merchants be transferred to his Western face? Would they see him as some sort of embodiment of those faceless speculators who had caused their currency, that symbol of

their national unity and pride, to be so massively devalued? He avoided
all prolonged eye contact and tried to look as unobtrusive as possible as
he picked his way through the detritus of smashed bottles and cigarette
butts in the gutters of the crowded streets.

He rounded one corner to see a gang of about ten jeering youths,
under the direction of a man in a filthy red headscarf who must have
been eighty, excitedly bouncing a small delivery truck on its chassis. They
chanted rhythmically with each bounce of the truck as its suspension
crashed and squealed in complaint, until they finally toppled it on to its
side. The Chinese ideograms painted immaculately on the truck, above
the more usual Bahasa lettering, were then daubed with some kind of
slogan, no doubt racist or obscene, by the old man, who produced a can
of spray paint from the folds of his sarong and wrote with a vitriol that,
to Emerson, was all the more shocking coming from such an old man.
He executed each stroke of every letter with a scowl and a flourish, each
one accompanied by a cheer from the onlooking gang. Once his graffiti
work was finished, he stepped back as his wrecking crew began an assault
on the vehicle with sticks and crowbars, or just anything they could lay
their hands on, before a can of petrol was produced and poured all over
the cab. The old man again was given the honour of tossing the lighted
cigarette through the driver's window, and as the flames took hold the
crowd of onlookers scampered back into doorways and behind trees to
shield themselves from the imminent explosion. Emerson found himself
carried along in the rush and squashed into an alleyway not twenty feet
from the scene, and when the deafening bang came, along with a ball
of flame which singed his eyebrows as it rushed past the entrance to
the alley, a huge cheer went up. Emerson ducked to shield his head
from the falling debris, and was appalled to see bits of various limbs and
heads raining to the ground all around him along with the fragments of
pressed steel, glass and rubber from the truck. Had the truck been full
of petrified Chinese hiding from the mob? Had the rioters known the
truck's contents or had they hit a lucky jackpot? It was only when one of
the children picked up a severed head and tossed it lightly to the boy to
his right that Emerson realized the truth. The limbs turned out to belong

to tailors' dummies and the van had belonged to the Chinese-owned clothes shop over the road. Nonetheless they were mannequins with Chinese features, and a furious game of *ad hoc* soccer ensued, with the hated Chinese head for a ball and the crowd baying in delight at the sight of that head being kicked all over the streets.

The atmosphere on those streets was unlike anything Emerson had witnessed before. The sense of lawlessness and anarchy, the power of the mob, the high background level of restless aggression which occasionally bubbled up into flashpoints of extreme violence at the slightest provocation, was a side of Asia Emerson had not seen. The serene grinning face of the Indonesians he had grown used to seeing in the last couple of days was gone – the furnace door, which normally hides the flames of passion behind a steel facade, had been blown off its hinges. The placid, acquiescent countenance had been contorted into an ugly, mangled grimace of hatred and fury as the pent up pressure of years of jovial passivity had been given an exhaust valve. And here in this district, on that night, it was all being channelled in one direction.

Emerson did not like the mood of the mob, and did not want to become the focus of its attentions, so he shrugged himself free of the crowd of knees and elbows which jostled his every turn and headed off down the nearest side street away from the worst of the rioting. A left, a right and another left found him in a very narrow, much quieter alleyway. He had no idea where he was, but for the first time that evening he found himself quite alone and was glad of the opportunity to collect his thoughts. He sat perched on the low window ledge of what appeared to be the back entrance of a disused shop of some kind, shuttered long ago and forgotten. It was dark here, no street illumination and no bonfires or torch-bearing mobs to light his way, but it was a clear night, and as his eyes grew accustomed to the darkness, he could make out an open drain running down the middle of the cobbled walkway, and dustbins overflowing with bags and bottles further along.

He didn't know it yet, but he wasn't quite alone. Most of the rats scurried past him in the shallow drain, making for the dustbins or more likely the rich pickings provided by such large numbers of people on the crowded streets a few blocks away. One larger, bolder animal paused, however, as it drew opposite Emerson, and ambled over in his direction. It was the size of a small cat, and its fur was soaked, plastered to its body by the indeterminate effluvia of the drain from which it had just emerged. It moved cautiously but confidently, and at slow speed its awkward, rolling gait belied the agility of which it was capable should circumstances require it. Its head was pointed and aggressive-looking, and the nose flicked from side to side as it walked, scenting the air and the filthy street for any traces of potentially more attractive sources of sustenance, but the rear third of its body broadened rapidly to a disproportionately large, bulbous vessel, gorged no doubt on the plentiful supply of waste food from the endless *warung* and other small eateries which proliferated around the night markets in this part of town. Emerson hadn't seen this particular rat. In fact, he only saw it when he felt a tugging at his shoe laces and looked down to see the creature, front paws scrabbling for purchase on the tooled toe-caps of his suede brogues, nose buried in the tangle of laces, attempting to retrieve the remains of some sticky rice dish which was now crusted into the top of his shoe.

The reaction of most normal people, were they to find an unusually large, and no doubt flea-infested, disease-ridden rodent feasting on their footwear in a dark and dingy alleyway in the back streets of the Chinese ghetto in Jakarta, would be a swift reflex knee-jerk to propel the animal as far away as possible before running in the opposite direction. But James Emerson was not normal. He watched it for a few seconds with a detached fascination, staying quite still, before his left hand flashed out and grabbed the creature firmly around the neck. The rat struggled madly for a second before Emerson brought his right hand around and, avoiding the snapping incisors, twisted the head as one might wring a sopping sock. He appraised the lifeless lump in his hands for a couple of seconds before tossing it by the tail with some accuracy into one of the nearest dustbins. It had been a big one, he thought. The biggest he'd ever done, but it worked just the same. He could still do it and he was pleased about that.

'When killing rats in this fashion, one must be 'ighly careful not to twist the 'ead too far.' Emerson could still hear the voice of his supervisor at the bakery in his student days, and he had learned the hard way during his time on night duty during his university vacations. 'The anatomy of the rat is such that one risks separating 'ead from body of said rat, thus,' and the resultant mess of gushing blood vessels still nauseated him. One of his duties had been to go around servicing the rat traps twice a night and dispatching in the approved manner those that had been caught but not killed by the traps whilst foraging for breadcrumbs. He had actually developed quite an admiration for the creatures during that time, and had none of the loathing or physical revulsion aroused in the majority of people by the mere mention of the word. He recognized them as a destructive pest, and health hazard, but admired them for their endurance as a species. They were the supreme scavenger, surviving on the by-products of mankind, a crumb here, a crust there, and notoriously difficult to trap. But he had become quite an expert.

When he had become a banker he had led a similar existence, growing fat on the accumulation of miniscule slivers, an eighth here, an oh-five there, skimmed from the many, enormous transactions. It was common to compare bankers to parasites, ticks or leeches, feeding on the life-blood of the community, tapping into the arteries to siphon off a small fraction of the liquidity being pumped around the markets, but Emerson preferred the rat analogy. Leeches were somehow passive, just there, on the surface, gorging themselves in full view of everybody. Some bankers were still like that of course, fat and stupid and easy to brush off, but they were the old school, the long-lunch merchants of another era who entertained their way to multiple chins, multiple houses, and the inevitable multiple bypass operations.

The new breed of financier was much more rat-like. They were mean and artful and operated in a kind of subculture below the surface of everyday life, actively seeking out new ways to feed, new ways to lend money, new ways to intermediate. Discover a new product, start a new market nobody else has thought of, and the crumbs left on the table are much larger than usual, at least for a time. The key is to gorge as much and as quickly as possible before the rest of the pack cottons on to the new food source and the pickings become meaner. Then on to the next thing. This breed will do anything, no matter how low, to get the deal at the expense of the competition, and, like rats, are not averse to turning against each other to eliminate a rival. It is survival of the fittest, but fitness to be a banker means an optimal combination of intelligence, underhandedness and an insatiable hunger to make more.

As he sat in that alleyway in Jakarta, hearing the muffled chants and the sound of shattering glass from the rioters in the background, Emerson pondered on his past. He had been one of those rats once.

CHAPTER 3

I T WAS HIS OLD FRIEND MAX COLLINS WHO HAD SOWED THE
seed in his head about going into investment banking, the easy
money waiting to be gleaned from the mostly very average people
who peopled the corridors of Mammon's palace, and Emerson had set
about securing a job with characteristic zeal.

He researched the leading firms, pored over their latest results for proof
of financial health, and talked to everyone he could about which had the
best reputation, as this was paramount. He wanted to be the best, in the
best firm. The best firm, for its part, would give him the best support, the
most products to sell, and most likely the best money. He wrote typically
forthright and individual letters to his three short-listed employers, and
invited *them* to pitch for *his* services. He interviewed all three (although,
again, they had thought they were interviewing him) and accepted the
offer from Steinman, Schwartz.

As one of the recruits to join the sales and trading team, he went on
their initial six-month training programme in New York, which involved
lengthy and intense classroom lectures in all aspects of the business,
followed every day by 'trading room experience', which meant trailing
around for a couple of hours a day behind a trader or salesman at work on
the vast dealing-room floor, toting a telephone handset to be plugged in to
eavesdrop on their phone calls at every available opportunity. He excelled
in most aspects of the course, to the extent that many of the lecturers,
all experienced traders or salesmen in their own right, suspected him of
having experience in the business already.

When it came to the two-week crash course in macroeconomics, designed for those unlike Emerson who had not studied the subject before entering the bank, he interrupted the speaker so often to correct him, or to ask difficult questions to which he already knew the answer, that the speaker, the MIT-trained, world-renowned monetarist, chief economist for the Steinman, Schwartz Group and managing partner of the entire firm, sarcastically inquired if Mr Emerson would care to continue with the lecture as he, the managing partner, had some garbage cans to empty.

The stunned, nervous silence which ensued, with everyone in the lecture theatre expecting Emerson to be thrown out, not only of the lecture, but also the firm and most likely the entire industry, became goggle-eyed as Emerson coolly rose from his seat, walked to the front, thanked the speaker for his kind invitation and proceeded to complete the lecture without notes or hesitation. The managing partner sat and watched in a kind of bemused trance, before addressing the auditorium at the end of the lecture to announce that James Emerson would be taking the rest of the economics module, which worked out just fine as he himself actually had a firm to run. From that point on, Emerson became a name known to everybody within Steinman, Schwartz, and his success was merely a matter of finally getting him on the phone to speak to some clients.

When he returned to London and was placed in the rôle of bond salesman, James Emerson quickly became a man obsessed by the pursuit of the deal. Squeeze the client, make a quick commission and on to the next transaction. He used to stop at nothing to 'get the trade done'; he would hide juicy ideas from his colleagues, lie to his clients, extract the maximum amount from them and then turn around and do the same to his trader sitting across the desk from him. And his bosses loved him for it. He had made a fortune in a short space of time for both himself and his employers, and his persistence in sniffing out an opportunity had been legendary.

He was constantly trying to outdo himself, for in his eyes he had little competition from the rest of the sales force, and it became something of an obsession with him to improve his 'numbers', month by month, week by week, day by day. He would stay late in the office every evening, going over that day's transactions, sometimes playing back in his head phone calls that he had made without getting a trade done. He would analyse his mistakes, assess his responses to clients' objections, and make notes as to how he would respond the next time in order to close the trade.

His success became so immense that any improvement became increasingly difficult, but he pushed himself for more and more, becoming volatile and depressed if one week's figures were worse than the last. As a discipline he began to look at his figures daily, trying to improve from one day to the next, and if he was honest with himself, he began counting hour by hour. It was around this time that he had begun to go over the edge.

Not content in staying late to read research or to go over his own day's performance, he began snooping round the unoccupied desks of colleagues, looking for information, trade ideas, evidence of neglected clients that he could then steal for his own list, anything that might make tomorrow's business better than today's. He became quite proficient at picking the locks on the small filing cabinets everyone had at their trading desks, rifling through notes and client records, and he got a taste for the thrill of access to illicit information. He felt special, justified in going through his own colleagues' personal files because he felt himself superior to them. He knew that he would be able to recognize things in thier clients' data that would be invisible to the regular sales guys; ideas would occur to him that the others wouldn't even understand, and therefore he should take those clients and cover them himself.

Some of his detractors in the office used to call him a machine, others a workaholic, but he simply didn't understand the negative connotations of those words. The thick personnel file on him, accumulated over the years and buried deep in a locked cabinet in human resources, labelled him more specifically as an obsessive-compulsive, which was presumably one of the reasons he had been hired in the first place. His managers' main responsibility had been merely to ensure that this tendency was channelled in the right direction, namely selling bonds and making money for the firm, whilst at the same time remaining within the law. For with this sort of character, the desire to fulfil the compulsion is more often than not greater than any balancing sense of propriety, ethics or even legality.

In some investment banks, propriety and ethics were, within reason, a dispensable luxury, and at Steinman, Schwartz they let him roam the trading floor late at night, rifling through people's desks, stealing ideas and clients. They knew he did it – the cameras whirred night and day – and he knew they knew. He wasn't even trying to hide it from them, or even from the colleagues whose desks he broached. It was merely more convenient to do it in the evening when no one was around to stop him. He had tried doing it during the day at first, by just telling one of the salesmen who covered an underperforming account to hand over the details. To him it was logical. He was the best salesman, and he should do whatever he could to unlock the potential for making money whenever he could. After all, these were clients of the bank, not of any individual. Of course, he didn't have the managerial responsibility or authority to reallocate clients, but he knew his bosses wouldn't object – they didn't want to annoy him, after all, and risk losing him to another firm – so he just went ahead and demanded.

That first occasion had led to actual blows being thrown, but Emerson's experience as a Cambridge boxer had merely led to the physical as well as the professional humiliation of the unsuspecting individual concerned. After that episode the bank's lawyers and management had had to work even more overtime to persuade the failing salesman in question not to press assault charges. Shortly after he had signed a binding statement to that effect, even before his fractured jaw was fully operational again, he was made redundant in the bank's next round of 'business rationalization', and went quietly together with a cheque for one hundred thousand pounds.

To avoid any further confrontation of this sort, Emerson had begun doing his night rounds when everyone had gone home. By the time the unfortunate victim returned to work the next day (and Emerson was always the first there, at his desk by six thirty), the client's details would have gone from his desk, the bank's database would have been updated to reflect the change, and more often than not the client would have already been informed of the change of coverage. There was nothing anyone could do to prevent it, but it invariably led to more business.

Emerson was a phenomenon. Some clients even requested a change of salesman, begging to be permitted to be covered by him, and promising more business to justify being allowed on to his list, so the management at Steinman, Schwartz indulged his arrogance and his flirtations with the bounds of ethical acceptability. His success was so great that the amount of business he did was several multiples of the next four best salespeople put together. And they were by no means poor salespeople. In fact, they would probably have been the best performers in any one of the other five bulge-bracket firms, but they were not extraordinary. They were not James Emerson.

He did so much business that, at first, the firm's compliance department raised questions as to the legality of his business practices. How could anyone do so much, they reasoned, without something illegal going on, without clients being bribed, without kickbacks being offered, the old brown envelopes stuffed with cash changing hands? So they listened to the tapes of his phone calls, every minute of every day over a one month period, for clues, suggestions of illegal activity. This in itself was no small undertaking, for James Emerson was never off the phone during his working day. From six thirty in the morning, when he would speak to every trader in the Tokyo and Hong Kong office for an update on what had happened overnight, through the meat of the London trading day, when the only circumstances under which he would stop speaking to clients on the phone would be to ask for a dealing price from one of his traders, until seven thirty in the evening when the last of his clients had gone home, and he had finished briefing the traders in the New York head office on the orders he had secured to be worked overnight.

So, every day, there were around twelve hours of tapes to be listened to. The compliance department had to listen to them through the night to keep up, and what they heard amazed them. For there was no hint of bribery and corruption, no suggestion of connivance with his clients to do business in exchange for favours, but simply an awe-inspiring breadth and depth of knowledge, imparted in a compelling and logical way that defied disagreement. The clients simply had to do what he told them to do or they were morons. Yes, he could have been accused of hyperbole, but what effective salesman can't? And of course, his approach was slightly more intimidating than most, but this was intellectual bullying, and which rule book legislates against that? The passion and logical strength of his argumentation meant that the ticket was as good as written before he even picked up the handset, and most of his clients knew, when they heard his voice on the other end of the phone, they had better find some cash from somewhere because the chances were that they would be buying something in the next five minutes.

For James Emerson didn't have time for dormant clients, and he always told them that he would no longer cover them if they failed to produce a certain amount of business every week, which was a threat most of them did not want to see carried out. In the unlikely event that one of his clients didn't perform, and it had only happened twice, not only did he drop them from his list after two consecutive weeks of sub-standard business, but he also advised the management at Steinman, Schwartz no longer to continue considering them as clients of the bank at all, due to the potential damage to the bank's reputation for being associated with a company that was so clearly lacking in the intellectual rigour demanded in today's increasingly complex capital markets.

So Emerson had been above board, in the bank's eyes. Yes, he was an arrogant asshole, obsessed, driven to be the best in all that he did, and that included killing rats and boxing, but he had turned himself into an incredible salesman in every regard. And they had paid him for it. In his first year out of Cambridge he made a bonus of two hundred and fifty thousand pounds. This was unprecedented at a time when all new graduate recruits joined on a basic salary of twenty thousand. And he blew the record books apart again in his second year, when his total compensation for the year amounted to just under seven hundred and fifty thousand. He could probably have doubled that in the third year with offers from competitor firms to lure him away, but he stuck to Steinman's. They were the best firm, after all, and he didn't want to sully his hands, or his reputation, by working for any lesser institution. Despite appearances, money itself, in fact, was not his real motivation. What got him out of bed in the morning was the desire to be better than everyone else in all that he did. So he turned down the massive offers from the other bulge-bracket firms, which he viewed as bucket-shops in comparison to Steinman's, and that year he made just over a million, a figure below which he never dropped in each of the subsequent eight years.

But that was all behind him now. He *had* been the best for a while, but he had been getting restless. He had turned into an obsessive without a cause, searching for a new focus, a new target for the energy that never let him rest. And then Hugh had died, and it had become immediately clear to him what he must do. And the end result of that decision found him sitting in an alleyway on the opposite side of the world, working for Jake Samuels, killing rats.

Emerson walked down the alleyway in which he had been sitting and set off back towards the source of the chaos and violence he had witnessed earlier. It was now well past midnight, but the background level of noise in the near distance showed no signs of abating. As he neared the end of the alley, the sound of scuffling footsteps around the corner, and urgent but subdued voices heading in his direction caused him to stop in his tracks and press his tall frame back into a darkened doorway. The noises he heard were of furtive activity, somebody up to dark deeds, and he had no desire to be part of it. The footsteps got louder, and he could clearly make out the sound of something being dragged and two if not three different voices. There was a sudden, very short muffled scream followed by a sharp slap and a guttural laugh. Whoever it was had now turned into the alleyway and Emerson risked a quick look around the corner of the doorway in which he was hiding. He was enraged at what he saw.

There were two men, young Indonesians no more than twenty years old, both with small Indonesian flags tied bandana-style around their heads. Between them they were dragging a Chinese girl, an arm apiece, into the shadows of the alley. She was barefoot and struggling wildly, legs kicking and back arching, but the more she protested the more the men seemed to enjoy their sport, and any form of scream was met with a swift slap to the cheek.

They stopped short of Emerson's doorway and set about their task, hoisting her effortlessly on to one of the overflowing rubbish bins so that she was perched on top of a mound of stinking, sodden cardboard and discarded, catering-sized cans of cooking oil. A cluster of rats that had been foraging behind the bins scuttled off into the open drain. By now the girl was more subdued, and sobbing, as her immediate fate became more apparent. The larger of the two men went behind her and pulled her backwards, pinning both arms behind her as he did so, whilst the other man came around the front and grasped both her ankles, so that she was now stretched over the bin and completely helpless. As he parted her legs in readiness for the violation, he realized he had neglected to prepare himself in the necessary way, and wedging himself between her thighs, briefly let go of one of her legs to begin fumbling with his own trousers. The girl sensed her opportunity and with one final effort, she drew the freed leg back up to her chest and smashed the heel of her bare foot against the nose of her distracted assailant. Emerson heard a sound very familiar to him from the boxing ring, one of shattered bone and pulped cartilage, as the man screamed and wheeled away in agony, stumbling over his jeans which now hung loosely around his ankles. This was Emerson's chance to intervene, and he took it. He leaped out of the shadows and screamed with the full force of his lungs, a wild, primeval scream, as he lunged towards the other man who still held the girl pinned over the dustbin. It was four swift paces away from his hiding place, but his target was transfixed by the sight of a tall, howling white man in a suit and tie emerging from the night, and was unable to move out of the way in time. The girl felt the wind on her right ear as Emerson's fist whistled by her head and broke the jaw of the man who held her. He immediately let go of her arms, and as he did her rear end sank further into the mound of rubbish in the bin, and she sat screaming with great rhythmic lungfuls of air, arms and legs flailing helplessly. The man Emerson had punched picked himself up out of the slimy scum into which he had fallen and ran blindly out of the alley. The other man still lay on his back, stunned and whimpering in the open drain, clutching his smashed nose. His trousers were still tangled around his ankles and his exposed genitals bobbed in the fetid water which lapped at his scrawny frame.

Emerson hauled the shaking girl out of the bin and carried her fireman-style over his shoulder back to the nearest main road. Her bare legs, coated in a slimy mixture of cooking oil and rice, hung down over his chest and he could feel her tiny hands gripping tightly to the back of his linen jacket. As he walked back amongst the crowds of angry rioters and looters in Glodok's main square, he no longer felt afraid. His brush with violence in the alleyway and his sense of responsibility for the girl over his shoulder kept his adrenalin levels high, and he now viewed the local troublemakers with contempt. He noticed that, in his absence, the army had moved on to the streets and was beating the mob back with batons and tear gas. The occasional loose round from a trigger-happy, nervous rookie whined through the night air, and he once had to leap aside to avoid falling debris from an upper storey as the fire service began to make safe some of the looted and burned-out buildings. He spotted a taxi stopping to let out a three-man film crew from CBS television, and he risked both their necks dashing across four lanes of traffic to catch it before it left for the relative safety of downtown.

He dumped her fairly unceremoniously into the back seat and pressed a twenty-dollar bill into the driver's palm to silence any complaints at the mess or the smell. He then got in himself and the taxi raced back to his hotel as best it could, dodging police blockades and columns of protesters. The girl spent the journey cowering in the far corner of the backseat, peering at him over the knees she hugged tightly to her chest, and saying nothing. The sobbing and screaming had stopped, and the shaking had subsided, and Emerson maintained a constant soothing monologue for the entire journey, as he bandaged his bruised and cut knuckles with his handkerchief and made a mental note to get a tetanus jab as soon as he possibly could.

There were plenty of raised eyebrows as the unlikely couple walked across the polished marble lobby of the Borobodur Intercontinental. She barefoot and filthy, leaving a slug's trail of grease from the revolving doors to the lift bank, he coated in a thin film of oily slime and shedding rice from his trouser turn-ups as he walked. They were left the lift to themselves to travel up to Emerson's sixth floor room, and it was only when they were safely inside and the door chained behind them that she spoke her first words to him.

'Thank you, *Bapak*. It normally two hundred for full massage and five hundred on top for blow job, but for you, on the house, yes?'

CHAPTER 4

CAMERON DODDS FLEW INTO GRAND CAYMAN IN THE EARLY EVE-
ning. He had to come. He needed to see Annie. He craved her.
She was not expecting him, but he liked to surprise. He knew
he should not really be leaving his post in London. Pegasus needed him
there to continue trading, to continue driving down the prices of the
vulnerable assets until they were ready for their next landmark victim.
But it was almost New Year. He could afford to miss a day, surely? And
for all his efforts he felt he deserved a long weekend in the sun. What
was the point of making all that money and working so hard if he could
not allow himself the occasional indulgence? He had not brought any
drugs with him. He did not want to risk getting caught at customs, and
he really wanted to show Annie he could do without, could be clean if
he wanted to be, for afterwards. He checked the address in his organizer
and directed the taxi to her beachfront apartment.

'Special delivery!' he yelled into the intercom at the door, and his pulse
quickened as he heard her muffled voice on the tinny loud speaker.

'Just a minute, just a minute. I'll be right down.'

Her saw her first through the glass doors to the building, walking down
the stairs into the lobby area. She was dressed in a bathrobe and her hair
looked as if she had just got out of bed. Of course! How stupid of him! She
worked the night shift and slept during the day. She'd be off to the office
quite soon. Still, when she saw him surely she could wangle a day off.

He kept his head bowed as she opened the door, and the peak of his
pink baseball cap shielded his face. The parcel he had brought with him
was held aloft, together with a clipboard for her to sign for delivery. She

took it from him, bleary-eyed, and scrawled a signature in the box he had indicated.

'Thanks.' She turned almost immediately back into the lobby and let the door begin to close in his face. He stopped it with his foot.

'Any chance of a cold drink, ma'am?' he mumbled, disguising his English accent. 'Thirsty work in this goddam heat all day.'

'Sorry. Have to go to work. Try the bar on the corner.'

'Gee, then I guess a blow job's out of the question?'

She wheeled round in sudden fury to find a grinning Cameron Dodds, minus the hat, leaning against the door frame.'

'Cam, you crazy son of a bitch! You scared the shit out of me! What are you doing here?'

'I refer the honourable lady to the question I asked a few moments ago.'

'Come in, you maniac, come in. What on earth am I going to do with you!'

'Well, I refer . . .'

'Yes, yes. Come in. Jesus! I have to rush to the office. You can come with me if you like. Meet Saul.'

'Can't you . . . ?'

'No. Absolutely not. I have to go in. There's some stuff I need to do today if we're to stay on track. With Braxton I mean. Danny Brookes is sending some figures over tomorrow and I need to be prepared. And Scott Turner has just left for Ireland.'

Dodds walked into the lobby and followed her upstairs, lifting the hem of her bathrobe as he did.

'Cut it out! Not now, Cameron. Later maybe, but not right now.' They entered her apartment and he sat on a sofa whilst she dressed in the bedroom.

'Well, we knew Turner would be going, didn't we?' he shouted through the slatted doors.

'You and I did. But Bradley doesn't. Not yet, anyway. And nor did Scott until a few hours ago. We have to let Bradley find out from Scott himself. We can't let either of them suspect anything.'

'But can't it wait until after the New Year?'

'Cameron! Please! You above all people know what we can do to these fuckin' markets on New Year's Eve. That's when we go for it, and you need to be back in London by then.'

'But that's the day after tomorrow! I only just got here. I'd have to leave tomorrow afternoon.'

'Which leaves us just about time for something along the lines of your earlier remark. But later Cameron. Now come on.' She emerged from the bedroom in a loose linen dress and, apparently, very little else. She had scraped her hair together into a prim ponytail, and she clutched a bunch of car keys in one hand. 'You coming or not?'

They spent the next half hour on the way to Colliers Landings catching up with events in the markets and their lives.

'I've been clean for three days now Annie. See? Told you I could when I wanted.'

'Let me know when it's been three months and I'll be a little more impressed,' she retorted impatiently, irked by the subject, as the car drew to a halt outside the old mansion that housed Xenfin. The sun was just disappearing below the headland to the west, and the last strains of low, scarlet sunshine picked out the outline of her figure beneath the translucent linen dress.

Seated at her desk in the dealing room, they started to go over the trading reports of the previous day, and checking the market activity from the New York closing levels. Back in that environment, Dodds assumed his professional persona.

'T-Bonds are down across the board,' he pointed out to her, 'but the curve has steepened big time. Everyone's piling into the short end.'

'You're right, Cam. Credit jitters. And look – Asian sovereign spreads are out another fifty beeps. Even Hong Kong.'

'Well the currency peg is under pressure again. They have to let it go soon. It'd help us a lot if they did.'

'But we can't count on that. We should concentrate on Indonesia some more, that's easy pickings, then crank up the pressure on Korea.'

'Jenner & Phipps have them on watch for a downgrade already. The market's spooked so that shouldn't take much pushing either. We've seen a lot of people trying to buy protection at Steinman's in London. Default swaps, credit-linked notes, you name it.'

'And while you're at it, do some of those for us, will you? We'd love to sell some protection on the quiet if I can get it away without Saul seeing. He wouldn't understand it anyway and it'd prime us nicely for the big bang later. SAUL!'

'Hi Annie. Who's your guest?'

'Saul, I'd like you to meet Cameron Dodds. Head of EMG derivatives at Steinman, Schwartz in London.'

Krantz looked Dodds up and down, taking in the day-old growth, tie-dye T-shirt and ripped jeans. He had clearly thought Dodds had come to change the water bottle on the dispenser or clean the pool or something. 'Happy to meet you, Cameron. Can I get you something or is . . . ?'

'Oh, Annie's taking care of me just great, Saul, thanks. We're just talking about credit derivatives.'

'Well that stuff is beyond me, guys. But I'm sure Annie knows what she's doing. That's why I hired her, after all! Means I can sleep a little easier in my bed.' They all laughed. Everyone in the markets knew that Saul Krantz hardly slept at all. Out of choice.

Krantz wandered off on a tour of the floor, leaving Dodds and van Aalst to themselves.

'He seems quite a guy.'

'He is. An amazing employer. Makes me sort of feel bad, you know, what's going to happen.'

'What's his background?'

'Look, Cameron. I'd love to sit here chatting with you all day, but I need to get on. Read this. That's pretty much all there is on him. We'll order up some dinner in a couple hours.' She thrust a photocopied article at him, one from a pile on the desk beside her which they were used to dishing out to visitors, and Dodds settled down in the chair next to Annie to read. The trading floor was strangely quiet at the beginning of the night shift, and the dimmed lights and the hum of the screens soon had him engrossed in the article. It was from *Business Week*, and about a year old.

WHO IS SAUL KRANTZ?
By Mary Bloomfield

Everyone knows Saul Krantz, or at least of him. His name is heard in the same breath as George Soros, Julian Robertson and Paul Tudor Jones, but his company, Xenfin Asset Management, is among the most secretive on Wall Street, or should I say, in the Caribbean. But what do we know of the man behind the legend?

Some people claim him to be of Polish extraction, others say he is Russian. What is known is that he first came to the US in 1971 at the age of twenty-six. He arrived on a tourist visa for six months, but was married within three, and applying for a green card shortly after that. He had, as you can imagine, been heavily investigated by immigration, but they had not been able to find anything wrong.

This reporter has seen his file at the Naturalization and Immigration Office in Washington, and I can confirm that Krantz began his career in Europe for an Austrian commodity-trading outfit, which took him most places in the world, but especially the Middle East. The contacts and the reasonable, but in no way startling, means he had assembled during this period, together with the information culled from various interviews with the apparently happy couple, left the US authorities in little doubt that he was a) not a communist, b) unlikely to be a drain on the national purse, and c) totally in love with his new bride. If it had been a marriage of convenience, then they had made a pretty good job of concealing it.

Divorced a year later, and thus the subject of a new Immigration Department investigation who were worried they might have been over hasty in welcoming Mr Krantz into the eagle's nest, he started his first company. Krantz Ventures Inc. was a venture capital firm, dedicated to pumping money into start-up companies in the US which he felt deserved a helping hand. The money was Arab, gleaned from contacts formed in his earlier days, and it was enough to get the authorities off his back.

Within five years he was a naturalized US citizen, an achievement he celebrated by winding up Krantz Ventures with tremendous profits for the original investors, and, to the enormous chagrin of the IRS, moving his operation offshore to the Caymans, the location of his current operations.

Now he could come and go in the US as he pleased, and he set about immersing himself in the hazy, ill-defined world of offshore fund management. The seventies was a time of innovation and great progress in the arcane world of portfolio management theory, and a go-ahead Krantz leapt at the emerging work of Markowitz and Sharpe with great enthusiasm. Always on the cutting edge of new thinking and quantitative techniques, his new company did exceptionally well in a short space of time, such that, by 1981 he was able to purchase the freehold on twenty-five acres of East Island property to include an abandoned, rundown mansion called Colliers Landings. He set about restoring the mansion to its former magnificence, and beyond, and in 1983 incorporated the Xenfin Limited Partnership as a Cayman company with seed capital from his original Saudi investors.

Dodds interrupted his reading to check on Annie. She was curled up in her chair, painted toenails twiddling nervously as she scanned her trading screens. He watched her tap some numbers into a calculator and pick up the phone. 'John. It's Annie. I want to sell some more won. What sort of size is doable at the moment? Then do that, at market, and work the balance of five hundred down fifty ticks from there. Thanks.'

Dodds smiled. It was good to see her in action first hand. He normally only heard her on the phone. She was good. Calm, in control. He returned to the article.

The returns Krantz generated for his funds, largely by means of technology and leverage, were way beyond what was being achieved in the conventional asset management industry. Money attracted more money in its own magnetic way, and in 1986 he celebrated having his first billion under management with an extravagant party aboard a rented yacht in West Bay, in full view of the opulent hotels and residences of Seven Mile Beach.

He was an extremely hard worker, but he also liked to play hard. His client entertaining became known for its extravagance, and for his rather eccentric sense of humour. Invitations to his parties were much in demand, and he would litter the venue with outrageous practical jokes which would leave his unsuspecting guests with singed eyebrows or ruined clothes, and they loved it. The society pages of the local press reported on his exploding bowls of whipped cream and collapsing chairs with glee, and they dubbed him 'The Cayman Clown'. And despite the serious nature of his business and its conservative image, not to mention the enormous amounts of money involved, he revelled in the frivolous nickname. But he could afford to.

By that time his business was beginning to achieve mainstream status, and the trend towards increasing sophistication and specialization in the financial markets necessitated the hiring of more staff to help him manage the mushrooming amounts which were being wired into his care from all over the world.

He looked to the bulge-bracket investment banks of Wall Street, Goldman, Salomon, Morgan Stanley, at this time in a boom phase of their own, and paid unheard of sums to cherry-pick the leading traders and analysts away from their hassled seats in downtown Manhattan, London and Tokyo. They came gleefully to his island hideaway with its gourmet food, laid-back life style, and unparalleled reputation. He made the approaches personally – he had little time for headhunters – and a 'call from Saul' became a byword in the industry for a passport to the better life. But he only hired the very best.

'Say, Annie. Says here he only hires the very best. How did you get in?' She ignored him and continued watching her screens, but the talk of Krantz's background and the mention of her joining Xenfin meant she could not help but think back to that time.

*   *   *

Annie van Aalst had got her 'call from Saul' one wet Friday morning in London in November 1996, at around eight a.m. as she sat, bored, at her desk in Salomon's cavernous trading room near Victoria Station.

'Annie, this is Saul Krantz. I think you probably know what this is about. I know it's real difficult to talk right now, but I would like to meet with you as soon as possible. If you would like to meet with me, make an excuse to your boss right now to leave the office for the day, walk downstairs and take the train from Victoria to Gatwick. My plane is fuelled and waiting for you in the South Terminal. Just ask for the Private Enclosure. It is three a.m. in Grand Cayman right now. I figure we could have a late lunch together. Do we have a date?'

She just about managed a strangled, 'Sure,' before leaving her desk to go to the bathroom to think. When she returned, mumbled embarrassment about 'female problems' was enough for her flustered boss, and she left the Salomon dealing room for the last time. The weekend she spent in Colliers Landings seemed like a blur to her now. The intensity of his questions stretched the limits of her knowledge, and she talked more about her background and motivation than she had ever done to anyone ever before, including her parents. By the time she returned in the Xenfin jet on Monday morning, not only was she totally committed to Krantz, it was inconceivable she could work for anyone else. She felt unable to face returning to Salomon's office, and she phoned to arrange a lunch meeting with her boss at La Finezza, a favourite Italian haunt around the corner on Sloane Street.

He had been first to arrive at the restaurant and was sitting nervously eating breadsticks when she arrived. 'Look Annie, I don't really know what all this is about, but let me tell you a little about the plans we have for Annie van Aalst at Salomon Brothers this year. First, let's get comp out of the way. You have had a great year and we intend to recognize that. I have in my pocket an envelope with a letter signed by Max himself which guarantees your bonus this year will be a *minimum* of . . .'

She quietly held up a hand to stop him in his tracks. She did not want to humiliate him, nor did she want him to feel he had failed. She did not even want to hear the numbers. 'Chris, I'm going to work for Saul Krantz.' Those were the last words they spoke on the subject. He knew there was nothing he could possibly say to dissuade her, and they spent the rest of the lunch chatting about old times and exchanging war stories about the markets in the way that traders do. As they parted on the pavement outside the restaurant, she handed over her security pass and company AmEx, and gave him a brief peck on the cheek. She had never worked in London since.

'Annie? Annie?' Krantz was back at her desk. She snapped instantly out of her reminiscences to see the great man standing over her. 'Your guest, Annie. He's fallen asleep. Don't you think you should look after him a little better? Look, it's a quiet session. Why don't the two of you head off for dinner. Out of the office I mean?'

And Annie woke Dodds, and they left Xenfin's offices immediately. But they did not bother with dinner. They returned straight to Annie's apartment, where they spent a fun hour or two reacquainting themselves before the jet-lag caught up with Dodds's drug-starved body and he fell exhausted across her bed. The next morning he awoke to find his things packed and a taxi waiting to take him to the airport and the London flight.

'You have to go, Cam. New Year's Eve will be too important to miss. I need you there. Thanks for coming though.' She kissed his nose. 'I had a great time. We'll be together soon, I promise. Put some thought into where you'd like to be based, OK?'

And Dodds left in the steamy sunshine of the Cayman morning to return to the stormy streets of the City of London.

CHAPTER 5

THE HELICOPTERS AND LIMOUSINES HAD STOPPED ARRIVING at the lakeside castle, now an opulent hotel on the west coast of Ireland, about an hour earlier. Their passengers, senior government officials from most of the G-10 nations, and a few more besides, were all safely ensconced in their rooms, preparing their notes for the extraordinary summit meeting that had been called only twenty-four hours earlier by the Americans. Holidays had been cut short, airforce transporters commandeered for the flights to Shannon from the European and North American capitals, as well as Moscow, Beijing and Tel Aviv, and a security cordon thrown around the small village of Cong the like of which had never been seen before.

The locals had no idea what was going on, and the hotel had been hermetically sealed from the outside world. Staff working there had been asked to stay overnight for the three days of the summit, and all incoming calls were routed to a message machine which politely informed any callers that the hotel was closed for minor refurbishments. All outgoing calls were barred, except for the visiting dignitaries and their entourage who mostly used their own secure cell phones, and the hotel management had been sworn to secrecy in the nicest but firmest possible way. The gates to the hotel's considerable grounds were chained shut, and a variety of security guards from the various governments involved, muttering messages into headsets in ten different languages, patrolled the estate in regular sweeping formations. On the lake, Lough Corrib, which guarded the approach to the hotel on two sides, a handful of black, semi-rigid inflatables with powerful outboard motors buzzed up and down the shoreline, scanning the choppy waters through the persistent drizzle and murky gloom for any signs of unauthorized entry. In short, for the duration of this highly secret meeting, no one was to be allowed in or out and there was to be no communication with the outside world.

To satisfy the curious, and to provide a false trail for later dissemination after the guests had left, word was put around amongst the hotel staff that this was a top secret security summit to build a new international framework for peace in Northern Ireland. Following the problems of the Good Friday Agreement earlier that year, and much talk in the press of a covert re-arming amongst the more radical Republican splinter groups, this was largely accepted by the army of waiters and chamber maids forced to leave their homes and families whilst the meeting was in progress.

But the truth of the matter was rather different. The government officials present on the west coast of Ireland on that grim, late December weekend were indeed there to discuss an escalating crisis, but it was nothing to do with the Real IRA or Loyalist factions. And the security guards were not there to prevent attacks by terrorists. Because the crisis being discussed was a crisis of a different sort, a crisis of confidence in the global financial system, and the mere fact that it was being discussed at the highest level, should it be leaked to the world by the press, could cause the situation to worsen to the point of no return. In this case, terrorist attack meant an assault by the press.

Very few of the VIPs present at the talks were well known to the public at large, at least physically. They were the finance ministers and central bank governors of all the nations represented, most of whom could have walked down the high street in Cong village in complete anonymity. To avoid the risks of the more familiar Irish or British representatives being spotted on their way in, they had been helicoptered directly into the hotel grounds, out of sight of the gates. The others had all arrived at Shannon Airport and been ferried by darkened limousine courtesy of the Irish government with outriders from the Garda – all, that is, except the American contingent.

Like the delegates from Beijing and Moscow, they had arrived in a military transport aircraft, but theirs was a Lockheed C-5 Galaxy. It is not every day that an extraordinary aircraft such as this arrives at Shannon airport, and when the nose cone opened, and the 'kneeling' motors in the landing gear lowered the plane's belly to a mere three feet from the Irish soil, ramps were rolled out to allow a presidential-style motorcade of six, black Chevy Suburbans to race out of the aircraft, headlights blazing in the middle of the afternoon, and head at top speed over the tarmac to the airfield's nearest perimeter gates. No customs or immigration formalities for these visitors.

It was a sign of the seriousness that the Americans had assigned to this meeting that they had sent their own transport, each car carrying seven passengers, including personnel from the security services, central bank staff and government officials, for a total delegation of forty-two. Bringing up the rear, and at a more sedate pace was a two and a half ton M35 truck in State Department dark-blue livery, which carried the heavier equipment they had brought with them. The main bulky items were the large, eight-man inflatables to be shared by all the security forces when patrolling the lake, and a certain amount of weaponry and ammunition. Given the importance of secure communications to the entire exercise, and the vital embargo on unauthorized signals getting out, there was also a large amount of electronic equipment, most of which was dedicated to jamming the broadcast frequencies of any unauthorized cell phones within the compound, and, should the need arise, disabling any electronic eavesdropping equipment should somebody choose to point it in their direction.

Unbeknown to the other countries represented, there was also a small shedful of computer equipment sent with an owlish operator from the National Security Agency headquarters at Fort Meade, Maryland. His day job was actually Chief Liaison Officer for the Echelon eavesdropping project, the main go-between for the enormous NSA listening station based at Menwith Hill in Yorkshire and the head office in Maryland. But for this trip, rather than eavesdropping on personal e-mails between private individuals in Hamburg or the like, his responsibility was to listen in to whatever messages the representatives from the other countries at the summit were sending back to their own governments, decrypting them wherever necessary, and reporting directly to the Treasury Secretary. He was to listen to everything, and everything was to be passed on. No message, however trivial it might have seemed to the NSA agent, was to be overlooked, and anything that required translation was to be transmitted first by secure e-mail to a team of waiting linguists in Fort Meade, who would then send back the English version by return.

The Chairman of the Federal Reserve Bank, the most influential banker in the world, rode in the second car in the motorcade, along with the US Treasury Secretary. Between them, these men controlled the behaviour of the world's largest economy, and the knock-on effects of their policies, actions, even their best intentions were felt throughout the world. And by far the most influential of the two was the Fed Chairman. For it was his responsibility to set the level of interest rates in the United States, the rates at which the unimaginably large amounts of money in the American economy were lent and borrowed, and to supervise the banking system. His decisions and even his whims or moods would have a direct effect on the level of the US dollar, the bond markets and the stock markets, and by extension, on all of those things in the markets of their major trading partners and beyond. But he was new to the job.

Byron Powell had taken over five short weeks previously from Alan Greenspan, probably the most successful and highly thought of central banker in history, and had found himself mired in a financial crisis that threatened the very economic stability it was his job to protect. And on top of that he did not get on particularly well with Treasury Secretary Dick Brightwell. This was his first trip with the politician, and in the course of an eight-hour flight from Washington it had become startlingly clear that they agreed to differ on everything – the likelihood of the New York Giants beating the Washington Redskins in the imminent Super Bowl, the verisimilitude of the ending to the latest Scott Turow blockbuster, and the most important aspects regarding the setting of monetary policy. But worse than that, Brightwell smoked, and had been desperate, after an eight-hour smoke-free flight, to light up a huge Macanudo as soon as they had got into the car.

'Jesus, Dick, can't you wait till we get to the hotel?'

'Screw that. Privilege of office. If you don't like it, ride with the spooks in the next car or open a window.'

As the high-speed motorcade reached the perimeter gates to the airfield they slowed down to be waved through. The airport security guard on duty was Fergal O'Shaughnessy, and he knew nothing of the identity of the VIPs he was ushering into Ireland that day. He had just heard that there was some bigwig conference happening at the fancy hotel in Cong, and that was more than he needed to know.

But of all the people in and around Shannon Airport that day, Fergal O'Shaughnessy was probably the only one who would have recognized the face of Byron Powell, newly installed Chairman of the US Federal Reserve Board, as he lowered the deeply tinted window of his official transport and hung his head out of the window to escape the impossibly dense fog of smoke with which his colleague Dick Brightwell had managed to infest the car in the half mile from the aircraft to the gate. Powell's head passed within two feet of O'Shaughnessy's as he stood at his security station and saluted the cars as they passed him. Why he saluted he could not have explained. He had no military background, and he had no idea who was in the cars, but it seemed like the thing to do. Probably something to do with the headlights being on. But Powell, new to the business of being in the public eye, and enjoying every minute of it, caught his eye and smiled at him as he went by, and O'Shaughnessy smiled back. Powell's was the only face he saw, as the other cars in the motorcade zipped through the gate with blackened windows firmly in place as they had been instructed, and it took O'Shaughnessy a few minutes to place the grinning banker. But he knew him, or at least of him, for sure.

For Fergal O'Shaughnessy was one of a new breed of Irishman. He would still go down to his local most nights and sink six pints of Guinness, but instead of the talk being of horses and racing and women and the Troubles (in that order) as it had been for so long, these days the old regulars were more interested in talking about the property boom and the soaring values of their share portfolios. Because Ireland had been a major beneficiary of European monetary union, forced as it was into having an interest rate that was probably three whole percentage points below what it ought to have been, for the sake of European harmonization. And those low rates caused businesses to boom, property prices to rocket and share prices to jump off the charts. There was a new prosperity, and on the back of an inheritance sixty-one-year-old Fergal O'Shaughnessy had become a student of the markets.

Upon his father's death two years before, he had sold the Waterford farmhouse he had inherited, and in which he had been brought up, for seventy-eight thousand punts, and put the lot in the bank. At three per cent. But he had soon realized he could do much better, and he had become an avid reader of the financial pages. Within a few weeks he had taken the plunge and bought his first stock, a blue chip Irish name which, a week after that was the subject of a hostile takeover bid by a German conglomerate. The price had rapidly doubled and Fergal had sold just as quickly. But he was hooked. Thereafter he had built up a diversified and international stock portfolio, across a broad range of markets and industries, until his holdings, on that day in December almost two years to the day since he was granted probate on his father's estate, stood at a market value of two hundred and seven thousand Irish punts.

In euros it was more, but he did not care for the euro, nor for its proponents. And he had been very glad to read in his *Wall Street Journal*, or *The Journal* as he had taken to calling it, ever since he put in his subscription order to his very surprised neighbour and newsagent in Hurles Cross, County Clare, that the new Chairman of the Fed was a confirmed eurosceptic himself. And it was in *The Journal* that O'Shaughnessy had seen a picture of Byron Powell for the first time, not a photograph but one of those funny pen-and-ink type sketches they always use in that paper, upon his appointment to the post a month or so ago. And he was adamant, he would have staked his entire portfolio on it in fact, that the face he had seen hanging out of the car window was the same man. What on earth was he doing here, he thought, the day before New Year's Eve, on official business? And who was in all the other cars? And that army truck? It must be something big, he thought, and then he thought back to the other comings and goings he had seen that day. One after another the official planes had arrived, the limousines had been waiting, and the occupants had been whisked away. He'd thought nothing of it until he'd recognized Byron Powell's face, thought they were low-level politicos or businessmen for some conference or other. Then the Chinese plane had arrived, and the Russian. Both of those aircraft had been parked in separate, remote corners of the airfield, illuminated by portable floodlights and generators for security and each with a handful of armed guards to warn off any prying eyes. What in God's name was going on? If Powell was here it must have a financial angle. And if the Russians and the Chinese were involved it must be big, must be *global*.

He enjoyed using the buzzwords of his new-found hobby, amazing his drinking mates with talk of bulls and bears, long bonds and emerging markets. Only, those damned emerging markets had cost him thirty thousand in the last week since all that stuff had started going wrong in Asia, and he was a bit worried that all the palaver in Shannon Airport that day had something to do with it. Why else would the Chinese be involved? And hadn't they had an unscheduled stop earlier that morning from a Japan Airlines Jumbo? They'd said it was a precautionary check on a faulty air-intake, but they could easily have dropped someone off. Maybe Konushi from the BoJ was here, or even Hyatama? (He always referred to the world's financial luminaries, Soros, Kaufman, Krantz *et al* by their surnames these days, as amongst academics and peers.) One thing was for sure: he did not like the sound of it, and he had not trebled his money in two years by being indecisive. So, after the motorcade had passed and he had safely closed the gates in the perimeter fence, he retreated from that windy, exposed section of the airport's most remote access point, to the warm shelter of his security cabin, put on the kettle to brew some tea, and used the phone to make two calls.

First he spoke to his second cousin, who was features editor on the *Limerick Leader*, and told him about County Clare's eminent visitors that day. Byron Powell's was the only face he had seen for sure, but his keen sense of drama provided a few other 'certain' sightings for the benefit of a good story. Callum O'Connor took the call himself, and promised he would see into it. First thing to do was to get up to Cong itself and try to get some snaps. O'Connor set off straight away on the two-hour drive, eager for a chance to scoop the nationals and the English dailies.

Then O'Shaughnessy called his broker in Limerick and instructed him to sell all his holdings. At market. Straight away. For cash. And so it was that Fergal O'Shaughnessy, security guard at Shannon Airport, became the first portfolio manager in the world during the current crisis to liquidate his entire inventory of stocks. He would not be the last, or the largest, by a long way.

From his twin room with en-suite facilities and teamaker at Ashford Castle in Cong, Scott Turner placed one call of his own. For he too had been on the Galaxy flight with Byron Powell, Dick Brightwell and the other thirty-nine representatives of Uncle Sam's finest. But unlike the Chairman of the Fed, his goals at that stage of his career were not to promote economic stability. In fact they were quite the opposite.

It was beyond Wallace Bradley's wildest dreams to have a Pegasus member within the United States Federal Reserve Bank as one of the key officials on bank supervision and capital adequacy, at a time when the world's banking system was on the verge of a complete loss of confidence. Turner's promotion to this rôle was extremely timely. As far as the goals and aims of the Pegasus Forum were concerned, that is. It was tantamount to having Louis Farrakhan in on the Arab-Israeli peace negotiations, as chief adviser to the Knesset.

'Professor, it's Scott Turner. I would have liked to call earlier but there was simply no opportunity.'

'It is most unlike you to call at all, Scott. I assume it concerns a matter of some importance.'

'I must keep this brief, as there is a chance this call will be intercepted. We only just arrived, though, so I think the spooks probably haven't set up the equipment yet.'

'Where are you? And who is we?'

'I'm in a hotel on the west coast of Ireland. Ashford Castle in Cong,

County Mayo. Make a note of that. "We" is Byron Powell and Dick Brightwell, amongst others. Powell called an emergency summit and we all had to drop everything and get to Washington for the flight. Six hours' notice.'

'Summit? What kind of summit?'

'The crisis kind. And the top secret kind. Nobody knows we're here. Oh, and there's a few other folks at the party you might've heard of too. Try Hyatama. And Bertheau from Canada. Donnelly of course, he's the host, and his rich cousin Peter from Westminster. All the usual suspects – central bankers and politicos.'

'G-7?'

'G-10. Plus a few interesting extras. Chao is here. And I mean Chao senior. And Gorodkin too. Moscow sent their best man.'

'Has something specific happened to prompt this? Or is it pro-phylactic?'

'I'm hearing that some German banks and more than one major British bank are close to the edge. There's going to be some tough talking, and some tough decision-making. I think Powell wants to agree a united stance on government intervention. Either we let the banks go under, or we try to bail out the whole system. But it has to be consistent. As he sees it, there's no point in the Brits letting some banks go in the name of the free market if the French are going to print some more money and nationalize at the first signs of trouble in their own backyard.'

'And where does he stand, Powell?'

'Oh, he's a confirmed *laissez-faire* diehard. Survival of the fittest, level playing-fields, all that macho jock bullshit. He was very vocal in criticizing the government during the Savings and Loan crisis in the eighties. Couldn't believe they caved in and threw 'em a lifeline. Whatever happened to the American ideal? He's a firm believer in the American dream, the possibility of rags to riches on the back of a lot of hard work. But he also believes that, if the dream is to be possible, then the nightmare has to be possible too, otherwise the dream is tarnished. The carriage has to be able to turn back into a pumpkin.'

'And nobody knows about this meeting?'

'Correct. That is why I am calling. They're about to impose a communications embargo on the hotel. They're worried someone'll find out they're worried. You should see the security here. It's like the Pope, the President and the Queen went for a stroll on the beach. We can still use our official cell phones, but you can bet your ass they'll be listening just as soon as they plug in their scanners, so I won't be able to call you again. You know, Professor, in terms of Pegasus I'm thinking this would be an excellent time to break the news to the world that the people in charge of all our finances are as scared as hell. Let the press know who's here and why. And then we'll see the markets in some serious shit.'

'I will take care of that, Scott. Excellent work, and I'll let Annie and Cameron know what is about to hit the world's newswires too. They can certainly make matters much worse.'

Scott Turner stood at the window of his room in the thirteenth-century tower and stared out over Lough Corrib. It was three in the afternoon, yet the light had almost gone from the sky, leaving the lush green lawns, normally Ireland's finest shade of emerald, swathed in a uniform, muted dullness. A vaporous but persistent drizzle filled the atmosphere and smudged the contours of the grey-stone castle walls, blending them into the seamless matt backdrop of lake and sky. The mullioned window was slightly ajar, and he could just about hear the powerful, high-pitched motors of the patrol boats carrying across the water in the distance as they started to criss-cross the lake in search of intruders. There was an occasional flash of light as their searchlights turned momentarily in his direction before circling round to head back out towards the far shore. Other than that there was complete silence.

In the rooms below him in the castle he imagined the world's finance ministers and most senior bankers going over their notes and briefings in readiness for the imminent talks, planning their stance, receiving constant updates on the markets and the losses being racked up by the mighty financial institutions in their charge. But Turner had done all his own work, and was ready. He knew the seriousness of the situation in the United States better than anybody, as he was himself one of the most senior officials in bank supervision within the Fed, and had been quietly concealing the truth from the Chairman for several weeks. The asset base of the US banks had been eroding steadily for some time, and their exposure to the Asia-Pacific region had never been higher.

In plain terms, America had lent more money to the likes of Indonesia and Korea than they had ever lent to any other region. Even during the Latin American debt crisis, and the ensuing Brady plan, the American banks were in better shape than they were now. And the potential for disaster was immense, as the problems in Asia had only just begun to unravel. Things were going to get a lot worse, and the statistics, the real statistics, which he was now ready to present to Byron Powell and the assembled decision makers, would make their eyes pop out of their heads. He would leave them really no option in that meeting, such was the mess he was about to reveal. They would have to let the banks go.

In fact, even in the US, they couldn't afford to do otherwise. The Federal budget was in massive surplus, but a bail-out of the major banks would plunge it back into a catastrophic deficit. And he didn't expect much opposition from the politicians. Dick Brightwell was a Republican and one year into a first term in office. He wouldn't be worried, at this stage, about popular measures to win votes. He'd probably figure that the masses, the small savers, would be protected by the FDIC insurance anyway, and they'd be glad to see him getting tough with the big corporations. And besides, he was just too stupid to see the real scale of the problem.

But Scott Turner was not. And he liked what he saw.

He had probably the lowest profile of all the members of the Pegasus Forum, and had had no direct contact with any of the others apart from Wallace Bradley since they had left Oxford. Externally at least, he was not a radical firebrand, like Johnnie Quaid, nor an aggressive trader-type like Annie van Aalst. His subdued, understated temperament was ideally suited to government work, and he had slotted easily into his career at the Federal Reserve Bank. People whispered behind his back that his rapid advancement was down to positive discrimination – the board was keen to fill their quotas of ethnic minorities, and to have an African-American in such a prominent position suited them just fine – but the truth was that his career progression had been entirely based on merit. He was simply better than the others, harder working, better organized and above the office politics – but his own passions bubbled behind the calm exterior. And Wallace Bradley had done well to spot the clue to those passions in his CV, submitted to St Mary's College so many years ago. There had been only the slightest indication, but Bradley had sniffed it out.

On the application form, under the section 'Interests/Clubs/Affiliations' he had written, amongst other things, the letters 'SDC'. This had meant nothing at all to Bradley initially, but his search for potential candidates for Pegasus meant that he left nothing to chance in his research. After some investigation into the Strategic Defence Command, the Society of Dyers and Colourists, and even the Sacramento Drama Circle, it turned out that these letters stood, in Turner's case, for the Sudanese Development Campaign, a charity registered in the United States, founded to solicit funds from Sudanese migrants abroad and wealthy philanthropists in order to relieve misery in the Sudan. For Scott Turner was originally Sudanese.

Until the age of eight he had lived in the Red Sea coastal town of Suakin, actually a small island linked by a causeway to the mainland of Africa, and forty miles or so south of the principal port in the country, Port Sudan. Until the nineteenth century it had been a thriving trading centre itself, but the magnificent pink coral buildings, constructed with the wealth from that trade, began to crumble when demand for their most precious commodity died off. For that commodity was black slaves, destined for the outer reaches of the Ottoman Empire and many points further west, and Suakin had been the gateway into bondage for hundreds of thousands of press-ganged Sudanese.

Turner himself had been christened Francis Ajang, born to a comparatively affluent family in Khartoum. Both his parents were educated people, his father a physician and his mother a librarian in the local Christian primary school. But times were hard for the indigenous black population in the years following independence from Egypt and the UK in 1956, and the steadily increasing influence of Islam and an Arabization of the entire country forced the family out of Khartoum after young Francis's birth in 1961. They fled north, which was a bad decision as that part of the country rapidly became the stronghold of the Arab population. But the small port of Suakin was cheap and relatively peaceful. Although far from its former glory in the slave-trading era, Suakin managed to escape the worst of the famines and fighting which blighted the rest of the country in those early years of independence, but life was still far from easy.

As a citizen of the very largest and also one of the very poorest countries in Africa, a seven-year-old Francis Ajang used to stand on the shores of the Red Sea and gaze out over the waters towards one of the richest countries. For the coast of Saudi Arabia, the mighty city of Jeddah and the shrine of Mecca, lay a mere two hundred miles or so away, and if he stood on the crumbling breeze-block wall which separated his parents' blistering shack from the beach, he fancied he could see the golden mosques shimmering on the horizon in the afternoon sunlight. And as a forty-year-old American citizen now known as Scott Turner stood staring into the rain on Ireland's west coast, looking out over Lough Corrib on that late December afternoon, he could clearly recall those boyhood moments of fantasy, imagining his own country of birth in possession of the fabulous wealth of the Arabian oil reserves. And wanting desperately to do something about it.

His family had finally fled when he was eight, taking their life's savings and purchasing passage on board one of the American tourist liners which still occasionally put in to Port Sudan on their way down the Red Sea from Egypt. They stayed with the ship all the way back to New York, and claimed refugee status upon arrival. They were disappointed to discover that their own romantic dream of the Ellis Island Immigration Center and its gateway to freedom for the world's oppressed had actually closed in 1954, but they were processed nonetheless in a faceless office in Brooklyn, and subsequently granted permission to stay. This was almost two years to the day before the arrival in America of another immigrant in rather different circumstances, a certain Saul Krantz. The Ajangs chose the name Turner, after a couple they had met on the ship, and citizenship came five years later, when Scott Turner, as he now was known, turned thirteen.

He was a bright thirteen-year-old, and it was clear he was destined for academic success. His father, Bok Ajang, now Wesley Turner, couldn't get his Sudanese medical qualification accredited by the New York State Department of Health, but he put in long hours working as a paramedic, ambulance driver and subway cleaner in an attempt to save enough to put his only son through college when that time would come. His mother Batul, now Betty, worked in kindergartens for African children in Harlem and added her own contribution to the Turner nest egg.

At his inner-city high school, Scott excelled. He was mature for his age, and aware of the world and his surroundings. He still remembered his early childhood in the Sudan, took a strong interest in Third World matters generally, and Sudanese issues specifically. It was at the age of seventeen that he got involved in the SDC, and was soon organizing fund-raisers at his school and in the community at large. People at home were still starving to death, and the black population of Sudan, still in the majority, were being displaced by the Arabs. Nearly five million people had been forced from their homes and were roaming the country, and those that were not starving were being murdered by government forces or, incredibly, being sold into slavery again. The wheel of history had come full circle and the trade which had made his childhood home of Suakin rich in the seventeenth and eighteenth centuries had started up again.

But what bothered him most of all was the attitude of foreign governments and business to their plight. They ignored the mass genocide, the ethnic cleansing that it would become so fashionable to condemn in Rwanda and Bosnia much later, and continued to lend money to the corrupt government.

Sudan, one of the poorest countries in the world, had an external foreign debt of almost thirty billion US dollars, which was like a destitute bag lady having a million-dollar mortgage. Those IOUs amounted to around a thousand dollars for every man, woman and child in the country, where unemployment was running at thirty per cent and inflation at twenty. And the charges on that debt were crippling. How could the banks continue to lend, when the money they threw at the problem merely ended up in the pockets of the few and made the problem worse? He viewed the banks as glorified loan sharks and wanted to do anything he could to raise the profile of these issues and do something about it.

At high school he continued to excel in most subjects, and his student careers counsellor persuaded him to study economics at college, with a focus on Third World affairs. He won a scholarship to Stanford, which enabled the Ajang-Turner family to use the money they had been saving for Scott's education to uproot and move together to the West Coast. He continued to impress, even when promoted to the Ivy League, and graduated *summa cum laude*, whilst at the same time founding a chapter of the SDC in California, which quickly spread all down the western seaboard.

He applied for a Rhodes scholarship almost by accident; or rather, his teachers did for him. It was just the thing to do for a student of his talents looking to progress to the next hurdle, and his tutors put his name forward for consideration automatically and without asking him. They were aware of his straitened circumstances and assumed he would be happy for any assistance. When he received the letter informing him that he had been selected as one of the thirty-two lucky Americans to be sent, all-expenses-paid, to Oxford for a couple of years of graduate study, he frowned.

Frankly, the prospect of being sponsored in his education by Cecil Rhodes, a man who, in his eyes, embodied the worst kind of possessive, white imperialism, troubled his conscience and his sensibilities. He was very much in tune with modern Africa, despite having left that continent at the age of eight, and was a vocal supporter of the campaign to remove Rhodes's remains from his grave in the Matopo hills above Bulawayo. It was inconceivable that he could possibly accept a scholarship funded by the man's estate, and in a polite but terse letter to a bemused panel of adjudicators, he became one of the few applicants actually to decline a Rhodes Scholarship.

Wallace Bradley had a copy of that letter in his file on Turner, and it was the phrases 'ravening expansionism' and 'exploitative profiteering' which caught his eye. The information came to his notice courtesy of the private investigator hired to look into Turner's background, and it reinforced Bradley's suspicions that Turner would be not only ideally suited from an ideological point of view to become a member of the Pegasus Forum, but eminently qualified to desire and obtain employment, following his time at Oxford, in a field of potentially enormous support to its aims.

Turner was woken from his daydream by the insistent, shrill pulse tones from the pager clipped to his waist-band. The message was from his boss, the Chairman of the Federal Reserve Board of the United States, who, in the adjoining room, had just completed his customary pre-meeting, mind-sharpening ritual, returned the box of tissues to the bathroom and the copy of *Playboy* to his briefcase. The message was brief: 'Connaught Room. Now.' Turner opened the window wide and leaned his head right out, gulping in a huge lungful of the damp, frosty air which tasted better to him than a glass of spring water. The lake was by now almost invisible, and the combined efforts of gathering dark and thickening mist conspired to allow nothing to penetrate the air save the occasional twinkle from the boats' searchlights and a muffled hum from their engines.

When journalist Callum O'Connor had received the phone call at his Limerick news desk from his cousin at Shannon airport, he had wasted no time in getting to Cong. He didn't want to share the scoop with anyone, so he hadn't taken a photographer with him, but instead he had borrowed a couple of SLR bodies, a tripod and a 'Long Tom' 600 millimetre lens, amongst others, from his bird-watching friend who ran the local dry cleaners. He parked his car on the high street in Cong and walked into the nearest pub, his equipment hanging over his shoulder in a nondescript green canvas bag. He figured the landlord would be the best starting place for information on goings-on in the village, and a couple of Guinnesses later, he knew exactly how many cars had entered and left the castle hotel that day. He was particularly interested in the six black Chevy Suburbans with American plates which had roared through the village nose to tail without consideration for the 'Kill your Speed, not our

Children' signs along the way, before turning through the castle gates at around two o'clock. But nobody knew what was going on, nor who was visiting. A couple of helicopters, military, had been and gone, and Daisy Ryan, waitress in the hotel and daughter of Tommy the butcher, had been asked to stay overnight and to bring enough clothes until Tuesday. Tommy himself had been asked if he could supply some kosher beef, to which he had replied in the affirmative, waited a couple of hours, and then delivered ten pounds of his regular brisket to the gate. He had not been allowed in, and he had stood there for over fifteen minutes, steaming in the cold, before the gate had abruptly opened and the meat virtually snatched from his hands with a guttural, incomprehensible grunt by a stocky, Mediterranean-looking type in a short black leather coat.

O'Connor mentally added the Israelis to the list O'Shaughnessy had given him, a list which now included the Americans, Chinese, Russians and Japanese, as well as the Brits and Irish.

The landlord told him of a good vantage point from which to observe the castle, which was Dorothy Gaskill's bed and breakfast on the brow of the hill just outside the village. He spent a cosy couple of hours in her attic bedroom, warmed and fortified by regular cups of coffee and intermittent nips of Bushmills, the long lens trained on the castle's floodlit southern facade, before he finally got lucky. A third floor window in the west tower opened suddenly and he managed to rattle off three clear shots of Scott Turner's black face leaning out before it disappeared back inside. O'Connor didn't know who it was, but that was the picture which adorned the front page of the *Limerick Leader* the following morning under the headline, 'WHAT'S WRONG AT CONG?', and a story about the world's financial leaders assembled in Ireland for crisis talks over the New Year.

Reuters Dublin bureau picked up the story as they did their regular trawl through the morning's regional press, and at round about the same time their London headquarters received an anonymous tip-off to much the same effect from a number which turned out to be a public telephone box at Carfax in Oxford. This was enough corroboration for them to run a newsflash on their 'NEWS' screen reserved for major breaking stories, which would appear instantly and simultaneously on the computer screens of around three million bankers, traders, salesmen and fund managers around the globe: 'DEBT CRISIS LATEST – G-10 FINANCE MINISTERS AND CENTRAL BANKERS IN SECRET EMERGENCY TALKS. CHINESE AND RUSSIANS INVOLVED.'

CHAPTER 6

THIS WAS AROUND TEN O'CLOCK LONDON TIME ON THE MORNING of 31 December, a day on which most dealing rooms in most banks had at best a skeleton staff. The majority of traders and fund managers were away over the holiday period, a fact which made markets much less liquid at that time, large amounts more difficult to trade, and prices more subject to big movements should something surprising happen. For Cameron Dodds, sitting back at his desk in Steinman, Schwartz's London office, this was no surprise. He had received the call from Wallace Bradley the night before, but he already knew what to expect.

Annie van Aalst was equally ready. In Grand Cayman it was only five in the morning, but she had been there all night, preparing for the announcement of the talks, and deciding which course of action from her would have the maximum possible impact. On the desk in front of her she had two documents. One was a computer printout headed 'Highly Confidential – US Federal Reserve Bank, New York'. It was a summary report of the current risk positions of the top one hundred banks in the United States and was a carbon copy of the report Scott Turner had with him to present to the assembled luminaries in Ireland. The second document she had was a secure e-mail she had received the previous evening from Danny Brookes, their accountant and analyst in London. In it he laid out his opinion as to which of the banks on Turner's list was the most vulnerable, given their current holdings and the state of the markets. It was all to do with risk.

Risk. What didn't she know about the subject? She was a professional risk-taker after all. That was her job. But it wasn't such a big deal. It sounded grand but she knew only too well that judgements of risk were being made in one form or another, by every living person, everywhere on Earth. All of those people were able to remain sane and functioning members of society by either formally or subconsciously assigning probabilities to certain risks and acting accordingly. Everyone knew there was a tiny chance of being hit by a falling meteor whilst standing on the seventeenth tee, but the chances of it happening were so small that it did not hamper their swing. More risk was taken when crossing the road, but most people could fairly accurately assess the likelihood of reaching the other side before the approaching car hit and they adjusted timing and speed accordingly. Life insurance companies took significant risk when they agreed to pay us when we die. Their risk was that they might have to pay out on a million-dollar policy if somebody got hit by a falling meteor or a bus after paying only his first month's premium. They assigned probabilities to our life expectancy based on how other similar people have survived in the past and they charged us accordingly.

What she did every day as a fund manager was no different, and banks were the same. They took risks with their own and their customers' money in the financial markets, and there was a rigorous protocol for measuring how much risk was being taken, and what was the likelihood of the financial meteor blowing the bank and all its money into oblivion. This was the measure Scott Turner had compiled on all those banks under his surveillance, and which Annie van Aalst now perused.

It was a measure known in the business as 'value at risk', and was a method of calculating, at a certain confidence level, the maximum possible daily loss under normal market conditions. This number was, by the very nature of markets, a guess. And, like most assessment of risk, it was a guess about the future based on what has happened in the past.

A bank would compile lists of all its holdings every day in all the different markets – what stocks it owned, what bonds, what currencies, what derivatives, what credits. For each of those asset classes there was historical data available on how the prices of those assets had moved, every day, over the last several years, and what the incidence of various daily price movements had been. Thus it was possible to say that, for a given bond, they knew that over the last forty years, the price had only changed by more than, say, five dollars a day in one per cent of cases. In other words, if they owned that bond, there was judged to be only a one in a hundred chance that they would lose more than five dollars in any one day. A typical bank would hold a very complex combination of different assets, all of which could be assigned their own daily value at risk, some of which reinforced each other, doubling up or tripling up the risk, or even more, whereas others cancelled each other out, so-called 'hedges'. The bank could then compute the overall daily value at risk of the entire institution.

What Turner asked the banks under his supervision to supply every day was a daily value at risk at a ninety-nine per cent confidence level. This meant the maximum amount the bank could expect to lose in any one day if the markets turned sour – the worst case scenario in ninety-nine per cent of cases. Of course, this did not mean it was impossible for the bank to lose more, just that it was only likely to happen one per cent of the time. The higher the value at risk, the more the bank was staking; the lower the confidence level, the more danger there was of greater potential losses actually happening.

The great weakness of the system of risk assessment was that it only worked if nothing untoward happened, in *normal* circumstances. And the circumstances Wallace Bradley and the other members of the Pegasus Forum had conspired thus far to provoke were far from normal. This was the nub of Bradley's strategy. This was the rôle of the members of the Pegasus Forum. Together they would engineer as many 'exceptional' events as they possibly could, which, in combination, would effectively create a new environment in which the events of the past would be a very poor predictor of what would happen in the future. It would be as if a meteor shower were raining down on the Earth, and those rare events, those 'exceptional' cases, would become commonplace. In essence, even without doing anything, the banks were effectively taking more and more risk every day.

The entire banking system was set up to protect the banks and their customers' money under those trusted, familiar, 'normal' circumstances of the past. The amount of money the banks had to set aside as a reserve to protect against possible losses was prescribed by the authorities, and that amount was based on what any potential future losses might reasonably be expected to be. But the definition of 'reasonable expectations' had changed, thanks to the actions of the Pegasus Forum, and things would only get worse as the 'exceptional' events became more and more frequent. The reserves in the banking system would be woefully inadequate to survive this new environment, but the authorities did not know this yet, because they did not yet understand the extent of the problem.

James Emerson *was* beginning to understand the extent of the problem, at least in human terms. In Jakarta it was five in the afternoon on New Year's Eve, but he had no desire to celebrate. The memory of the scenes of rioting he had witnessed the previous evening still haunted him, and the girl he had rescued was soaking away the last traces of her attackers in his bathtub.

He had not spoken to her much since he had brought her to his hotel suite. She had sobbed her way through most of the rest of the night, curled tightly in a ball on the floor of his sitting room like a wounded animal, until a merciful and deep sleep had enveloped her at around six in the morning. He had picked her up gently, still in her stinking, soiled clothes and laid her on his bed. He had then taken the sofa for himself and catnapped spasmodically until three in the afternoon when he had ordered room service and watched the news on CNN while she continued to sleep.

The aerial view of Ashford Castle from the news helicopter in the pouring rain and mist seemed an entirely different world from his own, and he listened intently to the reports of the secret summit meeting and the repercussions it was already having on the markets around the world. In the thin, holiday markets, the European exchanges had already fallen by around eight per cent in value in the first two hours of trading, and the world was holding its breath in anticipation of the opening in New York in a few hours' time.

The second story was of the failure of a bank in Germany, citing heavy losses in the Asian markets, and a grainy, black and white picture of Jakob Lichtblau filled the screen. He had been caught in the flash of a press photographer on the doorstep of his house as he returned home. He looked startled and scared, and the dim outline of a dishevelled and distressed Ilse Lichtblau could be made out in the darkened hallway behind him. Anti-Semitic graffiti, swastikas and stars of David covered the wall of his house. The reporter went on to say that three synagogues in Munich had been vandalized, and queues had begun to form at cash-machines all over Germany. Banks would close at noon for the holiday, but there were widespread fears of a panic to withdraw cash after the New Year's break. This was the first sizeable bank to go under in Germany since before the Second World War, and the size of the losses, and the speed with which it had been closed down, had astonished a nation used to the stability and reliability of their financial pillars.

He had watched the news until he heard the girl he had rescued beginning to stir in the bedroom around four. He had gently pointed her in the direction of the bathroom with a robe, a stack of clean clothes and a promise of a meal when she was ready. A little under an hour later she emerged looking like a different woman, almost a different species to the creature he had saved the night before. She was wearing one of his polo shirts, a dark-green one which drowned her tiny frame but which she had managed to make presentable by buttoning it up to the top and rolling the sleeves back several times. The spare acres of fabric below the waist were scrunched into the waistband of a pair of his khaki shorts, which she had managed to secure with one of his belts by tying it in like a sash. She had completed the outfit by again rolling up the legs of the shorts to something approximating her own size so that they hung somewhere around mid-thigh. Her feet were tiny and bare and her toes gripped the pile of the carpet with each step as she walked hesitantly across the sitting room towards the sofa where he was sitting. Her hair, jet black and shiny from the shower, was pulled taughtly off her forehead and combed straight down her back, where it hung just above where he imagined her waist to be within the voluminous folds of fabric. She stood right in front of him and gave a formal Indonesian bow, palms pressed together before her as if in prayer.

'Thank you, sir, for what you did last night. My name Tamana. I most graceful.'

'That you are, but you mean grateful, and you must call me James. As for last night, I just did what any man would do in the circumstances. And you helped me a lot. That's quite a kick you have there.'

'Karate. I have two older brothers. *Had* two older brothers. They experts. I learned from them.'

'Well I think those two monsters came off worse than we did in the end. Any damage?'

'No. But I still shake at memory.'

'You must stay here for the next few nights. Enjoy the comfort, watch some TV and order room service. Then you must go home. That is a dangerous line of business you're in, especially with a face like yours in these times. Don't you have a . . . I mean, someone to look out for you?'

'You mean "pimp", don't you? You can say it. It does not shock me. Nothing shocks me now. Yes, I am prostitute, at least at night. But I do not have pimp. I do it for me, or at least, for my sister-in-law. She need money. She have kids. I work.'

'But for a Chinese girl in these riots . . .'

'I not Chinese. I Japanese. Half Japanese. I have day job as secretary in bank. Same bank my brother used to work in. He dead now. That is why I sell body at night. Help his family, his children.'

And for the next several hours, they sat and ate and talked. She told him about her past, how her grandfather had been an officer in the occupying Japanese forces in Indonesia during the war, how he had deserted in 1945 and escaped capture by the liberating Americans. He had fled to northern Sumatra as a peasant with one of the Japanese geisha who staffed the officers' comfort station in his barracks. Together they had started a new life amongst the fierce Batak people, masquerading as 'Chinese' immigrants. It was a simple rural life, and her father had been born shortly after, but when he was only three the family was exposed for what they were – not Chinese but the hated Japanese. It was a chance encounter, a chance in a million really, but a man in their village actually recognized her grandfather from the Javanese internment camp where he had been imprisoned. A confession was forced with sharp knives and hot coals and both parents were executed, beheaded, whilst the three-year-old boy watched. And then they were eaten. The boy was spared his life but forced to participate in the feast.

The Batak reputation for cannibalism was largely historical, but they revived the tradition, it seemed, for that special occasion. Every detail of that day was burned into her father's brain, and her own strongest childhood memory was of being woken almost every night by his screams as he relived the experience in his dreams again and again.

She herself had learned the truth of her grandparents' fate on her thirteenth birthday, when her father decided she was old enough to know, and she had begun to understand his fierce Japanese patriotism. He had forced her to learn the language as soon as she was able, as he had forced himself as a teenager when he fled his adopted Batak parents and returned to Java in search of fortune in the big city. She took pride in speaking it. It had got her a job, the day job she still held, in the Jakarta branch of the Osakumi Bank of Osaka, where her brother had worked as a senior foreign-exchange dealer.

'So is this the brother who died? Is it his family you are helping to support?' asked Emerson. He had been silent during most of the girl's story. It was largely involuntary, as he was at a loss for words during most of it, but he had grasped her slender hand which had crept into his own as she recounted the ordeal her father had witnessed as a young boy. Her hand was still there, and he squeezed it a little more tightly when she began to speak of her brother. He too had lost a brother and the comfort he attempted to convey with this shared physical contact was not entirely one way.

'Yes, my brother died one month ago. He was trader in foreign exchange. Dollar-rupiah mainly. They say he commit suicide.'

'Why, Tamana?'

'Because of losses. Huge losses. His boss at bank say he been hiding them and been found out. There been big selling of rupiah against dollar since all troubles begin, and that his book. They say he not cope. I do not believe it.'

'What do you think really happened?'

'I am not sure, but I do not believe he take own life. Suicide very common in Japanese people, I know, face very important. But in his case . . .'

'People do irrational things in time of stress, Tamana. It is impossible to understand sometimes.'

'But what they say he do! He never do that. He never throw himself from top of Monas!'

'The what?'

'Monas, the Monumen Nasional in middle of Merdeka Square. You know, huge tower! Symbol of Indonesia's independence.'

'But why wouldn't he have done that?'

'Two reasons. First, he hate the thing. He hate Indonesian nationalism, and this was symbol of forces which killed our father's parents. He never go near it, and *never* use it to take own life.'

'And the other reason?'

'Heights. He had terrible fear of heights. He could never look out of window, even in office, and we only on third floor. Monas over one hundred metres. It not possible for him to go up there alone. No way, José.' And then she began to cry again, quietly and steadily. 'He was murdered, *Bapak* James. Murdered, I sure of it, and I think I know why.'

In Cong, County Mayo, the first day of the secret summit had come to an end. A fair amount of time had been wasted investigating the source of the leak of their presence in Ireland, but Scott Turner was in the clear. He had made his call to Wallace Bradley before the listening apparatus had been set up, and the fact that the initial scoop came in a local newspaper diverted attention to the villagers or staff at the hotel. An indignant catering manager spent his New Year's Eve closeted with aggressive secret service personnel from the United States and Ireland, whose questioning lasted well into the night before they were satisfied. The Chinese and Israelis wanted their own people to 'interview' him, but the Irish Government interceded to prevent it.

Of course there was much accusation and counter-accusation between the various national delegations that the leak had come from official sources. The Italians blamed the French, the French blamed the Canadians, the Germans blamed the Dutch and the Russians and Chinese blamed everyone else. For good measure and appearances' sake the Americans had a go at the Japanese, but they knew it was not them. In fact, they knew it was none of them, for the owlish man from the NSA had been up all night reading translated transcripts from his covert eavesdropping operation on the other delegates, and they had all come out clean. No calls to newspapers, no unsecure communications, no loose words to chamber maids (for they had bugged all the bedrooms whilst the first conference was in session). In fact, the most interesting information they had discovered was the sexual proclivities of a senior Belgian official who had made an improper suggestion to the room service waiter when he had delivered a bottle of champagne at three in the morning, and that one of the Chinese central bankers had a private brokerage account in Liechtenstein which he had liquidated by telephone when the press broke the news of the summit.

Annie van Aalst and Cameron Dodds had been especially busy. The markets were closed in London now, but Dodds remained at his desk long after everyone else had gone home to celebrate the New Year. The lights were dimmed on the enormous trading floor of which he was the sole occupant, and the phosphorescent glow from his bank of four trading screens provided the main illumination by which he worked. For it was five hours earlier on the eastern seaboard of the United States, and New York was still trading, as was Annie van Aalst in Grand Cayman.

Rumours had been flying around the market for most of the shortened trading day, mostly based on the closure of the German bank whose name nobody could pronounce yet on which everybody in the market suddenly fancied themselves to be an expert. And the buzzword of the day was 'contagion'. For now the problem was no longer confined to the Asian markets. The financial sickness which had begun in Thailand, and rapidly spread to the rest of the Asia-Pacific region as currencies plunged and companies defaulted on their debt, had taken their first Western victim. Analysts all over Wall Street and in the City of London were rushing to dredge up statistics on which of the Western nations had the most extensive trading links with Asia, and which were likely to suffer most. Beyond that, they tried to come up with lists of loans made by specific banks in Europe and North America to Asian companies who were now unlikely to be able to repay them.

But Annie van Aalst, thanks to Scott Turner and Danny Brookes had the definitive list, and between them they had been putting it to good use.

One American bank stood out from the rest as a prime target. Braxton Federal, based in Miami and named after one of the original signatories of the Declaration of Independence, was America's sixth largest bank. For most of the twentieth century they had been a small but highly profitable regional bank, servicing the needs of private and corporate clients all over the state of Florida. In the early eighties, a new CEO with international ambitions had taken over, and had begun to grow the bank beyond the State line. With a number of high profile and highly leveraged transactions, he had acquired control of several other regional banks in the southern states, as well as starting an investment banking operation on Wall Street. For this they had spent a lot of money hiring key executives, and opening a glitzy new headquarters in mid-town Manhattan. They had begun to specialize in Latin American debt trading, given the heavy preponderance of Hispanics in their home state and their own long-standing connections with Mexican corporations looking to expand north of the border, but the new CEO had other ambitions. Competition in Latin America was fierce, with both North American and European banks active in the region, whereas Asia was relatively underbroked. And for Eric Chen, a third-generation Asian-American, the Orient was a natural area in which to expend and expand.

Within five years he had built a portfolio of assets in Asia, direct loans and bonds, which totalled thirty-five billion dollars. On top of this, his trading operation had a reputation as the most aggressive in the United States when it came to the secondary trading of other people's bonds, and loans they wanted to get rid of. At its height, that trading book reached seven billion dollars in short-term holdings. This total was reached on 31 December, and it was largely due to enormous sales to them by Annie van Aalst.

For she knew that Braxton Federal was trading at the limit. According to Turner's statistics, they had a daily value at risk of around four hundred million dollars. The bank had ten billion dollars in capital. Using those numbers, the capital would disappear in around twenty-five days of those supposedly 'maximum' losses. Only she wanted it to happen more quickly than that. For she was going to try to create the extreme circumstances – the one per cent of cases not covered by all those theoretical calculations of 'maximum' losses. And once into those extreme market conditions, there was no maximum, only the black hole of insolvency.

She also knew from Turner's numbers that Braxton already had unrealized losses on its loan book of around five billion dollars. These were effectively reduced valuations on the loans they had made to Asian companies that they had yet to take into account, or even make provision for. So she was going to assail Braxton Federal Bank on all sides; it was going to be predatory trading at its most extreme, and she was going to use all the weaponry at her and the rest of the Pegasus Forum's disposal to push that bank into receivership.

They had done it fairly simply in Germany. They had identified a single major asset of a relatively small bank and reduced its value mercilessly by massive selling. The loss had rapidly become more than that bank could swallow and continue to function. In Braxton's case it would be more difficult – the bank was much larger and there were fewer tangible targets, but it was important. At this stage, they had provoked a bank failure in Asia, several in fact by now, but mainly small ones; Lichtblau had followed in Europe, but they needed one in North America to get the feeding frenzy going, to complete the chain of events that would provide critical mass and leave those marvellously unfettered market forces to do the rest of their work for them.

But it was important for another reason also. Everyone depositing money with a major bank in the United States was protected by insurance provided by the government, up to a certain limit. That limit currently stood at one hundred thousand dollars, an amount deemed by the government to be sufficient to protect the majority of 'small' investors. The US Government's insurance company, the FDIC, collected insurance premiums from the banks in return for guaranteeing those deposits and conferring 'fail-free' status upon those banks. This gave the man in the street confidence to deposit his money with that bank, knowing that the government would repay him if the bank went bust. The insurance premiums collected by the government were held as a war chest should the need arise to bail out a bank that was failing. To undermine confidence in the American banking system, therefore, it was not sufficient merely to undermine confidence in a few banks. The very guarantees provided by the government had to be called into question.

CHAPTER 7

WALLACE BRADLEY PLANNED TO SPEND HIS NEW YEAR'S EVE in Oxford, closeted in his suite of sixteenth-century rooms in St Mary's College. There was still an hour of trading to go in New York, but at five in the afternoon in Oxford it was already dark and he had drawn the heavy curtains to muffle the rain and howling wind from their assault on his senses. The room was filled with the mournful strains of a Bach cello suite, and a dozen candles scattered around the room on saucers and in empty bottles provided the only illumination. Spirals of incense smouldered in ashtrays and the air was thick with the sweet, intoxicating fragrance of patchouli and bergamot. He was sprawled on his sofa, the same sofa on which he had seduced Patsy O'Connor, and he would, to the casual observer, have appeared unconscious. An almost empty bottle of malmsey sat on the rosewood table at his elbow and his blank, glazed eyes were fixed on a spot above the mantelpiece.

Hanging there was a sword. A *katana* from the seventeenth century, a long sword with a gently curving blade of about three feet, a Samurai sword, a Japanese sword.

The temperature outside in the ancient quadrangle was close to zero, but sweat accumulated on Bradley's brow and top lip, an alcoholic perspiration augmented by the overheated atmosphere of the room. Only the depth of his breathing betrayed the extent of the activity in his brain, but he was oblivious to all external stimuli apart from that sword. He was transfixed by its image, and his unblinking gaze caused the long slim form of the ancient weapon to float in the air as if suspended by invisible strings; and, as he stared, the image of the sword strobed back and forth, flashing between positive and negative, detached from the background by his febrile, narcotic trance. The clock in nearby Lincoln College chimed five but Bradley heard nothing of it.

The sword hovered in the air before being grasped by black-gauntleted hands, and the faceless silhouette of a man, a warrior, shimmered into focus, flailing the weapon above his head in great, ceremonial sweeps. A pregnant woman lay naked and supine on a stone altar, writhing in the throes of labour, her hair a knotted mass of squirming snakes, her stretched belly distended and distorted by whatever pummelled her from within. In two rapid strides the warrior was on her, and with an extravagant flourish, the blade of the sword flashed in the last glimmers of a dwindling sun before plunging to her neck with lethal finality. The swordsman stooped to retrieve the severed head, seizing a great handful of snakes and thrusting it aloft in triumph. The dripping skull, suspended now from its serpentine tresses, which hissed and spat in defiance, slowly span around to reveal a face, a familiar face in black and white, beaming out from beneath a starched, crisp Red Cross cap.

Bradley's gaze dropped to the remains of the severed torso. Foaming torrents of blood gushed in systolic spurts and gathered in deepening puddles which already lapped at the altar on which the body lay. A vast stallion, dappled crimson, rose before his eyes from the lake of gore, a ferocious animal, snorting and champing and thrashing its hooves, cavorting spastically in the bloody shallows before rearing up, every sinew in its hindquarters stretched to the limit, every muscle twitching and throbbing with the effort as two huge wings unfolded from its body and with one supreme downward draft, propelled the beast into the skies. It soared heavenwards and Bradley watched it dwindle to a red spot in the ether, to be met by an equally red, rising sun which emerged from the horizon at time-lapse speed.

The warrior sheathed his sword and turned to face Bradley, the light from the rising sun illuminating his features in a red wash. Bradley knew the face. He knew it very well, and he screamed in ecstatic terror as he rose from his sofa and stumbled forward to meet it.

*   *   *

Danny Brookes, accountant to the Pegasus Forum, whistled tunelessly to himself as he trotted up the oak staircase to Wallace Bradley's first floor rooms, clutching his oversized briefcase and another large bottle of Madeira to fuel their planned New Year's Eve celebrations. Standing outside the heavy door he paused before entering, as he heard a scream, a muffled shriek in a language he recognized from his schooldays. The language was ancient Greek, and the cry he heard from within Bradley's rooms was the same word, over and over again, '*Eleytheria!*' Freedom. He then heard a kind of dull, rhythmic thumping, followed by a noise that sounded like shattering glass, and he rushed inside without knocking. As he burst in, his eyes smarted from the skeins of incense smoke which clouded the room, and it took him a second to find his bearings and his former professor. The banging noise continued in spite of his presence, and he finally saw Bradley, lying on his back, arms splayed either side of a enormous heavy gilt mirror which now lay on top of him. Much of the glass lay shattered on the ground, and Bradley lay amid the fragments, thumping his head again and again against the now bare backboard, shards of glass buried in his cheeks and lips, oblivious to Brookes's presence and the blood which trickled down over his collar.

Brookes dropped the case and bottle he had been carrying and picked his way through the mess. He wrapped both arms around the mirror from behind and gently prised it away from Bradley's grasp. It took all his strength to raise it into an upright position and free Bradley who lay pinned beneath it. The professor's head lolled back as he allowed himself to be led away, still feverishly mouthing that same Greek word, again and again, as Brookes hauled him back on to the sofa and proceeded to remove the worst of the glass from his face. Bradley's eyes remained wide open, staring but unseeing, and it was a minor miracle that they had been spared damage from the splinters of glass which littered the rest of his features. Once he had satisfied himself that no major vessels had been severed, Brookes left the stupefied man on the couch for a second to make a phone call.

Christopher Blake, in his hotel room at the Randolph in Oxford, answered on the first ring.

'Chris, it's Danny. You'd better get over here straight away. Bradley's hurt. He's out of his brain and seems delirious. It looks like he's had some kind of fit.'

The two men spent the rest of the evening tending to their leader and mentor. They bathed his face and assessed the damage, concluding that he had been extremely lucky not to have incurred any major injury. He passed in and out of consciousness, muttering incomprehensible phrases which Brookes's schoolboy Greek was not up to deciphering, as they plucked tiny pieces of silvered glass from his face with Blake's eyebrow tweezers. On one occasion he suddenly sat up, bolt upright with eyes ablaze, and proclaimed, in English, 'Poseidon will pay!' before slumping back into unconsciousness. During his periods of sleep, they pondered on what he had been doing – what had he seen in the mirror which made him attack it as he apparently had and pull it down from the wall? His constant repetition of the Greek word for freedom meant nothing to them. Freedom of whom, and from what? And the Poseidon reference escaped them both. They both knew he was god of the sea, or something like that, but why should Bradley be obsessed with him? Maybe he had confused Poseidon for Pegasus? An easy slip given the state he was in. They also failed to notice, as they tidied up his room, that the Samurai sword which had been hanging over the mantelpiece was missing from its mounting and lay under the sofa where it had been kicked in the confusion.

'What do you mean, you think he was murdered? Why on earth would somebody do that?' James Emerson sat clasping the hand of Tamana in his Jakarta hotel room. It had just turned midnight, and the explosions of the New Year's firework displays and the shots of rubber bullets from the Indonesian riot police in the street below were indistinguishable.

'My brother's name was Shin. I could tell he worried. He had told boss about it, then me. It was all to do with new customer of bank.'

'What was the problem?'

'They selling so much. Rupiah. Against dollar. And they didn't seem to care about price. Client was handled by Tomi, Shin's boss, and because Shin main trader for dollar-rupiah, all selling went through his book. He made prices.'

'But everyone's selling these days, aren't they? There's no law against it.'

'I know, but it was the way they did it. They were brand new client, introduced by Tomi, but they became bank's biggest forex client within two weeks. They start dealing straight away, and always in huge size. And what is more, they not care about price. Shin always trying to miss business, it too big for him. He not so experienced. So after while he make bad prices, sort of prices he know stupid, but he still keep getting hit. Wave after wave of selling. It all happen so fast, he not keep up. They sell fifty million dollars in rupiah, and ten minutes later, before he have time to unload position, they call up again and do fifty more. Sure, he losing money, but not his fault. He more worried about client. To him they seem like money-launderers, doing sort of thing bank warned about. Very large amounts, unprofitable deals, stupid prices . . .'

'So what did he do?'

'He go to boss, to Tomi, and tell him suspicions. Tomi very rude to Shin, tell him to mind own business. The only thing he find out is that they some kind of fund based in Switzerland. Shin reckon they acting for someone else. Third party.'

'Why was that?'

'Timing. The trades almost always happen early morning our time. Between seven and nine. In Switzerland, that between one and three middle of night. He never heard of Swiss fund manager doing night trading before.'

'So where did he think the shots were really being called?'

'The States. It early evening there. East coast, or maybe offshore. He had suspicion it really one of big US hedge funds, you know, in Bahamas or Virgins or somewhere; they try to conceal identity by putting trades through Swiss company.'

'What was the name of the Swiss client?'

'That another thing. They called Sukon. Nobody ever hear of them. And suddenly they dealing in billions of dollars.'

'So what did he do after Tomi gave him the brush-off?'

'He tell me what he going to do. And he tell wife. And we both support him. We only think he risk job, we never think he . . .' She closed her eyes and paused to regain her composure. 'And then he tell Tomi. He tell him he going over head, report Sukon's trades to Central Bank, to supervisors. He say it his duty as trader and employee. Tomi furious, tell him he crazy. He say bank making fortune on commissions. So what if Shin lose money on trading book? He sack him right there.'

'And then . . .'

'And then next day he get call. At home, from Tomi himself. Say he sorry about losing temper. That he not sacked no more, that he come back to office. He even offer raise 'cause he try to protect bank's reputation. He say he understand concerns, he arrange meeting with Sukon guy that week. One of their big cheese visiting Jakarta. Customer say he want for Shin to come too, as thank you for all good dealing prices.'

'And the meeting was at the Monas?'

'No! He never do that. They had dinner at Café Batavia. Next thing I hear from Marissa. That his wife. They find him on south side of Monas. Strangled in suicide nets.'

This was exactly what Emerson needed. A way in, an angle on the story he'd come to investigate that he could really get his teeth into and which would spark the interest of Samuels and, with luck, the readers. But he needed Tamana's help. She worked at the bank, and in a clerical position she may well have access to the files he needed to see. But he also needed the help of someone else, someone rather special. Over the next couple of hours, they hatched a plan for her to go back to the office after the New Year's holiday and dig out some information for him. This was one way of gathering intelligence. Outright, physical theft, using an insider within the target organization. The information warfare people called it 'social engineering', which was usually a grand name for charming the password to the MD's computer from a drunk secretary during a 'chance' meeting in a bar after work. In his new career as a very effective, if sometimes unscrupulous, investigative journalist, James Emerson had become particularly adept at this technique. But sometimes, old-fashioned charm could not keep pace with technology. Sometimes he needed some tactical, strategic back-up, and for that reason he ignored the hotel phone, picked up his cell phone, and, via a series of satellite hook-ups, dialled Max Collins, aka Cubit.

'Dude, this is more like it. No more phreaking cell phones. Some real deep dark action. That is what I like. Now, gimme gimme. Name of target institution, name of suspect individual and the sort of shit you're looking for.'

'Osakumi Bank, Jakarta branch. Tomi Lubis is the guy, and we're looking for anything you can find on a company called Sukon. I've been doing a little social work myself, and have an asset within the bank who will hopefully corroborate what you dredge up.'

'OK, cool. Now Osakumi is a huge bank, am I right?'

'Second largest in Japan.'

'So the Jakarta branch is a small offshoot, right? They must be hooked into the bank's main network back home. So if I can get into the network servers at head office, I should be able to take a peek into the Jakarta branch files without too many people knowing. May have some problems with the Jap nature of the crack, however. From a purely language point of view.'

'If you need any help with translation, e-mail me. I have a girl here who I can trust and who'll help. She speaks Japanese and Bahasa.'

'A girl, eh? I bet you have, you son of a bitch. Talking of Jap cracks, is it true what they say about Orientals?'

'I don't know Max. At least, not yet. Get cracking.'

It was a very innocent phrase. Yet those words, used effortlessly, and perhaps rather thoughtlessly, by James Emerson in Jakarta started on a very long journey.

The miniscule air vibrations produced by the highly structured inter-
action of vocal chords, teeth, lips and tongue entered the mouthpiece
of his mobile phone, where they were picked up by a tiny, fingernail
size microphone and rendered into digital form by an almost as tiny
microprocessor and circuit board.

The digitized signal was then beamed directly by the handset's inbuilt
antenna, using a modest portable power source known as a battery, to
the nearest terrestrial antenna of the GSM network several miles away,
before being flashed a further several miles, this time straight up through
the ionosphere, to the Pacific Ocean Intelsat satellite, which hovers in
geosynchronous orbit above a fixed spot on the Earth's surface. From
here, the signal was transferred across a chain of similar satellites known
as Iridium, before making landfall again in England, seven thousand
miles away, at a receiving station somewhere in Kent. The final leg of
the journey was from there up to London, where the particular code
input by Emerson into his handset in Jakarta, known as a telephone
number, enabled the signal to be received by a similar device held by
Max Collins in his Chelsea townhouse.

There, the throaty, somewhat hoarse words uttered by Emerson
after a night without sleep in a riot-torn city, were re-translated into
analogue form and emitted by Collins's phone, again in the form of air
vibrations which set up similar resonances in the membrane of his fragile
tympanum. These pulses then continued the last short stage of their
journey, via a series of vibrating bones and hairs, to the auditory cortex and
ultimately directly into Collins's brain, where his mental processes were
able to translate those vibrations into meaningful words. And even more
meaningful silences. *I don't know, Max. At least not yet. Get cracking.*
Meaning: no he hasn't slept with the girl yet, but would like to. And
hurry up.

Total journey time: a little under one second.

This whole process was nothing more than a simple telephone conversation, and billions of them take place every day, all over the world.
But unbeknown to either communicant, that particular telephone conversation had gone on another, entirely separate journey.

A red alert flashed on the work station of Samuel Bron, a technician at the Yakima Research Station in Washington State on the west coast of America.

Yakima was one of a chain of NSA listening posts which spanned the globe, and part of the international Echelon project, designed to trawl for suspect traffic through the mass of electronic, digital and microwave communications used throughout the world by people sending information to other people.

Bron had worked there ever since the station opened in 1971, but he had never experienced a red alert. He folded his copy of the *National Enquirer* and clicked on the warning message. A red alert meant that the computer had picked up some form of communication relating to a very small number of top priority issues, identified and specified by the various participating governments. There were no more than two dozen or so red alert issues worldwide, and they included things like planned nuclear launches, military invasions and assassination attempts on the President or the Queen. Since Max Collins had disappeared from GCHQ and the face of the Earth almost eight years ago, taking his considerable knowledge and abilities with him, he had since been charged *in absentia* with the murder of Alastair Pynne, the then Director-General, and the abstraction of many millions from the payroll accounts. The British Government had accorded red alert status to any information relating to his whereabouts.

It would be highly unusual for Yakima Station to pick up a red alert. The principal function of that particular listening post was the illegal and unauthorized eavesdropping on all communications from the Pacific Intelsat Satellite, known as an ILC or International Leased Carrier. This was a satellite which rented out its capacity to a variety of international telephone and television companies who used its power to carry their traffic worldwide. Red alerts, by their very nature, tended to relate to issues of a highly secretive, mainly military nature, and such transmissions were unlikely to be entrusted to a commercial communications device such as the Intelsat 'bird'.

Bron's computer told him nothing about the content of the intercept, merely that it related to a British Government-specified issue, and therefore should be passed to them immediately.

The contact point for all British-related intercepts was the GCHQ liaison officer at the NSA-run listening station at Menwith Hill in Yorkshire, England. This was the largest installation of its kind anywhere in the world, and it was staffed by twelve hundred US civilians and servicemen. In addition to the Americans, a small number of GCHQ staff was seconded there to help analyse and process any information of special interest to the British Government. Bron simply punched a few keys and the information was transmitted across the Atlantic, via the NSA's Pathway Network, in a matter of seconds.

Menwith Hill was a massive complex, covering hundreds of acres, the principal distinguishing feature of which was a series of dozens of enormous white golf-ball-style constructions, known as radomes, running east to west across the camp and housing the satellite receiving dishes for the territory monitored by Menwith itself. This was mostly Europe, the Middle East and Eurasia, and the station had played a crucial role in, and indeed received commendations for, intercepting hostile military communications during the Gulf War.

Deep beneath those Yorkshire moors was a radiation-hardened facility known as Steeplebush II. This was the nerve-centre of Menwith Hill, and housed the incredibly powerful and sophisticated computer equipment which processed the data as it was intercepted by the satellites. The latest piece of equipment to be installed there was a machine known as Copperhead. It was an incredible machine, capable of scanning fifty-six thousand communications channels simultaneously, whether they be voice, fax or data transmissions, and extracting three thousand voice channels at any one time. It was a machine manufactured by Applied Signal Technology of Sunnyvale, California, and had been shipped and set up by the manufacturer only three weeks previously. Once sorted by Copperhead, the various signals could then be sieved by the battery of enormous 'Dictionary' computers which were programmed with TextFinder applications to look out for certain pre-identified, individual keywords, and, more recently, whole topics, on the Watch Lists supplied by the government analysts.

The entire system was capable of processing fifty million messages a day, mostly faxes, telexes, e-mails and phone calls. Of these, approximately three hundred thousand a day would be flagged by the computers' automated intelligence gathering software as being of potential interest. Twenty-five thousand of these would then be forwarded to the various interested parties in the Echelon project worldwide, of which around two hundred and fifty would finally be selected as being of genuine interest.

On average, twenty-five messages a day from the original fifty million were deemed by the human analysts to be of sufficient importance to deserve being reported up the chain of command to senior governmental officials.

But the phone intercepts had always been a problem. It was easy for computers to analyse data and written transmissions, and it was easy for satellites to intercept phone calls. What had always been problematic was getting a computer to 'listen' to voice communications and search reliably for the same key words it could find so easily in written material. The infinite variation in human anatomy, language and dialect, not to mention the quality of the phone lines, had always made it impossible. Until very recently.

Progress had been made initially by the British Government's Joint Speech Research Unit, in conjunction with a Montreal-based computer consultancy and the Cognitive Science department at MIT. Alongside their efforts, a Belgian company in the private sector had been making more substantial progress in the field. They were located in the unlikely-named 'Language Valley' just outside Ypres in Flanders, an area which had set itself up to vie with the rest of the world for progress in this much sought after technology. When it became to clear to Gus Routh, the new Director-General of GCHQ, that this company was on the verge of making a major breakthrough, above and beyond anything the government effort had yet achieved, the Belgian company was seen to go quietly bankrupt. What had really happened was that the combined resources of GCHQ, the NSA and the more junior members of Echelon, had made an approach to the partners of the company, Dick and Willem Verstaffen. It was one of those offers they could not refuse, and they had retired to obscurity in the Dutch Antilles with more money than they could realistically spend in a lifetime and an unveiled threat of retribution should they open their mouths, in exchange for their latest research and a five-year commitment to their new employers from their leading technologists. This was one nationalized industry which did not make it on to the front pages of the papers, nor into any published government budgets.

The combined team of linguisticians and computer experts had begun by abandoning the traditional idea of trying to identify individual words. Speech was unlike text. Spoken words flowed together in one fluid continuum without neat white spaces delineating where one word ended and the next began. Humans understood the spoken language long before the written by getting the gist for whole sentences in context. Out of context it was very difficult to decide whether a speaker was saying 'fish 'n' chips' or 'fission chips'. The team had finally succeeded in developing a reasonably reliable system of continuous speech recognition which could identify whole topics of conversation from intercepted voice communications. All of a sudden this rendered accessible the vast mass of telephone calls on which they illegally eavesdropped every day; for instead of employing thousands of human 'listeners' to trawl the calls in real time for signals intelligence, which was clearly not practical, they could let computers get on with it for them.

Several years previously, Gus Routh at GCHQ in Cheltenham had personally specified the keywords for the Echelon search for Max Collins. These had included both of his names, of course, as well as a number of key computer-related and cryptographic or mathematical terms. Any of these appearing in combination would trigger a red alert. Over the years since Collins's disappearance there had been a large number of false alarms. A number of bewildered men had been dragged from their beds in the middle of the night and innocent computer equipment seized by the lorry-load, only to be returned by a red-faced Gus Routh the following day. There were simply too many Maxes and Collins in the world, and too many cryptographic and mathematical terms in everyday use, for their quest to be targeted precisely enough. They had wasted countless man-hours making these fruitless raids and Gus Routh had signed enough formal letters of apology to last him a lifetime. But they persisted in their attempts. They had to. Collins was too dangerous, and indeed too valuable a commodity to be at large. They constantly refined the list of key words on the Echelon computers, until the volume of red herrings slowed down to a trickle. When James Emerson had uttered the words *'I don't know Max. At least not yet. Get cracking,'* on a mobile phone in the middle of the Indian Ocean a few hours earlier, Routh's criteria had once again been fulfilled. Although they would not know it for another few hours, after eight years of looking they had their first lead on Max Collins.

CHAPTER 8

COLLINS HIMSELF WAS OBLIVIOUS TO THIS. IN HIS TEMPEST-shielded, Chelsea cocoon he felt secure, almost invulnerable. The words so casually uttered by Emerson had not struck him as being significant. It was just a bit of banter between male friends about women. And besides, the advances that had been made by the authorities in voice-scanning were top secret. Even Collins was unaware of the strides that GCHQ had made in that direction, and thus he viewed any voice-calls as being relatively secure.

He was still, of course, extremely security conscious. He knew he was a wanted man, and the ease with which he flitted around undetected within the world's computer systems was a constant concern to the security services. In the years since he had fled Cheltenham he had continued to develop his techniques, and nobody, not the NSA or GCHQ or even James Emerson, his closest friend, was aware of the extent of his capabilities now. He had also amassed a considerable fortune, stolen money of course, but stolen from sources he considered unworthy and therefore justifiable. He was a self-styled, modern-day Robin Hood, stealing from the powerful to protect the vulnerable, but his main currency was information. In his one-man campaign to rein in the power of government and large corporations, he would leak secret information to newspapers, post confidential papers on the internet for all to see, and constantly needle and irk the authorities he despised so much. He would crash their computers on a regular basis, wipe their servers and databases clean, transfer money from government accounts to charities and other worthy sources selected by him, all in the name of personal privacy and freedom from government interference.

At first he had mainly been active in the UK, but before long he had turned his attentions to the United States, where there was so much more to be done and where he perceived the individual to be so much more vulnerable. So although Max Collins and his past were an unknown quantity to the American authorities, as Routh and his cronies had hushed up the significance of his flight to cover up the breakthrough they had made in decryption techniques, Collins's internet alias Cubit, under which he pursued his cyber-terrorism, was very much known to them. The NSA, in particular, would have loved to have a half an hour alone with their tormentor.

But Cubit had a job to do for his friend James Emerson, and he wasted no time in setting about the task. In his antiseptic and chilly inner sanctum, the windowless bunker which housed his computing power beneath the streets of Chelsea, he fired up the bank of processors which would enable him to access the database of the Osakumi Bank in Tokyo. It was to be a classic dial-up hack, and for a man of his abilities, incredibly simple.

He began by searching for the bank's website, as any other internet surfer might do, by using one of the commercial search engines. Once on the site, he looked for the contact phone numbers for the bank, and was pleased to see that, in the spirit of using the web as a marketing tool, plenty were given for all the various departments. He was also pleased to observe that all the numbers had the same three digit prefix, 696-XXXX, differing only in the final four digit extensions, the direct lines to the key individuals mentioned on the bank's website. This meant one thing. In all likelihood, every phone line used by the bank went through the same exchange, and that would probably include the modem lines for the bank's various internet connections. Because those were the numbers he was really looking for. Those were the numbers he would attack in order to gain access to the system.

Most large corporations had very sophisticated internet security, nor-mally in the form of a corporate firewall, a barrier of sorts to discourage intruders, set up around the company's main internet gateway. Typically, however, and despite the best efforts of computer security experts to clamp down on it, there would also be old, so-called dial-up connections, still in operation. They were a legacy of the days before ISDN and other broadband connections that most large companies now used for their employees to access the internet. In a company of ten thousand employees, the chances were that a few of them were still connecting by means of their slow, old modems, forgotten by their IT department, unaudited and unmonitored. And unprotected by the firewall.

Once Collins knew the telephone exchange that Osakumi Bank was using, it would be simply a matter of time to check all ten thousand of the remaining possible four-digit telephone numbers in the hope of finding one that was connected to a modem. He could have picked up the phone and dialled every number in Osaka from 696-0000 to 696-9999, listening to every one for the tell-tale crackling and buzzing of a responding modem. However, he also had a wardialler, a clever piece of software which he had adapted himself from a commercially available product, combined with an extremely powerful piece of equipment which had the dialling power of one hundred phone lines. All this land-based telephony activity was a TEMPEST risk. The phone lines did actually run into his house from the outside, and when connected provided a potential risk from TEMPEST snoopers. But he had devised a clever means of physically severing the connections with the outside world when not necessary, and he always limited his connection times to minimize risk. Used together this set-up would enable him to check all the numbers in less than one hour.

He was lucky. Within ten minutes, his wardialler had hit gold.

Having found an access point to the bank's internal network, the next step was to log on as a *bona fide* user. This meant finding a user ID and a password for one of the bank's employees, and then logging on as if he were they. Finding the user ID would be fairly easy. They were typically not very secure, and allocated to the various users within the company by their IT department. In a large company, with thousands of employees, it was beyond the scope of most system administrators to come up with a different, obscure user ID for every employee, and more often than not they simply used the name, or some variation thereof – last name, first name; first initial, last name; either continuously written or separated by the ubiquitous dots. He had printed out a list of the bank's key employees as advertised on their website, so he had a few names to experiment with. It wasn't long before he had figured out the format: it was last name in lower case, followed by the first initial in upper case, no dots.

That was the easy part. The next obstacle was finding the password for that user. Typically, individual passwords were chosen by the employees themselves and remained unknown to the IT department for security and privacy reasons. Most of these personal passwords, however, were weak in that they were susceptible to guesswork. A lazy employee would not want to choose a long and complicated password, as it takes too long to type in and is easily forgotten. Furthermore, they tended to make the password something personal to themselves, a nickname, a pet's name, the name of a loved one or a significant date. In an incredibly high number of instances, they simply either repeated their user ID as the password, or used another version of their name. In Collins's experience, the more senior the employee, the less secure the password was likely to be as these people tended to be less computer literate and thus less aware of the dangers of intruders.

All the names posted on the bank's website were departmental heads. In a Japanese bank the size of Osakumi, this meant they must have been men in their fifties who were probably more concerned with their golf handicap than the integrity of the bank's computer network.

There were a number of automated password-guessing programs on the market, most of them available for free on the internet. Max Collins was responsible for most of them. Over the last few years he had compiled an amazing variety of them, which allowed the user to specify what language the password was in, even the city of residence and sex of the target, so that the most popular names of sports teams and local landmarks could be included as possible guesses. Also included was a dictionary list of the thirty thousand most common words in whatever language it happened to be in. Shakespeare had got away with writing his plays using a vocabulary of only around three or four thousand words, but most modern college graduates had an active vocabulary in the order of twenty or so thousand. Once the 'guess-list' had been personalized to include the target's name, sex, city of residence, and padded out with the top five hundred personal names in that country along with common nicknames and animal names, to cover the possibility of the password being the name of a spouse, child or favourite pet, the list had probably risen to around thirty-five thousand words. An ordinary home computer could scan through that list in a matter of minutes. Max Collins's rather special little system had gained access in a little under ten seconds.

He was now logged in to Osakumi Bank's internal network in the name of Nobuhiro Ashida, who, according to the bank's public website, was the departmental manager responsible for the accounts of high-net-worth individuals within the entire Osakumi group. His password turned out be KODAKU, which is the Japanese name for one of the Pokémon characters Collins had included in his Japanese 'dictionary' at his most recent update. Mr Ashida must have a young child.

However, despite the seniority of the user he was purporting to be on their system, Collins needed higher, more privileged access in order to gain entry to the files on Tomi Lubis's PC in Osakumi's Jakarta branch office. He needed to be able to masquerade as one of the system administrators. He quickly saw that the bank's operating system was Windows NT, the most widely used corporate operating system in the world, and for most hackers, notoriously difficult to gain privileged access to. But Max Collins was not most hackers. He had hacked NT many times in his career, and had developed a technique whereby he could plant a simple Trojan within the system. This was a latent program of his own design which, when executed, would add a new user to the list of administrators. He would be that new user, with his own user ID and a password chosen by himself. And he would, of course, grant himself unlimited access, 'super-user status'. He would then be able to log on to their system at will and perform all sorts of tasks without anyone knowing. The bank's computer alarm systems would not even register the break-in, as he would be set up within the system as a legitimate user.

Within five minutes of cracking Nobuhiro Ashida's password, Max

Collins had re-logged on as himself, and was reading Tomi Lubis's e-mails and account details from his sleeping computer in Jakarta, whilst Lubis himself was out welcoming in the New Year into the small hours.

The British motorcycle courier on duty at Menwith Hill, Yorkshire on New Year's Eve had not been expecting any work that evening. He had had two beers with his sandwiches at suppertime, courtesy of the American who ran the postroom at the base, and, as midnight approached, the festive atmosphere and camaraderie among the skeleton staff on duty that evening, persuaded him to have a nip or two from the bottle of single malt which was doing the rounds in the office.

When the red alert had come in from Yakima Station in Washington State, the GCHQ liaison officer on duty that night had listened briefly to the digital recording of the conversation between an unknown man, James Emerson, and the man they suspected of being Max Collins, and quickly made a copy on to audio tape for further analysis. The tape had been parcelled up and sent down to the courier station for immediate despatch by courier to GCHQ's Westminster office. If this was Collins, and they suspected it was, then he was capable of anything. For all they knew, he could be tracking their own computers remotely for any references to himself, and if the recording had been digitized and sent down to London by e-mail, Collins could have been alerted.

The courier groaned at the prospect of a three-hour ride down the M1 to London in the dark and pouring rain, but took the parcel and set off at top speed. He made good progress despite the weather, and a little under three hours later was in London and heading down Baker Street towards Westminster, where Gus Routh, called into the office from a party in Knightsbridge, was waiting for him, along with a team of sound technicians.

The biker did not even see the car that hit him. It was a nineteen eighty-five Ford Fiesta which pulled out on to Baker Street, a one way street, against the flow of traffic. There were four seventeen-year-olds in the car, all of whom were drunk and all of whom were killed when they swerved in a futile attempt to miss the oncoming motorcycle, and crashed into the shop window of Marks and Spencer's flagship store. The bike itself flew twenty yards through the air before landing in the same window amongst the mess of broken glass, twisted steel and ladies' underwear.

The courier himself was alive but unconscious when he was removed by the emergency services to St Mary's Hospital in Paddington. His motorcycle and its valuable contents were taken to the nearest police pound for examination.

It was two hours before the motorcyclist's next of kin had been found and informed of the accident, and another hour before the news reached Menwith Hill. From that point it took the GCHQ crew a further hour to track down the location of the bike wreckage, and to secure the necessary authority for one of them to go down to the police pound and remove the tape from the bike's pannier.

Had Gus Routh and his team received the tape four hours earlier, and had they then performed the voiceprint analysis, which compared the unique modulations of the voice on the tape, the frequencies and amplitudes of the sounds made, with the known pattern of Collins's voice held on file, and had they then promptly traced the number called by Emerson to a cell phone registered in the name of one Alex Little at a swish address in Chelsea, then Max Collins would have been at home when a rapid response unit of the Metropolitan Police's Special Branch pulled discreetly up to his front door in two unmarked cars.

As it was, Collins had already finished his work on Tomi Lubis's computer in Jakarta and had gone out at three in the morning on New Year's Day to get himself a self-congratulatory kebab from the kiosk on the Fulham Road. When he rounded the corner to his street, clutching the steaming mound in both hands, chilli sauce dribbling down his fingers and smeared around his lips, he immediately saw the two burly men standing in the shadows of the porch to his house, arms dangling at their sides clasping clearly identifiable weapons. He quickly took in the official-looking cars parked nearby, full of similarly short-haired people, and for the second time in his life, made an instant decision. Just as he had one day in Cheltenham eight years ago when his world had been shattered by the death, under 'friendly fire', of his girlfriend, he now had to disappear again. With remarkable cool he stood there for a while on the street corner, munching his kebab like any other late night drunk in search of grease, and then slowly turned back around the corner before strolling off into another new life and yet another new identity.

As he did so, he pulled out his mobile phone again and dialled a number. When he was connected, he punched in a twelve-digit identification number and hung up. The entire bank of computers in the underground bunker at what he already thought of as his old house whirred into life. Only this time, they were not scanning or sniffing or cracking or denying service to some other computer on the other side of the globe. They were wiping themselves clean and rendering irretrievable any information and all of the ingenious, genius software Collins had spent the last eight years creating and refining.

After ten minutes the computers shut themselves down and ten stainless steel cylinders, each about four inches long and an inch in diameter, clattered down from ceiling pods on to the tiled floor of the computer room. Each one was tightly packed with a mixture of powdered sulphur, aluminium powder and starch, and had a one-inch fuse, already ignited electronically as the last action of a dying computer. They were home-made, but highly effective incendiary devices.

Within twenty minutes, around thirty million dollars' worth of computer equipment and four million pounds' worth of prime London real estate was in the clutches of a high intensity blaze too hot for the fire department to consider tackling until there was very little left worth retrieving.

Whilst waiting for Max Collins's reply to his request for information on Tomi Lubis and Sukon, Emerson had spent the rest of the New Year's Day morning in Jakarta in pursuit of two of his favourite activities: watching television news programmes and having sex.

He had tuned in to CNN again to find more coverage on the secret summit going on in Ireland, and there was still much speculation as to its agenda and the identity of the participants. It was being officially denied by all suspected participating countries that there was any crisis meeting involving finance ministers or central bank chiefs, but the network helicopters still clattered overhead at Ashford Castle and the long lenses of the world's press were still trained on every window of the hotel in the hope of glimpsing a Byron Powell or Dick Brightwell or some other recognizable official. But all windows remained firmly shuttered. The markets had feared the worst on the last trading day of the year, and had all closed sharply lower. There was talk of a US bank, Braxton Federal, being in trouble, but no senior officials of that institution were prepared to comment. Eric Chen, the CEO, was away on vacation and couldn't be reached. In the meantime, the markets, and the world, held their breath until the resumption of trading on the second of January. In the absence of more hard evidence about the summit, the world's media concentrated on the one tangible clue they had.

The photograph of Scott Turner leaning out of his hotel room window, taken by Callum O'Connor, features editor of the *Limerick Leader*, from the loft bedroom in Dorothy Gaskill's bed and breakfast with a borrowed camera, had been syndicated all over the world. Every newswire, TV station, magazine and newspaper had bought it, and O'Connor had made more money from that than he had in all of the previous year. James Emerson was seeing it now for the first time.

It had been digitally enhanced by the news network's imagery wizards to improve upon the slightly out-of-focus, low-resolution image supplied by O'Connor's scratched lens. This process had had the effect of rejuvenating Turner's appearance somewhat, smoothing the lines and the pores, brushing out the blemishes, making him look as he had a few years back. The world's press was screaming to know the identity of that face, and CNN screened the picture above the caption: 'DO YOU KNOW THIS MAN?' together with a phone number to call. *Paris Match* and *Der Spiegel* had apparently joined forces to offer a one hundred thousand dollar reward to anyone who knew who it was and would give them an exclusive.

James Emerson did not need the money, but he knew who it was. At least, he had seen that face before. If only he could put his finger on where, and a name.

His concentration was interrupted by the arrival back into the room of Tamana, who he had despatched to the bedroom to call her sister-in-law and bring her up to speed on their plans to investigate the death of her husband. She crossed the room silently, barefoot on the soft carpet, and nestled in beside him on the sofa. Resting her head on his shoulder she reached across to his lap where the TV's remote control lay. One tiny, slender finger extended to the 'Off' button, and she prodded it gently. Turner's face disappeared from the screen, but the memory of that soft pressure, applied indirectly to his groin area by that one finger, pushed other buttons in Emerson's brain.

'Enough television, *Bapak* James,' she whispered. 'It New Year, and we celebrate.' Her hand still rested on the remote control in his lap, the pressure still applied but now increasing. He shifted position slightly and the control slid from his lap to the floor, but Tamana's hand remained where it had been, the contact now direct and active. She leaned across and kissed him softly on the tip of his nose. 'You save my life, James. And my honour.'

'But there's no need . . .'

'I do not do this to thank you. I not working now. This is for my pleasure, and yours. We have much in common.'

She removed her hand from its probing and placed it on his shoulder, pushing him gently backwards so that he lay supine beside her. She then stood up and allowed her shorts, his outsize shorts that she was still wearing, to slide to the ground. She stepped out of them and reached down to her knees to grasp the lower hem of the polo shirt she had borrowed from his wardrobe and which hung on her frame like a nightdress. In one smooth motion she pulled it over her head and held it aloft, pulled taut between her outstretched arms, and remained thus for a minute, allowing him to peruse and appraise her.

In the few hours since her rescue from the squalid rape scene, stretched over a dustbin in the back streets of Glodok, their status had been gradually equalized. There was no more sense of gratitude or of favours owed. Apart from her initial, reflex outburst when she had first come back to his hotel room, there never had been. She was a selfless, educated woman trying to avenge a lost brother.

In Emerson's loss she sensed a bond, a common factor which united them, even if Emerson himself would not recognize that the death of his brother was still a motivating factor in his life. For he pursued his new career as a journalist with the same obsessive zeal that he had applied to his old job, a zeal that had been prompted and ignited by that death. He liked to think he had been ready for a change, that he would have packed the banking in soon enough anyway. He would concede that, in taking over 'The Emerson Bulletin' when Hugh died, he had been doing his father a favour, but that was as far as he would admit. The rôle was his now, in his own right. Nothing to do with Hugh.

But she knew different. She had seen it in his eyes when he had shared with her his experiences of those few days, the inquest, the funeral, the massive hole in his life. And she heard it in his heart and felt it inside of her when they made love. In her experience, no man acted with such intensity for himself. The passion with which James Emerson was now pursuing every goal in his life was not for himself. But he was not simply doing it as a tribute, *for* Hugh or for his memory; he effectively *was* Hugh. His brother's life had been tragically cut short, and James Emerson was trying, in the only way he could, to complete that life for him.

As they finally lay still, the sweat on their bodies chilling in the blast from the air-conditioning, James Emerson *was* thinking about his brother. But not in the way that Tamana was thinking. For he had remembered. The face. The black face in a black and white photograph peering out from the grey walls of a medieval Irish castle. The face which had filled the TV screen before a girl from the street, but not of it, had turned it off and him on at the same time. He knew where he had seen it before.

He jumped up from the sofa, and walked naked to the phone on the console table. He felt Tamana's eyes watching him move, looking hard at his body, but now he had other things to do. He dialled the familiar number. As he waited for the connection Tamana busied herself tidying up the room. She too was naked, but moved about the room with an utter lack of self-consciousness or embarrassment, neither when bending to pick up the cushions from the floor, nor when stretching to close the blinds to the already darkening skies. It was four in the afternoon, which made it nine in the morning in London. Or more specifically in Dorset, which was still in the same time zone as the capital, even if it didn't seem that way at times. As the phone rang and rang, Emerson imagined the frosty fields stretching out into the distance around his father's house, and the two cracked leather chairs in the study in which they had sat only a week earlier before he had left for Jakarta. It seemed an awfully long time ago. The phone continued to ring, and Emerson suddenly remembered it was New Year's Day. Nine in the morning. His father would probably be in bed with a fierce hangover, or even still out somewhere, having stayed over with friends. Never did leave the message machine on. Still, he knew that if he let it ring long enough, the machine would switch itself on. On the thirtieth ring he was rewarded with his father's voice.

'If you can bear to talk into this infernal device, do me the pleasure of telling me when and why you disturbed me and I will consider returning the compliment. Goodbye.'

'Father, it's James. And the very happiest of New Years. Do you think you could make your message a little more grumpy? You risk not getting the Cantankerous Old Fool of the Year award if you're not careful. Anyway, all is well over here, but I need a bit of a favour. Your brains, if you have any cells left after last night. I know it's painful to go back, but it's rather important. I'm trying to put a name to a face. A face I've only seen once before, and that was at Hugh's funeral. Black chap, quite good looking, thinning hair. I'd rattle on about cheek-bones and jaw line but I don't think Hugh had so many black acquaintances that I need to go any further. Anyway, if a name springs to mind, give me a bell. I'm at the Interconti in Jakarta. Cheerio.'

Then he had another thought. That idiot from the British Embassy here. He said he'd known Hugh at college. If the black face at the funeral was a college acquaintance, surely he'd know who it was? He dug out the crumpled business card he'd been given only two nights before, and looked for a personal number. There was none. Only the direct line in his office, and he'd never be there at this time on New Year's Day. Still, while he was about it, he could at least leave a message on the voicemail so he would get it first thing the next day.

A tinny, synthesized voice, irritatingly sincere, informed him that he had reached the extension of Morley Lafarge.

'Morley, it's James Emerson. Good to see you the other night. Thanks again for dinner. One small question: you mentioned you knew my brother Hugh at college. Did he by chance have any black friends that you are aware of? One that might have come to his funeral? Not terribly PC of me to phrase it that way of course, but I thought you'd probably not mind.'

The jade green angle-poise lamp on Morley Lafarge's desk threw a pool of light over an assortment of scattered papers. The rest of the room was in darkness. Lafarge's plump frame sat back in his chair and replayed the message he had just heard. For he was in his office. He'd gone in to escape the family and to make some long-distance calls. To Bradley and to Blake. He picked up the phone to make the first of those calls.

He was surprised to hear the plummy drawl of Christopher Blake answer Bradley's direct line.

'Morley, good to hear from you. Happy New Year and all that. I'm here because the professor had something of a funny turn the other night. Brookes and I stayed with him all night. He's perfectly fine now. Seems to have slept it off. Probably the stress of everything combined with a drop too much of the sauce. Doesn't remember a thing of it. Now, what gives your end?'

'It's Emerson, Chris. James Emerson. Hugh's brother, you know.'

'How could I forget. He's out your way isn't he? Didn't Bradley tell you what to do?'

'Yes, yes. And I did it. Sent him out into the riots, put him on a wild goose chase at the Finance Ministry, tied him up in enough paperwork to sink a battleship. All that. But he's been asking some difficult questions. Specifically, he wants to know about Scott Turner.'

'Turner? How in hell's name did he find out about Turner?'

'I don't think he knows anything. Yet, at least. I bet he saw that photograph that's all over the media at the moment and the face rang a bell. Possibly from Hugh's funeral.'

'Well it's no big deal, is it?'

'It could be. I mean, he knows *I* knew Hugh, and all of a sudden Turner's face crops up on TV. If he starts digging into his background and comes up with the St Mary's connection, he could find out about Pegasus . . .'

'And what of it? A perfectly respectable dining society. He knows Hugh was in it, anyway. After that bloody inquest, who could forget it? Anyway, he has no idea what we're up to.'

'But you know what he's like! He gets obsessed, man. Once he starts delving, he'll find things. You know he will.'

'So what are you suggesting. You don't want to do a "Hugh" on him, do you? Christ man, do you intend to wipe out the whole bloody family?'

'I may have no alternative. I have a little more to be worried about than the rest of you, you know.'

'Why? Because you drew the short straw at Hugh's little absentee trial? You certainly acquitted yourself admirably. One firm push and over he flew. And you were the obvious choice, after all. What with your cloak and dagger training. Don't they teach you about that sort of thing at Sarrat? Anyway, it was down to you, me or the professor. Dodds and van Aalst would never have gone along with it. They must never know. And as for the Kraut and our Chink friend, well, their sort don't really have the stomach for all that sort of thing. No, you were the only man for the job. But maybe you *are* right. Maybe James should disappear from the scene. We can't jeopardize Pegasus at this stage. We just need that Yank bank to go under for some serious excrement on the old Xpelair.'

'So what are you saying?'

'Morley, my dear, I am saying that if you are worried about your ample neck being on the line for Hugh's death, and that dangerous James is hot on the scent, then you should do whatever you deem necessary to circumvent that eventuality.'

Tamana was standing at the minibar, still naked and fixing them both a drink when Emerson hung up the phone.

'James, your laptop is making noise. Beep-beep! Beep-beep!' she giggled. 'You been sending e-mails or something?'

Emerson suddenly remembered his request to Max Collins for information on Tomi Lubis and Sukon. He'd left the laptop on-line so he would know immediately when Collins replied. He dashed over to the desk and went straight to his e-mail folder. There it was. Or at least, it looked like it. The message header said it came from Cubit, but it was from a different address than usual. He'd also used the Pretty Good Privacy encryption program, an off-the-shelf product which was unusual for a man of Collins's inventiveness. Emerson understood as soon as he read the first line of the message.

James,

This is Max. No time to explain but the Alex Little identity is compromised. Consider him dead. They almost got me too. House gone, address gone, spooks everywhere. I have reserve identity and bolthole set up with emergency facilities. Will send details soonest. Sending this from cyber café for anonymity, as your need sounded urgent. Attached file will give details of Lubis and Sukon. Very dodgy. See for yourself. Included a few frequently called numbers from Lubis's telephone log. Sorry, no time to check out who they're to, you might have to call them yourself.

Best.

Max

Emerson marvelled at his old friend's knack for survival. He knew he was paranoid, but never for a moment thought he would be found, or that he was worried enough to have established an alternative identity. Or even to have maintained an escape route.

Emerson clicked on the attached file, and it opened immediately. On the screen in front of him were details of every single transaction handled on behalf of Sukon by the Osakumi Bank in Jakarta, and the numbers were astounding. That unknown Swiss money manager had, in the course of three weeks, sold the equivalent of four and a half billion dollars' worth of Indonesian rupiah. This was an enormous amount for one client, and an enormous amount even in terms of the size of the Indonesian economy and its money supply. But just as incredible was the fact that a lot of the rupiah sold by Sukon had been borrowed. Tamana's brother Shin hadn't known that of course, because Lubis had arranged the loan with another bank. All Shin had seen as the forex trader was the selling. But the fact that Sukon was borrowing the rupiah meant that they were selling short. Selling something they didn't have. Speculating in massive amounts. And that didn't sound like the activity of a *bona fide*, conservative Swiss money manager. It sounded like Shin had been right. They were acting as an intermediary for another institution, and a hedge fund in the US time zone seemed the most likely candidate.

As well as details of the transactions, Collins had included the basic account information held by Osakumi on Sukon, information normally required by bank regulators when a new account is opened. It gave an address in Geneva, and the names of the directors. F. Charvet, M. Kötzli, C. Blake, G. Langenscheidt. In Emerson's experience of bogus corporations, the so-called 'brass-plate' shell companies set up to conceal the real beneficiaries of banking or investment services for tax purposes, the directors' names meant nothing.

They were normally the names of the lawyers used by the parent company when setting up the company in the foreign jurisdiction, and the same lawyers would have set up hundreds of such companies. Their names appeared on the articles of incorporation of *all* of those companies as directors, but they did very little after the initial incorporation. They wouldn't appreciate the analogy, but they were rather like the witnesses dragged in to make up the numbers at those one-stop wedding chapels in Reno or Las Vegas, only without the red satin curtains. Any enquiry to the law-firm concerned as to the ultimate ownership of the company would merely receive a polite brush-off. Especially in Switzerland. And if the parent company was especially serious about concealing its identity, it would have set up a series of companies, like a nest of Russian dolls, each one owning the next. Anyone wishing to chase up the ultimate owner would have to jump through a lot of hoops and be very determined indeed.

The final files sent by Collins were the phone numbers most frequently called by Lumis. And here Emerson stopped in his tracks. It was not that there were no calls at all to Geneva, nothing with the '41-22' prefix Emerson knew so well from his own days as a bond salesman; nor was it the plethora of international calls to a country with the international dialling code 345, which he did not recognize. It was the number at the bottom of the list. A local number, called six times over a two-day period three weeks ago. A number he recognized.

James Emerson had been known, amongst other, less complimentary nicknames during his time at Steinman, Schwarz, as the walking tele-phone directory. He had never used the speed-diallers built into the phone system as he had known his customers' numbers by heart, he called them so frequently. Even the fax numbers. But he had no need to exercise his prodigious memory in this case. The number was fresh in his mind. It was a number he had called five minutes ago. The direct line to Morley Lafarge, economic attaché at the British Embassy in Jakarta.

CHAPTER 9

KILLING HUGH EMERSON HAD BEEN EASY.

The Pegasus Forum reunion dinner had been a drunken affair, and when, at Bradley's suggestion, they had all climbed the winding stone staircase to the top of St Mary's College gate tower to view the old Fellows' Library, Lafarge had been ready. Hugh had been feeling a bit queasy, and a few of them had gone from the claustrophobic confines of the windowless cell, where the valuable manuscripts were displayed, up on to the roof for some air. Lafarge had looked after Hugh, who had seemed as if he needed the air more than most, and Blake and Bradley had made sure that the others were looking at the view of the Radcliffe Camera on the east side of the tower. Hugh had wanted to vomit, and Lafarge had encouraged him to lean between the low battlements to do it into the square below. Just for a lark.

The parapet wall was shin height, perfect tripwire level. Hugh placed a steadying hand on one of the battlements and poked his head between them for maximum projection. Lafarge moved his own comforting hand to the small of Hugh's back. There, there. Better out than in. Come on now, Hugh. One last heave. And he had done it. A smart shove, so easy. So clean.

The scene in the square below was not so clean, as Emerson junior and the last contents of his stomach had hit the ground at the same time. Who had proved that would happen? Was it Newton? Or maybe it was Galileo? Anyway, something to do with diced carrots and human bodies falling at the same rate. More colourful than cannon balls and feathers. Lafarge had been pleased with himself. No hint of suspicion, just a bit of feigned shock to satisfy the authorities and the other members of the Forum, and it was all over. A shame really, as Hugh had been so good at his job. His press coverage of the crisis would have been a marvellously potent tool, if only he hadn't got all moral on them. It was ultimately Bradley's fault, he felt. He hadn't done his homework well enough when he had recruited Hugh. Although he could probably be forgiven for that. Nobody could have known that his commitment to the cause would have stopped short at bankrupting a few rotten countries.

As he sat in his darkened office on that first day of January, Lafarge knew it would be more difficult to take care of Hugh's big brother. But he still had the element of surprise on his side. And he was on 'home' turf.

When Jake Samuels, editor of the *Gazette*, called his roving reporter in Jakarta later that same day, he found him in the bath. Tamana knelt beside the tub, soaping his back, and passed him the phone.

'James! It's Jake. How goes it? Any dirt for us to print yet?'

'Nothing in writing, Jake, but I've got a good angle.' He looked at Tamana.

'Can't say too much right now, but you'll have some copy soon.'

'Well don't leave it too long, James, or we'll have nothing left to report on. This thing is getting really ugly, really quickly. There's a German bank gone already, and talk of Braxton Federal in the States being in trouble.'

'I know, I know, Jake. But that'll only be the beginning if it really gets out of hand. You should see the civil unrest here. It's anarchy on the streets. If things go as badly back home, we'll have the same problem.'

'Well don't forget to use the embassy, if you need them. You should let them know you're there anyway. Can't be too careful. Rioting and all that.'

'Actually, you just reminded me of something. They seemed to know I was here already. Did you tell them?'

'Not I, James.'

'Maybe your secretary did, when she booked the tickets?'

'No. Definitely not. It's not policy. If we're dropping someone into a war zone, then we do inform the FO, but always on my instructions. Besides, things weren't as bad when you left as they are now. I didn't think it necessary.'

'So who else knew I was coming?'

'Nobody, James. Just me and Emma. And whoever you told.'

'Well you didn't leave me much time to tell anyone, did you? I just told Dad.'

'Oh hang on a sec. I remember now. I mentioned it to our silk. You know, Chris Blake. He's the one who keeps you out of jail and our newspaper in business from time to time. You should get to know him one day.'

'Well the embassy here knew somehow. And they didn't find out from the flight manifests. Still, it's probably nothing.'

Emerson thought hard. He'd completely forgotten about Lafarge's lie over dinner a couple of nights ago. He had said he had got Emerson's arrival details from the airline. It had seemed insignificant then, just confirmation of Lafarge's general slipperiness. But now that Max Collins had found a connection between Lubis and Lafarge, the embassy official's lie took on greater meaning.

He handed the phone back to Tamana who replaced it in the cradle by the washbasin.

'What's wrong, James? You seem worried.'

'No, no. Not worried. Just thinking. Get some clothes on. Your stuff from the other night's been laundered. It's hanging in my wardrobe. We're going out to dinner.'

It was the first time Emerson and Tamana had set foot outside the hotel since he had saved her in Glodok forty-eight hours earlier. The New Year had arrived, and with it there were renewed scenes of violence on the streets. The intensity of feeling and fighting he had witnessed in the Chinese quarter had clearly spread across town now, and it was mostly centred around the banks. The first business day of the New Year would begin in a few hours, and enormous crowds of people had already formed around the doors and ATM machines on the streets. As the couple drove across town in a taxi, they saw armoured personnel carriers patrolling the main thoroughfares and trucks with water cannon prowling the back streets. The riot police had given way to the regular army, and troops toting automatic weapons as well as tear-gas grenade launchers were everywhere in a high-profile presence. Emerson doubted the banks would dare open the next day, as the vaults would be stripped bare of the little they had left in a few hours, and there would still be millions of people insisting on getting their money. In fact, he was right. The President had already privately ordered the banks not to open, and the new military presence was in readiness for the fury of the mob when the news filtered out. Diesel fumes hung heavy in the air from the military vehicles, although the streets seemed lighter of civilian traffic that night. Fear, and a siege mentality appeared to be descending on the city.

Emerson told the taxi driver to stop briefly at Tamana's apartment, and she ran in to pick up a few extra clothes and a photograph of her brother Shin that James had asked for. Then they carried on to the restaurant.

They had no reservation, but at the Café Batavia it was early enough for that not to be a problem. In fact, at that hour they were just about the only diners, but Emerson wasn't really interested in food.

'James, this is very expensive, you know. You are very kind to me.'

'Well, I'll be honest, sweetheart, I'm really coming here for some information. Now, look at the menu, and give me the picture of your brother.'

Emerson took the photograph and wandered over to the bar area. The bartender was not the same one who had been working when he had dinner with Morley Lafarge a couple of nights ago, but he folded a couple of large-denomination bills into the palm of his hand and approached the man who was busy polishing glasses and arranging bottles of liqueurs.

Emerson placed the photo on the bar, and cleared his throat.

'What you like, *Bapak*?' said the barman, without turning around or looking at his customer.

'Information. The man in this picture. Have you seen him in here?

He came in three weeks ago, on December twelfth. Were you working that night?'

'Can't say.' The man didn't look at the picture. Emerson demonstratively unfolded one of the bills and placed it on the bar. It was a fifty-thousand rupiah note, the largest in circulation. A month's salary for this man. Two weeks previously, when the exchange rate was about five hundred rupiah to the dollar, it would have been worth the equivalent of one hundred dollars; today, with the exchange rate hovering around fifteen thousand, it was worth around three. The face of former President Suharto smiled up from the bill, with the motto 'Father of Indonesian Development' emblazoned proudly beneath. The barman glanced back briefly to see what was on offer, but did not seem impressed. Emerson unfolded another bill of the same size, and placed it next to the other one. This was one of the new ones. No picture of Suharto, just a portrait of the writer of the national anthem. The barman turned around, pocketed the new note, took the old one and tore it in two.

'Our money not worth much, *Bapak*, these days. But *this*,' and he brandished the torn halves of the old note, '*this* is worth nothing.' And with that he threw it in the ashtray. Then he took up the photo of Shin and looked at it closely.

'*Cina*? Chinese, *Bapak*? No. I know no Chinese shit.'

'Japanese, you greasy fucker. Japanese. And he's dead. So you'd better help me or there could be trouble.' Emerson had found long ago, when after information, it did no harm to behave like a policeman. He never actually claimed to be one, but people tended to infer it.

'*Jepang*? Sorry, *Bapak*. Sorry. I not working that night. Maybe you ask Maître Dee or band. Sorry, no help.'

The band were setting up their equipment in the corner. It was the same band, Moe's Batak Stompers, who had played the other night, so maybe they were a regular fixture. He walked over to the leader, the short wiry one in the outsize tuxedo and wispy moustache who looked like an Asian Sammy Davis Jr. He showed him the photo and immediately the old man's face creased into an enormous grin. He began nodding enthusiastically.

'Yes! Yes! Me remember! Him come in here before Christmas. Very nice, very nice. Me remember, he love music. He come over and make request. Me remember. He ask for "Me jolly good friend milk-man". You know, *Bapak*? Fats Wally? He cool cat. He tinkle ivories somethin' bad.'

'Yes, yes, of course. But how can you be so sure it was him?'

'He speak Batak dialect, *Bapak*. Batak. We Batak people. Good singers. We love to sing. Very rare, *Bapak*, very rare you find China-boy speak Batak. Me very happy. Me remember. Me remember everything!'

'And do you remember who he was with? It was a business dinner. He was here with two other people.'

'Yes, *inggris*, me remember. One guy, short, no hair. Him look like Dizzy. Big cheeks. No tip when hat come round. Me notice.' This was Tomi Lubis. Tamana had given him a rough description.

'And the other?'

'De other guy? You know de other guy, *inggris*.'

'What do you mean?'

'Me remember everyone in here, chief. Me remember you. You in here few days back. You like music, see it in your eyes. Cool dude. You like it all. Nina Simone, Johnny Mathis, the greats.'

'Yes, I was here, but so what?'

'Other guy, with you that night. Another *inggris*. He no hair neither. And fat. He come here often. "God Save da Queen". Me play that when he come in.'

'I remember. What of it?'

'He with China-boy that night too. Jammin' on down, he was. He groove with chicks at the bar. We sing "play dat funky music, white boy!"'

Emerson could have kissed him. Instead he pressed a wad of huge notes into his hand and requested a song. Now he knew his suspicions were on the button. The man Tomi Lubis had presented to Shin as the client from Sukon, the man who just happened to be in Jakarta at the time Shin got fired, re-employed and then dead, was none other than Morley Lafarge.

Why on earth was a senior official from Her Majesty's mission in

Jakarta running around pretending to be a Swiss fund manager? The whole thing stank even more than Moe's breath, but he was on the brink of a great story. As he walked back to the table, Moe's Batak Stompers started up their set with 'Pennies from Heaven'.

Wallace Bradley awoke on the first trading day of the New Year with no recollection of his experiences of the night before. Blake and Brookes, who had stayed with him all night, told him everything that had happened, but he offered no explanations for his ramblings in Greek or the reference to Poseidon. He put it down to too much alcohol, and brought the conversation back to the matters they had intended to discuss the night before. It was a status report of the current situation, and the timetable for the next phase of their plan.

Bradley began: 'The rate of contagion in the Asian region pleases me. It far exceeds my own expectations and means we can proceed to the next step without delay.'

'I'm glad to hear it, Professor. In fact, I believe that Annie has already begun the groundwork for the US market.' Daniel Brookes opened his briefcase.

'Have you chosen the target?'

'Yes. It's to be Braxton Federal.'

'Really? You surprise me. It's a larger bank than I anticipated. Is it really necessary? Given the panic in the markets currently, I would have thought a run on a smaller bank would be both easier to achieve and sufficient to cause a stampede on the rest.'

'Yes, Brookes. What do you have to say to that. It seems to me the professor is right. Aren't the risks of going for a bank the size of Braxton not only too great, but superfluous?' Blake butted in.

Danny Brookes had always been irritated by Blake, especially his habit of taking whatever the last speaker had said and rephrasing it in his own words, as if he had thought of it. Still, he bit his lip and made his speech.

'We have to aim big, Chris. Just because of the structure of the US banking set-up. This is different to the Löwen-Krugman attack. They were relatively small by comparison, and we saw what happened there. We were flexing our muscles and sowing the seeds of doubt in the minds of the world as to the stability of the banks. They went under, but they were too small to take others with them. It was very important for us nonetheless, as it symbolized the reality of the Asian problem infecting a major institution in the West, and very quickly and directly. They were small enough for us to be able to bring them down virtually on day one. A nice power play. But what we want to do in this stage of the process is go for a whole system, not just one bank.'

'So what is the difference?'

'The difference is the FDIC. They're huge.'

'The what?'

'The FDIC. Government insurance of depositors' money. If you have up to a hundred grand in a US bank, you're protected, even if the whole bank goes under.'

'So how can we get around this?'

'Well, they operate on the basis of any other insurance company. They can afford to make pay-outs as long as everyone doesn't claim at the same time. There are around eight and a half thousand banks in the United States, many of them small. In 1988, *two hundred* of them failed. In 1989, slightly more than that. But the FDIC was able to cover everyone who held money there. There was turbulence in the markets but no mass panic. For our purposes, an attack on a small or even medium-sized bank just won't get the psychological effect we want to achieve. Small banks go bust over there all the time. In fact, since the FDIC was formed in the thirties there have been just over *two thousand* bank failures. They've been paying out money at an average of eleven million *a day* for over sixty years, and they're still in business.'

'How is that possible. Forgive my ignorance, Danny, but the intricacies of the accounting profession do elude me.' Blake was condescending as ever, even when confessing to ignorance.

'It's not intricate, Chris. The government gave them a load more money. For each of the eight years between eighty-four and ninety-two the FDIC actually paid out more in claims than they received in premiums. Now any insurance company can have that sort of cash-flow shortfall occasionally, but not *eight years in a row*! They were technically insolvent at one point, but as I said, the government recapitalized them.'

'So what is to stop them doing that this time? Can't the Federal Reserve just cough some more up from its phlegmatic coffers and keep everyone happy?'

'Not any more. In 1991 a law was passed. The FDIC Improvement Act. It effectively stopped the Fed from lending money to banks in trouble. And it helps us out enormously.'

'Couldn't they just change the law again? Emergency measures and so forth?'

'You lawyers always have a nose for business, don't you? Well yes, I suppose, it is technically possible, but doubtful. The political will isn't there at the moment. They've had ten consecutive years of economic boom there. If the banks aren't in good shape after a run like that, I can't imagine Capitol Hill will have the stomach to step in. And besides, this time we won't be talking small banks. Braxton is big stuff. It's bound to take some others lower down the food chain with it.'

'So what are the numbers, Daniel?' Bradley interjected.

'Well, the current reserves of the FDIC stand at around twenty-eight billion dollars. Simply put, Braxton Federal has eligible, insured customer deposits of around thirty billion. If we can cause a bank of Braxton's size to fail, we would exhaust the reserves of the FDIC in one fell swoop. The confidence of individual depositors in other institutions would be shot to pieces, because they would know that, if another bank failed, the FDIC would have no more money to repay those depositors. And if a bank like Braxton could fail, why shouldn't another, even larger one go the same way?'

'It's mass psychology, Christopher. Provoke hysterical herd behaviour in an industry, the banking industry, in which the participants are already so closely interlinked, and you have a lethal cocktail, the recipe for chaos.' Bradley was in his element. 'Anyone who invests in markets knows they are taking a risk of some kind – interest rate risk, market risk, credit risk and many others. But one sort of risk is strangely neglected – systemic risk, the risk that the whole *system* will implode. In most other businesses, if one company fails, its competitors will likely benefit. The banking industry, however, is unique in its structure. A major loss or failure by one bank can quickly spill over to other banks, so intertwined is the system with itself. Banks deposit money with each other, and borrow money from each other, all the time. Any default on a loan will be quickly passed on down the line.'

'But aren't the authorities aware of this? Surely measures are taken to ensure . . .'

'Exactly! Because of this inherent fragility in the system, the banking industry is probably the most highly regulated industry in the world. But that regulation is deeply flawed. In my view, and the world will see before long that I am right, the system of regulation and explicit government support for the banks actually increases the fragility of the system. With the support of a cheap government safety-net, banks are effectively encouraged to take *more* risk and to operate at *higher* leverage. And ironically, despite this increased risk, the clients of the banks feel safer, better protected.

'But there is more. The system of regulation, such as it is, is dangerously fragmented. We have a *global* financial market, my friend, which never closes and through which the money sloshes around at breakneck speed more or less without barriers. But we have no global policemen. There are very few organizations with the power to legislate beyond their own borders, and there are quite simply too many nations, too many vested interests and too many politicians ever to agree on a coherent policy for a universal code of supervision and regulation.'

'Sounds like an uneven battle to me.'

'Oh it is. The odds are heavily stacked in our favour. Even if we were to be exposed, I'm not sure there is much the authorities could do about it now. At least not after Braxton. The banks are the linchpin, the glue, the facilitators, the conduits for the flows of which we speak. Weaken the American banking system and we will have achieved our goal.'

Bradley closed his eyes as he finished his speech. For now he was thinking of something else, his own personal goal, and he would soon be in sight of the ultimate prize. Because he did not merely want to break the banks. Oh, that was the story for the rest of his team, and they swallowed it. They *wanted* it. But he, Professor Wallace Bradley, wanted more than that. Bradley was going to bankrupt an entire nation.

There was a country, a country not that much less significant than the United States in economic terms, but much more vulnerable. It too had had an economic miracle, but that had been ten years ago. Right now it was mired in the deepest recession in its post-war history, and showed no signs of recovery. This was the real reason Bradley had chosen to activate the Pegasus Forum. He had to hit now, as the victim would be too weak to respond. Saddled with debt, more debt than it had ever had, its government could simply not afford to spend more on a bail-out of the banks. For years it had been the world's greatest lender, lending huge sums all over the world, financing the deficits in other great economies around the world, but now, in the midst of this debt crisis sparked by Bradley and his cohorts, it would buckle at the knees when those countries could not repay those loans. They were the rich uncle of the region, and had lent more to the likes of Korea, Indonesia, Malaysia and the Philippines than any other nation. The government of that nation had done it and its banks had done it at their government's urging. As he liked to repeat again and again to his protégés, they were all in it up to their necks.

Bradley opened his eyes and stared at the Samurai sword, now back in its spot on the wall. It was a fearsome weapon, an instrument of war, and in Bradley's eyes he was waging a war. An economic war. And in an economic war, he was the ultimate weapons expert. Exchange rates, balance of payments, debt-service ratios, he had a mastery of them all. But above all he was a master of the ultimate payload, the nuclear warhead in the financial warrior's arsenal: *confidence*. Money wasn't worth a thing if the credibility of the validating authority was undermined. Currency used to be backed by gold, actual ingots held in reserve which could theoretically be claimed in exchange for the paper money that was so much lighter to carry around. But that had been abandoned long ago.

Nowadays the system of money being accepted in exchange for goods only worked if the vendor of those goods *believed* in the money. The Bank of England promised to pay the bearer of its notes on demand, what? Gold? No. There was not enough to go round. Securities? Well they were just more paper, just as worthless as the rest!

But it was not the Bank of England Bradley wanted to bring down, nor the *bank* of anywhere. He wanted to bring down Japan.

Japan would finally pay for the crimes it committed, long ago, during the war. Japan would pay for the actions of one man in particular. The man who had destroyed his mother. The man who had beaten and raped and sodomized and humiliated and tortured and starved the only woman in his life for whom he had ever felt anything. And he, Wallace Bradley, was finally in a position to do something about it. The sixteen-year-old boy who had discovered the truth about his mother's past all those years ago, a boy on the brink of adulthood who had become the man of the house overnight, had wanted revenge. It had driven his entire life from that point onwards, but he had always been maddened by his impotence in the face of forces much greater than his own. Now he had finally amassed the power, intellectual power, which would enable him to fulfil that boyhood vendetta.

'Professor? Professor? Are you all right?' Brookes was concerned that Bradley was going into another of his trances. He had been silent for a few minutes.

'Excuse me, gentlemen. I was elsewhere. Yes, fine. Braxton. Braxton sounds excellent. Someone must let me know when things get under way and I will continue to direct from there. The UK must be next, and then France. Any news from Turner yet? That summit must be nearly over by now. It will be amusing to know how the authorities are going to react to our little crisis.'

CHAPTER 10

BRADLEY WAS RIGHT. THE SUMMIT HAD COME TO AN END AND Scott Turner was delighted. He wanted to get the news to both Bradley and van Aalst as soon as possible, but he had to wait until they had all been escorted off the premises at Ashford and the communications curfew had been lifted.

The governments of the world were still insistent on playing the charade that nobody knew they were there, and so everyone in turn, from senior finance ministers down to lowly officials waited their turn to stand in line in the hotel's great hall until their name was called. They were then escorted to the door, where a temporary dark-green canvas awning had been erected, allowing the dignitaries to board their shuttered limousines away from the eyes of the world's media. There was a similar procedure to be followed at Shannon Airport, and from there the various planes scattered to their home destinations, unpestered by the press. Apart from that one picture of Scott Turner, who had been identified to *Der Spiegel* by a very happy former room-mate at Stanford, now one hundred thousand dollars richer, and an alleged but unconfirmed sighting of Byron Powell, Chairman of the Federal Reserve, reported in the local press, the publicity black-out had been complete. Or so they thought.

With the security forces focusing on the helicopters of CNN and Sky News, and with the NSA and GCHQ making sure that no unauthorized transmissions were made from within the castle, nobody had reckoned with the bow-and-arrow wiles and local knowledge of Callum O'Connor of the *Limerick Leader*.

Flushed with his success in gaining the only scoop of the summit so

far, he had become something of a local celebrity, but he was determined
to build on his advantage. He had paid his cousin Fergal O'Shaughnessy
well for the information received, and since security had tightened around
Cong and the castle as the summit got into full swing, O'Connor had
given up his hideaway at Dorothy Gaskill's bed and breakfast and spent
most of the following three days holed up with the airport security guard
in his cabin on the airport's perimeter fence, awaiting the return of the
VIPs and plotting his next move. That was three days of instant coffee,
Bushmills whiskey and talk of the stock markets and Pulitzer Prizes.

When it was radioed ahead by the Garda that the cavalcade of black
Chevy Suburbans ferrying the US delegation was approaching, the
Irishmen's plan swung into action. O'Shaughnessy was the security
consultant. He had witnessed the arrival and had watched plenty of
Mace Neufeld films. He knew the protocol. Security people in the first
car, most senior VIPs in the next one. That was how it had been on the
way in, and he reckoned they wouldn't change the order on the way back.
Byron Powell and Dick Brightwell would be in the second car and that
was their target. O'Shaughnessy opened the gates to allow the motorcade
in and stood firmly in the way. As the first car approached, it slowed to
a snail's pace to avoid running the security guard down. He stood back
to allow it past, and as it crawled by he rapped it sharply on the roof
twice. This was intended to be the universal signal: 'You're in the clear.
Off you go.' It also created a precedent for the following drivers. As the
next car, their car, approached, he did the same thing. Two sharp raps
on the roof. Only this time he left them with a gift.

Fergal O'Shaughnessy had seven children, and as the Chairman of
the Federal Reserve and the US Treasury Secretary sped away from the
security cabin on the final leg of their trip to the waiting C-5 Galaxy,
they were completely unconcerned with his paternal expertise. But they
should have been, for suction-cupped to the roof of their car he had left
a battery-powered baby-monitor.

Now these devices only had a useful range of about twenty yards, and
the journey to the aircraft was over half a mile. To overcome this problem,
Callum O'Connor, the scent of glory in his nostrils and acceptance

speeches already written, had commandeered, with O'Shaughnessy's help, one of the airport's baggage-handling trucks. He had been parked alongside the security cabin, gunning the engine, and as Powell's car had pulled on to airport territory and accelerated off towards the plane, O'Connor had followed, orange lights flashing, driving a parallel course at the limit of his home-spun listening-device's capabilities. He had the parental receiver wedged on the passenger seat beside him, turned up to full volume, and his ace-reporter's dictating machine was lashed to it with duct tape. They bounced around over the tarmac, but no matter how much they bounced, the tape recorder remained firmly glued to the receiver, picking up every word that was spoken inside that car. This was analogue recording at its most crude. But no one, neither the rest of the world's press, with their high-resolution lenses and parabolic microphones, nor the NSA with their frequency jammers and circling satellites, was even close to getting the results of those two Irishmen that day.

After they had watched the gigantic aircraft heave itself into the sky and point itself in the direction of the setting sun, O'Connor and O'Shaughnessy regrouped in the cabin and huddled around the table. With bated breath the dictating machine was produced and placed between them. The rewind seemed to take an age, but finally it was ready.

Initially there was a great deal of noise, and some folk tunes from a local radio station O'Connor had been listening to whilst he waited for the motorcade to arrive. Then the music was silent, and all that could be heard was the truck's engine ticking over, with the occasional surge of revs to prevent it stalling in the freezing January temperatures. Then came a muffled banging noise and some static, as O'Shaughnessy had stuck the transmitter to the roof of Powell's car, and then gold. It was astonishingly clear, given the conditions, and neither man could believe what he heard. It went as follows:

'Can you finally put that fucking cigar out? I'm dying in here.'

'Listen, Powell. Shut the fuck up. We'll be on the plane in a minute. And you can be sure of one thing at least. Read my lips. We won't be travelling together again. I mean, you're the new boy, but you ain't gonna last. How the hell can you recommend to these guys that we let the banks go?'

'There is simply no alternative, Dick. We can't afford to do otherwise.'

'So you're gonna recommend to the President that we don't intervene? Am I right? You, the guardian of the nation's banks are gonna hold up your hands and say "too bad, guys"?'

'That's right. That's my job. Unless you want to bankrupt the nation. It could come to that you know. But if we let them go, and the worst of them go under, we'll come out healthier in the end. You don't have an election to worry about for three years. It'll be all over by then.'

'Jeez, I can't believe we're gonna do this.'

'You heard what Turner said. The situation is too severe. And if we bail 'em out we'll be breaking the law.'

'Yeah, but we make the laws. We can make a new one.'

'And then we'll be back to the eighties again. Do you want to preside over a massive budget deficit? Back to the bad ole days? And the other countries are all on board. No one can afford to throw good money after bad. Only the French want out, but the EC won't let 'em. It's gonna be carnage for a while, but we'll survive.'

'Well I'm glad I'm not the one who's gotta tell the President. And I bank with Braxton in Palm Beach, for Christ's sake. Turner said they're one of the shakiest, didn't he? I'm closing my accounts as soon as we get home. Move it offshore somewhere.'

'There may not be anywhere safe to move it to, Secretary.'

Then a lot of static and bumping noise indicated that the car had entered the nose cone of the aircraft and the signal went dead as O'Connor's car peeled away from the Galaxy and headed back to the perimeter fence.

'Holy Mother of God. Would you listen to that!' O'Shaughnessy gasped. 'We've done it, Callum. We've only gone and fuckin' well done it!'

'This is it Fergal. This is the big one. Guard that tape with your life! We are in business. If the papers were prepared to pay up for that snap of the black guy, think what they'll pay for this! We'll make thousands.

Thousands! I'll get a job on the *Times*. Or maybe I'll go freelance! I'll need an agent . . .'

'Better make sure they pay you in cash, Callum. Cause judgin' by what yer man was sayin', cheques aren't gonna be worth nothing.'

'I'll tell you something else for nothing, Fergal. If they really go ahead and do this, cash ain't gonna be worth nothing neither . . .'

James Emerson had been struggling to get his head around it. Lubis and Lafarge had got Tamana's brother Shin to go to dinner. Lafarge was masquerading as a client, and Lubis was probably on some sort of kickback from Sukon to keep everything kosher within Osakumi Bank. That night, Shin ends up dead, having allegedly committed suicide from the highest point in Jakarta. Not bad for a man terrified of heights. And why would he have committed suicide? The bank said he had racked up huge losses and was concealing them. But according to Tamana, he wasn't too worried about the losses. The markets were in freefall and *everyone* was losing money hand over fist. And besides, his boss had just offered him his job back after firing him the day before, so Shin can't have been worried that the bank was displeased with his performance. No. It had to be related to Sukon. Shin had threatened to report their activity to the authorities as suspicious, and Lubis had gone berserk. Fired him on the spot. Then all of a sudden, second thoughts. Invited him back to the firm, and arranged a meeting with the 'suspicious' client to smooth things over. Why the sudden change of heart? Lubis had spoken to Lafarge. Collins's e-mail detailed three calls to his number on that day. Lafarge must have realized that Shin, as a disgruntled *former* employee, was just as dangerous, if not more dangerous to whatever scam they had going. He would still have been able to go to the authorities, and in fact it would probably have looked worse for Osakumi and Sukon if it had then come out that Shin had been fired for being a responsible corporate citizen.

So how could they have shut him up? Short of taking him into whatever the scam was, and that was by no means reliable, not to mention subject to blackmail attempts in the future, they had had to shut him up permanently. And that is what they must have done. But why was Lafarge, an embassy official, involved in something so murky?

Could the British Government be behind Sukon? Could they be secretly selling out of huge government holdings in the Indonesian rupiah at the worst possible time for the markets, and trying to keep it quiet? It seemed unlikely, but that was the best idea he had at this stage. He had to find out more about Sukon. He had to chase down the ultimate owners. But for that he would need the skills of Max Collins, and Collins was temporarily out of commission until he heard from him again.

He glanced again down the few details on Sukon that had been held on Osakumi's client records. There wasn't much, really, just an address and a telephone number. Of the four directors listed, one did not include a telephone number. C. Blake. Now, hadn't he heard that name somewhere recently? Common enough name, of course, Blake. But still. He didn't like coincidences of that sort. Where had he heard it? Who had mentioned it to him? He ran through a mental list of all the people he had talked to in the last two days. It wasn't many. He'd been holed up with Tamana for much of that time. And then he got it.

'Oh yes. I remember now, I mentioned it to our silk. You know, Chris Blake. He's the one who keeps you out of jail and our newspaper in business from time to time.' Jake Samuels's words to him yesterday. Not only had he referred to a Blake, but to a C. Blake, and that Blake was also a lawyer. If it was the same C. Blake, surely he could help them out with some information on Sukon. If he was lawyer to the *Gazette*, Samuels would be able to get him to help him. He should call him.

But then something struck him. It *was* Jake Samuels who had mentioned a Blake, but in the context of people who had known about Emerson going to Jakarta. Blake was the only other person who knew. Maybe it was Blake who had told Lafarge about Emerson's trip? In which case, it meant that Blake was not just some faceless lawyer used by Lafarge to set up an offshore tax vehicle, but that he was actually involved with whatever Lafarge was up to out here.

*   *   *

Morley Lafarge was glad to hear from Emerson, as it saved him the bother of arranging a meet himself. Emerson had suggested a rendezvous in Merdeka Square, right in the centre of Jakarta and the site of the Monas, the National Monument from which Shin had taken his fall. This was not ideal for Lafarge, as he had his own plans for engineering Emerson's death, but he was certain he would be able to manoeuvre things to suit him.

Merdeka Square is enormous, one square kilometre of baked, down-trodden grass offering scant opportunity for a murder. Unless, mused Lafarge, you happen to be one hundred and thirty-seven metres above it at the top of the Monas with a drugged foreign exchange trader. He smiled at the memory. So easy. Easier even than Hugh. Now for the brother.

James Emerson would be the third death chalked up to the Pegasus Forum, the fourth if you included Chumsai in Bangkok. Or around the two hundredth, if you included the dozens killed by rioters, looters and arsonists, not to mention government forces, during the street fights, demonstrations and mass hysteria in the capitals of the South East Asian nations during the last few weeks. There had been over sixty deaths, mainly Chinese, in Jakarta alone. But where did you stop counting? Did you include the Jews who had been torched to death in the synagogue in Munich following reprisals by Neo-Nazis over the failure of Bankhaus Löwen-Krugman? Or the crazy American who pulled a gun and shot the sales clerk in the fashion boutique where his Braxton Federal Visa card had just been refused? One more death would surely not make much of a difference. But it was an important one. Emerson appeared to be on the trail, and he could screw up the whole thing if he did it quickly enough. How much did he actually know? How much had he put together? He might even be able to reverse the crisis if he exposed them now.

But not after Braxton. Braxton was key. Nothing could stop it then. The dam would be well and truly broached. Nothing would be able to stop the tidal wave, the mega-tsunami, engulfing everything until the waters had levelled themselves out around the world. A little redistribution of liquidity. That is what Lafarge craved.

He knew Braxton's fall must be imminent, and that would be the point of no return. But he could not risk leaving it. He could not run the risk of Emerson finding out and ruining everything. They were so close to achieving all they had set out to achieve. He simply had to die, and today.

They had arranged to meet at the entrance to the Monas on the south side of the massive tower. There were thousands of people in the square, and the military presence was considerable. Merdeka Square had always been a focal point for demonstrators during times of unrest, which in recent Indonesian history had been plentiful. It was a natural place of assembly, and the National Monument in the middle and the Presidential Palace on the north side of the square were irresistible magnets for protestors against the system. The banks had failed to open that day, the first business day of the year, and the people were venting their spleen. Their savings, what little was left by now, were inaccessible. Food prices had trebled in a week, and all over Indonesia, even in Jakarta itself, the fifth most populous city in the world, there was a real danger of people starving to death. There was chanting and banners and isolated brawls amongst the protestors, which the soldiers attempted to break up with batons and heavy boots. There was much burning of flags, mainly American, in protest at their lack of support for an IMF relief programme to such a corrupt nation. Lafarge battled his way through the crowds, and found Emerson waiting for him at the doors to the monument's interior lift.

'James, so good to see you! We couldn't have chosen a worse place to meet.' He had to shout to make himself heard.

'You're right, Lafarge. Let's get out of here.' He looked around, but the crowd completely filled the square. Half a kilometre in all directions was a sea of ugly, scowling faces and fanatical chanting. He looked up, and saw the massive gold-tipped torch of the Monas. 'Let's go up there. At least we'll be able to hear ourselves think.' The two men paid their entrance fee, and rode in the lift to the very top of the tower, emerging on to the viewing platform high above the square. The scene of Shin's death.

It crossed Lafarge's mind that maybe he could manage a repeat performance with Emerson, but dismissed the idea just as quickly. Emerson was bigger than he, and undoubtedly stronger. If it came to a struggle, he would definitely come out worse off. Shin had been different. He had been doped up to the gills and scarcely capable of standing. And he had had Tomi Lubis to help bundle him over the retaining wall. Strictly speaking he shouldn't have involved Lubis with that. No outsiders were to be privy to the Pegasus activities, but then Shin's death had not been sanctioned by Bradley or Blake. In fact, they didn't even know about it. It had been his own enterprise. And besides, Lafarge didn't want them to know about the problem at Osakumi. After all, he had chosen the bank, and Lubis, as the ideal conduit for Xenfin's foreign exchange dealing. He had recommended it to the Forum and they had gone with it. He would have been criticized, maybe even thrown out of the group, if they realized he had made such an error of judgement. He just had not reckoned on coming up against Shin, probably the only ethical trader in the whole of the Jakarta foreign exchange market.

'Been up here before, Morley?' Emerson asked casually.

'Only once. Not that keen on sightseeing actually. Not my bag.'

'Hell of a way down. Gives me the willies. Terrific view though, through all the smog. Must be spectacular at night.'

'Yes. I suppose it must.'

'Tell me, did you get my message this morning? Left a message on your voicemail last night.'

'Ah, yes. Sorry, quite forgot to call back. You were asking about Hugh's funeral. Something about having seen some black there and wondering who it was.'

'That's it. Thought maybe it was someone from Hugh's college days. Wondered if you might have an idea who it was.'

'Well I'm sorry, James. I can't help you. You see I wasn't at the funeral myself. I'd had to leave Oxford rather quickly. Pressing business at the FO in London. And to my recollection, there were no blacks at St Mary's during our time there. No males at least. Maybe it was a friend from the *Gazette*? Or a reporter himself? The tragedy was covered quite extensively, I seem to remember, in the local and the national press.'

'Yes, I seem to remember that too. Funny. Well thanks anyway. It was a bit of a long shot anyway.'

But Emerson already had his answers. In his former life as a salesman he had been the master of getting his clients to volunteer information. Every salesman thrives on information about their clients, their opinions, their likes and dislikes, their activities. And Emerson would store every little nugget away. Any remark, no matter how casual, could potentially be used in making a sale in the future. Information gave him a hook, something to latch on to, a launch pad for a trade. And more often than not, his clients were not aware that they had said anything of significance. So it was with Lafarge.

'*No males at least*', Lafarge had said. Well Emerson hadn't specified that the black face in question was male. In his phone message he had merely asked about 'a black friend'. This gave Emerson two vital pieces of information. Firstly, that the black face in question *was* known to Lafarge, and, by extension, to Hugh; and secondly, that the identity of this person was important enough to Lafarge to merit concealing it.

But it was what Lafarge had said subsequently that had caused a tight knot of uneasiness to develop in Emerson's gut. He was so surprised, in fact, that he had had to use all of his self-restraint, not only to avoid betraying the fact, but to avoid beating Lafarge to a pulp there and then and hanging him over the edge of the parapet until he had given him the answers he wanted.

It was not that Lafarge had claimed he was not at the funeral. Emerson had not expected him to be. Lafarge had never said he was a particular friend of Hugh's, merely that they had known each other whilst at the same college together. Both Lafarge and Hugh were eight years out of Oxford when Hugh died, in entirely different careers. Lafarge was a diplomat, more likely to have been in Hong Kong or Seoul at the time than in Oxford.

But he had been in Oxford. He himself had just blurted it out. The reason he had not been at the funeral was that he had '*had to leave Oxford rather quickly*,' on business. But by implication, Morley Lafarge *had* been in Oxford around the time of Hugh's death. And the knot in

Emerson's stomach was ratcheted several degrees tighter. Two deaths. Both uncharacteristic falls from a high building. One, a man with a morbid fear of heights, the other a boy, for he could not prevent himself from thinking of his younger brother in those terms, who rarely drank and yet was supposed to have fallen in a drunken accident. And Morley Lafarge had known both victims. It was the sort of coincidence, seven thousand miles and three years apart, which James Emerson did not believe in.

'What say you the two of us go and have a spot of lunch, James? It's awfully smoggy up here, and we'll have to fight our way through that mob down there.' Lafarge gestured down to the hundreds of thousands of baying protestors now tightly packed into the dull, scorched square below. 'I know a nice little place. A bit downmarket, but clean and cheap and awfully good grub. Is the old stomach up to trying out the local fare again?'

The last thing Emerson wanted to do was spend another couple of hours across the table from a man he now suspected of murdering not only his girlfriend's brother, but also his own. But he had to do it. He had to find out more, and if he gave Lafarge's mouth the reins, he would undoubtedly find out more.

'Love to, Morley. But it's on me this time. And why don't we eat in my hotel? I still don't think I could manage dog balls, or whatever it is they eat round here, and besides, there's somebody I'd like you to meet.'

The Xenfin Limited Partnership was one of the largest single shareholders in Braxton Federal. It was a position they had accumulated naturally over a number of years, and Saul Krantz was a good friend of the chairman, Eric Chen. The successful recent expansion of the two companies mirrored each other, and Xenfin currently held around thirty-five per cent of the common stock of Braxton in their various funds, as well as significant amounts of the preferred. Braxton was happy to have such a well-thought-of, and friendly, major shareholder, and their association had, over the years, been to their mutual benefit. The bank even acted as custodian, clearing-house and banker to all of Xenfin's trading activities. It was an extremely close relationship, and one that Annie van Aalst had gently encouraged since she had joined Xenfin. But now she could smell blood. Only in this case, the blood was dripping from the balance sheet of Braxton Federal. Now was the time to cut loose, to sever the Braxton-Xenfin relationship and, in doing so, to mount an attack.

Her attack was on three separate fronts: the assets of the bank, the shares of the bank, and the reputation of the bank. Her tactics were relentless. When a guard was put up on one front, she would switch her attentions to another. If they put out a press release denying their problems, protecting their reputation, she would sell the stock heavily on the New York Stock Exchange, massive body blows, block trades which inevitably had to be reported to the public by the exchange and thus weakening the stock even more. If buyers of the stock came in and she couldn't depress the price any more, she would sell short hundreds of millions of dollars worth of bonds, bonds issued by countries and companies, mostly in Asia, that she knew Braxton had lent to heavily thanks to the privileged information supplied by Scott Turner. And if the bond prices temporarily reached a floor, she started spreading rumours.

This was the easiest bit. Wall Street, the City of London, Frankfurt, Milan, Hong Kong, all of the world's great trading centres relied on information. For it was information that moved prices. But that information had to be new. Old information, by definition, was already reflected in the current market prices. Braxton's share price at any one time was a reflection of all the news already in the public domain – latest earnings, projected earnings, expansion plans, analysts reports – but if new information was introduced and, crucially, if the source of that information was reliable or trusted, then the share price, the value of the company, should move to reflect those new 'facts'.

But facts were cheap. Language was cheap. For the price of a phone call to a few well-placed market professionals around the world, Annie van Aalst could introduce new information on Braxton which may or may not have been true. But given the reputation of Xenfin, their close relationship with the bank, and the exceptionally high level of paranoia prevailing in nervous markets, it would be judged to be true. Of course, if these rumours became widespread, Braxton could issue a statement rebutting them, but by that time the damage would be done. And van Aalst could switch her attentions to selling more stock, or more bonds. And of course in this, she was ably abetted by her colleague at Steinman, Schwartz in London, Cameron Dodds.

'Barnesy, I'm hearing Xenfin is thinking of selling out its holdings in Braxton. You heard anything? Talk is, they're going under.'

'Bill, it's Cameron. Any truth in the story that Eric Chen has had a heart attack? You know, the CEO of Braxton?'

Dodds loved the theatre of it all. He was not telling malicious lies, just acting a part. Van Aalst was equally convincing.

'Jim, it's Annie. I'm sniffing around for some levels on Korea Globals, Bakrie 08s and China Telecom 10s. They're on the Braxton list . . . What? You haven't seen it? I'll fax you a copy. They're big holders, and if what I'm hearing is true, they're going to be forced sellers quite soon. Wouldn't want to be the last one out if *they* start to unload . . .'

'Annie here at Xenfin. We haven't spoken before but I hear you're still showing a bid for Braxton perps . . . yes, the sub tranche. How many is that good for?'

Braxton's share price had started the day at \$111¾. By lunchtime, it was down to \$40½. Billions had been wiped from its value in four hours of trading. All of a sudden, van Aalst was aware of a figure hovering at her shoulder. It was Saul Krantz. He looked stern.

'Annie, what are you doing? I had a call from the exchange. There are some big block trades going through in Braxton stock. Merrill, Goldman, the Bear, they've all seen some. Rumours are flying around the street. Apparently, we're the seller. I want some answers, Annie, and I want them right now.'

She had been expecting this. At Xenfin, she was a bond fund-manager, specializing in emerging markets. Now, all of a sudden, she was selling the hell out of a blue chip US stock. It wasn't her job. Xenfin's holdings in Braxton were parked in a variety of stock and mixed funds, all of which were run by other managers at Xenfin, equity specialists.

'Saul. I know it seems odd. But my remit is to make money out of the emerging markets. What is going on in Braxton stock right now is because of their exposure to the emerging markets. They bet the ranch on those markets and they're losing out. Big time. I spend all my time looking at emerging markets. I know who's involved. I know who's over-extended, over-exposed. It is because of my involvement in the region that I found out about Braxton's problems ahead of time, and I thought I should act. We owe it to our investors. If there's an opportunity to make money, we should grasp it.'

'But it's not your stock, Annie. The shares you are selling are in other funds. Did you speak to the equity managers?'

'No, Saul, but frankly there wasn't time. And they're dinosaurs. They're not used to moving quickly, or in size. They think too much. They always find a million and one reasons not to do something. In a fast market like this, you have to act.' She knew it was thin, but at this point, she didn't really care. Krantz could fire her. He probably should. But at this point, it didn't matter. Braxton's demise was all they needed to make the whole thing unstoppable. Pegasus would win. She could go back to Oxford and help Bradley and Dodds from there with the final stages. Bradley still had his ace in the hole, and they had already set everything in motion. The markets had gathered their own momentum. From a trading point of view, there was little they needed to do now to keep the ball rolling on its downward spiral, and Dodds was capable of doing that. He had enough fire power to carry it on. She could afford to be brave. 'And besides, I'm not selling the shares Xenfin owns. I'm shorting.'

'Shorting? Are you crazy? According to the exchange, we've sold twenty per cent of the outstanding shares in Braxton this morning. You won't be able to borrow them. You'll fail to deliver. And I'm not going to let you borrow the stock we hold. Start buying them back, Annie. Start now. I want you to have covered that short by the close of trading today. I don't care how much it costs. The newswires are full of it. "Xenfin pulls the plug on Braxton." "Krantz declares war on Chen." "The Rat deserts the Sinking Ship." I won't have it, it's not true!'

'True! What is true, Saul? I'll tell you what is true. Braxton is going down the tubes. Whether you or Eric Chen like it or not. Just because we happen to own stock in a failing company doesn't mean we have to stick with them through it all, does it? Just because you play golf with the guy! It doesn't work that way any more, Saul. You got where you are today, and built Xenfin into the force it is, by making smart investments. People trust you with their money because of it. That is why we are sitting on billions, but don't be fooled. It's not *your* money. It belongs to all those people out there, people who have faith in your judgement. The biggest mistake a trader or a fund manager can make is to forget who owns the money he throws around the market. OK, so you feel like a big shot, you get big balls by being associated with big amounts, but we're not free to do what we want. We can't do a favour for Eric fucking Chen with other people's money. It would break Xenfin. Everyone would want out! They'll all be hollering for their money back, and you'd have to wind up the whole operation. And imagine what chaos *that* would cause. Do you have any idea what our total positions are? We have thirty billion dollars of cash, plus or minus a nickel. As we speak, our current leverage stands at around a factor of forty. Do the math. That means we have cash positions, long and short, of just over one point two *trillion* dollars. Add to that all the forward trades, the options positions and the swaps, and we're well over *two trillion.*'

'Annie, you are crazy! Since when was our leverage so high?'

'Since a week ago, when you gave me the go-ahead, Saul, to do whatever I needed to do to get us out of the emerging markets and more besides. I told you we could make money out of it, and we have. My fund is *up* close on forty per cent in the last two weeks alone! With the markets in free fall! And that is entirely due to being short and leveraged. You pull the plug on me now, and Xenfin will fall. I'll bet my ass on it. And if you think that Braxton going down is big news, wait till you see what happens when Xenfin has to get out of *two trillion* dollars' worth of positions in a market as shitty as this one. LTCM was small fry compared to that. But if you still want to play golf with Mr Chen and flirt with his wife, then be my guest. Buy the stock back yourself. But you'll be doing it without me.' This was her finale. Either a bravura *tour de force*, or her swan-song at

Xenfin. It could go either way. And the whole of the Xenfin trading room was hushed, waiting for Krantz's reply.

'Don't you blackmail me, van Aalst. You're threatening me. How dare you . . .'

'Saul! Look at the TV!' One of the other traders in the room yelled across the banks of screens and computer hardware. 'There's more big news coming out!'

All heads in the room swivelled up to one of the various TV monitors suspended above the trading floor. They were all tuned to news services, CNN, Bloomberg Television or CNBC, and they were all carrying the same broadcast. It was a press conference in London, run by Sky Television. Callum O'Connor's agent had done him well, and the Irishman sat there proudly at the table in front of an assembly of the world's press. A cluster of microphones were arrayed before him, each with a label and logo declaring their ownership by any one of two dozen radio and TV stations. There was a hush in the Xenfin trading room as the Sky presenter rose to speak.

'I have with me Mr Callum O'Connor of the *Limerick Leader*, who has brought us a quite extraordinary scoop. The world's press, including ourselves, have been trying for the last three days to get some conclusive evidence of who and what has been going on at Ashford Castle in the Republic of Ireland. There has been intense speculation that there was a crisis summit of finance ministers and central bank chiefs to discuss the current debt crisis which is rocking the world's markets, but little concrete evidence. Mr O'Connor now has such evidence and is happy to share it with us. Mr O'Connor.'

Callum O'Connor rose from his chair. He was indeed happy to share it with them. Five hundred thousand pounds happy in fact, for that is what Sky paid him to secure exclusive world-wide broadcasting rights to his bootleg tape. His voice had a slight tremor as he spoke to the world's media, and indeed to the world:

'Thank you ladies and gentlemen. The tape you are about to hear is a secret recording of a private conversation between yer man Byron Powell, Chairman of the Federal Reserve Bank of the United States of America, and Dick Brightwell, United States Treasury Secretary. It was recorded by myself at Shannon Airport last night. I hope you find it interesting. I'll be taking questions at the end.'

During his brief introduction, messages flashed up on Reuters and Telerate screens on trading floors across the world. 'New York Stock Exchange, London, Paris, Frankfurt, Milan exchanges – trading suspended pending announcement.'

The world was holding its breath, waiting for Callum O'Connor to push a button.

The sound people at Sky had done an amazing job cleaning up the quality of the recording. All extraneous interference, including the car engine noise and an inadvertent fart of O'Connor's had been suppressed, and the voices themselves had been digitally remastered for clarity. Two enormous pictures of the two speakers were projected on to a screen behind the podium and the lights were dimmed. They had done their best to make it as apocalyptic as possible.

Nobody spoke during the playback, but there were some gasps, especially when the booming, unmistakable bass tones of Dick Brightwell were heard to say:

'How the hell can you recommend to these guys that we let the banks go?'

'There is simply no alternative, Dick. We can't afford to do otherwise.'

'So you're gonna recommend to the President that we don't intervene? Am I right? You, the guardian of the nation's banks are gonna hold up your hands and say "too bad, guys"?'

'That's right. That's my job.'

When they got to the bit about Braxton being the shakiest bank, the traders at Xenfin left their huddles around the televisions and ran for their desks. They hit the phone lines and started barking orders to their brokers in New York.

'Sell Braxton! 50,000 at market!'

'Where's Braxton? Waddya mean? Trading's suspended?'

They hadn't seen the announcements on the Reuters and Telerate while they'd been watching Callum O'Connor present his prize catch.

One by one they wandered glumly back over to Saul Krantz and broke him the bad news.

'We're screwed, boss. Couldn't get any Braxton away. Trading's suspended until further notice.'

And then Krantz spoke. Very softly, very calmly.

'There's no need to worry.' They all looked him in astonishment. 'Thanks to Annie's prescience here, we're already short of that stock, and we'll stay short.' And then his voice rose again. 'Now, gentlemen, I suggest you all go back to your desks and see what markets *are* open, and see what you *can* actually sell the shit out of! Do you hear me? At the end of the day I want us ninety per cent cash. Correction. Not cash. Commodities. Metals, precious ones, oil, anything you can get your hands on. We'll get on with it, and the quicker the better. These markets are all going to the Devil, and I, for one, do not want to be along for the ride!'

And with that he marched away from the trading turrets and back towards the haven of his office. As he reached the door he paused and looked back.

'Oh, and gentlemen? I forgot to mention. Until further notice, Annie van Aalst is in charge.'

Callum O'Connor had finally sunk Braxton, but he had bailed out Annie van Aalst. At least for now. She was still in her seat at Xenfin, and in charge, but Krantz would be watching her like a hawk from now on. For his part, O'Connor was delighted. Five hundred grand. Not a bad night's work. Of course, Fergal had got his cut, but that still left three hundred. And O'Connor needed every penny. He too had a large family, and then there was the rest of the O'Connor clan who would want looking after too. Five thousand here, five thousand there. All of a sudden, the five hundred big ones didn't seem like so much after all. He'd have to sell the film rights, or write a book or something like that. Anyhow, he'd be fine for now. And he'd be able to make up for a fairly meagre Christmas in the O'Connor household.

CHAPTER 11

ONE MEMBER OF THE O'CONNOR CLAN HADN'T MADE IT HOME for Christmas that year. Callum's niece Patricia had made her excuses and stayed in Oxford to work over the vacation. She was the bright one, the one they all had hopes for, but if there was one member of the family who could have used an easy five grand at that time it was she.

Patsy O'Connor had moved out of her room in college after her affair with Wallace Bradley had come to such a messy conclusion, and now lived in a bedsit well up the Iffley Road. She had made it as homely as she could, with pictures of family, a few plants and posters, and a certain thrift-shop chic, which enabled her to make the sum of fairly uninspiring parts into a reasonably habitable whole. But it was well out of town.

She had wanted to be as far from Bradley as she could possibly get, and did not want to risk bumping into him in the city centre. She had given up going to lectures for the same reason. Bradley was often to be seen stalking the corridors of the economics faculty building, and a chance encounter would have been more than she could have borne. She only went into town once a week on her bicycle for her weekly tutorials, anorak hood up against rain and recognition, and she always left immediately afterwards to return to her lonely room and her books. For since she had stopped getting the extra tuition from Bradley, her grades had deteriorated dramatically.

It was her final year and her examinations loomed large, only six months away. She needed to study all she could, and had immersed herself in her books completely. As far as her few friends were concerned, she had dropped off the face of the earth. She never ate in hall, never went to parties, and had given up on rowing and the Christian Union. Most surprisingly of all, she was never in chapel. Her contralto Irish brogue had been one of the mainstays of the college choir, but she had not turned up for weeks now, not even for the Christmas concert. She had been sighted once by her former tutorial partner, pedalling furiously up St Giles, but she hadn't responded to the frantic cries and invitations for coffee. It had been a warm autumn morning, but she had been bundled in shapeless sweatpants and the ever-present anorak. The friend reported the sighting to her former crowd, adding merely that she did not look well and seemed to have put on some weight. All that microwave convenience food, no doubt, so beloved of those fending for themselves beyond the nurturing confines of the college walls.

But at least she had a job. She had taken it in November, waitressing at a greasy café in Woodstock, almost eight miles north of Oxford. She cycled there and back every day, a miserable journey, but she was glad of the exercise. She had never been slight of build, always 'on the well-nourished side' as her mother used to say proudly, as if her being overweight was somehow a sign of their prosperity. But since she moved out of college, her weight had become more of a problem. She did not eat the best food, it had to be said. A diet of crisps and chocolate kept her going at her desk into the small hours, hours which became longer and longer the closer she got to her examinations. But she had to do it, as the café kept her busy from four in the afternoon until seven, when it closed, and she desperately needed the four pounds an hour they paid her, plus the occasional tip. Sixty pounds a week, cash in hand. For now it was a race. A race against time.

The owner of the café where she worked had noticed it first, or rather her husband. There had been no customers at four o'clock one rainy Tuesday afternoon in December, and she had been alone with him behind the counter, busy drying spoons. He'd come up behind her, very close, and clamped his hand on her right breast.

'Lovely pair of jugs you got there, darling. Like that do you? I bet you do, the way you wear those tight shirts. Been waiting for me to do that, haven't you? Just begging for it, I bet! I know you college girls. At it all day long, I bet!'

She had screamed and shrugged him off, running into the kitchen in tears and into the arms of Deirdre, the doyenne of the Blenheim Grill.

'Sit yourself down, dearie. What's the matter? Tell me everything.'

And tell her she did, and Deirdre Mattock abandoned the frying pan she had been scraping, and strode imperiously into the dining area. Patsy heard every word, but could not believe what she was hearing.

'What is wrong with you, you filthy pervert! You ought to be ashamed of yourself! Get out, now! Get out before I throw you out. And don't think you're sleeping here tonight! Groping up a pregnant girl like that . . .'

Pregnant? What was she talking about? She wasn't pregnant. She couldn't be. She had stopped sleeping with Bradley ages ago, and besides, she had had her period since then. At least, she thought she had. It had come at the right time, but had been a lot lighter than normal. Come to think of it, she'd only bled for a couple of days. The doubt set in.

That night on the way home, she made a detour to a chemist's shop she knew would still be open in Summertown and bought herself a testing kit. When she got home, she took one of her chipped mugs and sneaked into the bathroom shared by all the residents of the converted house on the Iffley Road. She managed to get most of the urine all over her hands as she held the mug in the flow, but she caught enough. It surprised her how warm it felt, even through the thick ceramic mug, and she crept back up two flights of stairs to her room, clutching the precious beaker of fluid and praying she wouldn't meet anyone on the way. It was an hour later, an hour of staring at that mug on her desk, before she plucked up the courage to do the test. Her urine was cold now, as she imagined it should be, and smelling rather. It was also a much darker colour than it had been when fresh. She wondered if this mattered, but wasn't about to repeat the process, even though she quite wanted to go again already.

The testing kit had five of the litmus-type strips, and Patsy O'Connor used them all before finally accepting that the fine blue line, vividly apparent in all of the little plastic windows, meant that she was, in fact, pregnant.

The next few days were spent going to the local library, furtively looking at the books on pregnancy and childbirth, and counting days on the calendar. She didn't know much about the process herself, even though she came from a large family where people were having kids all the time. Her Uncle Callum had five of his own, and Fergal seven. But she didn't understand how she could be pregnant. She had not had sex with anyone since her last period. Bradley had been the first and the last. Maybe sperm could survive inside the body for longer than she thought? Maybe Bradley's sperm had been lurking inside her for weeks, concealed in some fallopian backwater, waiting for its opportunity to pounce on her unsuspecting egg when the fresh batch came through, just as he had pounced on her on that sofa in his rooms. She shuddered at the thought, and looked in all the books, but couldn't find anything at all about that.

She prayed and she prayed, seeking guidance, a sign, anything from an unresponsive and silent deity. She convinced herself she was being punished, visited with a terrible infestation for her immoral affair, for her plotting to cheat the examiners, and for neglecting the chapel choir and the Christmas concert. And she became angry at God's apparent lack of concern. How could He not help her? She deserved better! She was not a bad person! She was trying to help her parents, to do well in her exams so she could get a good job and send home money! That was why she had gone to Bradley in the first place. That was why she had plotted with him. And that was why she had neglected her friends and the Christian Union. Didn't He understand all that? Her good intentions?

And it was during a bout of such thinking that she resolved to take steps. She would show Him what she could do. He could not control her body in that way. She was in control. To Hell with Him and her Catholic parents. She would have an abortion.

And that was when the race had begun, because she was turned down for the operation by her local doctor. He was an old man close to retirement, and, in her eyes, a sanctimonious old fool. But he did not believe in abortion on demand, and furthermore threatened to inform the college authorities *and* her parents if she persisted. So she needed money. She found a private clinic in Headington which booked her in, no questions asked, under a false name and without the embarrassment of an examination, but it would cost. She reckoned that, assuming conception took place soon after her last period, she was currently three weeks gone. She thought she had read in one of the books that abortions can be performed up until the twentieth week. That left her seventeen weeks to get the money. Seventeen times sixty pounds was just over a thousand. That would cover it, with a little left over for extras and some spending money in the meantime. If she was running short, she was sure Mrs Mattock would let her work longer hours at the Grill. And besides, if she carried on cycling to work every day in her condition, she might just lose the baby anyway. Her Auntie Morag, Fergal's wife, had tried that when she was pregnant with number eight and it had worked. Maybe she would get lucky too?

She hadn't been. But the extra hours she had put in for a sympathetic Mrs Mattock meant that she had saved up enough for the operation by what she calculated to be her seventeenth week. She had phoned the clinic and they had had some free slots, as they liked to amuse themselves by calling them. So she had brought her appointment forward to the second of January, which meant not going home for Christmas, but that was probably just as well. She was showing quite a lot, and with a family of expert breeders such as hers, no amount of baggy jumpers and elastic-waisted trousers would be able to conceal the truth. And, as Darren Mattock had been so quick to notice, her breasts were getting bigger by the day.

And so it was on the second day of the year that she lay in her bed at the Headington clinic, watching TV. The doctor had already examined her, an excruciating experience of bright lights, stirrups and a cold speculum, and had left the room to prepare. The clinic was a fancy one, she noted, with fresh fruit and cable TV. She flicked through the channels, and was amazed to see her Uncle Callum on Sky News giving a press conference about some secret summit meeting in Cong. She loved Cong and Lough Corrib, and as a child had dreamed of staying at the big hotel there one day. Maybe Uncle Callum had made some money out of all this, she wondered. Maybe he could afford to send the whole family there now!

Her dream was interrupted by the doctor returning to the room with a nurse. They were both smiling, and the nurse came to sit beside her bed and hold her hand while the doctor remained standing at the foot of the bed. It was he who spoke.

'Patsy, as you know I've examined you, but I'm afraid there seems to be some mistake.'

Her heart leapt. She knew it! She wasn't pregnant. It was all rubbish. Mrs Mattock had been wrong all along. The test was wrong – she knew she should have used warm urine. The swelling in her stomach was psychological. A phantom pregnancy. She seemed to remember reading about it somewhere, and it wasn't all that uncommon, especially at times of severe stress. And the prospect of her finals was certainly stressful.

'Patsy, you say you think you are seventeen or eighteen weeks pregnant. That is definitely not the case.'

She was right! And think of all the money she had saved! She'd be able to treat herself, maybe go on a short holiday somewhere before term started!

'By our estimation you are currently in the thirty-eighth week of pregnancy, and the baby's head is fully engaged. You say you have been experiencing some stomach cramps lately, well those are called Braxton-Hicks contractions. They're a kind of pre-contraction contraction designed to soften up the birth canal. In fact, my dear, I'd go so far as to say that you are in the early stages of labour. The good news is . . .'

She didn't hear the rest. She didn't feel the nurse squeezing her hand, she didn't hear the doctor saying that the baby seemed perfectly healthy. She didn't even remember the ambulance transferring her to the local maternity hospital. Her waters broke on the way but she had no idea. She thought she had wet herself in all the upset. The baby was born eight hours later, at two in the morning of January the third. To Wallace Bradley, a son.

As Lafarge and Emerson sat down to lunch in the restaurant of the

Borobodur Intercontinental Hotel, they could have been in any international hotel in any major city of the world. A piano played bland, vaguely seasonal music in the corner, and the smarter tourists and businessmen went about their daily lunch ritual. Uniformed waiters bowed and served, and the noise level barely rose above a discreet murmur from the parties of four and five, deep in conversation or negotiation. But for the taped-up plate glass windows, there was little evidence of the chaos in progress on the streets of Jakarta outside the doors. Emerson's own facade, as he smiled indulgently at Lafarge, bore similarly little resemblance to the tumult raging in his head.

Could this really be the man responsible for his brother's death? Was he sitting down to lunch with a killer? And had this man, this overweight, pompous boor also killed another man, the brother of a girl he was rapidly beginning to care for? He had to find out before he turned his evidence over to the authorities. He had to get *more* evidence. And he had to find out what it was all for. If he was right about the British Government being involved, he had to be careful. If it *was* some sort of dirty tricks campaign designed to save the government some money, or to avoid a political embarrassment, and Lafarge had killed twice in its name, then he, James Emerson, could be in danger also. The authorities might be the last people he should turn to.

'Excuse me for a second, Morley. I said there was somebody special I'd like you to meet, and there is. She's in my room. Quite a girl. I'd appreciate your opinion.'

'By all means, old chap. Glad to see you've wasted no time in getting to grips with the locals. Go ahead and call her.'

'She should be on her way down. In fact, here she comes now.' Both men rose as the girl approached the table. Now she had access to some of her own clothes, she looked even more stunning. A simple, fuchsia-pink linen pinafore dress, fitted and tucked in the appropriate places, stopped around mid-thigh, and cream, ballet-style pumps completed the entire inventory of clothes she was wearing. She walked towards them with the natural confidence of one who knew the admiration she was arousing, chin slightly raised, jet-black hair braided in one thick rope jangling between her shoulder blades, arms swinging with the grace of a catwalk model.

'Christ, James. Where did you find her?' Lafarge whispered as she approached.

'You wouldn't believe me if I told you.'

'Well I wouldn't mind having some of your sloppy seconds if you could sort it, Jimmy. They go for that, you know, the Chinks. Can't get enough of the old white man's trouser snake. And those legs! I love the slightly bandy legs. Just made for wrapping around your waist. They piss in parenthesis. Who was it who said that?'

'Tamana, this is Morley Lafarge. Morley, meet Tamana Wang.'

Lafarge didn't blink at the mention of her surname. Emerson couldn't be sure if he was an extremely good actor, or if he just wasn't listening as he ogled the new arrival from head to toe with unconcealed lust.

'My dear, how lovely that you could join us. Now, tell me. Where did James find you? He's being very coy, and I've not seen you working around here. What's your patch? Glodok, with the other Chinese girls? More likely Menteng. Classier, more your style. I bet you're a favourite with all those businessmen and diplomats, aren't you?'

'I work financial district.'

'Really? I would have thought it was fairly deserted at night round there. Still, I suppose those traders are working all hours these days, what with the troubles at the moment. Probably glad of a nice Chinese girl like you waiting on the doorstep to take home and bang after a hard day banging the currency. What, James?'

'Tamana does not *work* the financial district, Morley. She works *in* it. She's PA to the MD of the Osakumi Bank, actually.'

'Really? I must apologize, my dear. You see I thought . . .'

'I know what you think. It OK. I used to it. If you live in city like this, you have to be.'

'What was the name again?' Lafarge was thinking he could get Tomi Lubis at Osakumi to arrange something after Emerson had been taken care of. Now here was another reason to sort that out without delay. His hand tightened around the small glass vial in his jacket pocket.

'Wang. Tamana Wang.'

Lafarge had not been listening earlier. That was now apparent as the mention of her family name registered and he knocked over a glass of water as he reached across for the butter.

'Sorry, James. Sorry. Here, allow me.' As Emerson mopped up the puddle in his lap, Lafarge recharged his glass with the bottle of mineral water on the table. The slightly increased effervescence as he added the two grams of soluble powder from the vial now concealed in his palm was noticed by nobody.

'Wang, Wang. That name rings a bell.' Lafarge attempted to cover his surprise by confronting the topic that had provoked it. He felt more confident now. He knew Emerson's time was limited. Two grams of the stuff was probably a bit much. He didn't really want it to kick in until after lunch, when he'd be long gone. Better not have a dessert.

'You probably read it in the papers, Morley.' Emerson watched him intently. 'Tamana's brother, Shin Wang, died recently. Fell from the Monas. They're calling it suicide, but Tamana doesn't believe it. Maybe you can help?'

'Well my deepest sympathies, my dear, but I don't see what I could possibly do. Have you tried the Japanese Embassy?'

'What could the Japanese Embassy possibly do?'

'Well, they could speak to the police. Get them to re-open the case.'

Emerson could stand it no longer. He could no longer hold back.

'Why the Japanese Embassy, Lafarge? You've been calling Tamana Chinese ever since you met her. And now, now you know Shin Wang was her brother, all of a sudden you suggest we go to the Japanese Embassy. Know him did you, Lafarge?'

'Well, as you said, I must have read it in the papers. Not every day that someone flings themselves from the top of the Monas.'

'It didn't make it to the papers, Lafarge. Not, that is, unless you read Bahasa, which I don't believe is the case. There was a tiny article in the local paper. One column inch, page thirty-seven, December seventeenth. Believe me, I checked. And it didn't mention that he was Japanese.'

'Well, really. I don't see . . .'

'Now, cut the crap. You knew Shin Wang, didn't you? You entertained him at the Café Batavia on December twelfth. You and Tomi Lubis. And then somehow you got him to join you at the top of the Monas, and you threw him over the edge. You killed him, Lafarge, and I want to know why!' Emerson was quite calm.

'You are mad, Emerson. Quite mad. How dare you lure me here to lunch, confront me with some bereaved whore and accuse me of murder? Do you have any idea who I am? I could have you thrown out of the country. Or the military police might quite like you to themselves for an hour. This is an absolute outrage! I shall call the ambassador at once. This is going to mean trouble for you, Emerson, and your paper.' Lafarge's defiance was total, due in no small measure to the glass of water still sitting at Emerson's right. Just half of it would be enough. Maybe one sip.

'Oh, our paper can look after itself. We have great lawyers. I believe you know one of them. Christopher Blake. He's on the Sukon board as well, isn't he? Must be quite a company. Because you moonlight for them too, don't you? Quite the financial experts, the two of you. And Tomi Lubis. Where does he fit in? Washing your dirty trades for you? Since when does the British Government get involved in shady dealings? I'm sure Jake Samuels would love to print a story about the Treasury or the Bank of England causing a run on the currency of another country.' Emerson was firing in the dark, but he wanted to hear the reaction. He had to find the connection.

'Treasury? Bank of England? Are you quite insane? You've finally lost it, man. You're just like your brother. Can't take the drink.' As if to underline the fact, he raised his wine glass and took a defiant mouthful. His eyes were closed with pleasure and a smirk hovered around his lips as he swilled the liquid around his mouth. His smirk broke into an unrestrained grin when he saw the sight which greeted him as he swallowed the wine and reopened his eyes with the satisfied sigh of a glutton. Emerson was clutching a tumbler of water.

'I'm not drinking alcohol, Lafarge. And I'm stone cold sober.' He raised his own glass in turn and drained its entire contents. 'But you have finally overstepped the mark.'

'And you are a dead man, Emerson. Another respect in which you will shortly resemble your brother.'

Emerson could restrain himself no longer. He leapt to his feet and reached across the table, hauling Lafarge upright by his lapels before beginning the onslaught. He pounded away at Lafarge's padded chin for almost a minute before the screams of Tamana and the people at the table to Lafarge's rear filtered through to his consciousness.

'James! Stop it! Stop it!'

'It's OK, it's OK. I'm stopping. Somebody call the police. And the British Embassy. This man is a murderer!' As he let Lafarge loose from his grip both men slumped face down on to the table. Lafarge was unconscious, Emerson was sobbing.

Emerson was released from questioning after four miserable hours. *Why had he been punching the man?* He had killed his brother. *What evidence did he have?* None. *Who was the girl?* The sister of another of Lafarge's victims. *Who?* Shin Wang. *But he committed suicide.* Again and again and again. Finally, another British Embassy official arrived to remove him from police custody, on condition that he leave the country on the next available flight to London. Morley Lafarge was still in hospital having his jaw reconstructed.

Emerson packed his things straight away and checked out around suppertime. He'd just be able to make the Air France flight to Paris, and get a connection back to London from there. In truth he was glad to be heading back to London. There was no more reason to stay in Jakarta, as he had the seeds of his story for the 'Bulletin' and Lafarge had served his purpose. Sukon was based in Geneva, but there would be nobody there but lawyers. And the only lawyer he wanted to see was Chris Blake, who was in London. He had to find out who was behind Sukon. If he was right, and it was the British Government, then clearly London was the place to find out. But the story had taken a new twist. The markets, the speculation, the financial crisis that was flooding the world, all this was somehow linked to Hugh. For now he was also investigating the murder of his brother. And that had happened in Oxford.

Tamana Wang travelled with him to the airport. In the taxi on the way he made one last attempt.

'Tamana, is there absolutely no way I can persuade you to come with me? I'm a good cook, and I'm sure you could get a job in a Japanese firm in London?'

'Sorry, James. I have to remain here. I so graceful for everything you do for me. You save my life, but you do much more than that. You give me back rest of my life. You found killer of my brother. The name of Shin Wang is clean, and doubt and shame of suicide is gone for ever. Once you leave, I give information to police about Lubis and Lafarge, and I continue to help Shin's wife.'

'Well I don't think . . .'

'Not in the way I do it before. I crazy then. Not thinking, grieving. But I must stay and help her. And if I can find out more about Sukon for you from bank here, I tell you.' She kissed him again, a deep, lung-bursting, confident kiss which left him in no doubt as to what he was going to be missing by returning to London. 'But you are needed in England. By Hugh and your father. You must tell him truth now.'

As Emerson's Air France jumbo jet soared into the skies over Jakarta that evening, another ambulance was back at the Borobodur Intercontinental. A twenty-one-year-old bus-boy in the restaurant, a local power-lifting champion everyone described as being strong as an ox, had been found dead in the hotel kitchens. He had had a massive heart attack. The obsessive genes Emerson had inherited from his father had saved his life. His earliest recollection of visiting cafés as a child was his father's curious insistence on always drinking left-handed from his tea-cup, so as to avoid lip-contact with the more commonly used side in case of poor washing-up. This eccentric quirk had become so ingrained in Emerson's own behavior that it extended even to drinking vessels without handles, which he automatically took from his left side. The glass of water he had drunk belonged to Tamana. His 'own' glass remained untouched until the thirsty bus-boy in a hot kitchen drained it later.

PART 3

Poseidon

'Annual income twenty pounds, annual expenditure nineteen nineteen six, result happiness. Annual income twenty pounds, annual expenditure twenty pounds ought and six, result misery.' (Mr Micawber)

Charles Dickens, *David Copperfield* (1849–50)

CHAPTER 1

SCOTT TURNER CALLED WALLACE BRADLEY AS SOON AS HE GOT in to Washington, and before he caught the shuttle back to his offices in New York.

'Professor, I have some excellent news.'

'We've heard.'

'What do you mean?'

'There was a leak. Byron Powell's car was bugged. I wish I'd thought of that. It's been all over the media while you've been flying home. Brilliant publicity for us. We understand that an agreement was reached.'

'Yes, absolutely no financial intervention from any government or central bank to shore up a failing bank in their country. It's every man for himself. Of course, the central banks will do everything in their power to stop the situation getting to that point, or by forcing strong banks to prop up the weak ones, but no government money is to be used.'

'And there will be no strong banks. Not for long, anyhow. They can't afford to do it either. Will all the countries comply?'

'I think so. Apart from the Chinese and the Russians, of course, but we don't really care about them. And maybe the French. Otherwise, most of the governments are right wing. Free-market fundamentalists. *Vive le marché libre!* Couldn't be better for us.'

'Indeed. It almost looks like somebody planned it all, doesn't it?'

'Ha ha. Now, about Braxton . . .'

'Braxton could be history as early as tomorrow.'

'Jeez. That was quick.'

'Confidence, Scott. Faith. Credibility. Remember all those words we have spoken about for so long? They are very slippery commodities. Very difficult to nail down. Hard to build up and even harder to keep. Once they start to ebb away, they're gone before you know it. The market is cruel. It is implacably quick to punish and bears long grudges. Braxton has lost the faith of the market. Chen is a pariah. Even if the FDIC pays up for *his* customers there'll be nothing left to cover the next Braxton Federal, and the next. And before long it will be the UK, and France and Italy and Germany again, but big this time! And then Japan. But we will save Japan till the end. For I have something rather more special lined up for then.'

'Professor, don't you think we're coming to the end soon? I mean, we set out to punish the banks, to destabilize the world's financial markets and to send the world a wake-up call. We all had good reasons for wanting that. But don't you think we're pretty much there? Another week or two and it'll be utter chaos. Beyond then I daren't even think. Professor? Professor?'

Another one! A weak one! He thought he'd have weeded them out by now. Bradley sat in his Oxford study, breathing hard. He could feel his pulse pounding in his temples, and his fists were pressed tight against his ears, but he could not block out the sounds of his thoughts. A black, a weakling. How could he have been so short-sighted? How could he have trusted one? A do-gooder at that. He opened and closed his mouth several times to its very widest extent in a kind of mute scream, the effort stretching the skin tightly across his face so that the cuts from his New Year's Eve injuries reopened and the blood trickled down his face. He tasted it on his lips, the salt, the humanity, and he thought of her. He thought of his mother, and her injuries, he thought of her tormentors, her principal tormentor. And he began to feel aroused.

He never understood why this happened, but it always did. At first he had been repulsed by it. Then he had been only seventeen, but it had not been long before he had learned to enjoy it. At first this had always been alone, but as he had begun to travel the world, especially to Asia, the first port of call would always be a brothel. It could never be the same one twice, as his behaviour and his treatment of the girls generally ruled that out. For he had been surprised to discover that he was not a considerate lover, nor gentle. He actually enjoyed the violence. It excited him, and the scale of it had escalated over the early years. For this reason he had avoided women at home in his younger years until he had learned to control his urges a little better. But now he could do that, if he wanted to at least, and the students were the best prey. They marvelled at his erudition and, latterly, at his fame. And he could spot the weak ones, the vulnerable ones, just as well as he could spot the weak and vulnerable banks and the overexposed countries. They never lasted long. A week or two was the norm, as they tired of his demands and, in some cases, became a little scared of his practices. But it didn't matter. Each one left him plenty of material for his imagination. He was like a camel in the desert, each encounter an oasis of experiences with which to survive the barren trek to the next one. He barely remembered their names, or even their faces. Just their bodies, but those he remembered in extreme detail. Photographic detail, in black and white.

Emerson sat in Jake Samuels's office with his head in his hands. He was exhausted. 'It's incredible, Jake, absolutely incredible. Quite how I ended up involved in this escapes me.' And with weary resignation, knowing there was little point in leaving anything out, he told Samuels everything. He told him all about Morley Lafarge, how he had somehow known Emerson was going to Jakarta, and his suspicions that Chris Blake was the conduit. He told him about meeting Tamana, and the death of her brother Shin at the hands of Lafarge and Tomi Lubis. And he told him about the mysterious Sukon Corporation, and his suspicions that they were a front for illegal currency dealings by the British Government. He told him about his final confrontation with Lafarge, and last of all he mentioned the familiar black face he had seen on TV and who had been at Hugh's funeral.

'Scott Turner was at Hugh's funeral?'

'Who?'

'Scott Turner. He was the African-American plastered all over the papers during the Ashford summit. He was sold out to *Paris Match* or someone like that for a hundred grand by an old room-mate. We know who he is now. Runs some department at the Fed. Something to do with supervision of banks. That's why he was at Ashford.'

'But why was he at Hugh's funeral?'

'Don't get me wrong, James, but are you absolutely sure? You were pretty upset . . .'

'And I suppose you're going to say that I think one black face looks pretty much like another! Well screw you. I am positive. And Lafarge felt it was important enough to lie about.'

'So where do we go from here?'

'I'll look into the Turner angle, if you can talk to Blake. Find out if he did talk to Lafarge, and if so, why. He knows you best. He'll trust you. And I'll try and corner him through the Sukon connection. If it is the same C. Blake, that is.'

The news of Braxton Federal's closure hit the newswires later that afternoon. The stock had never resumed trading following its original suspension at the time of Callum O'Connor's press conference, and the bankruptcy proceedings were set in motion immediately. The bank had effectively been assassinated.

'You see,' Danny Brookes explained to Chris Blake in his chambers at Fig Tree Court, 'it's all a question of balance.'

'Ah yes. The scales of justice. Or maybe the balance of power? We hear about it all the time.'

'No you fool. Balance sheets.'

'Indulge me.'

'Assets and liabilities. What you have and what you owe. For a bank, for any company in fact, what they *have* has to equate to what they *owe*.'

'And a bank has . . .'

'Its own money, capital if you will and . . .'

'Investments?'

'Exactly. Loans that they make, bonds that they buy, stocks that they own.'

'And they owe . . .'

'Depositors. Amongst other things. The people who entrust their money to the bank so that they won't have to worry about it under the mattress. Those people can demand their money back at any time. The banks owe it.'

'But the bank doesn't have it in the vaults?'

'No. The bank lends it to other people.'

'So if I want my few guineas back, the bank has to get them back from whomever they lent it to.'

'In principle, yes. Only if that third party has gone broke, then . . .'

'I start screaming.'

'Exactly. Now if you were the only one asking for his money, the bank could just call it in from anybody else. Doesn't have to be the exact same person they lent your cash to in the first place.'

'But if we all want it back at the same time . . .'

'Then we have a run on the bank. I'm sure you've seen *Mary Poppins*. The bank panics and starts having to flog off their investments to get your cash back. Only . . .'

'If they're selling everything at the same time, that forces the price of what they're trying to sell down.'

'Correct. Which means they don't have enough to pay everyone back. We've come full circle. What they end up with, the proceeds of their car-boot sale, is not enough to pay off what they owe to their depositors.'

'Insolvency.'

'Yes. Braxton, in a nutshell.'

'But the government steps in and pays everyone anyway.'

'In Braxton's case they'll be able to pay most people. Everyone who had less than a hundred grand anyway. But now the cupboard is bare. Braxton's claimants have cleaned them out.'

'Right. The insurance company is broke. All those other policies they've written, to cover all those other depositors at other banks, aren't worth a penny.'

'And all those people get nervous. What if *their* bank goes under? They won't be compensated. So . . .'

'So they get in their cars and drive to the bank, or they pop out in their lunch hour and go to the cash-machine, and start to try taking out all their money. Better to have a fistful of dollars than a worthless bank book.'

'And we get a run on all the other banks. More car-boot sales to satisfy demand, lower prices and . . .'

'More insolvent banks. It feeds on itself. You just have to set the ball rolling. Our accomplice the free market does the rest. That was how we started it all in the first place in Asia. When Chumsai's company went under, that was the hole in the dam. No amount of little Dutch boys could plug the hole for long. The floodwaters were too strong. That was the beginning of the erosion, but in this case it was not major earthworks but asset prices. And Pee Seuar Land Holdings was in a particularly sensitive sector.'

'House building?'

'Property. Banks have fallen over themselves lending to property developers in Asia. The valuations were astronomical. Question those valuations and the scales fall from the eyes. The emperor is not only naked, he's fat and ugly as well.'

'And now you will take your turn on the stage Mr Brookes?'

'Yes. The time for subtlety is over. Accountants have been propping up these businesses for too long. SmokeandMirrorsdotcom is about to have the lights switched on and the stage turned around. All the public sees is glossy annual reports with pages of impressive numbers validated by fancy accountancy firms. It may be all well and good in the West, but in Asia it's bullshit. The numbers are crap. If Sanderson, Toomey, McClintock say they're kosher, everyone's happy. Nobody bothers to check. The accountants are God. We could make it all up and analysts would lap it up. If we say, "Yes! It's true! Phat Phuk Chicken Farm's sales have quadrupled in the last ten minutes!" the stock price will rocket. And all the stockbrokers take *our* numbers to validate their own analysis.'

'So, you are the worm which will turn, Danny Boy.'

'Precisely. I have enough material stashed away, not only to put

Sanderson, Toomey, McClintock out of business, but to call into question the very validity of the profession. Who will believe what a company is worth any more, once I reveal the extent of the corruption within the accountancy profession? They're all bean-counters to a man. And nobody has yet questioned their ability, or rather their willingness to count accurately.'

'My dear chap, it's all so wonderfully fundamental, isn't it? Truth versus lies. You believe me, I'll believe you.'

'More like, "you scratch my back, I'll give you a blow job and put seven figures in a numbered account in Liechtenstein."'

'Let's drink a toast.'

'Amen to that. The professions.'

'May they sink like a stone.'

Wesley Turner still called himself 'Dr', even though the Californian authorities, like their counterparts in New York thirty years ago, refused to acknowledge his Sudanese qualification. And 'Dr Turner' sounded a lot better than Doc Bok, as his patients in Khartoum and Suakin used to call him.

'Good morning, Dr Turner,' beamed the local butcher in Carlsbad, a small town just north of San Diego to which they had retired shortly after Scott moved away to New York and his job at the Federal Reserve Bank.

'I'll take two pounds o' dose soya sausages, please Dwayne, and two chick'ns, big 'uns. Family comin' in from da East Coast.' He still had not lost his African accent. Or rather, he tried not to.

'That boy of yours, Scott, in town? You must be real proud. Boy like that, workin' for Byron Powell. That'll be twenty-seven ninety-eight please Dr Turner.'

'I've no cash wit' me, Dwayne. I'm on me way to da bank. I'll have to give you a personal cheque.'

'Certainly, Doctor. Ah. Franklin Intercontinental. I'm afraid not, sir. You haven't heard? After Braxton closed yesterday, Franklin went into voluntary bankruptcy proceedings this morning. I'll keep everything on one side until you get the cash, sir, if that's OK. I'm sure you understand.'

When Wesley Turner got to the bank, the doors were closed. There was a small crowd of maybe twenty people waiting outside. A notice pinned to the door read:

FRANKLIN INTERCONTINENTAL – IMPORTANT NOTICE
AS OF THURSDAY JANUARY THIRD, FRANKLIN
INTERCONTINENTAL INC. IS IN LIQUIDATION.
NO MONIES CAN BE DISBURSED AT THIS TIME.
PLEASE ADDRESS ALL ENQUIRIES TO FDIC REGIONAL
OFFICE IN SAN DIEGO.

There were no lights on inside the bank, but a couple of frightened faces could be seen occasionally peering from a second-floor window at the ever-increasing crowd below. A single motorcycle policeman stood to one side of the door, keeping an eye on things. In truth, his thoughts were elsewhere. He had an account with San Luis Savings, and talk was, they were next. But he was on duty. He couldn't get away to withdraw any cash. And he had a son in college.

Wesley Turner had twenty-eight cents in his pocket and his car ran out of petrol on the drive back home. Betty always left it on the red. Why did she never top it up? He set off to walk the four miles to the nearest gas station. It was a beautiful January morning, close to seventy degrees already at nine thirty in the morning, and the Pacific breakers crashed against the rocky promontory below the coast road along which he now trudged. Gulls dived and shrieked as they plunged into the foaming waters, searching for food, and it struck Turner that they didn't actually have much in their own refrigerator. At least there was the credit card.

When he got to the gas station there was a line of twelve cars, and a blackboard propped up next to the pumps which said '$20 cash per customer only. No personal checks or credit cards.' It turned out that the oil company banked with Braxton. All their lines of credit had been frozen and the tanker drivers were on strike. They had not been paid yesterday. It wasn't that the oil company did not have the money. At least, the latest statements said they had plenty, but Braxton's accounts had been frozen by the liquidators. The depositors just could not get at it. It was as good as not having it.

Turner turned around and started back along the coast road. He passed a mailbox on the way and that reminded him to post the letters he had in his jacket pocket. He prided himself on being very careful with his finances, and his son had always lectured him on the time-value of money. The longer it sat in his account, the more interest he earned. Which meant that he always left it until the very last minute to pay his utility bills, always waited until the final threatening disconnection notice before posting off the cheque. It made him feel as if he was beating the system. Now he had a sickening feeling. He could see in his mind's eye the crest of Franklin Intercontinental at the head of the cheques he had written that morning to the power and phone companies. Those were worthless now, and in a couple of days he'd get to see if their threats of disconnection were good.

All along the coast of southern California and, on the other side of the country in Florida, Braxton's home state, similar scenes were taking place, and the reaction of most ordinary people in the face of the problems was to look after themselves. The people of America had never been so prosperous. Everybody had money, at least on paper, but the ink figures in their bank books could not be used to buy the groceries. It was a different sort of paper money that was becoming important now. In just a couple of days, it had turned into a cash-only society. And it was beginning not to matter which bank you were with. Merchants were reluctant to take cheques from anyone, even the really big boys like Chase or Citibank, as they couldn't be sure they would be honoured. And as for credit cards, well even if the card purchases were sanctioned by the little electronic machines at the check-outs, that didn't mean to say the shopkeepers would be reimbursed at the end of the month by the bank. No one trusted anyone. Confidence in the ability of banks to pay had evaporated, and cash was king, at least for the time being.

For now, at least, people still believed in the value of the greenback. But the amount of notes in circulation was limited. Substitutes had to be found.

Police noticed a distinct rise in the frequency of muggings and burglaries. The criminals were targeting anything that was portable and valuable, which included cash of course, but also jewellery and bearer bonds. In the wealthier neighbourhoods, where ironically the residents were less used to having actual, hard cash than the production-line workers and manual labourers, the cannier shopkeepers had installed scales and jewellers loupes at the till side to assess the value of gold and gems that people without cash brought in to barter for goods and services. Before long there was a thriving secondary market in forged valuation certificates from reputable jewellers and auction houses, which respectable people would attempt to pass off with their costume necklaces and earrings.

Gold prices were soaring, and at current valuations a good lunch for four at the Breakers came in at around two ounces of eighteen carat. For the male residents, that meant another link out of the chunky graduation bracelet. In fact, in Palm Beach it was not uncommon to see shopkeepers at the check-out looking up the stock price of a particular company before accepting a bundle of share certificates from middle-aged Chanel-clad ladies in exchange for a freezerful of groceries. But only at around sixty per cent of the previous day's closing price. The volatility in the markets was such that one never knew what those stocks would be worth at the end of the day. Another week and the street barter-value was down to only forty per cent.

The President had declared a state of emergency in Florida and southern California, and Byron Powell was doing everything he could to alleviate the situation. He was putting ample liquidity into the system, at least into those banks still operating, and he had cut interest rates, but it made very little difference. He could boost money supply, but he couldn't boost confidence in the system. Whenever he tried to do that, in a speech to Congress or some Senate committee, it had the opposite effect. Rather like someone shouting 'Don't panic!' in a burning building.

For the past ten years his predecessor, Alan Greenspan, had attempted to put a brake on the booming stock market. Whenever he commented on it, or advised caution, the market simply went higher. The simple psychology was that, if Greenspan felt it was worth commenting on, it must be in danger of going much higher. So buy! Now the opposite was true. If Byron Powell tells us not to worry about the banks, there must be something worth worrying about. Get your money out while you still can! And the rest of the world watched in horror.

It was a cliché in the language of the markets to point out that when America sneezes, the rest of the world catches a cold. In this case, America was HIV positive and the rest of the world had been having unprotected anal sex whilst sharing needles with them for a very long time.

CHAPTER 2

'ARE YOU SERIOUSLY TRYING TO TELL ME THAT CHRISTOPHER Blake was at St Mary's Oxford?' Emerson couldn't believe what Jake Samuels was telling him.

'I am, James. He was wearing the tie. Bold as brass. And I looked him up in *Havers' Guide*. It's true.'

'So that makes three. Hugh, Blake and Lafarge, all at Oxford at the same time, all at St Mary's College. And did you establish if your Blake is the same one on Sukon's board?'

'Short of getting a signed confession, yes. "The colour of a man's neck speaks louder than words." One of your father's, James.' He poured Emerson a large slug of Scotch from the bottle in the bottom drawer of his desk. It was almost midnight and, for once, the *Gazette* offices were deserted. The hum of the floor polishers on the floor below was all that could be heard.

'So what about your end? Anything on Scott Turner, or Sukon?'

'No. Blank on Turner. No CV, no nothing. Nothing on the web, no personal website, Federal Reserve Bank completely unhelpful.'

'Hmm.' Samuels pursed his lips. A germ of an idea was beginning to form in the old newspaperman's mind. 'I have an idea. You still got any of the Steinman, Schwartz letterhead from your days there?'

'Fraid not. But I know what it looks like. In fact, we could get the font and the logo from their website and do a mock-up. Cut and paste, you know. Easy as pie. Add the address and the usual disclaimers in tiny letters at the bottom, and bingo! What do you have in mind?'

'I think we should send a fax to the Fed. Public relations department.'

'Go on.'

'Steinman, Schwartz International in London are having a conference. You know the sort of thing. Get the clients along, feed them up, talk about this and that. At the Savoy. Get a few key-note speakers in. "Whither Capitalism?" You know the form. Well we would very much like to invite Mr Scott Turner, Director of Bank Supervision at the Fed, to be one of those speakers. "Risk Management in a non-Bell-Curve environment." Something along those lines. Only, we're not sure if he's suitable. Or willing. Would it be possible to see a brief résumé? Something we could include in the handouts for the clients to show just how eminent our speakers are?'

'You're brilliant, Jake.'

'Well, I think they'd be a little more likely to send the relevant information out for something like that than give it to pushy hack *extraordinaire*, James "the Ferret" Emerson, don't you?'

After fifteen minutes of fiddling around in Microsoft Word, Emerson and Samuels had produced a fake Steinman, Schwartz letterhead to fool anybody. The only way in which it differed from the real thing was perhaps the right shade of aubergine for the corporate logo, but as it was being faxed in black and white that did not matter. And of course the return fax number. That was the number of Jake Samuels's personal fax next to his desk in his office. They then spent another ten minutes composing the invitation, and faxed it off to the number they got from the main switchboard at the Federal Reserve Bank offices in New York. It was seven thirty p.m. in New York, and the chances were that the PR people had gone home for the day.

Annie van Aalst, on the other hand, had just arrived at Xenfin's office in Grand Cayman. There too it was seven thirty p.m., but unlike the minus ten degrees excluding wind chill they were suffering in New York, on the eastern headland of Grand Cayman it was still a healthy sixty-five, although the sun had set two hours previously. She stood on the terrace of the old mansion, the highest point on the island, and stared out to sea.

The breezes whipping in from the east plastered her loose linen clothes against her body, and she inhaled huge lungfuls of ozone and seaspray, unlike her partner Cameron Dodds the only stimulant she needed to prepare herself for another night's trading. With Braxton gone, and now Franklin Intercontinental too, she really just had to wait for the sign from Bradley.

For she was the only one he had entrusted with any of the scenario for the final act of the theatre they had stage-managed. All she knew was that there was likely to be some dramatically bad news about Japan, and she had been told to set up Xenfin's risk profile to be hurt to the maximum when the news broke. For that was to be the other side of the coin.

Xenfin, Saul Krantz's baby of thirty years, was to be the other final sacrifice. Up until now, Xenfin had done extremely well out of the debt crisis. After all, most of the investment decisions were being made by Annie van Aalst herself, and she knew pretty much what was going to happen next. But now, after the Braxton episode, she had won her position of precarious trust from Krantz, and effectively controlled the entire Xenfin dealing room. Which meant she could set it up to burn, financially speaking, no less effectively than Max Collins had done in his own Chelsea headquarters. One last night of trading and she would be ready. But this was the tricky part, because it went against the broad guidelines that Krantz had set them all. Cash and commodities. She needed to keep Krantz out of the way for the night, stop him looking over her shoulder, or at least keep him happy, and for Annie van Aalst there was only one way she could think of to achieve that end.

She walked uninvited into Saul Krantz's office at Xenfin and flopped with feigned exhaustion into the leather swivel chair across the desk from him.

'Hey, Boss. Any last words for the troops before we go back in to battle?'

'Annie, you're early today. Don't normally see you until around ten.'

'I thought we might go for a little walk along the beach, Saul. Just you and I. We haven't done that since that weekend you flew me out here and persuaded me to leave Salomon.'

'A walk along the beach was not part of the contract! With the money we pay you, you could buy your own beach!'

'Aw, come on Saul. What happened to the playful guy who hired me? Lost your sense of fun? Haven't seen any of those famous practical jokes in a while, have we? This place is getting pretty boring to work. Has the Cayman Clown gone all serious in his old age? Come on, Saul. Just half an hour. It'll be a blast!'

Krantz swallowed the bait. The age jibe had hit home. The Cayman Clown would not be outdone. 'OK, Annie. Things do seem a bit calmer on the Street today. Give me five minutes.'

And together they scrambled down the shrubby headland, part sliding, part controlled tumbling, until they fell, giggling and exhilarated, in a tangle of sandy linen and silk on to the beach. This was not part of the Xenfin estate, and the landscape was a world away from the manicured lawns and ingenious water features of the Colliers Landings' sterile, quasi-municipal parkland. It was a public beach, but well off the tourist trail, unkempt and unswept. Driftwood and seaweed accumulated in serpentine garlands along its length, and the wind fashioned the corrugations in the shifting sand, unmolested by beach boys and their rakes. There were clusters of rock pools, and shiny white crabs scuttled unselfconsciously from one to the next, without fear or expectation of being disturbed.

Van Aalst threaded an arm through Krantz's as they strode along the beach into the teeth of the warm wind which now assaulted them from the front.

'You know, Saul. This should be part of the contract. Four hundred thousand a year, twenty per cent of the net return on top, plus one hour a month with our founder, leader and pastoral guru Mr Saul Krantz, on the beach, after dark.'

'Annie, you *are* nuts!'

'No, I mean it. I'm serious! Don't you find it easier to think down here? Back to nature, away from the central air and fluorescent light and tinkling fountains of Colliers Landings? You should do it Saul. One hour a month, one on one, with everyone. You'd learn a hell

of a lot. About your staff, about your work, even about the markets.'

'But I think I know you all pretty well.'

'Oh, you know what we like to eat and drink, and you checked us
all out pretty good before we joined. But do you bother to keep it up?
I bet no.'

'Well, I . . .'

'There you go. I bet you couldn't tell me what my favourite thing to
do is on a clear night with a full moon. That's the sort of stuff you really
need to know to keep the staff happy. We're not in it for the money any
more. You've seen to it that we don't have to be.'

'OK, Annie. So let's go with the experiment. Tell me, what is your
fav . . .' He turned to look at Annie van Aalst, and found her standing
entirely naked before him on the beach. She was completely relaxed, arms
hanging loosely at her side, eyebrows raised in gentle enquiry. Her sun-
bleached chestnut hair hung loose just above her prominent collar bones
and blew in wisps around her cheeks. She raised both hands to tuck it
behind her ears, and as she did so her breasts lifted, inviting inspection of
the roseate nipples, visibly hardening in the evening breeze. She allowed
him a good long look before she spoke and he liked what he saw.

Even in the moonlight he could see that her skin was perfect, a
uniform shade of melted demerara, no bikini lines, no elastic marks
from constricting underwear, and her body was firm. Firm, but not
over-sculpted, the stretched and toned muscles sheathed in a coating
of padded velour, subcutaneous Martinis.

'See. I knew you'd never guess! Skinny-dipping, Saul, that's what I
like to do! Come on, you old prude. Get your kit off!' And with that
she turned and sprinted off towards the ocean. He watched her run
for a moment, each loose, languid stride accentuating the muscles in
her buttocks, before he began to tug at his own belt and within seconds
was racing after her. He caught up with her at the ocean's edge and they
splashed, high-stepping through the shallows side by side, shrieking with
laughter, until the gently shelving beach began to steepen and Krantz
plunged full length into the waves.

Now it was Annie's turn to watch. For a man in his forties he would have been in excellent shape. For a man of fifty-five, he was phenomenal. And Krantz was a swimmer. As he ploughed through the surf, every muscle in his broad, powerful back was laid bare with each stroke of his arms. He swam butterfly, and he did it on purpose, as each twin surge from his splayed arms was followed by a violent, undulating thrust from his buttocks, the water foaming and cascading over his body as it jack-knifed through the waves at remarkable speed. Annie was spellbound by the sight, and she stood quite still, watching this display of virtuoso masculinity, and imagining the pleasure she had still to come.

He was some way out now, well out of his depth, and she saw him turning back towards her. She knew he could see her, and she stood waist-deep in the swell, one hand clasped behind her neck, her upper body an open invitation, the other in front of her but below the water level. She didn't move as he surged towards her, and now she could see him from the front. His eyes were open, oblivious to the spray, and glued on her. His breathing, in time with each mighty revolution of his arms and each glimpse of his chest as his torso reared up out of the water, was ferocious and rhythmic, gasping and exploding. He was getting closer and closer with every stroke, yet somehow he was increasing the tempo. She found her hips swaying back and forth, was it in time with the waves or with his own undulation? And trembling slightly in anticipation of the storm she imagined soon to be unleashed on her body, Annie let herself float back into the water and started off towards the shore in a slow backstroke.

The sight of her moving away from him, her stretched out form rocking gently from side to side as she swam, breasts bobbing above the water, forced him to an even greater speed. And as the water became too shallow to swim, he sprang to his feet and raced the last few yards to where she already lay on the sand. She was lying on her back, limbs splayed like a beached starfish, water lapping at her toes. Krantz stood over her, feet astride her waist, seawater dripping from him on to her squirming stomach.

She gazed up from where she lay, and this time she took a proper, unabridged look at the Colossus of a man who bestrode her. The flashes of his physique she had glimpsed in the moonlight through the surf had barely done him justice, and as he stood over her, panting hard with the effort of his swim and unable to speak, she marvelled at all aspects of the display he presented for inspection. She reached up behind him with one hand and ran her fingertips over his left buttock. The memory of the Krantz backside thrusting its way through the waves was an image that would never leave her, and the close-up reality did not disappoint. The skin was like taut latex, stretched to the limit across a mass of muscle, pumped and swollen from its exertion, and Krantz didn't flinch as she stroked and probed, testing the limits. He just continued to stand over her in silence, his panting subsiding slightly to be replaced by an altogether deeper breathlessness.

Annie didn't know how much longer she could wait, and the Krantz anatomy was beginning to demand more and more attention. She had been impressed by its lively condition and considerable girth, even when Krantz was fresh from the cool evening waters of the Caribbean, but now it was obviously warming up. He saw her admiring it and smiled down at her. He'd seen that look in the eyes of women before.

'Not bad for an old guy, eh Annie? It won't bite, you know . . .'

And she reached up again, but this time with both hands. It was definitely a two-handed job, and she grasped it, one fist above the other, and squeezed hard. She was shocked by two things. Firstly, and for the first time in her own considerable experience, two hands were not enough. Not nearly enough. And secondly, and no matter how hard she squeezed, the fingers and thumb of her hands could not be made to meet.

'That's quite a grip you've got there, Annie. Do you play golf?'

She could barely speak. 'Never with a club like this before, Saul.'

'I call it my number one wood. Maybe we could do some work on your approach play?'

'I find keeping my head down has always been my biggest problem,' she grinned, and Krantz had to brace himself as Annie van Aalst, still holding on to him with both hands for all she was worth, pulled herself up into a sitting position between his legs, looking up into his eyes as she did so.

'You know, you should always keep your eyes on the ball. I could help you with that.'

'Oh, I'm sure we'll get to that later, Saul. There's plenty of time. But first of all, let's forget the golf. I'd like a swimming lesson . . .'

James Emerson was woken at six in the morning by somebody ringing the doorbell to his Docklands penthouse. Very few people knew his address. He was relieved to see a familiar face on the security monitor.

'Max! Get yourself up here!' he yelled into the intercom. 'Type the following security code into the keypad. Today's number is . . .'

'It's OK man, I already figured that one out. I'm on my way.'

Collins flopped on to the daybed and kicked off his shoes.

'I'm whacked, man. Got any chocolate?' Collins looked terrible. His shaven head hadn't been clipped in days and he was getting a sort of post-chemo growth in isolated thickets around his crown and nape. His eyes bore the strain of days without sleep, staring at computer screens, getting himself back in business.

'I'm back in business, Jimmy. Cubit rides again. They thought they had me, those suckers, but no friggin' way.'

'What happened?' Emerson sat cross-legged on the floor in T-shirt and boxers, still trying to come to from the deep sleep Collins had interrupted.

'I was blown, man. They found me. At least, they found Alex Little. Must've heard me on the mobile, I guess. That's the only way. They probably lucked into our pow-wow in Jakarta.'

'But how did they know we'd be speaking?'

'Oh, they didn't. They just listen to everyone all the time. At least the computers do. You know man, the spy in the sky. Echelon or whatever. They must've made some major-league progress on voice recognition. I'll bet Routh's behind it. He was always the brightest of a dim bunch.'

'So what now? You can stay here if you like.'

'No need, dude. I had a bolthole set up just in case. Can't be too careful, know what I mean? Never know when the enemy's gonna make a quantum leap.'

'But what about the old place?'

'Torched it. Gonzo. Not a trace, not a fragment that wasn't vapourized first. But never fear. I have a duplicate set-up at the new place in Hampstead. Not quite so much hardware, but the software's all the same. That's because I wrote it. There's no TEMPEST protection, of course, so I'll have to spend a little less time on-line. And please, no mobile phones. Too easy to trace if they do have this voice-scanning system now. If we must speak on the phone, never use my name and never mention computers or anything to do with them. Don't use your name either, for that matter. If they did hear our chat in Jakarta, they're probably listening out for you too now. Better to e-mail. Encrypted of course. I brought you a disk to load on to your laptop, a better one than last time. Five-twelve bit, uncrackable. I mean, for them.'

And Collins talked for ten more minutes. He gave Emerson his new address and phone number, and his new alias, Charles Lewis. He ate three bowls of Coco-Pops, with chocolate milk, and left as abruptly as he had come. For the first time in a few days, Emerson felt a lot more secure himself. His secret weapon was back and more or less fully armed.

Annie van Aalst had been at her desk for a little over four hours. The first hour had been wasted, spent as it was in quiet contemplation of the preceding two. Krantz had been amazing, and she still felt him, rather as she imagined an amputee can still feel a missing limb. They had not stayed on the beach long – despite their level of energy it had quickly become too cold – and they had abandoned their clothes to the waves and sneaked naked back through the lobby of Colliers Landings. The had been like an eloping couple in a Whitehall farce, giggling and praying that they would not bump into an IT technician or some other member of the night shift at Xenfin, before reaching the sanctity and security of Krantz's on-site quarters. For him it was a *pied-à-terre*, a place to put his head down occasionally if his round-the-clock habits got the better of him, but it was several factors larger than her own home, all white linen and beige chenille and iroko. They had sunk into the granite plunge pool for warmth, and emerged half an hour later, re-energized. And then she had taken control. She had shown no quarter, no mercy, giving and demanding in equal measure, a flurry of tanned limbs and pink velvet, until she had finally finished him off. She had left him snoring gently under the covers, and pulled on a pair of his sweat pants and a T-shirt before padding quietly back to her trading desk, ready for a session of suicidal trading.

Leeson had accidentally destroyed two hundred years of Barings' history in a few months. She had what was left of one Tokyo trading day, around seven hours, to destroy thirty years of Saul Krantz's patient genius. But there was a difference. This would be no accident. She knew exactly what she was doing and seven hours would be more than enough. She started to make the calls.

At first it was quite hard going. She was a brilliant trader, technically peerless yet with an instinctive touch that could not be learned. Krantz would not have hired her had she not been, but because of her success, making deliberate mistakes did not come easily. It was like a concert pianist being asked to play wrong notes, and the first money-losing trades she executed jarred discordantly with her money-making instincts. But she soon picked it up, her fingers flying over the keyboard to check prices, barking ludicrous orders into her headset telephone at astonished brokers on the other side of the world, until she was single-handedly performing an entire atonal concerto of catastrophe, rising to a crescendo with the final cacophonic combination of bonds, stocks and options that she knew would lose most of their value in the next day or two, Phipps permitting.

When the Tokyo market finally closed, she had done enough. Enough, at least, to cripple Krantz and Xenfin. Their investors would do the rest, merely by demanding their own hard-earned money back and forcing them to unwind the enormous loss-making positions they would soon find themselves in. But she would not be around to see it. The Xenfin Gulfstream was fuelled and ready at Owen Roberts Airport to take her to London. Krantz had sanctioned the trip a couple of days before, ostensibly to attend the Chancellor of the Exchequer's Mansion House dinner and meet the other leading lights of London's financial community. But she would be sending the Gulfstream back empty, along with her letter of resignation. She was going with one almighty bang, and she could hardly wait to witness the fall-out. She called Cameron Dodds at his desk in London.

'Holy smoke, Annie. Was that you?' Dodds had been watching the pyrotechnics in the Japanese markets since he had got into the office. He knew she had had one last hurrah to do before joining him in London, but even he had not been trusted with exactly what it was to be. Nor did he know about the proposed annihilation of Japan.

'Yes, Cameron. And now I'm done. I'm coming now. Right away, OK? I can't be around here when Krantz finds out. Let's go to the dinner together tonight, can we? Meet me at the Halkin at five. I have a room for a couple of days and then I'm staying with you.'

Dodds could not remember hearing her so weary, so needy before. The enormity of what they had been doing was beginning to sink in to both of them at the same time.

After Collins had left his apartment, Emerson decided to make use of the extra couple of hours in the day to go into the *Gazette* offices early. He pulled on his tracksuit and set off to jog along the river into the City and Fleet Street. It was cold and subdued at that time in the morning, the Thames a ribbon of mist threaded amongst the towers of the capital's trading rooms, and Emerson joined the flow of commuters already disgorging from London Bridge Station and streaming over the bridge to rejoin the fight against the markets which threatened to destroy their livelihood.

It was a curious mix of bodies at six thirty in the morning when the two opposing ends of the spectrum of City life crossed paths. For this was the time when the highest earners arrived, the proprietary traders, the star fund managers, the keenest salespeople eager to steal a march on the competition; but it was also the time when the night cleaning staff were leaving, the other end of the financial food-chain, who had been labouring all night to polish the screens and hoover the carpets which cosseted the tread of the slippery-soled shoes of success. They passed each other in the marble lobbies, heads lowered in mutual embarrassment.

Emerson skipped amongst them all, dodging briefcases and umbrellas, glad he was no longer of that world, away from targets and bonuses and sleazy sales strategies, and he continued his run through the heart of the Square Mile, exhilarated at his freedom to do as he pleased.

There were very few bodies in the *Gazette* offices at that time. A few hacks from the financial pages were there, catching up on the night's events in the Far East and preparing their rehash of the myriad Reuters and Dow Jones newswire reports which piled up on their desks. Emerson joined them, pulling up a chair below a television turned to CNN.

'James, unusual to see you here at this hour. What was her name, and why did she kick you out into the cold?' The jibe came from Si Newman, a jolly, rotund fifty-year-old who had been the mainstay of the *Gazette*'s pink pages for twenty years. He smoked cigars and wore red felt braces and was the only one in the office besides Emerson capable of using the Bloomberg, which he guarded jealously, his own personal oracle. The truth was, he had not written an original word in twenty years, but as long as nobody else knew how to delve into the Delphic mysteries of Bloomberg, he felt he was safe. The *Gazette*'s own guru. He knew Emerson knew how, and was always rather guarded. Emerson teased him mercilessly.

'Morning Si. My favourite plagiarist. How's the speed-reading going? Got enough to write anything yet?'

'Research, James, it's called research. Something you would do well to note.'

'OK then, Guru, fill me in. What's the word?'

'Well, James, it looks as though the crisis might be coming to an end.'

'Really? Why?'

'We've had a huge rally in all the Japanese markets. Somebody somewhere has been buying the bollocks out of the stocks, the bonds, the currency. You name it. Never seen anything like it. The Nikkei is up over twelve per cent, twelve per cent in one day, and volume is three times average. It's the same story on the index futures, massive volume, and JGBs have rallied six points.'

'What's behind it? Any news? IMF package for Indonesia, maybe?'

'No, that's the funny thing. No news at all. Just huge buying right out of the blocks. And led by one name.'

'Not the Post Office? Are the Japs trying to buy their own way out of trouble again? The MoF been powering up the printing presses?'

'No no. Not Japanese. Offshore.'

'Surely not Soros? Last I heard he was extremely negative about the whole thing. Maybe Tiger?'

'Word is on the Street that it's Xenfin. Saul Krantz himself, apparently, waging a one-man war.'

'Xenfin? Wow. They're normally pretty low-profile. I mean huge, but they don't like their name on the tape.'

'I know. Tried to get a quote from Krantz but he wasn't available. Spoke to some girl, van Dyck or something, no, van Aalst, that was it, van Aalst. She said it wasn't company policy to comment on market rumours regarding their activity, but off the record she could confirm that they had been buying heavily. Japan. Thinks everything's undervalued. Thinks they've suffered enough already on the back of the bloodbath in South East Asia, and that we'll all be thinking these prices are a steal in two weeks' time.'

'She may be right. Sounds like she's got balls. Let me make a quick call to one of my old buddies at Steinman's in Tokyo. He'll tell me what they've been seeing. Maybe get you some fresh material for that story yet.'

'Hi Jamie. Long time no hear. So you want to know about all this Jap buying, I take it.'

'Right. Talk is it's Xenfin who started it.'

'And carried it on, and finished it. Right on up to the close. We've never seen anything like it. They must've bought five billion dollars' worth of JGBs from us alone. God knows how much she did away from us. And the stocks! Jesus, they just didn't stop. Not just the big names, mind. Shitty ones too. The ones we all thought were close to the edge. Not any more! We had to stop dealing with them in the end.'

'Why ever that? No balls?'

'No lines left. They wanted to do all kinds of credit-sensitive trades too – write puts on the Nikkei, huge size, receive in twenty years, even bigger size. We didn't have enough lines in place for all of it. I reckon they alone are responsible for half the volume on Simex today. And they've put through some huge forex trades too. Dollar-yen mostly, always buying.'

'Well that's made some salesman's year in one day. Who's the lucky one? Do I know him, or is he after my time?'

'Oh, you know him, but he's not a salesman. That's the funny thing. Xenfin always insists on talking to Cameron Dodds. Remember him? He was a trader on the EMG desk in your day. Well he runs the desk now, and Xenfin will only speak to him, no matter what the product.'

'Really? That's weird. Is Dodds in Tokyo now?'

'No no. Still in London. He normally handles Xenfin's Asian business first thing in the morning when he gets in, before Tokyo closes. Or if it's urgent they call him at home in the night and he phones the orders in to us.'

'Holy shit, so Dodds executed all these trades from home? That's kinda dangerous, isn't it? I hope he has some screens there at least.'

'No he doesn't. But he didn't need them today. He spent all night in the office. He was there from the word go. Must've known they were going to be busy.'

'Really. By the way, what's the history here? Why does Xenfin speak to a trader like Dodds and not to a salesperson? The sales force must hate that. Xenfin is one of the biggest clients in the world.'

'Oh, you know. Same old story. The Dodds dick. He used to shag the fund-manager. Still does occasionally, so I'm told. Think they were at college together.'

His old colleague's words rang in his ears. '*Must've known they were going to be busy . . . think they were at college together.'* It couldn't be. Surely not. Xenfin and Steinman, Schwartz? Manipulating markets together? The implications were mind-boggling. Emerson leapt from Si Newman's desk where he had made the call to Tokyo, and left a bemused financial editor calling after him.

'Jim! Jim! What is it? Come on Jim! Tell me!'

He ran up the back stairs two at a time to Jake Samuels's office. It was closed and in darkness, but he burst in and switched on the lights. It was just as they had left it the previous night, even the whisky glasses were still there, an amber residue congealed in the bottom. But there it was! A single sheet lay face down on Samuels's fax machine. This must be it.

Heart pounding he turned it over and saw the imperious eagle at the head, the symbol of the Federal Reserve Bank. Quickly he scanned it . . . *Thank you for invitation . . . delighted to pass on information . . . Mr Turner is available on those dates . . . brief résumé . . . Sudanese immigrant . . . Bronx Catholic High School . . . Stanford . . .* cum laude . . . And then he saw it. He could scarcely believe it. *Marshall Scholarship, St Mary's College, Oxford. 1987–9.*

St Mary's College. The same one as Hugh, and the same one as Morley Lafarge and Chris Blake. Four of them. And if his old mate in Tokyo was right, probably Annie van something and Cameron Dodds too. That would make six! Same college, same time. They were behind it all! A lawyer, a central banker, a diplomat, a hedge-fund manager, a trader and Hugh. A journalist. Could the six of them have done this together? On their own? It was almost inconceivable. Almost.

CHAPTER 3

ANNY BROOKES WAS AN UNLIKELY MEDIA STAR, BUT WALLACE Bradley had decided this was the best way to secure optimum coverage of the revelations he was about to make. The original plan had been to release the story to the press by using Hugh Emerson's position on the *Gazette* to good effect. Following Hugh's 'withdrawal' from the project, however, and the inadvisability of feeding the story to his brother James in the light of his own investigation, television was deemed to be the way forward. Blake had voiced his own concerns that Brookes was not the best performer, and that the stresses of live television may cause him to buckle, but Bradley insisted. Time was getting short for the final move on Japan, and the damage Brookes could inflict on the faith of the marketplace in the very numbers which form the basis for much of their investment decisions was considerable.

Brookes himself had a deep loathing of the profession into which he had insinuated himself so successfully over the last ten years. Sanderson, Toomey, McClintock, the company for which he worked, was one of the top three accountancy firms in the world. They employed fifteen thousand people worldwide, a faceless army of analysts who would quietly beaver away in company records, verifying, checking and cross-checking that the numbers presented for public consumption were a true representation of that company's business.

Did you really borrow as little as you said you borrowed? Where are the loan documents? Did you really spend as much as you claimed on plant and material? Show me the invoices? Were sales as high as all that after such a poor year? Where are the order books? And earnings. What about earnings? Do your figures tally with the inventory positions?

Earnings were the key number in many cases, for this was probably the most significant figure in determining both the value of a company itself, and its ability to borrow money in the international capital markets. The value of any company was reflected in its stock price, and its ability to borrow was shown in its credit-rating. If the earnings figures were distorted, if they were shown to be too high, then in all likelihood both the credit rating and the stock price were too high as well.

But accountancy firms did not make stock recommendations, nor did they assign credit ratings. That was the job of stockbrokers, investment banks and credit-rating agencies. Accountancy firms merely gave their seal of approval that the numbers purported by the company to be true were in fact an accurate reflection of the facts. Stockbrokers and credit-rating agencies made mistakes all the time; shares went down when they were a hot tip to rocket, companies defaulted on their debt when they were viewed as being safe. But those mistakes, though often costly to the man in the street, were excusable. For they were nothing more than subjective, individual opinions of highly paid professionals, who did nothing else all day long but interpret the numbers. The numbers were the starting point, the given, and they were presented as gospel by the accountants.

What Danny Brookes was about to do was to call into question the accuracy of many of those numbers. He was going to blow the whistle, and he had good reason to do so.

In the late seventies, his father, Gregory Brookes, had liked to dabble in the stock market. He did not earn a lot of money, but the family was comfortable, and his minor successes had enabled the Brookes clan to take slightly more exotic holidays and drive a slightly higher model Ford than was the norm on their particular housing estate in the suburbs of Leicester. But that was before he had ever heard of Anglo-BioVac.

They were a small company based in Cambridgeshire and beginning to make waves in the embryonic but booming biotechnology sector. They specialized in developing vaccines for the medical profession, and caused several newspaper headlines in 1979 with talk of a new breakthrough in immunization techniques against, of all things, the common cold. This was big news, and the stock price had trebled in a matter of weeks.

Gregory Brookes had got the tip early from a friend of his in the pub, who had read of it in a share-tipping column in the *Sun*. The *Sun* journalist had copied it virtually verbatim from the first draft of a City stockbroker's report he had found left on the tube one evening on his way home from work. The stockbroker's analyst for his part had written his lengthy recommendation based on the figures just released in Anglo-BioVac's latest annual report to shareholders, which pointed to the recent sale to a major pharmaceutical company of a licence to manufacture three new revolutionary vaccines.

Those figures, the figures on which the firm of stockbrokers had based their strong 'buy' recommendation, had been duly audited and signed off by the local firm of Cambridge accountants still handling Anglo-BioVac's affairs. The senior partner in the accountancy firm played squash with the head research chemist at the company. He had even personally provided some of the original seed capital when the company was getting off the ground. He knew his client and he trusted him. He did not feel it necessary to insist on seeing the terms and conditions of the manufacturing licences his friend told him they had sold. He could see the money they had received for them, after all, and that was considerable. And besides, he was not a lawyer. It was not his job to verify the endless clauses and sub-clauses, contingent conditions and further testing requirements the pharmaceutical company had included. Was it?

Gregory Brookes was no rocket scientist when it came to investing, but he reckoned he understood a thing or two about supply and demand. He had heard of Warren Buffet and Benjamin Graham, and he liked their approach. Men will always have to shave (buy Gillette!); women will always have their periods (buy Tampax!); and he had only to walk into his local branch of Boots the Chemists and see the extraordinary range of over-the-counter cold remedies on offer to understand the enormous potential market for a vaccine of this kind. This was his way out of the estate. This was his ticket to Brookvale

Avenue and the double-fronted houses with carriageway drives and conifer hedges.

He had bought the new-built house from which he longed to escape, as a newlywed in 1961. He had paid twelve thousand pounds then, but almost twenty years of growth had seen its value rise to around forty-five thousand by 1979, and his mortgage was almost paid off. Another pal from the pub was a local surveyor. He knew Greg's house of old, and he didn't actually need to have a look at it to come up with a nice friendly valuation. He filled in the forms for the bank and estimated a valuation of fifty-five thousand. What did he care? He had his indemnity insurance didn't he?

Gregory Brookes's remortgage application was passed by the bank without a second glance. The valuation and structural report was by a well-known local surveyor, and Brookes himself had an exemplary payment history on the small outstanding mortgage he still had. The purpose of remortgaging was to make structural improvements and finance imminent school fees for his three children. Good, sound, valid reasons. He only earned eleven thousand a year, which made his application for a fifty-thousand mortgage somewhat above the normal earnings multiple allowed, but the bank's risk was limited. Property prices were rising and, if the worst came to the worst and the Brookes couldn't keep up with the payments, then they could just foreclose, couldn't they?

When Gregory Brookes spent his newfound fifty thousand pounds on one hundred and twenty-five thousand shares of Anglo-BioVac at forty pence a share, the price had never been higher. He was ecstatic. It had gone up a whole ten pence the day before. He knew there was no way he could afford to service the new mortgage he had just taken out for long, but then he did not anticipate holding the stock for very long either. His target for the price was one pound twenty. Triple your money. A hundred and fifty grand. The way things were going, he'd be able to sell in the next few weeks, repay the mortgage and move the family to Brookvale Avenue. He had not told his wife, of course. He wanted it to be a surprise. But he had already secretly been to have a look at a house that had just come up for sale.

As it turned out, Gregory Brookes had bought right at the top of the market. The share price nudged forty-two the next day, but nothing actually traded there, and then came the announcement. The pharmaceutical company which had 'bought' the licences declared that human testing had shown the new vaccines to be almost wholly in-effective outside the theoretical confines of Anglo-BioVac's animal testing laboratory. It also turned out that the money paid for the licences was actually contingent upon the success of those human tests, and was now returnable. The audited reports, which had listed those funds as hard, solid earnings, were meaningless, and the share price of Anglo-BioVac fell overnight to eight pence.

The accountancy firm which had approved the figures was dragged through the dirt, of course, and aggrieved investors sought redress through the courts, but it would be two years before the verdict was passed. It pointed to an overt failure on behalf of the senior partner to fulfil his responsibility of proper due diligence in examining the relevant documentation. It also blamed the board of directors of Anglo-BioVac for failing to point out the patent error in the accounts, and compensation for shareholders was agreed at an average share price of twenty-five pence. But there was nowhere near enough money to go round.

Anglo-BioVac had gone bust shortly after the announcement, as other creditors withdrew funding, and the accountancy firm had very few assets which could be seized to make a pay-out, especially as they had neglected to pay their professional indemnity insurance premiums for two years. The partners had ring-fenced their own property in offshore trusts or their spouses' names long ago, and the company cars and the leasehold on the offices in Cambridge city centre raised only a few thousand. The Institute of Chartered Accountants withdrew the partners' charter, of course, but if ever there was the case of a toothless self-regulator shutting the stable the door too late, this was it. And it was all much too little too late for Gregory Brookes.

Whilst the court case had proceeded, he had struggled to maintain the payments on the mortgage. But he couldn't bring himself to tell his wife what had happened, and their savings soon ran dry. The letter from the bank announcing their intention to foreclose on the mortgage had come the day after the fourth missed payment, and even at that late stage Gregory Brookes had spent the day scouring the press and Teletext for signs of any resolution in the long-running court case. He left work early that day, at three o'clock, in his Ford Cortina, the Ghia model with central-locking and electric windows. He knew no one would be home yet, and he was right.

Danny Brookes found his father when he got from school. He was still sitting in the car, but the car was in the garage and the engine was still running and his father was quite dead.

'And, run VT.'

'I have with me tonight Daniel Brookes, former partner of the renowned accountancy firm Sanderson, Toomey, McClintock from which he resigned earlier this morning. Mr Brookes, would you care to inform us of the details of your allegations? It seems you have damning evidence of a connivance between senior officers of the firm and their clients in, shall we say, the "window-dressing" of company accounts for public consumption.'

'That is correct Jeremy. The term "creative accounting" is almost always used with a smile, a nudge and a wink with the understanding that it is in everyone's best interests to "adjust" the facts to the best possible light. Well, in my opinion that is nothing short of fraudulent activity, and it can be profoundly damaging to the man in the street. I have with me documents and tapes, pertaining principally to our business in Asia, which show . . .'

The *Newsnight* story ran and ran. Within twelve hours of the original broadcast, stock exchanges around the world had suspended the shares of any company audited by Sanderson, Toomey, McClintock pending further investigations, and the credit-rating agencies put out blanket warnings that the debt-ratings of those same companies were under review for possible downgrade. But the aftershocks went further than that.

Fundamental questions were raised in various parliaments as to the desirability of self-regulation in the accounting industry, and independent bodies were set up to look into the establishment of government agencies for that purpose. The *Times* ran with a headline the next day asking 'Who audits the auditors?' and Jake Samuels unwittingly contributed to Wallace Bradley's blockbuster by paying a large amount on behalf of the *Gazette* for exclusive publication rights to the tapes and documents Brookes had abstracted from his employer's archives.

But more importantly than that, an enormous blow had been struck against the confidence of the public at large in the integrity of the financial industry. There was a widespread withdrawal of money from unit trusts and mutual funds, and especially in Asia, where Brookes had shown the extent of the nepotism, cronyism and unadulterated egotism prevalent in the markets. There was a bloodbath, but it was only a taster of what was yet to come.

But Danny Brookes did not care. He had had his hour in the spotlight and Pegasus was on track.

In Oxford, the oak floorboards had been polished, the cushions plumped and the semen stains scrubbed from the sofa, for Wallace Bradley was preparing to receive some very important visitors from America.

In many respects the people he would be greeting held more influence in the financial markets than Byron Powell or Dick Brightwell, or any hedge-fund owner, or any bank chairmen. At this point in the crisis at least. And they were vital in the final stages of Bradley's plan, for they held the key to the execution of his ultimate goal.

The debt crisis in Asia had been translated into a worldwide problem. His people, the Pegasus people, had lit fires in key places at key moments and fanned the flames with loose talk to the press and massive sales of bonds and currencies. No one element would have been enough on its own. You cannot bring down a system just by selling a lot of bonds, it has to be more fundamental than that, and that had been the genius behind Bradley's plan.

The system was flawed in the first place, and he had conspired to create a series of superficial events which, taken in concert, would highlight those flaws and undermine the basic fundamental precept, *confidence*, upon which the system depended to function. The very freedom of the almighty free market would be its own undoing. And with it would go not just the Japanese banks, but Japan itself. For he was now very close to that ultimate aim.

The three gentlemen who filed solemnly into his rooms that day were not government officials, nor were they bankers. They were actually accountants by training, and they represented an agency of such power in the financial markets that their actions alone could control the viability of not only private companies but entire countries. For, in Oxford that day, to hear the opinions of Wallace Bradley, were the chairman and two vice-chairmen of Jenner & Phipps. The largest credit-rating agency in the world.

For a century and a half, Jenner & Phipps had provided a service to the markets. Broadly speaking, for a fee, they gave an independent opinion on the credit worthiness of institutions. If Braxton Federal had wanted to lend money to Pee Seuar Land Holdings, they could have looked up the Jenner & Phipps report on the company and received an unbiased opinion as to Pee Seuar Land Holdings' ability to repay both the interest on the loan and the principal at maturity. To expedite matters, and to provide a quick and dirty assessment for the lazy loan officer who might not want to plough through a ten-page report before lending a hundred million dollars of his depositors' money to some property shark in Bangkok, they developed a system of easy-to-understand ratings. These ranged, in Phipps' system, from AAA++ all the way down to D, which stood for 'Default'. There were no longer many AAA++ rated entities in the world, and the few remaining tended to be major industrialized countries, such as America, Germany or the UK. Further down the list were the smaller, shakier nations of the world and the mass of corporations which provided the bulk of Jenner & Phipps' business. Jenner & Phipps themselves were fiercely independent, and had established over a long period a reputation for clear assessments and unbiased opinions.

These opinions also happened to have a direct impact on the cost of borrowing money for the companies and countries they rated. Banks lent money to just about anyone, it was all a question of the interest rate. The riskier the loan, the higher the rate of interest the banks demanded to compensate them for taking that risk – the risk that they would not get their money back either on time or at all. Jenner & Phipps' ratings provided a means of quantifying that risk.

Occasionally, the analysts who followed the various companies on behalf of the rating agency changed their minds. A company formerly rated AA+ might be downgraded to BBB following, say, a hostile takeover of a competitor, to pay for which they might have to increase sharply the amount of their borrowings. Such a downgrade had two effects. It increased the rate the company had to pay for any future borrowings, as banks saw the new, riskier rating and demanded a higher rate, and it depressed the value of old loans taken out when the company was in better shape and paying lower rates for its borrowings. For companies who habitually borrowed a lot to finance their ongoing business and any expansion, a downgrade in their Jenner & Phipps' rating was critical. The increased cost of servicing their debt would eat into profits, could turn profits into losses, or even put them out of business if the change was dramatic. The same could be true for whole countries. And that was what Wallace Bradley wanted. He aimed to put Japan Inc. out of business.

For five years now, Bradley had been acting as an external consultant to Jenner & Phipps on the Asian region. His reputation as the leading expert of his time on Asia, not to mention his rôle as adviser to several of the regional governments, meant it was quite a coup for J&P to have him on their books. Recent speculation that he could be awarded the Nobel Prize only added to his kudos. They doted on what he had to say. Whenever he mailed them a report, they took it as gospel and acted upon it as appropriate. And they had enhanced their own reputations immeasurably by doing so.

For Bradley had spotted the problems looming in the Thai property sector a full twelve months before the demise of Pee Seuar Land Holdings, and Jenner & Phipps had taken steps to downgrade the credit-rating of every company in that sector. Bradley was a guru and they had slavishly followed his advice. Of course, they had their own in-house committees and procedures to follow, but hey, what was the point of paying these outside consultants if you didn't follow what they said? Isn't that how management consultancies prospered? To the investors and lenders who subscribed to Jenner & Phipps' service they looked not just shrewd, but positively clairvoyant. Like the great Henry Kaufman in the eighties, Bradley had become his own self-fulfilling prophesy. And today he was about to prophesy catastrophe.

'Gentlemen, thank you for coming all this way to see me. I apologize for not having been able to come to you, but my work currently prevents it.' He neglected to mention he would himself be shortly travelling to Japan, but then that was personal. 'What I am about to say to you may seem dramatic, but this is a matter of the utmost importance, and I fear speed is of the essence if you are both to maintain one hundred and fifty years of unsullied reputation for Jenner & Phipps, and to protect the investors and lenders who depend so on your credit ratings and opinions. Please, do I have your word that no mention of our talks today can be released until any official announcement you might care to make is agreed upon? Any leak, any irresponsible handling of this matter, could be cataclysmic for the borrower concerned.'

'You have our word, Professor.' Bruce Phipps, the chairman, spoke. His Texan drawl and intense, staring eyes brought to mind a TV evangelist or cult leader, which in the eyes of the world's investing community, he actually was. 'Jenner & Phipps prides itself on its sensitivity in releasing market-sensitive information.' The jargon rolled in large pre-formed lumps from his tongue. He spoke all the time as if at a press conference, even to his wife in bed and to his four children on the rare occasions he ran into them at the breakfast table. 'The investors are only half of our business. We try to act as empathetically towards the borrower as possible when bad news is concerned. And I assume we are talking about bad news.'

'The worst possible news you could imagine.'

'And who is the borrower in question, Professor?'

'I have dragged you halfway around the world, gentlemen, to give you my opinions on . . .' Bradley's peroration was interrupted by the unmistakable sound of a screaming baby outside his door, the high-pitched bleat of a newborn, followed by a timid knock. 'Excuse me for one second, sirs.'

He leapt from his armchair and yanked open the inner door. The outer door, the oak, was also closed. He hadn't wanted any disturbances.

'Who is it? Can't you see I'm . . . Oh for Christ's sake, girl. It's you! Are you still at this university? Get away from me. I won't have you hounding me like this! And take your mewling brat with you, you ignorant little tart!'

Bradley took several deep breaths and returned to his guests.

'Gentlemen, please forgive the small interruption just now. I can assure you it will not happen again.' He could still see the pathetic image of Patsy O'Connor, snivelling in the corridor outside his room. Her cheeks were stained with running mascara and her shoulders with regurgitated breast milk. He still felt aroused, the sight of the red hair, pale complexion and full lips, and the breasts, much heavier than he remembered. God, he'd like another go at her. The presence of the child was just an unwelcome obstacle.

'Japan, gentlemen. Japan will be the topic of our conversation today.' If he was honest with himself, Bradley found himself more aroused at the prospect of screwing Japan than the idea of Patsy O'Connor's breasts. He could never think about Japan without that happening. Without thinking about what he was going to do to them, without thinking about what had been done to his mother. He sat down quickly and crossed his legs.

And then he began his lecture. He knew that his visitors were not professional economists, and so he did everything in his considerable power to bombard them with jargon. For if he knew Bruce Phipps, a true jargonaut himself, he would be impressed by Bradley's jargon even if, perhaps especially if, he didn't understand it. He spoke of money supply and velocity, he talked of the monetarization of debt, deflation, reflation, inflation. He drew equations on napkins, fired questions they couldn't answer and gave them the answer before they'd had time to admit they didn't know. And he talked and he talked and he talked for over two hours. It was full of statistics and percentages, ratios and equations, Greek symbols and Roman rhetoric. And at the end of it all, he flopped back exhausted in his chair and tossed a five-hundred-page report at each of them.

'This report, gentlemen, sets out in rather fuller detail the background to, and the reasons for, my concrete recommendations to which we will come presently. The conclusion, as I am sure you are aware, is that Japan, both in the public and private sector, has levels of debt which are quite extraordinary. Quite unlike anything in the industrialized world. And they are rising. The economy is deep in recession and tax revenues to the government are falling. I project that the debt burden will increase by 100 per cent of GDP in the next twelve months, maybe sooner. This is a classic public debt trap, gentlemen, such as was experienced in the thirties. They are trying to borrow their way out of debt. Many learned economists have advocated this strategy, but it is so clearly flawed in the context of what is happening elsewhere in the world. It is financial, fiscal and monetary suicide all at the same time.

'Japan, in my professional opinion, risks reaching the situation whereby the income of the entire nation, private and public sectors combined, is not capable of even servicing the debt they have incurred. They won't even be able to pay the interest. When this occurs, and you note that I say "when" and not "if", the Japanese yen will cease to hold any value as a currency. This is much worse than what is being observed in several US states currently. There we have bartering as a *substitute* for cash. Cash still works, it is just difficult to get hold of. Its value is unquestioned. If anything, its value is enhanced because of its scarcity. I am sure the United States authorities will take the necessary steps to ensure that the dollar does not become devalued.'

'But can't the Japs do the same?' Phipps had been following. Just.

'No. They have demonstrated over the past few years an asinine inability to manage their own economy. They borrow from Matsumoto-san to pay Suzuki-san. What is the point of someone accepting one IOU in repayment of an earlier IOU, when those IOUs are flooding the market? If they print more banknotes, those notes will be less valuable than toilet paper, and too slippery for the job.'

'So just what are you suggesting, Bradley?'

'Standard and Poors, your competitors, and Moody's, have Japan rated as an AA credit risk. They too cite the high levels of public debt as a cause for concern. You at Jenner and Phipps, the oldest and most influential agency in the world, still have them as a AAA risk. I challenge you now, gentlemen, to grasp the nettle. Regain the initiative from your competitors and tell your clients the risks they are currently running if they invest in Japanese Government debt, or indeed in the Japanese yen as a currency. Japan has the finances of a third world nation. If they were not so prominent in G-7, the IMF would be drawing the curtains and calling in the priest. They are like a bankrupt con-man in a millionaire's suit, and if we are not careful, they will relieve the more gullible amongst us of all our savings. As your consultant for the region,' Bradley spoke like a cancer specialist delivering bad news, 'I must advise you to cut the rating of Japan from AAA to B.'

There was a stunned silence in the room. Nobody spoke for almost a minute whilst Bradley's long-case clock ticked its countdown to the response. The two less senior men did not dare to utter before gauging the response of their chairman. Phipps was indeed the first to speak. And he spoke with the air of one who has experienced an epiphany. His eyes shone, he beamed and punched the air.

'Japan. Single B. I love it. It's so . . . perfect. So, outrageous. So . . .' And at this point he brandished Bradley's unread ream of statistics above his head like a prophet. 'Justifiable!' Then the other men spoke.

'Quite incredible.'

'They'll be below Indonesia.'

'And Russia.'

'Even Sudan will be stronger.'

'Exactly, my friends. And rightly so, because those countries all have functioning currencies and inordinately less debt than the Japanese. But mark my words, this will be only the first step. Because Standard and Poor's and Moody's will be forced to follow. They can't ignore the facts. And then we will downgrade again. In my considered opinion, the Government of Japan will default on its debt by mid-March. D for Default, gentlemen. That will be the ultimate target.'

And by then, thought Bradley, Japan will be on its knees. They'll be begging for money from the IMF, the World Bank, Oxfam, like paupers with their imperial caps in their pudgy little hands. But no one will be interested. No one else will care because they will all have their own problems. No other government will be *able* to lend them a penny. For what he had just suggested was indeed outrageous. And, if Phipps and his cohorts managed to bulldoze it through their credit-rating committee at the next meeting, he, Wallace Bradley, would have achieved the impossible.

For although he was not in the Japanese Government, the Japanese Ministry of Finance or the Bank of Japan, Wallace Bradley was, from outside the country, almost by remote control, about to effect a dramatic increase in interest rates in another country at a time when that country could least afford it. And the authorities would be powerless to prevent it, because it would be *what the market demanded*. This was nothing to do with governments, this was the free market pure and simple. It would kill off businesses by the thousand. It would paralyse industry, commerce and trade. The entire country would grind to a halt within the shortest of times.

When interest rates were raised or lowered by a government or a central bank, it amounted to fine tuning the economy for the long run. They moved them generally by a quarter or a half a per cent at a time. In extreme cases, extreme measures had been used. During the last sterling crisis, the Chancellor of the Exchequer raised interest rates by three per cent, and was quickly forced, *by the markets*, to reverse it. But Wallace Bradley had bigger ideas. This would be his *coup de grâce*.

For, thanks to the efforts of the Pegasus Forum, and thanks to the debt crisis they had precipitated all over the world, *the market* now demanded a huge premium for lending money to borrowers with a low credit rating. No lenders wanted to take credit risks and the availability of capital for borrowing had dwindled to a fraction of the normal amounts. In the international markets, the difference between the interest rates demanded of a AAA-rated borrower, and a B-rated one at current crisis levels was around *fifteen* whole percentage points. And this is what Wallace Bradley had wanted – if he was successful he would be effectively *raising* their interest rate by that incredible amount.

Jenner & Phipps were going to hold their next meeting to review ratings as soon as Bruce Phipps and his team returned from Oxford with Bradley's report and analysis. As long as they approved it, and he was sure that, with Bruce Phipps's evangelical backing, they would, the news would be released the following day into an unsuspecting market. It would be complete and utter chaos. He couldn't wait. And he would be there when it happened.

When his guests had finally left, Bradley went to his desk and pulled out another file. In it was an envelope. The postmark on the envelope was three months ago, and it had been posted at the central Post Office, Nanjing, in the People's Republic of China. He gently extracted the flimsy, almost translucent paper from inside the cheap envelope and laid it on the desk in front of him.

The letter came from a lady, once a professor of modern history at Shanghai Jiao Tong University. She was now in her eighties and no longer an active academic as far as the rest of the world was concerned, but to a select few she was known by another name: Madame Y.

She was the founder of, and still the main driving force behind, the Dragon Institute, originally based in Nanjing itself and now comprising several other, extremely low-profile and secretive centres scattered across China and the Pacific rim.

She had been in correspondence with Wallace Bradley for some twenty-five years, and this was the seventh letter he had received from her. He had even met her once, briefly, in 1985 at the Dragon Institute's anonymous headquarters adjacent to where the tower of the Jinling Hotel now stands. Bradley had been in Nanjing for the opening of a special memorial, a great hall of roughly hewn granite blocks and glass walls containing pile upon pile of human bones. This was China's very own Holocaust Museum, and it commemorated China's very own and largely forgotten Holocaust. For Nanjing was formerly China's capital city. In December 1937, when the Japanese Imperial Army had marched into town, fresh from their successes down the river in Shanghai, Nanjing was known to the outside world as Nanking.

Three hundred thousand deaths later, and after thirty thousand women, conservatively speaking, had been raped, disembowelled or had their breasts sliced off before being nailed to walls, the city became known as the site of the Rape of Nanking. Or for some, the Nanking Massacre.

And if the Nanking Memorial Hall was China's Holocaust Museum, then Madame Y was China's Simon Wiesenthal. At the age of seventeen she had wriggled beneath a stack of corpses, schoolfriends, classmates, and parents, as the bayonet blows lanced through the cadaverous flesh which protected her. And she remained there for three days.

Too terrified to move, she lay wedged beneath the bodies of her sister and mother, and she became obsessed. And her obsession remained with her to this day: to hunt down and expose any remaining Japanese responsible for the outrage at Nanking.

She had been remarkably successful. Most of them were actually rounded up at the time by official means and executed for war crimes in the nineteen forties. The few escapees met gruesome deaths after Madame Y's exhaustive researches had traced them, through endless rounds of bureaucracy and name changes, and passed their identities on to those young and zealous or bereaved enough to pursue the matter to its usually grisly conclusion. The last known Nanking fugitive had been executed at his home somewhere in San Francisco in 1971. There had been no shortage of willing volunteers from the local Chinatown to carry out the task.

Since 1971 she had enlarged the scope of her research to include any former Japanese soldiers known to be guilty of war crimes anywhere in Asia, whether they were senior officers of the *kempeitai* or brainwashed camp guards. It had kept her very busy.

The only war crimes trials held for forced prostitution had been run by the Dutch in Jakarta, then known as Batavia, in 1948. They were woefully incomplete. The names of the accused, and their victims, had been assigned to secret archives until their release date in 2025. When the names of those alleged perpetrators are finally released, it will be discovered that the majority of them died, thanks to the efforts of Madame Y. Several of them were imprisoned at the time of those trials, one for as little as seven years, but her reach was such that none of those convicted survived the first anniversary of their incarceration.

She had many nicknames in the circle of people known to her, most of which translated badly from the Chinese or Japanese. Those who assisted her in her searches called her, in Chinese, the 'Rogue She-Elephant' due to her legendary strength and long memory. Those who still lived in fear of a knock at the door from one of her 'missionaries', knew her simply as the 'Poisonous Walnut', a reference to her reputedly deep-brown skin colouration and wizened appearance. But to most who knew her, or knew of her and admired her, she was known simply as 'the Empress of Nanking'.

On Wallace Bradley's letter from the Empress of Nanking, written in English and typed on an old typewriter using a threadbare ribbon, there was no greeting, and no return address. It said simply:

Captain Kaifu Shimizu
Ship's Captain, Japanese Navy, 1933–1940
Commandant, Palembang Internment Camp, Dutch East Indies, 1940–1945.
Arrested 1945 pending trial.
Released, unconvicted, Dec. 1949 on termination of trials.
Forged death certificate in above name, dated Feb. 1950, recovered from Osaka Registry Office, Nov. 2000
Yoshimi Akira
Domestic Sales Manager (Ship-Building), Yokosuka Heavy Industry.
1950–64
International Sales Manager (Ship-Building) 1964–72
Managing Director, Yokosuka Heavy Industry 1972–84

Board Member (Business Development) Yokosuka Corporation,
Tokyo. 1984
Chief Executive, Yokosuka Corporation, 1990
Chairman, Yokosuka Corporation, 1992–Present.
Age and Health of Subject: 85, good

Below this, various headings had been added by a stamp of purple ink.
The blanks were filled in by hand.

Dragon Institute Comments:

Confidence: 100 per cent
Proof: Documentary, photographic, physical
Date of confirmation of identification: October 1st, 2001
Date of first application: March 4th, 1975
Address of applicant: Professor Wallace Bradley,
St Mary's College, Oxford, UK.

Below this was a final handwritten comment from the Empress of
Nanking herself. It said simply: 'This man was known as the "the
Cactus" in Palembang. If you should run into him, you might remind
him of this. As you see fit.' Every day for three months, every day since
he had received this letter, he had read it, and he knew every detail by
heart. So much had happened in that short time, but most importantly
of all for Professor Wallace Bradley, he had begun the final stages of his
move on Japan.

The fire had been lit in the nations of South East Asia; they had been
the kindling, the tinder-dry brushwood. The world's greatest takers of
foreign capital, and the most flammable. In Bradley's eyes the dispensable
sacrifice.

From there it had been sufficient to keep pouring fuel on the fire, and
the fuel for the most part had come from the massive balance sheets of
Xenfin and Steinman, Schwartz. The heat had built until the flames had
begun to lick at and singe the trunks of some of the smaller firs of the

Black Forest, the Redwoods of the west coast of America and the old oaks of England. Until now the delicate cherry blossoms of the imperial Japanese gardens had been spared from direct attack. Deliberately. Yes, they had begun to wilt, and smoke damage had blighted the early buds, but now the wind was about to change direction. A full force nine westerly was about to blow up the Korean Strait in the form of an announcement from those arbiters of reputation, of creditworthiness and trust, Jenner & Phipps. And Wallace Bradley was ready.

The name he had wanted from the age of sixteen, the man he had hunted down across the years, was within his sights. The whole of Japan would stumble and fall to its knees. That is how it must be. The man and his deeds could not have existed in a vacuum. The system must be made to suffer, but he also wanted the man. In three days' time Wallace Bradley, Nobel-nominee and world-renowned economist, had an appointment to meet with the eighty-five-year-old chairman of the Yokosuka Corporation, Japan's largest and most powerful industrial giant. This was a man known across the business world as Yoshimi Akira, captain of industry. A man known to the few hundred wretched inmates of the Palembang military brothel as Captain Kaifu Shimizu. A man known to the Empress of Nanking as the Cactus. A man known to Wallace Bradley of St Mary's College, Oxford as Poseidon.

The blood thumped in Bradley's temples. Again he jammed his fists into his ears to lessen the pressure, the pain. He stood swaying in his crumpled brown suit, eyes clamped shut to dispel the images, but they never went away. Poseidon! King of the oceans! Violator of Medusa! Naked and roaring with laughter, sprawled on a blood-drenched tatami; in one hand a mighty trident, in the other a huge cactus, a spiked, Priapic phallus. Poseidon – sire of Pegasus.

CHAPTER 4

AS HE GUIDED HIS JAGUAR OUT ALONG THE M40 IN THE LATE afternoon, James Emerson was lost in thought. One thing above all was clear: he had to go to Oxford, to St Mary's College. That was the source, that was the common factor which kept on cropping up. And as he thought, it all began to come together.

What was it Samuels had said? Out of the blue Hugh had requested a transfer from 'The Emerson Bulletin' to the financial pages. Some Indonesian story had sparked his interest. That would make sense. If they wanted to start a panic in the region it would be useful to have a leading journalist on their side, churning out bogus stories to a market eager to believe the worst. And Lafarge. He had obviously been used to set up the accounts in Jakarta. He'd posed as the Sukon executive. Lubis was just a stool-pigeon, a conduit for the trades who would ask no questions and take the kickbacks. Shin Wang had got in the way and he'd been killed. Hugh had obviously got in the way too, somehow. And he'd been pushed off St Mary's tower. Emerson was convinced of that now. Blake the lawyer must have been responsible for all the paperwork. Setting up the shell company in Geneva. What was it Tamana had said about her brother Shin's suspicions concerning Sukon? *'He had a suspicion it was really one of the big US hedge funds, you know, in the Bahamas or Virgins or somewhere.'* Try Xenfin. Try the Caymans. And then there was Dodds. Cameron Dodds. Trader at Steinman, Schwartz. A leading light at the leading investment bank on the street. Could they really have done it together? Could they really have caused all this mess? What was the motive? Was it a massive fraud? Did they have millions, or billions, salted away somewhere? What could they possibly gain from it all? Currencies were losing their value and banks were closing down every day, all over the world. If they were just stealing money, they didn't need to spark a crisis like this.

And maybe there were others! Out there, still plotting, conniving, the next step in the conspiracy. What was the connection between these people. How did they meet? They were all at the same college, but how did they get together in the first place? And who was the driving force? Not Hugh. He'd gone. Not Lafarge. Too stupid. Blake? Maybe Blake. He seemed pretty shrewd, according to Samuels. And what about Dodds or van Aalst? Were they capable of organizing this whole thing? He vaguely remembered Dodds from his own time at Steinman, Schwartz. Bright, but a rebel. Dyed, spiky hair, suspicious sniff, if he remembered rightly. Not a corporate citizen. Not a leader. Of Annie van Aalst he knew nothing. But he knew that Lafarge had been in Oxford when Hugh had died. He'd let that much slip. *Maybe he'd actually been at the dinner Hugh had been attending when he died.* Maybe that was the connection! That pretentious dining society Hugh had been so proud to be a part of. The Pegasus Forum.

It was five in the evening and already dark when James Emerson parked his car in South Parks Road and jogged the half mile or so to St Mary's College. It was the beginning of term, and the streets were full of earnest young men and women bicycling from steamy coffee house to tutorial to lecture, the depths of winter but only eight short weeks away from the glorious Trinity term, when rugby gave way to cricket almost overnight, and long summer afternoons in the parks or on the Cherwell were followed by croquet on the lawns and Shakespeare in the quad.

As he arrived, breathless, in the porter's lodge, Emerson almost knocked over three morose grey-suited types, single vented and button-downed, one of whom shot him prissy, staring looks as they all shuffled into the waiting taxi. A London taxi. Bruce Phipps had had it wait for them during his meeting and was taking it straight back to Heathrow.

Emerson marched through the lodge and into Cranmer Quad with his best proprietorial strut, ignoring the 'College closed to visitors' sign and allowing of no challenge from questioning porters. He stopped the first college scout he saw, obvious from the short white coats in which they were preparing to serve that evening's dinner in hall, and asked for directions to the library.

'Strictly for College Members Only', it said on the door he pushed open. He drew some glares from the few students there at that hour, getting in the last minutes of work before dinner. He was clearly an interloper. Too old to be an undergraduate student, too smart in his Calvin Klein to be a don. Maybe a parent, or rich foreign postgrad. He tracked down the college history section and was happy to see a shelf crammed with thirty or forty identical volumes, soft-bound in bright blue. It was a collection of the last forty years of the annual St Mary's College magazine, *The Virgin*, as the college was known to its competitors and detractors. An irreverent and radical JCR committee had introduced the title for the magazine in the twenties. In it was a round-up of college activities for the preceding year, including reports from the various sports teams, religious organizations and social groups. This latter included the notorious dining societies. St Mary's had its fair share of those, copy-cat moulds of the Bullingdon or the Assassins or the Loders, by those too poor or too boorish or too boring to be included in the real thing. He opened up the latest copy, for 1999, and skipped through the entries. There were accounts from the Blaze, the Jurassics, the Malthusians and the Turks, all vying to outdo each other in excess, with reports of which restaurants or college rooms had been smashed up that term, who had been rusticated and who had defecated in whose window box. There was no mention of the Pegasus Forum. Odd. Why wasn't it mentioned?

Hugh had been so proud to be invited. He had told his big brother it was one of the oldest societies in the university, even that it had briefly gone under in the nineteenth century, but that they had been responsible for resurrecting it. They and some don. What was his name? Was he still around? Emerson picked another copy of the magazine off the shelf, this time the 1987 edition, the year Hugh had gone up to Oxford. Again, in the dining societies section there were reports of the same old clubs, but nothing on the Pegasus Forum. He went to jam that edition of *The Virgin* back into its chronological spot on the shelf, but it wouldn't go in all the way. He pushed a little harder, and the thin covers started to crease. He stopped and inserted his flattened hand between the books in an attempt to squash the neighbouring volumes a little more together and enlarge the available gap. There was a bit of folded card at the back of the shelf, which had apparently been the culprit. It felt like an index card of some sort, the type the more anal students used for organizing their notes, and he got hold of it between the tips of his straightened index and middle fingers in a scissor-like action. It took some pulling, as it had got jammed down the back of the bookcase itself, in the paper-thin crack between the shelf and the back wall, and all he succeeded in doing at first was to pull off the corner, which came away in his fingers. But he looked at the fragment and saw it was actually a heavy bit of good quality stationery, gilded around the edge. Like an invitation. Unable to give up what he had now started, and wanting to leave the books as he had found them, he delved back into the tightly-packed shelf and yanked out the rest of the blockage. He was right, it was an invitation. An old one.

The President of the Pegasus Forum
invites you to join him for port and cigars
immediately following Freshmen's Dinner
in the Talbot Room, St Mary's College,
October 4th 1987

There was a red stain at the top of the card, apparently where a mark, a wax seal of some sort, had long since become detached, and the card itself was extremely dog-eared and creased. James Emerson shivered. Hugh must have received an invitation like this one. Maybe it was actually his? An invitation to his ultimate death. His imagination began to work overtime. He could now clearly envisage his younger brother Hugh, on the first day of his first year at Oxford, clutching an invitation like this one in his hand. Fifteen years ago maybe *he* had been in this library on his first day at Oxford – he had always been an assiduous student. And the bell would have chimed for dinner. Freshers' Dinner. And he would have panicked about being late, and dashed back to his room to pull on his gown, leaving the strange invitation lying on the table in the library. And some soul had found it and stuffed it into the shelf from which James Emerson had plucked it many years later. He read over the invitation again before folding it carefully and sliding it into his wallet.

The rooms available in Oxford and Cambridge colleges for use by societies and clubs were many and varied in size. But if it was anything like the Cambridge system, Emerson reasoned, they were generally all reserved centrally at the porter's lodge. His next task was to discover in whose name the Talbot Room had been reserved on the fourth of October 1987. For that would most likely give him the name of someone he would very much like to meet: the don involved in resurrecting the Pegasus Forum.

The man whose name James Emerson was trying to discover was at that moment struggling with a small but surprisingly heavy suitcase down the winding oak stairs that led to his rooms. In his pocket was his passport, and an airline ticket to Tokyo. British Airways, of course. He didn't want to have to suffer the Japs before he absolutely had to. It was only twenty minutes since the visitors from Jenner & Phipps had left, but Wallace Bradley was on his way to Heathrow Airport already. At the bottom of the staircase, standing in the shadows of the archway and just off the main quadrangle, he found Patsy O'Connor. He was furious.

'Professor Bradley! I really have to talk to you. It's about the . . .'

'I'll have nothing more to do with you, girl. Do you hear? And if you make any more fuss I'll just have to make your little cheating plan known to the university authorities. Now get out of my sight!'

'But I have had your . . .'

Bradley swept past her into the quadrangle, desperate to escape her, desperate to avoid a scene.

'Baby!!!' she screamed at the top of her voice, and the first sobs howled their way across the echoing cloisters. Bradley stopped in his tracks. The blood was pounding in his temples again. He couldn't stand the screaming, the noise. He had to stop the noise! And he turned around and took four steps back into the shelter of the entrance to the staircase.

For a second O'Connor thought she had done it, got through to him, brought him back. She heard the echo of his footfalls on the stone-flagged walkway, and momentarily paused her sobbing. She was crouched down, rocking like a child on the soles of her feet, arms wrapped around her knees, and she looked up at the figure of Bradley walking through the archway. As he filled the entrance, he became outlined in silhouette by the lamp over the arch now behind him. It became darker in the hallway where O'Connor crouched.

'Oh, Professor. Thank you for returning. You see, I need some help, some money. I need to . . .'

Wallace Bradley said nothing more. He raised the back of his right hand and ripped it viciously across her cheek, cutting her with the signet ring he wore.

'And let that be a lesson to you. Plaguing me like this. Begging! Blackmailing!'

But Patsy O'Connor did not hear his parting words. Nor did she do any more crying. The surprise blow had knocked her off her haunches and she had rolled backwards, banging her head against the corner of the stone-clad doorway. She lay unconscious on the floor as Bradley turned away to leave for the airport. Her five-day-old baby, still in the pouch strapped to her stomach, did the rest of the crying for her.

It had not taken Emerson long to get the porter out of his lodge. A hoax telephone call from his mobile, claiming there was a group of 'town' thugs painting anti-university graffiti on the outside of the college's west wall had sufficed. In the five minutes he was gone, Emerson sneaked into the lodge and dug out the book for the college's room reservations. It seemed the Talbot Room was not so popular. A couple of dozen bookings per year at most. The slim ledger, which had been pressed into service for this purpose in 1952, was not yet full. On the fourth of October 1987, however, the room was clearly booked out to one Bradley, W., the name filled out in the rather too neat and childlike script of the man who had since become the head porter. A quick glance at the current college room list, pinned on the wall inside the lodge, confirmed that there was indeed still a Bradley, W., professor now no less, resident on staircase VI, room seven.

Emerson found Patsy O'Connor now conscious but still sitting on the stone floor at the foot of staircase VI, cradling her child and dabbing away the blood from the cut above her right cheek-bone. It is rare to come across newborn babies in Oxford colleges, and it crossed Emerson's mind that this girl and her child might be a homeless pair seeking shelter. He remembered Hugh telling him that, in a fit of misplaced charity once in the seventies, St Mary's College had opened up their Junior Common Room to the indigent during the winter months. A rape and numerous thefts later, mainly alcohol from the Fellows' cellars and the odd bit of silver, and the policy had been reversed. But there was still the occasional drifter to be found wandering lost in the corridors, thinking the offer of shelter was still valid.

'Please help me, sir.' Her broad Irish accent confirmed his suspicions. Street-dweller, definitely. Not from round these parts

'I'm sorry.' He tapped his one empty pocket. 'No change.'

'No! You don't understand! It's not like that. Listen to me. I need help. I'm a student and I have just been assaulted. By a Fellow of this college!'

Emerson groaned inwardly. Another one to rescue. And not as promising as the first. Little did he know.

'What's his name?'

'Bradley. Professor Wallace Bradley. You must have seen him leaving. You must have passed him on the way here! Short man. Plump, fifties, crumpled brown suit. Glasses. Carrying a suitcase. A horrible man. A beast, a monster. The father of my son.'

Emerson had seen him. In fact, Bradley had actually handed in his room keys at the lodge, as he always did when travelling for an extended period, whilst Emerson had been illicitly occupied in there. And Emerson realized now that he still had the keys in his coat pocket, where he had inadvertently thrust them in his consternation at being disturbed in mid-snoop. So the Bradley he was looking for liked beating up girls, did he? Girls carrying newborn babies. It was the first Emerson had heard of Wallace Bradley and he had already made up his mind about him. He hauled Patsy O'Connor to her feet and helped her back up the stairs. The baby, her baby, Bradley's baby was still strapped in the papoose-style carrier at her chest, face buried deep in her bosom. It now seemed to be sleeping, Emerson thought, or it's suffocated in there. She followed him mutely back up to Bradley's rooms.

'You know, Patsy – you did say you were called Patsy didn't you? – I'm a firm believer in fate.' He was cheery, in a no-nonsense, blustering sort of way. It was his way of calming her down from the shock of the violence she had just suffered. 'Here I was, just arrived in Oxford, wanting to meet a man I now know to be called Professor Wallace Bradley. And, somehow, fate decrees that this man is, this very day, leaving to go somewhere with a suitcase. Probably be away for a while. And not content with that, good old fate has the man hand me the keys to his room on the way out. I will always believe in fate, Patsy. Mark my words. Much more useful than God or any of that other nonsense.'

'Now there I do agree with you Mr Emerson.'

'James, please.'

'James. God never done me no good either. Look at me. Not six months to go till my finals, and stuck with this little one.' Her Irish accent was somehow stronger than normal, as if she was retreating to her roots to find comfort away from the bland, ill-defined vowels of southern England which had insinuated their way into her speech over the last two years.

'Well, I think *Professor* Bradley owes us both a little hospitality, don't you? And as he's gone, and we have his keys, why don't we help ourselves?'

Patsy O'Connor followed him like a lamb. She was glad to have somebody take charge, and he seemed to be very much in charge. She marvelled at the casual way in which he proposed entering somebody else's quarters, but he seemed to feel as if he had a right. And after what had happened to her, she certainly felt as if she had a right. She also marvelled at her lack of guilt. Maybe she had finally dealt with that particular Catholic laundry-mark which used to guide her life so in the past? Maybe she had shaken it off? She certainly felt liberated, empowered almost, as she followed Emerson into Bradley's rooms and helped him look around.

The first thing she noticed was how unusually clean everything was. There were flowers in vases and the floorboards had been swept and polished. He must have had visitors, or been trying to impress someone at least. This was borne out by the presence of four dirty coffee cups on the table, which was more typical of the middle-aged slob she knew and hated. How could anyone leave on a trip without cleaning away dirty cups? The man must be so institutionalized. Those dons were all the same, so used to the scouts coming in, clearing up, making the beds, all in worship at the altar of the intellect, all to cushion the mega-brains from having to deal with the mundanities of life that might sully the brilliance of their minds.

'So what is it you'll be looking for, Mr, er, I mean, James.' She felt him to be so clearly superior to her in every respect that the familiarity of first name terms was not easy for her.

'I need to find out about something called the Pegasus Forum, Patsy. It's a club of sorts, and the professor here ran it. Or runs it.'

'Oh, I know a little about that already.'

Emerson stopped his searches and wheeled around to look at her. 'What do you mean? Are you serious?'

'Well, Pegasus. He'd be that flying horse, wouldn't he? The Greek one. Or was it Roman?'

'Greek. And yes. The flying horse. What do you know?'

'Well for starters, he has a dirty great statue of the thing in his bedroom. Silver. On his dresser. It's mostly buried in dirty socks and week-old underpants, but I used to look at it whilst he was humping me. Gave me something impressive to admire, at least.'

'Anything else?'

'Well, then there's his computer. Tons of stuff on there with Pegasus in the title. And TPF come to think of it.'

'How on earth do you know that?'

And for the first time Patsy told someone her story. She explained how Bradley had blackmailed her for sex, how he had kept evidence of her connivance in their plot to make sure he recognized her exam paper in her finals, and the proof was in her e-mail he had kept stored in his computer. She told how she had tried to get in there and erase it whilst he slept, but that it was protected by passwords and all kinds of things. But that she had a good memory, and the names of the other files stuck in her mind because so many referred to Pegasus, and he had that statue in his room, and she could never understand it because he was an economist, not a classicist.

'An economist you say?' Emerson was beginning to understand more and more. 'What was his field?'

'Oh, he's an expert on the Far East. South East Asia, Japan, you name it. Probably *the* best man in the world on that particular region. I was so thrilled to be having tutorials with him at first. It was so exciting. What a man, what a mind. But then, I didn't know what he was really like . . .'

'*South East Asia, Japan, you name it.*' The words rang out in his ears. '*Probably the best man in the world on that particular region.*' It was Bradley. Professor Wallace Bradley. A man whose name he had not heard until a few minutes ago. He was behind it all. He must be. He had somehow engineered this panic in the markets. But he had needed help, and so he had recruited from within St Mary's. Years ago. Blake, Lafarge, Turner, maybe van Aalst and Dodds. Others perhaps. And *Hugh*. How in God's name had he got to Hugh? And what was it all in aid of? It was time to call Jake Samuels. Let him know what was going on and to prepare the paper for a big one. And, besides that, he was going to need some help with Bradley's computer, for which there was only one man he could think of.

Max Collins got in to Oxford a little under two hours later. He'd never been there before and thought it was going to be just like Cambridge, but he was disappointed. Oxford was more of a grown-up Cambridge, a real city which had a university in it, rather than a film set of an ancient university with a pretty village attached. He felt a little threatened by the thundering buses and one-way systems and pedestrianized zones, but as a hunted man he liked the anonymity and uniformity of the McDonalds and the Gap and the other high street chains. As he trudged through the lodge of St Mary's College wearing his outsized overcoat bought in Camden Lock many years ago for a meeting that had changed his life, and with his clumpy but still shaven head angled down towards the stone flags, nobody gave him a second glance. Nobody guessed he was a mathematics genius and nobody guessed he was wanted by the security services of at least half a dozen countries. He was student vintage 2002 – grunge meets *Clockwork Orange* meets James Dean, except for the fact that the army surplus duffel-bag he carried contained a portable computer which, had it been available on the open market, would have eaten up the annual budget of at least half the students at St Mary's College that year.

He walked straight to the staircase Emerson had described to him and found Jake Samuels hovering outside the door to Bradley's rooms, trying to remember if Emerson had said Staircase VI, room seven, or staircase VII, room six. Collins did not know Samuels, nor had Emerson mentioned he had invited anyone else, so he brushed past him, gave a token tap on the door and walked straight in without waiting to be invited. Samuels heard Emerson's greeting and recognized the voice. He followed Collins into the room and the two men were introduced.

'Jake, this is, er, Max – the cleverest man you will ever meet, once you've got past the haircut. He's our sums man. That's all you need to know about him, and all you should probably want to know.' Samuels eyed him with interest. He knew Emerson, knew his methods, his thoroughness, his standards. If he was impressed by this Max character, then that was enough for an unsurprisable newspaper editor.

'And as for you, Max, meet Jake Samuels. The man who created "The Emerson Bulletin" in the first place. The editor of the *Gazette* and the most honest man in newspapers. Not saying much I know, but there you go. The best newsman in Europe with the ear of more presidents and prime ministers than you can probably name.' They quickly shook hands with each other and installed themselves in the armchairs ready for Emerson's briefing. They had been told nothing, except that something significant was cooking, but both men were surprised when Patsy O'Connor emerged from Wallace Bradley's bedroom with a baby strapped to her chest.

'Gentlemen, please meet Patsy O'Connor. She's helping us out while we're here. And that is baby Patrick. I've filled her in on you two already. Jake is the smart fat one, Patsy, and Max is the smelly scruff.'

'It's an honour to meet you both,' she blushed, and had to stop herself from curtsying. 'I've just been feeding the little one. He won't disturb us now for a couple of hours.'

'I'd like to thank you both for dropping everything and coming down here,' Emerson continued. 'It's useful to have everyone under one roof, and I'm going to need your help.'

'What's the scoop, Jimmy boy? Sounds big, man. Sounds big. What do you want with the Cubit Crack-Machine?' Collins was sprawled deep in the cracked leather wing-backed armchair and had his feet on Bradley's coffee table. He'd taken his boots off, and was displaying holed socks and calloused feet to the other occupants of the room.

'You're Cubit?' Samuels was wide-eyed. Impressed, even a little awe-struck.

'You've heard of Cubit, Jake?' Now it was Emerson's turn to be surprised.

'Anyone with a rebellious teenage son who spends the half of his life he isn't watching TV chained to the internet, knows that Cubit is a folk hero. I'm tempted to ask for an autograph. I scarcely dare tell my son I've met you.'

'Please don't, man. Please don't. Jimmy boy here, and now you, thanks to my big mouth, are the only people who know who Cubit actually is. There are a lot of other people who would like this information. Scary geezers with earpieces and bulges in their jackets. Keep it to yourself.'

'No problem. I'm rather relieved you're on our side, in fact. If half of what my son tells me you've done is true, I wouldn't want to make an enemy of you.'

'Let's get back to why we're all here.' Emerson cut back in. 'Jake, on Christmas Eve you asked me to find out what was going on behind the scenes in this financial crisis. That was only ten days ago, but in that time, South East Asia has come to a virtual standstill. There is almost complete lawlessness, anarchy, chaos, call it what you will. As a result of this, the markets in the rest of the world have begun to suffer to the point of extreme danger. Two major US banks have been closed down, with more to follow no doubt. And just this evening, the Prime Minister of this country has announced that three of the four largest clearing banks have also been closed down. Currency is hard to come by, the price of gold has gone through the roof and confidence in the banking system is non-existent. The world is on the brink of complete financial collapse.'

'Heavy stuff, Jimmy. Heavy stuff. But we read about it every day. What's new man? Why have you dragged us up here? What have you found out?'

'I'm coming to that. Starting in Indonesia, which bore the brunt of the initial meltdown, I was able to establish that one particular company, a Swiss company by the name of Sukon, was unusually active in everything that was going on. I believe they were a front for the largest hedge fund on this planet, the Xenfin Partnership, who were dealing in unbelievably large amounts. I have now established that a small number of people, including somebody at Xenfin, Chris Blake the lawyer who is known to you, Jake, a senior diplomat in Jakarta and a trader at the largest investment bank in London were all acting together. They were aided and abetted by a very influential man at the Federal Reserve Bank in New York, the American central bank.'

'Holy shit, man. You mean, these guys were doing this *deliberately*? They *wanted* all this stuff to happen?'

'Precisely. And the entire plan, I believe, was being orchestrated by one man. The man in whose rooms we are now sitting, Professor Wallace Bradley.'

'The economist?' Samuels's knowledge of world affairs was second to none.

'Yes. The man rumoured to be up for the Nobel Prize this year. An expert on Asia.'

'But why, James? What can they hope to gain?'

'That is what I do not yet know. I suspect they are channelling funds somewhere, huge funds, for their own use at a later date. Using the mayhem as a smoke-screen. But that is what we need to find out. And that is why I want you, Max, to break into this computer and dig out Bradley's files. He formed a group called the Pegasus Forum, a dining society, years ago. That is when he recruited all his people and I believe that to be the link. All of the people I mentioned had that in common. They were all at this college, St Mary's College, in the late eighties. They were all, I believe, members of the Pegasus Forum, and they are all guilty of conspiring to destroy the world's financial system.'

'Wait a minute, James,' Samuels spoke again. 'The Pegasus Forum. Wasn't that . . . ?'

'Yes, Jake. You're right, as always. You were at his funeral. Hugh was a member. That was the dinner he was attending when he died. I should say, when he was murdered.'

'What are you saying? Hugh was involved in this mess?'

'Was, yes. In the early stages, at least. I believe he tried to pull out when he saw what Bradley was really trying to do, and that is when he was killed. The same man who I think killed Hugh has killed again since.'

'So, what can we do?'

'Jake, I think it may be too late already to stop what they have started. Once markets get an idea in their head, it's pretty difficult to turn it around. And right now the markets are in self-destruct mode. I just think though, that if we can find some concrete evidence of the conspiracy, proof that the whole thing was deliberately engineered, we may be able to give the markets the excuse they need to recover. As long as nothing else happens in the meantime. But one more major incident and the damage will be irreparable – we can all wave goodbye to everything. Savings, pensions, property, the whole *system* which enables our society to function, even the value of currency itself, will be destroyed.'

'So where is this dude now?'

'Who, Max?'

'The Bradley dude. The main man. The puppetmaster. Fagin. The eco-terrorist.'

'I don't know. I saw him leaving with a suitcase this afternoon.'

'Sounds like he's clearing out. Believe me, I understand. I've done it a couple of times myself. If he thought we were getting close to mass going critical, he probably didn't want to be around when it happened. Or he's gone somewhere to plant the final charge, prime the fuse. Look at the coffee cups. It's like the *Marie Celeste* in here. He's gone somewhere in a hurry. Find out where he's gone, and why, and maybe we can stop him doing it.'

There was a lull in the conversation as the four occupants of Wallace Bradley's sitting room pondered on what had been said and what the next steps could be. Before anyone could add anything further there were footsteps on the wooden landing outside followed by a sharp rap on the door. Emerson looked at Samuels and Collins, but before they could act, Patsy O'Connor rose and motioned them into Bradley's bedroom, closing the door behind them. If anyone had a legitimate reason to be there it was she, and the reason was strapped to her chest. She walked back to the living room door and opened it to the visitors.

'"Oh lovely Pussy! O Pussy, my love, what a beautiful Pussy you are."'

'That's disgusting, Annie! What sort of pervert would write that?'

'Cameron, you are too much of a philistine. Just shut up and fuck me now.'

It was just ten hours since Annie van Aalst had finished setting Xenfin's massive funds to self destruct. The Gulfstream had taken her from Cayman to Gatwick whilst Saul Krantz slept, unaware of the time bomb ticking in Xenfin's various custody accounts all over the world. They were now ninety per cent invested in the Japanese yen, in Japanese stocks, in Japanese Government bonds, futures, options on futures and swaps. And whilst she lay back on the king-sized bed in the Halkin Hotel, with Cameron Dodds exploring every inch and opening of her body, she too was dreaming. Dreaming of a swimming lesson on a moonlit beach and Krantz's bull-like, mature body pounding her like a jackhammer, grinding her into the sand which cushioned her compliant form. Every nerve-end tingled with sensation and she gasped with pleasure both at Dodds's efforts and at the thought of the enormity of the destruction which was about to take place.

'Annie? You OK?' Dodds had never elicited a reaction such as this from her before.

'Oh yes, Cameron. Oh yes. Don't stop now. I'm just fine.' And she closed her eyes again and switched to her favourite fantasy.

How the mighty would fall! Her buying frenzy on behalf of Xenfin had driven the Japanese market to a high they had not seen in three months, back to pre-crisis levels, yet none of the brokers with whom she had dealt had questioned her activity. That was the beauty of dealing in the financial markets. As long as the company one represented was known to the counterparty, any amount of bizarre trading would be gratefully accepted by a greedy salesman, keen to do business. And Annie van Aalst represented Xenfin, the biggest name in the business. All the banks wanted to deal with them. In fact, any salesman doing business with them was to be congratulated, a feather in the cap, a scalp on the belt, a notch on the bedhead. Nobody would question Xenfin's ability to pay for what they were buying. They had a name, a reputation, the *trust* of the marketplace. There it was again. Trust. Credit. Faith. In a crooked world it was such an intangible and unlikely concept on which to build an entire financial system.

Of course there were checks and balances, but generally speaking, these checks only occurred at the end of the trading day. During the day, a *trusted* employee could perform all kinds of iniquity without being found out. And a trusted employee on a suicide mission could get away with much worse before the comptrollers and accountants and risk managers would notice what she had been up to. But by then it would be too late. The deals were done. The trades executed verbally on the telephone were legally binding. Daylight exposure, it was called. In Annie van Aalst's case, working her nightshift as she always did, it was more like moonlight exposure. And in this case, even the mighty Xenfin would not be able to pay for all the trades she had done in their name. *My word is my bond*. What a load of naïve crap.

The numbers Annie van Aalst had quoted to Krantz in defence of her assassination of Braxton Federal were all true. When she had spoken to him, they did have a total exposure of something close to two trillion dollars. But with positions of that size, they were creaking at the seams. All of their credit lines were full. She had borrowed to the maximum on just about all of Xenfin's existing lines. Forty times leverage on all of their cash positions, plus massive off-balance sheet bets in the derivatives markets. Yet in that one night of frenzied trading, she had significantly increased their positions. She had opened new accounts at banks she had never dealt with before, but who were gagging for their business and so took their trades on risk. They'd worry about formally establishing the credit lines the next day. Get the business on the books first, worry about the paperwork afterwards. That was how it worked in the less prestigious investment banks. Corners were cut, rules ignored, risks taken. And again, this was the beauty of working in the off-shore hedge-fund business – a complete and utter lack of transparency which nobody seemed to mind.

Again, it was the system's fault. She felt she had done nothing wrong. If, as an individual, you applied for a mortgage with a high street bank, it was illegal not to disclose your other commitments and loan facilities. Yet if you were a hedge fund applying to a bank for a credit line to trade in billions of dollars' worth of derivatives, the same stringency did not apply. Of course you had to supply financial statements. But those nicely audited statements could be over a year old, and generally bore no relation at all to the reality of the current financial situation of the company. Sure, the bank in question might ask for a statement of your current liabilities, but nowhere did you have to disclose what credit lines you already had with other banks, and to what extent they were still available. That information was proprietary. Secret. Market-sensitive. None of your business.

'Can we deal with Xenfin? Too bloody right we can.' And a thirty-year-old sales manager would override the compliance procedures of the entire bank in a second to avoid missing the business.

And as Annie van Aalst lay squirming below Cameron Dodds in the

Halkin Hotel in London, and as Wallace Bradley sat in the British Airways lounge at Heathrow Airport, fingering his first-class ticket courtesy of a certain Yoshimi Akiri, Chairman of the Yokosuka Corporation, the Xenfin Partnership, Grand Cayman, was sitting upon an obligation to buy almost one hundred billion dollars' worth of Japanese securities more than it could afford to pay for. And if Bruce Phipps delivered on his promise to downgrade the credit rating of Japan to the extent recommended by their guru Wallace Bradley, those securities would be worth next to nothing in twenty-four hours' time.

And she knew of at least one other person, aside from Wallace Bradley and herself, who would be delighted when it happened

A few miles west of London, a muffled announcement came over the tannoy in the lounge, calling a flight. Wallace Bradley rose from his seat, smoothed the tail flap of his crumpled brown suit and shuffled off in the direction of the gate.

CHAPTER 5

'DAD! I CAN'T BELIEVE IT!' JAMES EMERSON HAD HEARD HIS
father's voice and barged past an astonished Patsy O'Connor
to embrace him. 'How on earth . . . ?'

'Just ask your boss, my boy. Thought you might need a little help
landing this one.'

From his perch on the window seat across the room from the reunited
father and son, Jake Samuels smiled inwardly. As a newspaper editor,
these two working together represented the dream team. Ever since
Emerson senior had retired, Samuels had been trying to persuade
him to return, at least on a freelance basis. The occasional piece
to bolster the output of Hugh, and even James, on 'The Emerson
Bulletin', but Charles Emerson had always been stubbornly steadfast
in his retirement.

When Samuels had received the call from James, however, asking
him to come to Oxford straight away, he had sensed the younger man's
urgency, and thought that now would be the right time to enlist some
help. He had been lucky to track Emerson senior down to his London
club, and his old friend had promised to follow him to Oxford as soon
as he could.

James Emerson was a reporter of the modern age. He could track down
large scale scandals on the corporate level, he could distil the essence of
a balance sheet in a matter of minutes and he knew the markets. In fact,
for a while Samuels understood Emerson had virtually *run* the markets
in London.

But the older man was better. There had been no other like him for getting to the bottom of human psychology, for understanding the mentality of the traitor or the corrupt and recognizing their traits. He just knew when he was right, and his relentless pursuit of his quarry, and the stylishly economical way in which he induced them ultimately to expose themselves was a universe away from the son's world of hacking computers and strong-arming frightened fat cats. Between father and son they were capable of anything. If either one of them alone was capable of getting to the bottom of Pegasus, then together they may be able to turn it around.

Over the next half an hour James Emerson brought his father up to speed with the details of the situation. At one point the older man fell silent whilst his remaining son related what he believed to be the story of Hugh's death, and the resolve shone from his moistened eyes. It was a curious crew assembled there – the editor of the most respected and influential newspaper in Europe, a volatile and unstable mathematical genius, father and son journalists, and a twenty-year-old Irish Catholic girl complete with five-day-old baby.

Whilst they all listened to his tale, Bruce Phipps and his two directors were well stuck in to the vodka and tonics as the American Airlines Boeing 777 stretched its legs over the Atlantic on the short flight to New York. Also airborne, but heading in the opposite direction towards Tokyo was Wallace Bradley. His one suitcase, with which he had struggled through Cranmer Quad a few hours before, was safely checked into the hold. It was small enough to have fitted into one of the overhead lockers and to have allowed Bradley a quicker exit when he arrived at Narita Airport, but its unusual contents would never have been allowed in the passenger cabin of a civil airliner. The stewardesses gave up trying to serve him anything after the first hour, preferring to avoid the strange man in first class who just stared, silent and unblinking, at the bulkhead wall three feet in front of him.

The blood pounded in his temples.

*   *   *

Patsy O'Connor took on the role of waitress and housekeeper to the four men who sat discussing the next step in their plans to stop Bradley and the Pegasus Forum from causing any further damage. She ran out to the late night grocery shop in Turl Street, sleeping baby still cocooned at her breast, and returned with sandwiches, biscuits and coffee to find a hive of activity. The four of them were going through the contents of Wallace Bradley's desk. His father's desk. The desk. But they had found nothing besides plenty of lecture notes, research papers and a few old photographs. Seated on the floor amid a tangle of cables was Max Collins. He had moved Bradley's computer and seemed embarrassed.

'Jimmy boy? Is this Bradley dude some kind of computer freak?'

'No idea, Max. Patsy, you know him best. What do you think?'

'Oh no, sir. I mean, he could use one and all, but he wasn't comfortable with it. He was always complaining about losing files and stuff. Why do you ask?'

Collins replied. 'Well, I don't quite believe it, but I can't get in.'

Three heads turned to look at the odd figure now lying prone on the floor, tapping away at the keyboard.

'What do you mean, Max? Are you trying to tell me that the scourge of the NSA and GCHQ, the masked avenger of the cyber-plains, can't crack the password of some crazed old professor?'

'That's just what I'm saying. I've tried everything I can think of. I've used all my best tricks, tried thirty different languages. But there's some dark stuff going on in there. I can't figure it out. I need more time.'

'We may not have it, Max. If you're right about Bradley doing a bunk he could be about to take us over the brink.'

'Well, let me tell you. He's got some serious security in here. Not conventional at all. The nice thing about the rest of the world is that they all use similar software. They're complacent about it because they don't know about me. But *this* stuff is totally out in left field. Like nothing I've ever seen. Are you sure he doesn't have some kinda help with it?'

'Well maybe one of the other Pegasus members?' suggested Samuels. 'What do we know about them?'

'Not much. I only met Lafarge. He's a dinosaur and pretty stupid. I would doubt he could have helped. Jake, you know Blake. Is he up to it?'

'God no. The steam generation. There's Scott Turner of course, but that CV we saw from the Fed didn't show up any PC skills. Heavy duty economist, but not a computer whiz.'

'Of the members we know about,' Emerson senior cut in, 'or at least suspect, that leaves Annie van Aalst and Cameron Dodds. We know nothing about van Aalst, but didn't you say you used to work with Dodds at Steinman's, James?'

'Yes. Yes . . . Now you mention it, it could be him. He used to work in the quant group, the number-crunchers, before he became a trader. And no disrespect to you, Max, but he's pretty off the wall. Could he have come up with some clever system?'

'If he was at this college, we could find out his background.' All eyes in the room were on Patsy O'Connor. 'In the library. They keep a register of graduates and their subjects. And if they've published any papers, they'll be there too. I'll go and have a look. But one of you'll have to look after the baby. Can't have him crying in the library now. I'd be thrown out for sure!'

Emerson's father helped her untie the straps which held the pouch around her neck, and transferred the whole package to his own arms. The baby stirred a little, but to everyone's relief did not waken. The older man stood swaying gently as he cradled the child and O'Connor left in a hurry.

Whilst she was away there was little more Collins could do with Bradley's computer, and he sat broodily, gazing around the room, until after ten minutes he suddenly said, 'No drawer.'

'I beg your pardon, Max?' Old Emerson was curious.

'No drawer. That desk's got no drawer in the middle. It should have. Look at the thickness of the top.'

Both Emersons turned to look. The desk was a large knee-hole with two sets of drawers, one either side of the space for the sitter. The desktop itself was covered in green leather, worn and polished with use, let into a slab of mahogany almost six inches thick.

'There must be a secret compartment. Trust me. I've done a bit when it comes to antiques.' And in a second, Max had slid over to the desk and was kneeling in front of it, brandishing a long thin screwdriver he had been using earlier. He set about probing and pushing the carvings on the desk front. Two minutes later he found it. Gentle pressure on a panel on the underside of the desk top released the mechanism and a hatch dropped down. He pulled out a file and handed it to Charles Emerson who sat down with the sleeping baby on his lap and began to read.

Patsy O'Connor burst back into the room ten minutes later waving a slender pamphlet. 'You were right, James. Dodds was a mathematician here. Got a first. And there was one paper published. Here it is.'

Before Emerson could take it, Collins had jumped up from the floor where he had been quietly cursing over Bradley's computer, and snatched it from her. He read the title out loud: '"Steganographic Applications of Digital Imaging Incorporating Hash Function Cryptography." Holy shit, man.'

'Max, could you please translate?'

'This dude is into steganography. No wonder I couldn't find the key.'

'Max, please?'

'OK, sorry. Steganography. It's an old principle, all about hiding messages. In order to be able to crack a code you've got to know there's a coded message there in the first place. Most coded messages look like gobbledygook. A whole bunch of numbers and letters that pretty much give away that there's something there that needs protecting. But if the key to the code was dressed up to look like something innocent, like a passage from the Bible, it would be hard to recognize it as a code in the first place. Keeps the likes of me very confused. In a crude form it's like invisible ink. A blank sheet of paper is just a blank sheet of paper until you know there's a message hidden on it. And you can't go around checking every blank sheet of paper for hidden messages.'

'Isn't that rather basic?'

'God yes. But it's been used for centuries. Even during the last war. Suppose you send a message saying: "Dear Andrew, We need reinforcements against imminent defeat." If that message gets intercepted by the enemy, it looks like a piece of plaintext. Gets taken at face value. Human psychology takes the path of least resistance. The listeners will assume they've lucked into an uncoded message. Sloppy Huns, something like that. But what it really says, if you take the first letter of every word is "Dawn Raid". Dumb-ass example of course, but you get the gist. Nowadays, the techniques are a tad more sophisticated.'

'But what's digital imaging got to do with it?'

'Well, in the same way that you could hide a message in a passage from the Bible, you can hide a message, digitally, in a picture.'

'You mean like a microdot?'

'No. Not any more at least. When a computer digitizes an image, it divides the image up into pixels. Little dots. Lots of them. And each one must be assigned a specific colour so that when you put them all together, the image looks, like, realistic. There are three primary colours, right?'

'Red, blue and green?'

'Correct, Jake, my man. Glad to hear you were listening to those elementary school teachers. Now a relatively basic computer uses a combination of eight "bits", ones and zeros to you, the things that computers understand, to specify each shade of say, red. That gives you two hundred and fifty-six possible reds if you count up all the possible combinations of eight digits being either a one or a zero. Same goes for blue and green. Two fifty-six of each. And all the other colours are made up of mixtures of these, right? Multiply it out, two fifty-six by two fifty-six by two fifty-six, and that gives you almost seventeen million possible colours. Your average image scanner or digital camera isn't half so precise. Nowhere near that sort of definition. Which means that you could get away with storing an image on a disk using a lot less of the actual space required, and "borrow" a couple of the bits from the colour chart, so to speak, and tweak them to hide your message. The image would be indistinguishable from the original, only one version would have a message hidden in it. The change to the colour specification would be way too subtle for the human eye to detect.'

'So we're looking for a picture.'

'Yes. We'd never be able to crack the password itself. Most passwords, the crackable ones at least, are short. Eight or nine digits max. This one is probably very long. You could easily hide ten thousand words in an image file without changing the appearance of that image. But a password of that length would take rather a long time to type in manually. Not too practical for everyday use. So we'll have to look for a picture on file. A floppy of some kind which looks as if it just has a few holiday snaps on it, but one of them will conceal the password. And then we'll be in.'

'In the meantime, gentlemen, I appear to have details of Professor Bradley's bank account.' All now stared at Charles Emerson. In the excitement of Patsy O'Connor's return from the library they had forgotten the file that had been found in Bradley's desk.

'What does it show, Dad?'

'Fairly unremarkable really. No billions salted away in his current account at least. Normal outgoings, rather frugal really. Monthly credit for around two and a half thousand from the university which I take to be his salary, and then another regular credit. Actually, it's for more than his salary.'

'What is it? Does it give the source? Investment account perhaps? Was he transferring interest income from an off-shore account somewhere?'

'Could be, I suppose. I've lost track of the names of all those private banks in Jersey and the like. Sounds like a bank, though. The credit comes in every month from one "Jenner & Phipps". Anyone heard of them?' Everyone shook their head except James Emerson. As a former bond salesman he knew exactly who they were.

'"Jenner & Phipps" did you say? That's not a bank. It's a credit-rating agency. The biggest in the world.'

'Credit rating? You mean for people applying for loans or HP or something?'

'Well, sort of. Only they don't rate individuals. They look at companies and countries, check them out and give them a rating based on the soundness of their finances.'

'So why would Bradley be getting paid by them?'

'He could be a consultant. He's an expert on Asia, you say, Patsy?'

'Oh, he's the biggest name in the country. Maybe the world. He advises governments out there on all sorts of things. Budgetary planning, long-term financing, all the important stuff.'

'So he'd be very well placed to supply some advice to Jenner & Phipps on their ratings for borrowers in the region. That's quite a conflict of interests, if he's advising the governments at the same time. Unless . . .'

'Unless what, James?' Jake Samuels had been listening to every word.

'Unless it was part of his plan. Pegasus, you know. They've clearly been trying to cause mayhem. What better way to achieve it than by advising the government of, say, Indonesia, to borrow and borrow more in order to finance their economic expansion, as all those countries have been doing over the last twenty years, and then to pull the rug out by advising Jenner & Phipps to cut their credit rating. Talk about leaving them high and dry. It could cripple their finances in very short order. The banks did it, less maliciously of course, to millions of people in the eighties. It was boom time and they encouraged everyone to borrow, borrow, borrow whilst times were good. Everyone got in debt up to their neck and when the bubble burst, the banks turned their back on them. They called in loans, repossessed cars and flogged off houses when people couldn't keep up the payments. They bankrupted hundreds of thousands of their own customers. If Bradley's been doing that with whole countries, it's incredibly fiendish.'

'And damn clever. But why, James? We still don't know why.'

'I think the answer must lie in that PC, Jake. Max, how are you getting on? We've simply got to get into it. The clock is ticking.'

'Well I can't find the picture, Jimmy. I've looked everywhere. There are just no floppy disks in this room at all. We need this dude, what's his name, Dodds? We need Dodds or we need his gear to be able to have a crack at it.'

At that precise moment, Cameron Dodds was slicing into a perfectly sautéed medallion of foie gras at the Mansion House, the Palladian palace and ceremonial residence of the Lord Mayor in the heart of the City of

London. The Governor of the Bank of England and the Chancellor of the Exchequer were set to deliver speeches to the few hundred bankers and merchants of the City lucky enough to be invited, as they normally did every year in June. The speeches were always scrutinized by analysts and pundits for signs of a change in policy or hints at changes in interest rates. This time, the dinner had been brought forward to January given the urgency of the financial crisis around the globe, and the diners were agog to hear the officials' words, coming, as they did, a matter of hours after the announcement by the Prime Minister on national television of the closure of three of the United Kingdom's largest banks.

Annie van Aalst was sitting next to Dodds, and they were surrounded by the great and the good from the world's leading financial institutions. Liveried waiters hovered at shoulders and the chandeliers of the Egyptian banqueting hall shimmered in the cut glass of the crystal and the highly polished silver which dressed the long tables. It all seemed perversely opulent to Dodds in the light of the financial catastrophe that was building around the world.

The badge van Aalst wore still described her as 'Senior Fund-Manager, The Xenfin Partnership', and strictly speaking this was still the case as her letter of resignation to Saul Krantz was currently in the Xenfin Gulfstream, somewhere over Newfoundland, winging its way down the eastern seaboard back towards Grand Cayman.

Given the rumours of Xenfin's activity in the market the night before, the people sitting around her at that dinner were very curious to know if it was true. Had they been buying into Japan? Did they think the worst was over? And Annie van Aalst was very happy to confirm, off the record naturally, that they were very bullish on Asia now. When she mentioned the amounts they had put into the market, a variety of serious looking men and women in evening wear took turns in making their excuses to slip away from the table for five minutes, and the lobby of the Mansion House became scattered with people making urgent, whispered calls to their Tokyo offices, telling them to buy too. For in the financial world such was the gravity and consideration with which investment decisions affecting the livelihoods and pensions of millions of people were made.

'My lords, ladies and gentlemen, pray silence for the Governor of the Bank of England!' The background bubble of conversation subsided almost instantly as the Governor took the lectern. He was attempting to appear relaxed, and had indulged in a couple of glasses too many of the passable Montrachet to aid him in this. But although he was beaming at the assembled crowd, the strain of the previous night's events shone through the patina of good will.

'My Lord Mayor, Chancellor, ladies and gentlemen. I will begin by thanking you all for braving the foul January weather at such short notice to attend this extraordinary dinner for the bankers and merchants of the City of London. As you know, we normally hold this shindig in June, but frankly we were worried there wouldn't be any bankers or merchants left in the City of London to invite by then!'

If the best man had suggested that the groom was sleeping with the bride's grandmother it would have been less excruciating, and the Governor's attempt at frivolity was met with a jarring silence. He stuttered and appeared flustered, fumbling with his notes for what seemed like minutes.

'Shame!' shouted one silver-haired grandee suddenly, sitting close to the top table, and the cry was echoed by those immediately around him.

These interruptions were immediately followed by a well-aimed chocolate profiterole arcing in from left field, which hit the Governor squarely on the forehead and exploded, depositing sludgy whipped cream all over the man's face and shoulders. This met with a great cheer and a spontaneous round of applause, and the rest of the diners took this as their cue to follow suit. There was nothing the public schoolboy lurking within the massed ranks of the British establishment liked better than a good food fight, and before long cream-laden puddings rained in from all directions. Slabs of cheese, grapes and nuts peppered the top-table dignitaries as they cowered beneath the fusillade of food, but it was not until a considerable orange, flung with some vigour, rendered the Chancellor of the Exchequer unconscious that the brace of Special Branch detectives, tasked with his protection following the worsening of the banking crisis, stepped in to carry him away.

By this stage the younger and rowdier element amongst the diners were standing on their chairs, chanting for the Prime Minister to be brought on. Passions were high and the blood was up, but the most enduring and by far the most significant image of the evening, which was subsequently flashed around the world by the BBC cameras normally present at the occasion to film the speeches, concerned a very drunk Sir Peter Taverton, chairman of the two-hundred-year-old merchant bank which bore his name.

He clambered up on to the table before him and marched solemnly across the place settings of his neighbours, scattering cut glass decanters of port in his wake, until he reached the top table where he stood facing the Governor.

'You, sir, are a charlatan!' he boomed. The chanting of the crowd behind him petered out as he began. 'You profess to uphold the value of this country's currency, and the integrity of this country's banks! And yet you throw us to the wolves! You will ruin the future, not only of those assembled here tonight, but of millions of ordinary men and women who will see the fruits of their thrift wiped out! You have pissed on us all from a great height, and now, sir, I intend to do the same to you!' And there was a stunned silence as he proceeded to unbutton the flies of his Savile Row dinner suit and urinate copiously on to the untouched bowl of fruit salad still sitting before the Governor. Droplets of urine mixed with sugar syrup spattered the starched shirt fronts and boned bodices of all those within range, and when he was done, he marched back the way he had come, back down the long tables, watched by several hundred pairs of eyes in the great banqueting hall and several million more on television around the country. A slow, rhythmic handclap accompanied his progress, gaining in volume and tempo until the beats merged into one rapturous ovation of applause, as he reached his chair, descended from the table and tucked in his napkin beneath his chin before helping himself to a large portion of lemon meringue pie.

CHAPTER 6

WHEN HISTORIANS LOOK BACK AT MAJOR EVENTS IN WORLD history, and the Great Banking Crisis of 2002 would come in for much subsequent analysis, they like to focus in on key individual events, turning points if you like, which enable them to satisfy the cause-and-effect view of history. Thus we read endless accounts of the Assassination in Sarajevo, the Invasion of Poland and the Defenestration of Prague amongst many others. To these events, these flashpoints in the annals of world history, can now be added the Bankruptcy of Pee Seuar Land Holdings and what became known as the 'Taverton Micturition'. For most pundits later described this incident as *the* flashpoint, the validation for the hundreds of thousands of demonstrators, rioters, anti-capitalists and ordinary men and women who took to the streets that night. For on that night in January 2002 the United Kingdom experienced the most fierce and widespread violence and destruction since the Blitz.

Banks were vandalized everywhere, windows smashed, doors and walls daubed with graffiti and then set alight. No financial institutions were spared, not even the offices of insurance companies. These were the repositories for the millions of pension funds, life insurance and endowment policies with which the population of Great Britain were attempting to provide for their futures and for those of their children, and they too were visited with a vitriol unprecedented in the history of civil unrest. The poll tax and race riots of the eighties were minor scuffles compared to the sheer volume of bodies which emerged from the hearths of England and the rest of the

Union to protest against the negligence which threatened their financial well-being.

Further targets were any examples of conspicuous wealth – smart cars, expensive houses, even the exclusive shops selling designer clothes – and the fury of the mob towards symbols of what they would no longer be able to afford was relentless. But it was not long before the violence turned against individuals. In London and the surrounding area, the homes of known bankers and financial professionals were targeted, and even in the provinces accountants and bank managers cowered behind curtained windows, their wives and families sheltering under tables or in cellars from the bricks and other projectiles flying in through shattered glass.

Given the huge number of people out on the streets, the police were unprepared and powerless to act. The emergency services were stretched to the limit within a few hours as the number of casualties from broken glass and smoke inhalation grew exponentially. Contingency plans for such extensive outbreaks of civil unrest were woefully inadequate, and the rapid escalation of events caught planners and coordinators completely off their guard. Before the Prime Minister had addressed the nation to announce the closure of the first three banks, the Home Secretary had given instructions to the Chief Constables of all the counties to be prepared for demonstrations and outbreaks of violence surrounding the branches of those banks around the country. They had had all of three hours' notice to prepare. Leave was cancelled and officers drafted in from holidays to strengthen the forces, but it was too little and much too late. Throughout the night, the night of the fifth of January, panic-stricken calls were phoned into the Home Secretary's office calling for more help, more manpower, more resources. An emergency cabinet meeting was called at five a.m., and the ministers had to be picked up and driven to Downing Street in armoured police vans whilst protesters shrieked and whistled and threw rocks which clattered harmlessly against the security gates which protected the Prime Minister's residence from terrorist attack.

In that emergency meeting, a hasty decision was taken. The Home Secretary formally requested assistance from the Defence Secretary in the form of military support for his beleaguered police force. The request was endorsed by the Prime Minister and unanimously approved by the rest of the cabinet. By six a.m., armed regiments were being deployed around the country in a highly visible presence. Squads of three and four men fanned out through shopping malls, scanning before and behind at all times in a kind of synchronized dance movement. On their backs were the standard issue automatic rifles, the SA80 originally designed by Royal Ordinance and since modified by the private sector manufacturer Heckler and Koch following problems with jamming during the Gulf War and Kosovo crisis. The weapons they carried in their arms were rather different, and had been procured by the Ministry of Defence for just such an eventuality. Following the massive riots at the World Trade Organisation meeting in Seattle in 2000, British police and military leaders had visited the United States to consult with their American counterparts on the latest methods of unruly crowd control and what the Americans call 'non-lethal compliance technology'. The visit had resulted in a large order for a Californian arms manufacturer specializing in just such technology, and the military and police personnel patrolling the streets of Britain's major cities were authorized to use it for the first time that night. That decision would go down as a major mistake in the development of crowd control techniques in this country.

The weapons looked like conventional automatic rifles but fired a round pellet about the size of a large marble by means of a system of compressed air. Upon impact with the subject, or a hard surface, the friable plastic casing shattered and deposited a small quantity of oleoresin capsicum powder, a pepper-based irritant. Much more targetable than the conventional tear-gas grenades, the pepper projectiles could be shot at an individual troublemaker, rendering him temporarily incapacitated, or fired in volleys against a wall or similar hard surface to provide saturation coverage of a larger crowd. The idea was that the psychological impact of being 'shot', albeit 'non-fatally', plus the 'kinetic impact' of the projectile itself and finally the nauseating pepper cloud, combined to produce much improved 'compliance levels' from non-compliant mobs. It was a step down from the rubber bullets used widely in Northern Ireland, and a step up from the paintball globules used widely in corporate entertainment. The guns, or 'launchers' as the Home Secretary euphemistically liked to call them, fired at twelve rounds a second with a muzzle velocity of three hundred feet per second. The effect of the impact was comparable to a smart punch from an amateur boxer, but depending upon the point of impact, if the bone was relatively close to the surface, the skin could be broken. A volley of twelve rounds received in such a one second burst by the chest of a stocky adult at twenty feet would knock him down and induce heavy coughing, temporary vision impairment and most likely vomiting. The same Home Secretary who had introduced curfews for the under-twelves had now sanctioned chemical warfare on the streets of Great Britain.

But the weapon which caused most outrage, notwithstanding the thirteen-year-old who lost an eye when a stray pepper bullet caught him just below the brow bone, and the forty-seven-year-old housewife who suffered an allergic reaction to the irritant and died whilst trying to withdraw her final savings from a cash-machine, was the water cannon.

This was by no means a conventional water cannon, although those were deployed in Edinburgh and Glasgow as the new Scottish Parliament had not ratified the use of the new product. But in Moss Side, Manchester and in Brixton in London where the riots were at their most intense, the army deployed for the first time, in a vehicle-mounted configuration, a 'wireless stun-gun'.

This weapon delivered a single, concentrated stream of high-voltage electrified conductive fluid at its target over a range of around twenty-five feet, and was effective even through heavy clothing. To avoid electrocuting innocent bystanders the current could be switched on and off, spraying the crowd with harmless water until the targeted troublemaker was engaged and the current switched back on. The degree of current delivered could also be varied, making it potentially useful for delivering significant current to hostile mechanical equipment. Unfortunately for the government, and even more unfortunately for a group of around twenty, middle-aged demonstrators attempting to prise a cash-machine out of the wall on Acre Lane in Brixton, the sergeant in the Welsh Guards who was operating the equipment for the first time had got the setting wrong. The identification of the charred remains of those involved kept the Home Office pathologists and dentists busy for most of the rest of the week.

By the time day broke on the morning of January the sixth, the riots had calmed down somewhat, but the scenes in many of the United Kingdom's city centres were apocalyptic. Hardly a shop front was intact, fires smouldered everywhere, and broken glass lay ankle-deep in the gutters; the accident and emergency departments of the major urban hospitals were overflowing with the walking wounded and the not so lucky; crowds of marauding gangs combed the streets looking for property still to loot, or to trade for other goods, as cash was already largely unavailable. The Royal Engineers had erected barbed wire and sandbag barricades around the vicinity of major banks, and the City of London itself, the Square Mile of the financial nerve centre to Europe and the world, was a ghost town. Troops had spent much of their time driving the demonstrators out of the streets of the City, and erecting roadblocks on the major arteries which led into the Square Mile.

As for the markets themselves that day, they were closed. At least, those markets over which the British Government exercised control – the Stock Market, the Gilt market, the London Metal Exchange and Financial Futures market and, of course, the bank clearing system. The other markets, the foreign exchange markets excluding sterling, the eurobond market, and any other foreign stock, bond, commodity or futures markets could theoretically still be traded by anyone who wanted to. But in London the traders were not able to get to their desks.

It was not until ten that morning that the Prime Minister saw fit to address the nation again. He began by expressing regret at the lives that had been lost, which had risen to around one hundred during the course of the night's activities, but he underlined the need to remain calm. He talked of extreme circumstances demanding extreme measures, which most people took to be a justification for the use of the military and their 'non-lethal compliance technology', but turned out to be a whole series of government controls he planned to introduce immediately in an attempt to bring the situation under control.

These included fixed prices for basic foodstuffs such as bread, milk and potatoes and strict limitation on the amounts purchasable per household. There was to be no profiteering, no hyper-inflation and no hoarding. Because of the chronic shortage of cash, in addition to those banks already forced to close, all other banks would remain closed too, even the solvent ones, for an unspecified length of time. A selected number of bank premises would be commandeered by the government and staffed by police and military personnel for the limited distribution of cash to account holders in proportion, and that proportion was to be twenty per cent, to the amount of savings they had before the crisis broke. This money would be a special issue note, printed by the Bank of England as an emergency currency, and valid for a limited amount of time. It would be legal tender, except in Scotland and Northern Ireland, alongside whatever other cash remained in circulation for as long as the government stipulated it be so, and when the crisis abated, as he assured the nation it undoubtedly would, could only be redeemed for 'real' sterling with the Bank of England itself. The amounts distributed to individuals would be strictly monitored, and automatically debited from their old bank accounts for transfer to Treasury funds. It would not be possible to withdraw more.

So, he claimed, although the government was actually printing more money to alleviate the situation, it would not affect the money supply, as the amounts handed out would mirror the amounts debited from private accounts of individuals who were, due to the run on the various banks, unable to withdraw that cash. The government was not bailing the banks out as such. They were merely making funds available to account holders on behalf of the banks in an attempt to 'tide the banks over' until there was a recovery in asset prices. Or so the government presented it. In reality these were measures of which the Central Planning Committee of the Union of Soviet Socialist Republics would have been proud.

Any cases of severe need, and all those reliant on government benefits, would be dealt with separately. This would not involve distribution of money, but special food centres would be set up to hand out basic foodstuffs once a week based on the number of family members per household. The utility companies would be ordered to continue to supply heat, light and water to all households. There was to be a temporary moratorium on utility bills, and it would be illegal for any household to be cut off from the supply. Public transport would continue to run, and it would be free of charge. The government would reimburse the private companies which run the services, for the limited period anticipated that the crisis situation would continue.

The list of measures the Prime Minister presented ran on for twenty minutes, covering everything from the emergency services to fuel provision and the limitation on the use of private cars. It smacked of war-time contingency plans being hurriedly dusted down and adapted on the back of an envelope to accommodate an economic crisis and the complete breakdown of the system of currency and exchange. But it was full of holes.

And what was more, it was going to cost. For the Prime Minister closed his speech with an announcement of an immediate increase in the basic rate of income tax of five per cent for one year only. Again, he dressed this measure up as a prudent step. The emergency procedures outlined had to be paid for. In times of austerity we must all tighten our belts, and so on and so forth. And the end result of all these announcements, especially the one about the heightened powers of the police and military to order people off the streets and the imposition of a curfew, just made everything much worse. More people came out on to the streets. More buildings were burned to the ground. More people were killed. It could scarcely get any worse.

But of course it did. For before long the newspapers had got hold of what they thought to be a key statistic, and that was all the people were talking about. The total of all deposits held by British banks on behalf of private sector customers in the UK amounted to around seventy billion pounds. The total amount of banknotes and coins in circulation in the country totalled a little less than half that amount. In short, if everyone wanted their money back, they could not have it.

In fact, there was nothing unusual in this. This was the way the
system worked, with more than half of the private wealth of the country
existing in electronic form, figures on a computer screen, numbers on
bank statements. Theoretically, the missing billions were backed by
securities, bonds and stocks held by the banks which can be sold to
repay depositors. Unfortunately for the population at large, it was now
apparent that the value of those securities was less than the value of the
missing billions in good old hard cash. The *Sun*, the most widely read
newspaper in the United Kingdom with immense power of influence
over the masses, ran a headline that morning which read 'BANK OF
ENGLAND BUST!' In the less sensationalistic *Daily Telegraph*, the
most widely read 'serious' broadsheet, the satirical cartoonist 'Matt' had
drawn a picture of a destitute woman sitting on the pavement in front of
a columned portico with a hat upturned in front of her. A note pinned to
the hat read 'Please give generously. 35 million depositors to repay.' And
underneath, the caption ran: 'The Bag Lady of Threadneedle Street', a
reference to the Bank of England's more usual nickname, originated by
the Irish playwright Sheridan in the early nineteenth century, of 'The
Old Lady of Threadneedle Street'.

The worldwide reaction to these unprecedented scenes of chaos in the
United Kingdom was initially shock. In Europe, earnest commentators
and smug politicians counselled against fiscal and monetary imprudence,
praised their own systems of controls, of checks and balances, and warned
of the dangers of massed panic. But the florists of Amsterdam and the
dentists of Belgium and the merchants of Munich and Hamburg, were in
no mood for political platitudes. They were labouring under the umbrella
of a shiny new currency, the euro, which had been beset by problems
since its ill-fated launch in electronic form two years earlier.

And to make matters worse, the actual new notes and coins had
appeared on the streets of Europe for the very first time only four days
before. The timing could not have been worse. The currency, so pristine,
so freshly minted, looked too new to be worth anything. The notes had
a plastic feel to them, and the glistening new coins, in the aftermath
of Christmas and Hanukkah, bore more than a passing resemblance

to chocolate money. Nobody took it seriously and everyone looked for alternatives. European Monetary Union, a fragile concept at best during the preceding two years, now seemed close to breaking point.

It was almost axiomatic in the capital markets that there was a hierarchy of investment behaviour amongst the various different investor groups. When new information came into a market, the first to react were the professionals – the traders, the hedge-fund managers, the pension funds; then came the wealthy middle classes – the doctors and dentists, the businessmen, the readers of the financial pages; finally, when the news had long passed, it filtered through to the masses – the old people, the working classes, the small-scale savers. Typically, when it got to that stage, so the saying went, it was time for the professionals who started the whole thing rolling, to reverse their decision and do something else. But in this case it was different. The news had been spread all over the popular press. Everyone had access to the same information at pretty much the same time, and they all ran for the door at once. It was a long time since there had been armoured personnel carriers on the streets of Paris and Berlin and Amsterdam, but when it came to protecting the banks, the governments were given no choice.

In the United States too the situation was worsening. The failure of the two major banks, Braxton Federal and Franklin Intercontinental, had been followed by a raft of smaller failures, and the state of emergency in Florida and southern California had spread to Texas, South Carolina and Georgia. The crisis was rising up the country like floodwater, and if something was not done, it would not be long before the nation's capital and its financial heart were submerged also. The government ran a massive public information campaign in an attempt to restore confidence, that elusive quality the loss of which was destroying the system which relied on it to function.

Television cameras were invited to film the gold reserves still held by the US Government at Fort Knox in Kentucky and in the vaults of the Federal Reserve Bank of New York beneath the streets of Manhattan. The value of all major currencies used to be tied to the value of gold, but this 'Gold Standard' had been abandoned by most countries in the early 1930s, partly to expedite foreign trade by strategically devaluing a currency, and partly due to the dwindling supplies of gold. In the United Kingdom the pound's link to gold had been formally severed in 1931, although the United States had continued to use gold to define the value of internationally held dollars until as late as 1978, when it stood at a rate of just over one fiftieth of one ounce.

By inviting the cameras in, it was intended that the sight of the government's shimmering stacks of wealth would maintain the confidence of the people in their currency, but in fact it had the opposite effect. The good citizens of Ohio and Arkansas were shocked at just how little gold there appeared to be. The vault at Fort Knox in which the gold was kept was only eighteen metres by twelve. That was the size of the average church hall in the Midwest Bible belt. How could the wealth of the wealthiest nation on Earth fit into such a small space? It can't be enough, they reasoned, and in fact they were right.

Gold reserves had had an ever-dwindling role to play in central bank activity for some time now. In 1933, President Roosevelt had shocked the nation by confiscating its privately held gold. All of it, except that which could be claimed to have numismatic value. Of course, it was never 'confiscated', merely 'called in', like debts, but they took it all the same. Not until 1975 did the US Government begin selling it off. The British Government themselves had more recently embarked upon a high-profile and much criticized programme of gold sales into the open market. So called 'monetary gold', gold held by governments as a reserve, was an outdated concept in the brave new world of the 'fiat' currency, a currency that has value because the government says it does. It cost an average of three pence to manufacture a banknote – it had next to no intrinsic value – yet the Bank of England or the Federal Reserve or the Bank of Japan said it was worth fifty pounds, or a hundred dollars, or ten thousand yen. The moment one began to doubt the word of the upholders of the value of our currency, the currency itself could lose that value very quickly indeed.

And Sir Peter Taverton, by pissing into the Governor of the Bank of England's fruit salad, had triggered the doubts of one nation in the most graphic way possible.

CHAPTER 7

WALLACE BRADLEY WAS QUIETLY VERY PLEASED WITH HIM-
self, for he had precipitated a 'first'. Up until that point,
problems afflicting the world of electronic money had managed to remain confined within its own marble walls. Stock markets
had crashed in the past, banks had gone bust and currencies had been
devalued, but the real world impact of these events had been limited to a
theoretical markdown in value of investments which had recovered in due
course. For Bradley this would not have sufficed. He had needed more
than that, for his goals were rather more fundamental than bankrupting
a few billionaires.

What drove the market moves was information. New information was
emerging all the time, and the trick was to perceive what information
was relevant amongst the mass of reports, statistics and analysis being
delivered every minute of every day by the mushrooming cloud of
electronic newswires and reporting services.

Yet what was relevant? In those times of free movement of capital it was
simply defined as that to which the majority of people paid attention at
any one time, whether it was 'true' in any absolute sense or not. The mass
of information was synthesized into a gut feeling, an overall impression,
and once any particular trend was established, the market seized upon
any information which supported this impression as a further proof, even
if there may have been masses of contradictory data from other sources.
The trend reinforced itself. And despite the highly complex nature of the
information being fed into the market, and the market was nothing more
than the sum of the individuals who participated in it, the end result of all

that data had to be a simple 'buy' or 'sell'. For, like the computers which dictated an increasing amount of their activity, the markets operated in binary notation, a long series of ones and zeros. And so did the banks which operated at their heart. For them, everything was black or white: the market was either going up or down; we must either buy or sell; we must hire or fire.

What Bradley knew he had done was to tap into this and spread the crisis beyond financial circles. He had not created a trend out of thin air, but by engineering a series of high-profile events all pointing in one direction, he had garnered the attention of the market. He had caused the one-eyed giant to look momentarily in the direction *he* wanted, and once he had attracted its attention he had bombarded it with information that would reinforce a new worldview. His view. A view which amounted to a complete distrust of the institutions in, and on, which we normally bank. Those institutions were both physical entities – the banks themselves – and intangible concepts – the value of a currency, truth. And now he, or more precisely Bruce Phipps, was about to supply the body blow that would finish off the picture of the world he wanted to present. And finish off Japan.

As the British Airways Jumbo began its final approach to Narita Airport in Tokyo, the strange passenger in the front row of first class who had hardly blinked, let alone moved, during the twelve-hour flight was galvanized by an announcement over the public address system.

'Ladies and gentlemen, this is your captain speaking. As you have probably noticed, we have commenced our descent into Tokyo, where we should be landing on time in a little under twenty minutes.

'I feel I should apprise you of some developments which have occurred whilst we were in the air, and for which you should be prepared when you arrive.' There was a general murmur of interest from the first class cabin. Sleeping businessmen stirred from their slumbers and removed their sleep masks, stewardesses took up their positions on their fold-down jump seats, and the in-flight video screens were extinguished. 'There has been some dramatic economic news concerning Japan, released in America, which has apparently caused wide-scale panic. You are all aware of the situation back in the UK. Well, it seems that something similar has erupted now in Japan. Tokyo city centre has ground to a complete standstill with hundreds of thousands of people on the streets. All shops and businesses have been told to remain closed, and the police are struggling to retain control. A warning has been issued by the British Foreign Office, advising people not to travel to Japan in view of the dangers posed by wide-scale civil unrest. Unfortunately, we received this information too far into our flight to be able to turn back, or even divert to another country. Narita itself is partially closed to incoming traffic for the time being, and we are the last inbound foreign carrier permitted to land this morning. There is a large military presence in evidence at the airport itself, due to the enormous number of people trying to leave. Japan Airlines itself has been grounded indefinitely due to insolvency. I would advise everyone to exercise the utmost caution during their stay in Tokyo, and to remain indoors wherever possible. Thank you for flying with British Airways, and please try to remain calm. Our ground staff will advise you of any further developments when we land.'

Bradley was shocked. This could only mean one thing. Phipps had made his announcement early. It was a twelve-hour flight to Tokyo, but only seven to New York, and Phipps had had an hour's head start on him. That meant he must have arrived almost six hours ago. But how could he possibly have had time to convene the rating committee, make the decision and announce it to the world in that time? What Bradley had not taken into consideration was the other means by which information could be disseminated into the marketplace. Accident.

The first class cabin between London and New York was almost the exclusive domain of senior Wall Street bankers and corporate moguls. Phipps's own evangelical style made it almost physically impossible for him to talk in a whisper. He was constantly at the podium, addressing large crowds. Like many men obsessed with his own self-importance, he was also chronically unaware of those around him. Sitting behind him on that flight to New York was Joel Katzenberg, a senior fund-manager for a large fund-management company in Boston. He ran a modest international bond fund of around ten billion dollars, and had been in London to meet some European specialists. Katzenberg travelled a lot. As chance would have it, the previous week he had been in San Diego at a conference run by Bear Stearns to discuss the sharp widening in credit spreads in recent weeks, and to try to identify which issuers represented good value. The keynote speaker at that conference had been Mr Bruce Phipps, Chairman and Chief Executive of Jenner & Phipps, the world's largest credit-rating agency. The whiny, nasal Southern drawl of the man had irritated him then as it had irritated him throughout the entire seven hours of the flight to New York, during which Phipps had maintained an incessant dialogue with his colleagues in the neighbouring seats. Katzenberg knew exactly who he was, even without seeing him, but a strategic trip to the men's room gave him a glimpse of his face and confirmation. They were only about an hour out of JFK when Phipps made his slip.

Katzenberg could scarcely believe his ears. Japan! Downgraded to single B! It was unthinkable. Unimaginable. Totally devastating. It would destroy the Japanese economy and take many others with it. The impact on the US would be dramatic too. Japan was America's largest creditor. The US ran a huge trade deficit which had been largely financed by inward investment from Japan. Amongst other things the Japanese owned more US Treasury bonds than anybody else. They would have to sell them all to raise money back home. Interest rates all over the world would be driven up at a time the world could least afford it.

Surreptitiously, Katzenberg took his notebook computer from its case in the overhead locker and fired it up. The first class cabin of this American Airlines 777 was extremely well equipped. As well as first growth clarets, vintage port and fully reclining beds, it included both power and phone points in each seat which allowed executives to make use of their travelling time to the full. They could work for the full seven hours without the computer batteries giving up after two hours.

And they could send and receive e-mails. Within five minutes, from thirty thousand feet above the north Atlantic, Katzenberg had informed his astonished boss of what Jenner & Phipps were planning, and he had outlined instructions to his colleagues to liquidate as best they could every single bond holding they had. At whatever price they could get for it. All ten billion dollars of it.

It was also in the nature of market participants not to be able to keep a secret for too long. Information was the most precious commodity in the market, and Katzenberg's two subordinates were sitting on the biggest news to hit the bond markets in anyone's living memory. They were proud of it. It was theirs. But nobody would believe they had known it in advance once the news was in the public domain. Then it would lose all of its value, and they would lose all of their kudos. And on top of that, they both had friends at other fund management firms, good friends with whom they slept and drank and discussed strategy, who they would like to help out. For to them this was not only the sort of information which could ruin whole countries, this was the sort of information that could make or destroy careers, the sort of news that could make or break their employers.

So independently of and unbeknown to each other, they both made one telephone call to those friends. And one of them also called his father, a quality controller at General Motors in Detroit who liked to play around with his 401k funds on-line when there was nothing much on TV.

He happened to be at home sick that day, and was sitting at his PC when his son tracked him down. Within five minutes he had logged on to the pension fund's website and moved all of his retirement plan out of bond and stock funds, and into money market and commodity funds. For the same reason that his son had felt the need to inform one of his friends, the father had also felt a need to help other people of a certain age protect their futures. So he posted a remark on the website's bulletin board, urging other imminent retirees to do the same as he had, and why.

Within another five minutes it had been picked up by the Dow Jones Newswire, and was flashed, albeit as a rumour, on to traders' screens on all the mammoth trading floors of Wall Street. London was closed and Tokyo was still sleeping.

In a nervous, suspicious and highly fragile market, a rumour was all it took. Within ten minutes all markets had been suspended limit down.

These limits were the artificial 'circuit breakers' introduced after the crash of '87 to stop markets going into perpetual freefall. As soon as the order imbalances had been dealt with, the markets reopened, and immediately went limit down again. And so it was for the rest of the trading day. Stop, start, stop, start, the markets gapping down in huge pre-determined chunks, until the New York Stock Exchange and the Nasdaq and the Chicago Board of Trade and the Mercantile Exchange had finally had enough, and all colluded to cease trading one hour early. The idea was to give the markets a chance to digest the news overnight and, hopefully, to return with a rather more sane outlook the following morning. With what was about to happen in Japan, there was very little hope of that.

The decision to leave Wallace Bradley's rooms in Oxford was taken at around six a.m. Emerson and his assembled crew were dejected. Max Collins had failed to gain entry to Bradley's computer and was inconsolable. He sat in a corner like a punished child, muttering to himself, looking at no one. They had been unable to find the disk on which Collins expected to find a picture-password, and with the exception of his bank statements, Bradley's desk had yielded no helpful information. But they brought everything with them nonetheless, all the papers and files and reports for further examination in case something had been overlooked. Emerson borrowed a suitcase from under Bradley's bed and stuffed everything in, and while he was in the bedroom looked again at the silver statue of Pegasus on the dresser, half hidden under a mound of dirty socks and loose change. The exquisite beauty of the work had him lost momentarily in contemplation. He imagined Hugh looking at that statue, years ago, on his first day in Oxford, and being seduced by the whole concept. A handful of fresh young minds, flattered by their selection to join an élite group, the flickering candles dancing in the polished flanks of this magnificent animal, a trophy, a symbol, a cause.

And on an impulse he decided to take it with him. He wrapped it carefully in Bradley's dressing gown and packed it in the case along with his papers. If anything, it might help him get inside the head of the man they were now tracking.

Collins also needed Bradley's computer. The monitor could be left, but he packed up the small tower case which housed the CPU and put it into his duffel-bag along with his own equipment. And then they all left.

They staggered their departure, as it might have looked a little odd for five strangers, two of whom were carrying large bags, to be seen leaving the college at six in the morning. It was decided that Charles Emerson would take Patsy and the baby in his car. She insisted on staying with the group, and maintained that she may well be able to help with more background information on Bradley as their investigation progressed. So the two of them drove back to her bedsit up the Iffley road, where they stopped to pick up some clothes and supplies for her and the 'tike' as Emerson senior called the baby, before heading back to London. Jake Samuels drove back alone, and Collins slotted himself into Emerson's Jaguar.

As they drove through the centre of Oxford on their way back to the M40, Emerson was surprised to see the crowds of people demonstrating on the streets. Closeted in Bradley's rooms, they had not seen the broadcast from the Mansion House earlier that evening, and were unaware of the rising level of panic in the British people. As he stopped at traffic lights he lowered the window to ask a policeman what was going on.

'It's the banks, guv,' came the reply. 'Bloody government's gone and closed down three banks. The people want their money. I'd stay indoors if I were you. Get yourself home quick as you can. Specially in a car like that.' And with that he ran off to restrain a grey-haired man in his sixties who was quietly and systematically throwing stones through the windows of a local building society.

Emerson and Collins listened to the car radio news all the way back. They heard account after account of the spreading violence from reporters all over the country. Marches in Manchester; street fighting with petrol bombs in Leeds and Bristol; burnt-out bank premises in Northampton and Cardiff, and just about everywhere else. The radio presenter was flitting between phoned-in descriptions of violence from his roving reporters, rather like the sports desk on a Saturday afternoon doing the rounds of the football grounds for updates and goal-flashes. 'And now it's over to Liverpool, where news is just coming in of an arson attack on the house of a known bank manager . . . and back to Birmingham where I'm informed the police have just succeeded in stopping protesters from entering the Bull Ring . . . I must interrupt you there, Rod, as we're now going live to King Street in Manchester city centre, where we have the Chief Constable of Greater Manchester on the line for his comments on events thus far . . .'

Pegasus Wanderers, several billion – Society United, nil, thought Emerson grimly. He and Collins barely exchanged a single word during the journey. Collins, still brooding on his failure, eventually fell asleep. Emerson, lost in thought, continued to listen to the radio.

All the pundits had something to say, even the Church leaders. The Archbishop of Canterbury had been dragged from his bed and put in front of a microphone to urge restraint. When a journalist pointed out that Christ himself had turned over the tables of the money-lenders in the Temple, he stammered and said it was just an objection to the transacting of business in a house of God, and not to finance *per se*. A Muslim from Bradford phoned in, saying that his religion was opposed to the payment of interest of all kinds and that this financial crisis was the vindication of that philosophy. Somebody else called in to ask who it was in the Bible who had said 'Neither a borrower nor a lender be', and how right they had been? This temporarily stumped the presenter until another, more informed caller from Brighton pointed out that it was actually said by Polonius to Laertes in *Hamlet*, and although this may have been sound advice from anxious father to departing son, Polonius was not exactly a rôle model in the mould of Christ upon whose teachings we should base a whole society, and nor was Shakespeare. Emerson shook his head slowly. Confusion and chaos at every turn, people hanging on to half-formed thoughts, mislearned facts, driven by fear. And greed.

By the time they had rounded the M25 and joined the M4, they were caught up in a convoy of military trucks, also heading for London. It was a battalion of Welsh Guards coming up from Aldershot, and Emerson had to be at his most nimble to insert the low-slung Jaguar into a tight gap between two in a long column of covered troop carriers. The green canvas flaps of the truck ahead of him billowed open as the convoy thundered eastwards, and in his headlights Emerson clearly saw the faces of the men, tightly packed in two rows, facing each other and silent. The tension showed in their young faces. Domestic operations were not what they had been trained for. Not what they wanted.

Emerson soon managed to slip free of the convoy and pushed the car on back to London. Apart from the military trucks, there was very little traffic on the motorway. An occasional ambulance screamed past him, sirens howling, but no police cars. All manpower had been diverted on to the city streets. As he swept past Heathrow Airport, normally sleeping at this time in the middle of its brief, nightly lull, there was already a build-up of traffic on the slip roads to the airport. Most of the cars were packed with families, trying to get out of the violence no doubt, and taking their valuables with them. Quite where they hoped to go was a mystery to Emerson, for now the radio was beginning to report the results of the European fixtures. Copy-cat demonstrations in Brussels and Paris, three killed in Munich, and an apparent bomb attack on a forty-storey bank building in Frankfurt which was being put down to real terrorists attempting to piggy-back on the general civil unrest.

And then came the story which told him where Bradley had gone.

He almost missed it at first, as the newscaster clearly thought it an arcane detail to be glossed over as quickly as possible before getting back to the more interesting stuff back home. 'The American markets closed at a ten-year low today in response to an unconfirmed report that a leading credit agency was to lower the credit rating of Japan from triple A to single B.

'A man was stabbed in Hull this morning in a kebab shop on his way home from . . .'

Japan! That was it! Japan! Japan was his final gesture. Wallace Bradley, world famous consultant to Jenner & Phipps, had persuaded them to lower the rating to single B! It was inconceivable that they could do such a thing. Coming at this stage in the crisis it would mean complete and utter meltdown. On Bradley's part, it was genius. The logical final step. Borrowed money kept the whole financial globe spinning. Debt made the world go round, and Bradley had triggered a debt crisis. He had started by attacking the relative small fry, a few small but high-profile bankruptcies. A few hundred million here, a billion or two there. Digestible stuff. Not life threatening. But the world had become focused on the issues. On *his* issues. Credit. Trust. *Confidence*. The ability to repay. And then he had upped the stakes. That German bank, then Braxton Federal. Braxton for God's sake! And now three British banks, and God knows who would be next.

But if it were Japan! Japan would be the ultimate. Like the newsreader, most people would not understand the implications of that seemingly minor news item. But Japan was the world's largest *lender*. A huge proportion of all that money being borrowed all over the world, especially in the United States, came from the inexhaustible coffers of Japan. Only those coffers had been exhausted long ago. The Japanese Government and the banks and big business had been borrowing more and more for ten straight years. Borrowing, in order to go on lending. Japan had been in recession for ten years, they had no money of their own. If they could not borrow, they could not lend. And they could only borrow if they had a good credit rating. Take that away, remove that keystone, and, forget upturned tables, the whole Temple, the Temple of Mammon, would come crashing down. But the news report said the rumour was 'unconfirmed'. That meant at least that Jenner & Phipps had not done it yet. It had to be stopped.

Emerson put his foot to the floor and the Jaguar leapt forward. As he swept the car into London, past the barricades and through the gauntlet of the crowds baying for justice, a plan was forming in his mind.

CHAPTER 8

WALLACE BRADLEY WALKED AS IF IN A TRANCE THROUGH Tokyo's Narita Airport. Staring straight ahead of him at all time and shuffling amongst the crowds of Japanese thronging the ticket counters, he tried not to look at any of them. This was the moment he had been dreading, the time when he would have to experience 'them' *en masse* and at their worst. They screamed hysterically at each other, all fighting for places on the next outbound flights. No Japanese airlines were flying so they harassed the check-in clerks of the foreign ones, at first offering fistfuls of worthless notes, and then suddenly exploding into paroxysms of uncontrolled fury at their refusal to cooperate.

The sweat coursed down Bradley's back and arms, moistening his grip on the suitcase he grasped with its special contents, and the blood pounded in his temples as never before. It was an incessant, unbearable thumping, as if his entire head was beating to the rhythm of some diabolical drum. Curiously, there was no actual pain, just intense noise which was somehow much worse. There was no relief. At one point he stopped in the very middle of the crowd and gently placed his case on the ground by his side. People swarmed around him with no regard for his presence. He closed his eyes and jammed both tightly clenched fists into his ears in an attempt to block. But what? He knew it was hopeless, after forty years he knew, but still he tried. He had been trying, ever since he had been called out before his whispering classmates to be given the news of his father's death, since first he had read his father's dossier about his mother. But blocking his ears was no good, and closing his eyes was futile. For the sounds and images came from within.

They were of him, but they were not of his making. They were generated by the actions and crimes of a system, a nation, and specifically of one man, all of which he intended to eradicate. Only then could he experience quiet, only then would the pounding abate. Pounding blood. The blood of his mother's gaping wounds, the blood in Captain Kaifu Shimizu's throbbing phallus, and the blood which still pumped through his veins in the shape of Yoshimi Akira, Chairman and Chief Executive of the Yokosuka Corporation. Poseidon!

For tomorrow Pegasus would take to the skies. Tomorrow Medusa would be avenged! And he, Wallace Bradley, Piers Bellefoy, Bellerephon, would take his seat amongst the gods on Mount Olympus. Standing still amongst a sea of thousands of swarming Japanese, he threw back his head and screamed to the heavens.

'I'm afraid Mr Phipps is in a meeting, sir, and absolutely cannot be disturbed.'

'But you don't understand. This is of vital importance. I know what he is discussing in that meeting, and it can't be allowed to go ahead. I have to speak to him. It's about Japan.'

'If you are referring to the rumours circulating, sir, we are fully aware of those, and whilst it is regrettable that . . .'

'Listen to me. My name is James Emerson. I work for the London *Gazette*. I have information which . . .'

'I'm sorry, sir. Jenner & Phipps has a strict policy of not discussing with the press any corporate decisions that may or may not be forthcoming. Maybe if you call back . . .'

Emerson hung up in intense frustration. It was two in the afternoon of the sixth of January, and he had been trying to get through to Bruce Phipps, or somebody senior within the company, all day.

When they had all got back to London, Charles Emerson had dropped Patsy O'Connor and her baby at his son's apartment where she was to stay for a while. Emerson's father had then been asked to take the first available flight to New York. Amongst other things he was to attempt to confront Phipps in person. That would buy them some time to execute the rest of Emerson's plan, which he was refining constantly in his mind. Collins had retired to his own bolthole with Bradley's computer to continue in his attempt to break into it, and to begin preparations for his own considerable rôle in the theatre brewing in Emerson's brain. Jake Samuels sat perched uncomfortably on the edge of the same chair on which he had sat a little over two weeks previously, when he had set Emerson his assignment.

'James, we have to start talking to some of these Pegasus people. We can't just focus on Bradley. At least, not until we know exactly where he is. If we can't find the puppetmaster, let's at least try to sever the strings to some of his puppets. Blake, for one, I can deal with. Although I imagine he's not so important any more. I guess he did his work in the early stages.'

'But at least we can tell him we know what they're up to. Maybe he'll contact Bradley. Warn him off. He may not even know that Lafarge is unmasked. That should shake him up a bit. Maybe he'll talk.'

'Then there's van Aalst and Dodds. We know where they work, at least. We can get to them.'

'And to Scott Turner. Actually that's already being taken care of. I've given Dad a couple of errands to run.'

'Why not go to the authorities here? The Bank of England, the Serious Fraud Office? Tell them what's been going on.'

'And just what has been going on, Jake? What fraud? What have they actually done wrong? And what proof do we have? A bunch of old college mates bringing down the world's financial system? A few people selling a lot of something at the same time? A couple of bankruptcies?'

'But surely . . .'

'They've just exploited the weaknesses in the system. Free movement of capital. Huge amounts of debt. The banks all leveraged to the hilt and tangled up with each other. Kids with the ability to commit billions and billions and billions of dollars with nobody asking any questions. It's the whole system which is killing itself, Jake. They've just melted the glue which was holding it all together.'

'But what about Hugh? They killed him, surely. And your girlfriend's brother. What was his name?'

'Wang. Shin Wang. We're pretty sure they killed them. At least Lafarge killed them. But then we have no proof that would bear cross-examination. No. I think we hold off for a couple more days. Then I have an idea which may just work. And for that I'll need your help, and the particular talents of a Mr Collins. In the meantime you speak to Blake. I'll track down van Aalst.'

'So what's the plan, James? What help do you need from me?'

'Well, it goes something like this . . .'

And for the next hour, James Emerson told Samuels what he was planning to do. At first the Fleet Street veteran sat back in disbelief. And then he began to get interested. Within ten minutes he was taking notes and adding ideas of his own. When Emerson was done, Samuels made a couple of phone calls. One to Si Newman, his financial editor, and the other to a man named George Brand, 'Foreman George' to the team of men and women who worked for and worshipped him at the print works down in Wapping.

'I can do it, James. My end, that is. In fact, I'm committed to it now, so there's no going back.'

The two men spent the rest of the afternoon sitting at Emerson's kitchen table covering sheets and sheets of A4 with notes. Coloured tabs cross-referenced between the rapidly growing piles of paper, and by six that evening they sat back exhausted. The script was written. They were just about ready.

It was a spectacular morning in Grand Cayman. The early morning spring sunshine leaked through the slats in the shutters of Saul Krantz's office at Colliers Landings, tingeing all that it touched with a glow of freshness, a nacreous marbling of warmth and promise of the day to come. It washed over Krantz's back where he lay, sprawled across his desk. He was silent but not sleeping. Fuming. Weeping intermittently. The Xenfin Partnership was out of business.

He had received Annie's resignation letter as soon as he had risen that morning, and he had stared at the accompanying computer printout on his desk in utter disbelief. The billions of dollars, entrusted to his care by institutions and individuals all over the world, were effectively gone. She had blown them up with a calm ferocity that frightened him. The investors he had lured to Xenfin had trusted him and he, in turn, had passed that trust on to Annie van Aalst. It was all so flimsy, when you think about it, he mused. Those people had bought into his judgement, with no guarantees, and had granted him absolute discretion to do what he wanted with their money. All they had to go on was how he'd done last year. In the early days that had been fine. He had done it all himself then. But as Xenfin had grown, he had had to recruit and delegate. And so those same people who had bought into Saul Krantz's judgement as a fund manager, were also suddenly having to buy into his expertise as a judge of character and ability. A whole new realm. This was why he had always been so thorough in his recruitment. He felt a huge responsibility to get it right, to hire the right people, as they were effectively extensions of himself. But how do you defend against a *kamikaze*?

He was pondering who to call first. The amounts involved were mindboggling, and a disorderly liquidation of the positions entered into by van Aalst on her last day, as he, Saul Krantz, lay sleeping with the scent of her body all over him, could be catastrophic to hundreds of other institutions. He suddenly felt incredibly vulnerable and incapable. His *own* confidence was shot to pieces, and he needed help and advice to resolve the situation with the minimum pain possible. He was about to get it.

The phone rang and it was James Emerson.

'Mr Krantz, you don't know me. My name is James Emerson. Please do not hang up, because what I have to say is of vital importance. Not only to yourself, and I suspect to the survival of Xenfin, but to the continuing ability of the world's financial system to function.'

'Mr Emerson, I appreciate your concern. Those are grand words that you speak, but how can . . . ?'

'I know about Annie van Aalst, Mr Krantz. Your secretary informs me she has left your company.' This was true. When Krantz had received van Aalst's letter he had immediately informed his staff and sent telexes to all Xenfin's counterparties in the markets to that effect. This was standard practice when a key, authorized risk-taker left a firm, and vital to prevent them continuing to execute unauthorized trades by telephone in the name of a former employer. 'I suspect she may have left you in an awkward situation. I may be able to help you.'

And in a few words, Emerson explained to Krantz what had been going on. He explained about Wallace Bradley and the Pegasus Forum. He explained about St Mary's College, Oxford and how the students had been recruited. And he outlined the extent of their activities since the crisis broke. 'I don't have all the details yet, Mr Krantz. I don't even think I have a full list of all those involved. There are probably others. But Annie was one of the key players. She used your balance sheet, Mr Krantz, and the good name of Xenfin. A trader at Steinman, Schwartz was involved too, and a British lawyer who took care of the documentation. A diplomat in the Far East fed them information about developments out there, and arranged for huge currency sales to be channelled through a corrupt trader in Jakarta. We can only speculate on the rest. We can only guess at how they sparked the key failures in the banking sector which opened the floodgates.'

But Krantz could help him there. It all made sense at last, and his despair began to develop into a profound anger. He told Emerson about the call he had received from the German bank supervisory authority, and the complaint that had been made against van Aalst by Jakob Lichtblau at Bankhaus Löwen-Krugman. Complaints that he had dismissed on the word of Annie van Aalst. He told him about the massive sales she had made in the stock of Braxton Federal, for which he had almost fired her, but had instead promoted her. And he told him about the massive investments she had made in Japan the night before she jumped ship, the day before the rumour broke about Japan's credit rating being downgraded.

And suddenly James Emerson jumped back three years in his mind.

Three years ago he had been the leading salesman in the London markets. His reputation was legendary, the confidence he instilled in his clients absolute. They begged to do business with him. Now he began to work his spell on Saul Krantz. He knew it was vital that news of Xenfin's plight must not escape if something was to be salvaged, if there was not to be a return to a financial stone age. Five years previously another hedge fund had been on the brink of disaster, and the Federal Reserve Bank had quietly assembled a group of its major creditors and told them in no uncertain terms what the implications were should they pull the plug. But that was small fry compared to the extent of Xenfin's positions. The very news that they were somehow in trouble might be enough to precipitate the disaster. It had to be kept quiet for now. And Emerson was going to help them turn it around.

He talked at Saul Krantz for half an hour, and outlined exactly what he wanted him to do and why. He knew it was the greatest challenge of his life, the sales call to end them all, but if he could not gain the confidence, the trust of the man in that short time, then it was all over. Financial Armageddon. There it was again. It all came back to those words, every time. *Confidence. Trust.*

He had not lost his touch. At the end of that half an hour Saul Krantz saw James Emerson as the one hope. Despite his slip up over Annie van Aalst, Krantz was still an excellent judge of character, and he recognized the quality and sincerity of James Emerson's words. He promised to keep everything quiet for a further two days. Any more than that, and he would have to make an announcement. He owed it to his clients, his investors. He had a fiduciary responsibility. But as things stood right now, they weren't going to get their money back anyhow, and James Emerson's idea represented at least a chance. A last roll of the dice.

If ever an end justified the means, then this was it. If it failed, then it would probably be Emerson going to jail rather than Wallace Bradley or Annie van Aalst. After all, she was merely guilty of incompetence. She bet the ranch on black and it came up red. Malicious intent would be extremely difficult to prove and she had a blameless track record. And

Bradley was quite possibly insane, by the sound of it. God knows what sort of kick *he* was getting out of this all.

Saul Krantz could not quite believe what Emerson was proposing to attempt. He was not at all sure if it would work. If, indeed, it was possible. But he was sure of one thing: it was not legal.

'Can I fix either of you boys a drink, now? Looks like yous both could use one.' Patsy O'Connor emerged from the kitchen. In one hand she carried a frozen bottle of vodka she had found in Emerson's freezer, whilst in the crook of her other arm she cradled the statue of Pegasus.

'Isn't this a beauty, though?' she said and moved towards the table. 'Let me put it down here between yous, maybe it'll give you inspiration!'

'You mean the vodka or the statue, Patsy?' They all laughed. She went to place the statue on the table, but as she did so, the vodka bottle, still wet and slippery from the freezer, began to slide from her grasp. In a reflex movement she went to steady it with her other hand, and the statue of Pegasus tumbled from her arm and crashed to the floor.

'Shit, sorry guys,' she gasped, and bent to retrieve the damage. 'I can't believe it. It's broken. A wing's come off. Hope it wasn't valuable!'

'Pass it to me, Patsy. I'm sure we can get it fixed. Never mind. Just get some glasses for that bottle.'

Whilst she was gone Emerson examined the statue. The wing had snapped at its weakest point, the narrowing where it joined the horse's flank. But the statue rattled somehow. Maybe a small piece of silver had fallen inside the hollow body, he thought at first. But he shook it again, and the rattling came again. There was a metallic sound to it, but also a kind of plastic knocking. And a rustling. The more he shook it, the more he was sure. There was something inside the plinth of that statue.

The plinth itself was round and tiered, about ten inches in diameter at the bottom, narrowing to about six inches at the top where Pegasus himself stood. It was made of wood, highly polished walnut, he guessed, and about three inches deep. Turning it over he saw what he was looking for. There was one small hole, a couple of millimetres across at most, drilled just inside the edge, and an almost invisible seam, blended beautifully into the grain of the wood, running all around the circumference. He took a ballpoint pen from the desk, inserted it into the hole and began to turn, anticlockwise. As he did so the entire inner section of the base began to turn also. It was threaded. In a matter of seconds he had unscrewed the middle of the plinth and, righting the statue again, he lifted it away from its base. Samuels stared. Sitting in the palm of his hand on a beautifully turned, round platter of polished walnut, was a floppy computer disk and a single piece of paper. A flimsy piece of notepaper, folded in half. The disk would have to wait for Collins. But he unfolded the paper and read.

He was puzzled at first. Deep frown, pursed lips. The names of two people. Who on earth were they? And then he began to wonder.

He passed it to Samuels, who cottoned on immediately. For what they were reading was a letter from an old lady. The letter from the Empress of Nanking. And it was not the names of two people on that piece of paper, but the two names of one person.

Patsy O'Connor came back into the room armed with shot glasses.

'All I could find, James, sorry. We'll do it Russian style, shall we?'

'Patsy, sit down a second. I need to talk to you. You knew Bradley pretty well at one stage, didn't you? There must have been a point when you were friendly?'

'Oh, not for long, but yes. There were a couple of weeks at the beginning when it was all quite sweet.'

'Did he talk much about his background? His family? His parents?'

'A little. When he was pissed. I know he was an only child, 'cause he was always going on about big Irish families and how nice it must be.'

'And his parents?'

'All I know is that his mother was Australian and his father American. Wallace was born in the States and then moved here. He said he never knew his mother. She died of something nasty she'd picked up in the tropics, apparently, couple of years after the end of the war. She was a nurse, or something. His dad was a US Army doctor. That's how they met, he told me. During the war in the Far

East. The father was killed in a car crash when the boy was sixteen.'

Samuels looked at Emerson, and they were both thinking the same
thing. Emerson looked again at the letter in his hand. The dates matched.
Palembang Internment Camp, Dutch East Indies, 1940–1945. '*She died of
something nasty she'd picked up in the tropics.*' An Australian nurse. An
American doctor. A Japanese camp commander. Japan was his target.
Japan had been his target all along. And one man in particular.

'I need to get to Tokyo. Right away. Next flight . . . What do you mean,
there are no flights going in? Are you serious? What about overland?
OK. So book me on the flight to Seoul. I take the train to where, do
you say? Pusan? OK. And then the hydrofoil across to Fukuoka. How
far from there to Tokyo? Five hours by bullet train? OK. Here's my card
number . . .' Samuels and O'Connor looked at him perplexed.

'James, what is it? Is the plan off?'

'No, Jake, it's not. I think I know where Bradley has gone. I'll be in
touch by phone. We've written the script. You might have to play both
parts if I'm not back. But I shouldn't be more than a few days. Now, I
have to pack. Get me Max Collins, Jake, can you? I need him over here
right now, and tell him to bring a box of tricks with him. Tell him I need
Rembrandt to paint my door again. He'll know what I mean.'

It had taken Wallace Bradley two hours to get from Narita Airport to
his hotel in the Ginza district of Tokyo. The limousine driver whom
he had arranged to have pick him up thought twice about letting him
in the car. He was ashen white, and sweating profusely to the extent
the driver thought he must have malaria or something equally horrible.
He made a point of keeping the smoked-glass partition, which separated
the passenger area from the driver, firmly closed at all times, and he was
glad to see Bradley insisted on handling his luggage himself.

The journey took so long, twice as long as normal, because of the chaos on the streets. Like London, Paris and Frankfurt, like Jakarta, Seoul and now Hong Kong, Tokyo was gripped by a profound and widespread panic. Pavements and roads blended into one, as the crowds spilled on to the carriageways, mindless of the danger and mindless of the law. It seemed there was a river of people, flowing aimlessly around the capital, clogging its arteries; the city was in a coma and it seemed somebody had just switched off the life-support system. Its vital functions were shutting down.

The psychedelic neon tubes, the heartbeat of the city, which normally flashed their constant advertisements high above the thoroughfares, were a dull, lifeless grey. Traffic lights changed from red to green and to red again but nothing moved. In fact there were very few cars on the roads, just people. But the crowds were strangely quiet. Unlike at the airport, there was no hysterical screaming, very little violence, just a ghostly expression of revolt by a people used to smiling acquiescence and deference. And somehow it seemed all the more threatening for that. The latent anger, the sense of power flowing through those silent shuffling thousands, hundreds of thousands, was almost tangible. And yet their mute complaint was the same as that of the Londoners and Parisians and Jakartans and all the others who had taken to the streets before them.

They were the ultimate losers. The vast majority of the money that had been lent and lost, borrowed and not repaid, was theirs. For, ultimately, the money that was being borrowed had to come from somewhere. Banks borrowed from banks who borrowed from other banks, who lent to governments who lent to other governments. Japan lent to the world, but who lent it to Japan? Their people, was the answer, the smallest units, the simple cells of any economy. They were the ultimate source of the wealth, for they generated it. They worked, they assembled the cars, they sold the cameras and the TVs, they made the products and provided the services which generated the income. It was their money which went into the banks and got invested in stocks and bonds, and lent to P.L. Chumsai and the US Government and Braxton Federal. And it was their money that got lost. It was an economic war that Bradley was waging, but economic war was nothing more than a war against the people. The people *were* the economy.

Every side street, every six lane expressway, was full of people. Some carried banners which Bradley could not read, others simply ambled, a stunned look of disbelief on their faces. This was the end. The Japanese economic miracle, built from scratch after the American occupation, and the devastation of a ferocious war, had been levelled again. But this time it was an economic Hiroshima, in many respects a much more profoundly destructive explosion than its forebear, and one from which the fall-out would continue to settle for many years to come. For its damage was much greater than the mere physical destruction of buildings. Oh, it had destroyed many institutions already, and hundreds more would crumble before long, but what it had really destroyed was much more significant. Not only had it destroyed the actual value of those institutions, it had destroyed the *belief* of the rest of the world in them. And that belief could not be reconstructed with bricks and mortar.

Max Collins, complete with his ubiquitous laptop and Bradley's computer, strolled into Emerson's flat a little over half an hour later.

'Painting and decorating services at your disposal, dude.'

'Max. We haven't much time. I need to leave for the airport in an hour. I'm convinced Bradley's in Japan. I think he's gone looking for this guy.' He handed Collins the letter he had found, and told him what O'Connor had recounted about Bradley's parents.

'Holy shit, man. You mean you think Bradley's mother was in this camp?'

'Right, Max. And she died a couple of years later. When Bradley was a baby. I think he's after revenge, Max. But look. We've found a disk. Hopefully this is the one which will get you into his PC. And that should give us the confirmation.'

When Collins slotted the disk into Bradley's PC and ran the program, they were stunned by what they saw. It was indeed a picture, the picture which held the password to Bradley's files. But it was not the sort of

picture they had been expecting. It was a black and white photograph of
a naked woman, a barely living skeleton standing in front of a white wall
with horizontal black lines painted on it. This was the picture Bradley
had chosen to conceal his password. The picture of his mother from
his father's files. Nobody spoke for several minutes. They stared at the
image, the thing, the woman who stared out defiantly at them from
the screen.

'So this is what Pegasus is all about,' Samuels murmured at last. He
understood. Jake Samuels, the man for whom Christmas, in the words of
Charles Emerson an eternity ago, 'wasn't his bag' had lost relatives of his
own in camps, different camps, closer to home. But he understood. He
had seen many photographs like the one on the screen, many newsreels
and archive footage. He had visited the holocaust museums. For the
Gazette, he had even interviewed the Nazi hunters, the men and women
who devoted their entire lives to seeking out the perpetrators of these
atrocities. Yet the tendency was, given the enormity of the *Shoah*, to
forget the others, not the millions but still the hundreds of thousands
of others who had suffered a similar fate, but at other hands.

'OK, Max. Let's see what's in there.'

And now he had the key to entering Bradley's systems, Collins began
to delve into Bradley's files. They skimmed through page after page of
analysis, details of banks and governments around the world. Years of
work. They found the report written for Jenner & Phipps about Japan,
and its chilling conclusion: *'Japan has a corrupt, incompetent government
and the public finances of a weak Third World nation. If it were not in G-7,
the IMF would have imposed currency and spending controls long ago. As a
nation its long-term debt merits a rating no higher than single B.'*

And then they found the details of the members of the Pegasus Forum.
They found Bradley's notes, his research into all of their backgrounds, his
comments. *'Paid-up member of the Communist Party. Major grudge against
international capitalism.'* Johnnie Quaid. *'Broken home and neglected
childhood due to corrupt banker father. Alcoholic mother. Very bright. Idealist.'* Annie van Aalst. *'Prodigious mathematician. Hates the system. Rebel
without a cause. Can be directed.'* Cameron Dodds. *'Father undischarged*

bankrupt. Banks foreclosed on stuttering business.' Christopher Blake. *'First generation African-American. Passionate supporter of Third World issues. Strongly anti capitalist exploitation of Sudanese homeland.'* Scott Turner. *'Wishy-washy pinko. Father leading journalist, moral crusader. Anti-establishment.'* Hugh Emerson. And then an addition to the file: *'Expelled from Pegasus 3/98.'* Expelled was the word he used to gloss it. Expelled. March 1998. The date of Hugh's death.

'Quick! Come over here! Look! It's him!' Patsy O'Connor had turned up the sound on the TV in Emerson's apartment.

'What, Patsy? Who is it?'

'It's him! Your man! Bradley! They've only gone and given it to him! Jesus Christ. The Nobel friggin' Prize.'

And there on the television news was a picture of Wallace Bradley. Same glasses, same rumpled brown suit, squinting through the screen. James Emerson studied the face intently. This was the first proper look he had had at the man's face since he had learned his name only the day before.

'The Royal Swedish Academy of Sciences today awarded the Nobel Prize for Economics to Professor Wallace Bradley of St Mary's College, Oxford. Notwithstanding the current crisis, his work has gone a long way towards furthering the development of the emerging economies of South East Asia. In a statement this evening . . .' Emerson switched it off. He couldn't bear to listen to any more. The man's face was ingrained on his memory, as were his words. *'Expelled 3/98.'*

Patsy O'Connor's baby suddenly disturbed his thoughts with a plaintive cry from the spare room where she had set up its travel cot.

'I'll get it, Patsy. Don't worry. I'll bring him to you. Sounds hungry.' Emerson was glad of the distraction. The revelations of the last half hour had been a lot to take on board, and he went into the darkened room to get Bradley's son. He had yet to actually get a good look at the baby. He seemed to spend the whole time either squashed against Patsy's chest or sleeping, and Emerson scooped him out of the cot, taking care to support the head which now beamed up at him with a windy smile. Patsy had followed him in and took the baby straight out of his hands.

'Don't you bother, James. You've got some packing to do. Get off with you. You'll be needing some time to yourself.' He handed her the baby without a word. 'James? James! What's the matter with you? I'm only trying to help you catch that flight of yours!' He walked out of the room without replying. Could it be? His brain was working overtime, and now he had another call he needed to make.

CHAPTER 9

C HARLES EMERSON HAD INSTALLED HIMSELF IN HIS NEW YORK hotel room and was just about to leave for the offices of Jenner & Phipps when he took the call from his son. He listened in astonishment to the account of what they had discovered in the statue of Pegasus, and to the contents of Bradley's computer files. He drew a sharp breath and closed his eyes when he heard of Bradley's description of his younger son's 'expulsion' from the Pegasus Forum. But he had to sit down when told of James's last piece of information, a hunch he had not shared with the others.

'But James, are you sure?'

'Quite sure, Dad. It's unmistakable.'

'But wouldn't she have . . . ?'

'Not necessarily, not in her state. And she's naïve. It's been quite a week.'

'OK. Leave it with me. I'll check up on the feasibility of it, and get on to the appropriate authorities.'

'How will you know where to look?'

'My boy, you forget with whom you are speaking. There has not yet been a piece of information invented that this old newshound could not track down.'

Half an hour later Charles Emerson stood in the anteroom to the office of Bruce Phipps. His secretary was protesting. She didn't like the tone of the elegant but persistent older man who refused to take no for an answer.

'My dear, you simply do not understand. I will not move from this

spot until I have spoken to Mr Phipps. It is of the utmost importance.'

'I'm calling security.'

'You may call whomever you wish, dear. But if you don't wish your
antics to be spread all over the London *Gazette*, I suggest you inform
Mr Phipps I am here. Tell him, if you like, that I have an urgent message
from Professor Wallace Bradley. I have travelled four thousand miles to
deliver it. I *will* deliver it.'

One hour later, Charles Emerson left a stunned and chastened Bruce
Phipps in his office. Part one was complete. The planned downgrading of
Japan was cancelled, and an immediate statement to that effect would be
issued. No details of Bradley's duplicity would be given, not yet at least.
The groundless rumour of the downgrade would simply be ascribed to an
over-zealous reporter. To a certain extent, the damage Bradley wanted to
inflict had already been done. For an entire trading day the markets had
believed that Phipps would downgrade Japan, and in such instances the
rumour was just as important as the news. The markets were used to
official denials of rumours one day which then proved to be true the next,
but at least Emerson had ensured that the rumour would not actually
become fact. Damage control.

Phipps was also informed of the outline of James Emerson's plans
for the next two days. He was aghast, but in no position to refuse to
play along.

Visit number two would be a little more problematic. Getting to see
Byron Powell, Chairman of the Federal Reserve Board, was not the main
difficulty. Jake Samuels had accumulated some extremely influential
contacts over the years, and when the Vice President of the United States
called Powell's office to make an appointment for him to see a Mr Charles
Emerson from London, England, the central banker was in no position to
decline. Given the dramatic activity in the markets, Powell was spending
most of his time at the offices of the New York Fed on Liberty Street, a
few blocks north of Wall Street itself, and Emerson had a firm appointment. With Samuels's stringpulling, that had been the easy part. Getting
him to go along with what they had in mind was another matter.

But Charles Emerson was superb. The man was probably the most eloquent journalist of his generation, if not his century. In his meeting with Powell, not only did he turn the originally granted ten-minute audience into two and a half hours, by expressing himself with a clarity, an intensity and a passion which defied interruption or disagreement, but the two men emerged from the meeting as firm friends.

Powell had interrupted him only three times. The first time was after five minutes, when he picked up the phone to call the FBI; the second time was when he called a number in Grand Cayman, and spent thirty seconds reassuring an astonished Saul Krantz that he was onboard; the third time was halfway through Emerson's description of the details of his son's plan, when Powell interjected with a particularly clever and subtle twist on the overall idea.

Powell's first intervention bore fruit while Charles Emerson was still in his office.

The two FBI agents charged with the task started tracking Scott Turner's car on Kellogg Avenue in Carlsbad, where he had just left his parents' house. Ostensibly he had been spending the holidays with them. Dr Wesley Turner and his wife Betty didn't realize it at the time but he had really been saying goodbye. The agents tracked him northwards on the I-5 and I-405 for around an hour and a half as far as Los Angeles, where he swung off to head for LAX, the International Airport. They watched him park his car, unload one suitcase, and head off towards the Tom Bradley International Terminal. For the sake of completeness, they let him check in at the Egypt Air desk on the 12.50 p.m. flight direct to Cairo. They knew the case would stack up better if they could show he had actually attempted to leave the country. In fact they waited until he had handed in his boarding pass at the departure gate before they finally picked him up. In his pocket they found he had a one-way ticket. He also had another ticket, again one-way, for the connection on Sudan Airways from Cairo to Khartoum. He was travelling on a Sudanese passport in the name of Francis Ajang. In his briefcase was a letter of introduction from the Sudanese Minister of Finance, welcoming him to his new post.

At three p.m. Charles Emerson left the offices of the Fed and set off to complete his third task, the one given to him by his son at the last minute and the one which had caused him most surprise. As even he could not be in two places at once, and as time was of the essence, he decided to call in an old favour.

Hal Bramfield on the *Washington Post* was plainly very surprised to receive a call from his old sparring partner. He still wrote a regular feature for the *Post* but the heady days of Watergate and working with Woodward and Bernstein were long gone. Emerson had taught him many things about investigative journalism over the years, and Bramfield was happy to help out an old friend. Besides, it would be a good excuse to get out of the office. The vast offices of the National Archives and Records Administration were on Pennsylvania Avenue, and he knew a nice little coffee shop nearby which he would be able to drop by on the way back. He took Emerson's hotel details and promised him an answer by that evening.

Charles Emerson himself had another trip to make, and it would mean an overnight stay. But he didn't bother returning to his hotel for a change of clothes. He just flagged down the next cab to come cruising along Liberty Street and took it to JFK airport. An hour and a half later and he was bouncing down the runway in an American Eagle 35-seater Saab 340, praying for no turbulence and hoping that their aircraft were better than his experience of their cars. Charles Emerson was not a born flier. In the same way that he did not like to see recognizable body parts on his plate, he did not like to see moving parts on aeroplanes. He tried to ignore the horrifyingly inadequate-looking propeller which churned the air beyond his right shoulder, and instead concentrated on the task in hand. The flight would take a little over one hour, which would make it around six o'clock. The New York State Vital Records Office in Albany, the State capital, would have to wait until the following day.

By the time James Emerson arrived in Tokyo, after a gruelling journey via South Korea, the announcement by Jenner & Phipps, elicited by his father a few hours earlier, that they had no plans to downgrade the credit rating of Japan was beginning to have an effect of sorts. The silent millions who had flooded on to the streets of Tokyo in mute protest had largely returned to their homes. There were still pockets of protest apparent, but the Japanese are not by nature rebellious creatures, and the firm response by the authorities had sent most of them scurrying for cover. The civil unrest, at least, had been quelled. The markets were a different matter.

Most professional market participants were sceptical beasts, cynics bent on self-preservation. Bad news was accepted, as who would deliberately invent bad news? A good reason to sell. But good news? In the terrible overall market conditions prevailing at the time, good news needed twelve proofs before its validity was accepted. 'It's a false dawn', 'somebody's talking their book', 'somebody's long and wrong', 'the figures are a blip, an aberration . . . look at the seasonal adjustments', and so on. In the case of the proposed downgrade, the traders and salesmen who peddled information to their clients were more prepared to believe a rumour emanating from an overheard conversation on a flight than a forthright denial on live television from the chairman of the company concerned. 'Well he would say that, wouldn't he?' 'there's no smoke without fire', 'no one likes to be pre-empted by the markets', 'we just stole his thunder!'

And so the banks remained closed, those that had not been declared insolvent already. The insurance companies froze all payments, (they had nothing to pay with, anyway, and no means of paying it) and two hundred and six of the companies in the Nikkei 225 Stock Index were trading at a price below the magic one hundred yen level.

Before the crisis started, one dollar had been worth approximately ninety yen. As the economies of Indonesia and Korea and Malaysia crumbled, the yen had fallen to around one hundred and thirty to the dollar over a number of weeks. When Braxton Federal had failed, and the dollar had come under some pressure of its own, the yen had rallied briefly back to around one hundred and ten. On the day Joel Katzenberg had overheard Bruce Phipps on his flight from London to New York, the yen had fallen to two hundred and fifty to the dollar. The next day it had moved through the three hundred mark. On the day James Emerson arrived in Japan it was pushing four hundred. Which meant that those blue chip Japanese stocks were trading at prices of around twenty-five cents or less. Those behemoths of industrial success, those giants of technological marvels and efficiency had been reduced to penny shares. As one highly placed source at the Federal Reserve was anonymously quoted as saying by the *Washington Post*, 'Jeez, if Uncle Sam had any money left he could buy up Japan Inc. for the price of a Big Mac!'

After his five hour journey from Fukuoka, Emerson walked out of the Marunouchi entrance to Tokyo Central Station, a Japanese St Pancras or Grand Central built in red brick in the early years of the twentieth century, and somehow much more permanent than the glitzy towers of glass and steel whose occupants were now mostly bankrupt. The first thing he saw opposite him was the Imperial Palace, or at least one of the several entrances to it, a moated hideaway for the deified but powerless figurehead of Japanese society and culture. At the height of the Japanese property boom, this incredibly indulgent square mile of parklands and, by palatial standards, relatively unimpressive buildings in the centre of downtown Tokyo, the most expensive real estate on Earth, was worth more than the GDP of a few small countries combined. Right now, at the current exchange rate and land values, it was probably not worth much more than the price of a few brownstones on the upper east side of New York City.

He walked the few blocks to his hotel, the Seiyo Ginza in the centre of Tokyo's most fashionable district. This would normally have been an extravagance, with mid-price rooms running at one hundred thousand yen a night, a thousand dollars at pre-crisis levels. Right now it was more like two hundred and fifty US, or a hundred and fifty pounds, which is what it used to cost in a taxi from Narita Airport to downtown.

In another hotel room, far above Emerson's head as he strolled into the Ginza district, and looking down into the Palace gardens was Wallace Bradley. His room was on the fourteenth floor of the Imperial Hotel, and he stood in the window, quite naked. His sagging, hairy body was not a pleasant sight, but then nobody could see it. Not yet, anyway. That would have to wait for his visit to the Pink Cherry, a hostess bar he knew he had not frequented in the past, and which would therefore still be willing to accept his custom.

He held a bamboo cup of warm *sake* in one hand, by no means his first, and sipped away his pain. It was the only way he had found over the years to take away the noise, the pounding in his head, the black and white images. It usually subdued his senses, but occasionally his demons took strength from the alcohol and ran wild, became violent. It had been happening more frequently again recently, since Pegasus had become active, since he had received the letter from Nanking, and it happened most often when he was with women. He knew he had to be careful tonight. He could not afford a scene at the bar, he could not risk detention as had happened to him once in Jakarta when the British Embassy, in the form of Morley Lafarge, had had to smooth things over with the brothel owner and the police in order to get him out. Tonight must be calm. Because tomorrow was to be his day.

He took his suitcase down from the top of the wardrobe and placed it on his bed. Opening the lid, he removed the Samurai sword he had carried with him from Oxford. With great reverence, he grasped the black lacquer, finely ribbed *saya* in his left hand and, trembling slowly with excitement, firmed his grip around the four-hundred-year-old ray-skin binding, wound tightly around the handle of the ancient weapon. And slowly, very slowly and very carefully, he drew the sword for the first time in his life. His right arm was fully extended by the time the point of the three-foot-long blade escaped its sheath for the first time in over fifty years, and Bradley gazed at it in awe. The blade itself was not especially ornate, no carved dragons or chrysanthemums, but its utilitarian appearance, and its extremely shallow curve, somehow made it all the more menacing. It was not a flamboyantly arched, ceremonial sword, encrusted with jewels and precious metals, it was a warrior's sword, a fighting sword from some minor shogunate. And although it had not been drawn in over fifty years, and the blade not touched by human hand, its extreme sharpness was still very much in evidence in the apparent invisibility of the cutting edge itself. It dwindled away to nothing like a mountain peak lost in the mist, a tantalizing mirage of death, so fine yet so phenomenally hard. That much Bradley knew. The elaborate forging techniques of the master swordmakers, whereby the steel was hammered and folded on itself again and again, produced a durability without brittleness unknown to modern armourers. Bradley tossed the sheath aside and, grasping the handle with both hands now, raised the sword carefully above his head in practice.

James Emerson had been very busy since he checked into his Tokyo hotel. He arrived to find various messages, one from his father, now back in New York, and several from Jake Samuels, including a fax. A fax of a photograph.

He spoke to his father first.

It was seven in the evening Tokyo time, five in the morning in New York, but Charles Emerson had not really slept.

'James, I have the necessary. And one surprise.'

'Fire away.'

'Bradley's mother's name was Charlotte Drabble. Australian citizen by birth, nurse by profession. Parents both deceased. One of my old muckers in Washington tracked her down in the Immigration and Naturalization records. Came in to the States in New York, December 1945, in the care and under the sponsorship of one Dr Bradley. Immediately admitted to military hospital.'

'I can imagine why.'

'Well, you're right James. I can't believe it but you are.'

'And when did Dr Bradley and Drabble marry?'

'Civil ceremony in March '46.'

'Right. That fits too.'

'And young Wallace. Do you have his exact date of birth?'

His father told him.

'And when did the mother die?'

'Well, that's the surprise.'

'Are you going to tell me?'

'She didn't die.'

'What do you mean?'

'There's no death certificate.'

'Are you sure?'

'Positive. And there's more. You mentioned that Wallace Bradley and his father moved to the UK.'

'That's right. After the mother's death, I thought.'

'Well, on a hunch I checked out the records on that. New York State Commissioners of Emigration. They did leave, in January '49. But they left *en famille*, complete with a certain Mrs Charlotte Bradley, *née* Drabble. She went with them James. Very much alive, at least in January '49.'

'And tell me you've had someone run down to St Catherine's House to check the UK records?'

'I have indeed. Took him all afternoon. No death certificate there either. No dead Charlotte Bradley *née* Drabble of Australian descent in the last fifty years. Mrs Bradley is very much alive. And when I return to London I shall begin looking for her.'

His next call was to Jake Samuels.

'Got the photo, Jake, thanks.'

'Did it come out OK on the fax?'

'Yes. Very clear. The marvels of modern telecommunications. There's no doubt in my mind.'

'Patsy isn't dealing with all this too well.'

'I'm not surprised. Look after her, Jake. What about Max?'

'He says he's ready. Ready when you are. I'm ready too. I've had words with the boys in Wapping. We roll when you give the word.'

'OK. I phoned the Yokosuka Corporation. Said I was from the Nobel Institute, trying to track down the good professor. He has an appointment to see the old man at nine tomorrow morning. I'll pick him up then. I'm sure he'll come quietly when I tell him the news. The airport's reopened now, and I've booked us both on the British Airways flight back at one. No point in hanging around. Maybe you can arrange a reception committee? Then we can get going with our plan.'

CHAPTER 10

THE OFFICES OF THE YOKOSUKA CORPORATION ARE A TOWERING glass monolith in the heart of the Maranouchi business district of Tokyo, a short walk from Wallace Bradley's hotel. He had not slept that night.

The girl he had ended up with at the hostess bar had been a disappointment. Much too prim, too shy. Not into his sort of thing at all. He had tried to be good, tried to hold himself back, but the *sake* had thinned his reserve. He had been thrown out after an hour of her company. The proprietors of the Pink Cherry were used to odd behaviour. Some of their Japanese clientele had strange requirements of their own, and the management employed a wide range of girls to accommodate as best they could. To a point. But nothing like this. Fortunately for Bradley they didn't involve the police. An establishment such as theirs rarely invited the forces of law and order over the threshold, at least in an official capacity. But they made him pay more. Much more, in fact, to compensate them and the poor girl for the loss of income whilst the bruises healed and the nose was reset. The patches of hair would take longer to grow back, but that could at least be concealed with wigs.

Bradley left the hotel very early, before seven, and went for a walk in the Imperial gardens. It took him a long time to get around, however. It was not easy to walk with a three-foot-long sword concealed inside the trouser leg of a suit, no matter how loose-fitting and crumpled. But he practised, and after an hour or so was able to affect a reasonably regular if stiff-legged gait which he thought should suffice to get him in the building without raising too much suspicion. And thus he hobbled towards the Yokosuka building, a middle-aged man with a limp, an unremarkable man in a brown, baggy suit, a Nobel laureate, a man about to achieve his life-long ambition. One of the Empress of Nanking's less likely assassins.

Fate had been kind to James Emerson over the years. He had had things more or less his own way in whatever direction he chose to apply himself, and although in his youth he would have mocked the very idea of supernatural forces being at work, preferring to ascribe his success to a dedication and meticulousness which scared most people, he had mellowed to the idea more recently. But it seemed his supply of luck had been exhausted a few days earlier in the porter's lodge at St Mary's College, when a departing Wallace Bradley had inadvertently handed him his room key. For although he had been waiting to intercept Bradley outside the offices of the Yokosuka Corporation since eight that morning, an hour before the appointment, he missed him.

Looking back, it could have happened a couple of times. Either when a fracas outside the main entrance of the Osakumi Bank building next door distracted him momentarily, or when a loud American couple asked him to take their picture together standing in front of McDonald's. Either way, Bradley's anonymous, shambling figure entered the lobby unmolested at five minutes to nine and announced himself at reception.

He was happy that he had timed his arrival just right, as the Japanese found it equally rude to be too early as late, and heaven knows he did not want to offend the man whose life he was about to end.

Not one but two of the uniformed office ladies ushered him in a flurry of bobbing heads and plastic grins to the lift bank, and accompanied him as they were whisked silently up to the very top floor. They did not speak on the way up. Any man with an appointment to see their chairman, the redoubtable Yoshimi Akira, was immediately conferred with a status almost, but not quite, as elevated as that of the great man himself. And they were certainly not permitted to speak to him.

Once on the top floor, the two mute twins gestured effusively to a black leather sofa in a waiting area outside two enormous, highly polished doors made from what looked like solid rosewood. There was an Andy Warhol-style print of a dozen multi-coloured Mount Fujis on the wall, which on closer examination turned out to be the real thing, a work Akira had personally commissioned twenty years previously and unknown outside the Yokosuka building.

Bradley stood and waited. This was what it had all come down to now. The years of preparation, the years of study in pursuit of eminence in the one field in which he could do some damage, the years of searching for a man's name, had finally come to this. A meeting between two men. Bradley had replayed this moment in his mind a thousand times, a million times, over the course of those years. His feverish dreams, his nightmares, had prepared him for it, and as he heard the slow footsteps approaching on the other side of those double doors, and heard the rattling of the handle, he was suddenly aware that for the first time in forty years the pounding noise of blood in his temples had finally abated.

At 9.05 a.m. James Emerson realized that he must have missed Bradley going into the building. He dashed into the lobby himself and tried to make himself understood to the receptionist.

'This is most urgent. Do you speak English?' Nods. Blank expressions. 'I must speak with Mr Akira. He is in great danger. Professor Bradley is not what he seems. You must stop the meeting!'

'Ah-so. Professor Bradley. Yes. Meeting with Mr Akira. Please wait. You wish for tea?' A hand slipped beneath the desk and pushed a button.

'No, I do not wish for any bloody tea! You must let me up! Where is he? Which floor?' And as he tried to run towards the lift bank, two stocky security guards materialized from a door concealed in an apparently blank wall and blocked his way. They were used to this. Since the crisis had broken there had been all kinds of lunatics trying to get into the building. They were usually shareholders, desperate for retribution, but Emerson was the first *gaijin* they had had to eject. And this they did, with little ceremony. As he landed on the pavement outside, the revolving entrance doors were electronically secured to prevent him from trying again.

*   *   *

Forty floors above the pavement, two rosewood doors swung inwards to reveal a diminutive figure. Yoshimi Akira was no more than five feet two or three inches tall, and the grand scale of his surroundings emphasized it. Standing in that oversized doorway he looked like a framed miniature.

In the three months since Bradley had established his true identity he had seen many photographs of the man. These tended to be head and shoulder portraits of the type used in press releases and corporate brochures, formal studio shots designed to eliminate character. But in reality, Yoshimi Akira, Chairman of the Yokosuka Corporation was exquisite. The man stood in the doorway with outstretched hand, a man Bradley knew to be at least eighty years old, yet his warm, engaging smile and loose-limbed gait as he approached his guest, were entirely disarming.

He was dressed, not in the shapeless, elephant-grey flannel of corporate Japan, but, despite the time of year, in an expertly tailored, controversially green linen suit. A brilliant white, starched but soft-collared shirt and cubist-patterned woven silk tie completed the outfit. He looked like a New York art dealer.

'Mr Bradley, I should say Professor Bradley, forgive me. This a great honour indeed. And may I be amongst the first to congratulate you!' Akira grasped Bradley's right hand with both of his and shook heartily. His English was perfect, tinged with a west coast American twang, strong and vibrant. The voice of a much younger man. Bradley was nonplussed.

'Mr Akira. I too am deeply honoured. But may I ask, for what am I to be congratulated?'

'You mean you didn't hear yet? The Nobel Prize, Professor. You have won the Nobel Prize for economics!' He pronounced it in the American way. Eck-onomics.

Bradley closed his eyes for a second. There was the faintest hint of a throbbing noise returning, as if he felt the man gaining the ascendancy, slipping away from his own control. He banished the thought, felt the sheath of his sword close to his thigh.

'Well, no, Akira-san. I must say, I had not yet heard. I have been travelling for the last few days.'

'No matter, no matter. I am delighted to be the first to inform you. Please, come in to my humble office.'

Bradley followed the man, who positively sauntered back into the office from which he had come as if he was walking down the first fairway.

'Please, make yourself comfortable.' He gestured with a casual flip of both hands to a choice of chairs, and then to the walls. 'And I'd love to hear your opinion on my collection.' Bradley surveyed the pictures which hung at eye level around the beige walls, and had to restrain himself. At first glance he counted a Kandinsky, a Miró, three Matisse, and if he didn't know any better, what looked like a Rothko.

'I saw you admiring the Warhol outside.' Bradley had been standing well away from the picture when Akira had appeared. There must be cameras, he thought. 'Andy did it for me as a joke. Not long before he died, actually. Can't stand the cherry blossom crap we're expected to hang in the public areas. Andy thought that would be a neat compromise. Pop-Jap! A new genre!!' And he threw back his head and roared with laughter.

The little man was now perched on his chair, one of those orthopaedic constructions on which he sat as if on a motorcycle, knees resting on padded supports. His posture was entirely erect, and he held his chin slightly elevated as if he were constantly viewing himself in a hidden mirror. He had a thick mane of hair, swept back off his face and held there invisibly. It was largely black still, although Bradley estimated both its colour and its gravity-defying position was the work of some other modern artist. His lean face was almost entirely triangular in shape, and when relaxed, quite smooth. It was only when he laughed, or frowned, which was less common, that one had a clue as to his age. For then his face would splinter into a series of creased contours, a mass of rounded peaks and deeply riven troughs which combined to give the impression that the man was wearing his brain on the outside.

For the most part, however, his brain was only apparent in his conversation, and Bradley quickly realized that he was dealing with an individual of considerable intellect. Here was a man who had risen to the very top of one of Japan's mightiest and most impressive *keiretsu*, whilst being equally at home in the Western idiom. He talked at length about Picasso and Ernst, before switching to Chinese philosophy and then jumping on again to Chomsky, Pinker and modern linguistic theory. He flitted from subject to subject, but not in the manner of a dilettante, a butterfly barely disturbing whatever flimsy petal upon which he alighted; much more than that, he gave the impression of being one who sees a profound underlying structure between seemingly disparate topics, which he would then graciously, though without condescension, bind together for the benefit of a possibly less well-informed audience. 'So you see, Professor, or may I call you Wallace, it's all about perception, don't you agree? In the social sciences – and despite what some of your colleagues might say, eck-onomics is, if not quite an art, most definitely no *natural* science – a rose is only a rose if enough people agree it smells and looks good. Today a rose, tomorrow a toadstool! That is the problem we have now in the world with this financial crisis. A question of misguided perceptions.'

Bradley did not know what to say. He nodded earnestly with a thin smile. He was struggling not to like the man. He forced himself to think back forty years. To a summer's afternoon, to his father's desk, to a file he found that day.

'That much is quite clear, Akira-san.'

It is clear to the examiner that this woman has suffered the most severe form of physical, sexual and mental abuse that one human being is capable of inflicting on another.

'Now, to business. It's great timing that you're here, because we Nips could use some help right now. Things aren't looking so good. Maybe you can help reorientate those perceptions?'

Gross lice infestation with boggy, secondary scalp infection.

'I imagine you are enduring some considerable difficulties.'

Extensive bruising and superficial open lacerations around wrists, ankles and neck consistent with (recent) restraint.

'Hey, you Brits are still masters of the understatement! We're going bust. What could be worse than that?'

Moist, crusted yeast infection of groins and axillae. Snail-track ulcers on oral and genital mucosa; scabies burrows on hands and genitals.

'It is true, the erosion of credit-worthiness is probably the most insidious problem afflicting the financial markets at the moment, but I fear we have yet to experience the worst.'

Multiple traumatic anal fissures with secondary bacterial overgrowth. Purulent anal discharge. Active proctitis.

'Holy moly. Worse? The currency's worthless. The banks are bust. The government's broke too. What could be worse than that?'

Foul-smelling, mucoid cervical discharge. Extreme tenderness L. fornix with cervical excitation. Numerous vulval lacerations and contusions consistent with vaginal insertion of abrasive foreign objects.

'I agree with you, Akira-san, but civil breakdown, widespread lawlessness and, ultimately, popular revolution could put this country back in the dark ages.'

The abnormally high level of sodomitical activity in this case, unusual for Japanese males generally, is indicative that this woman was given no respite from her abuse, even during times of menstruation and vaginal infection.

'Well maybe that would do us all some good, Bradley-san! A return to the age of the Samurai! A little fiscal discipline, some old-fashioned medicine!'

Regular injections of Salvarsan were administered, a toxic arsenic compound more properly referred to as arsphenamine. This has been ineffective in this case in preventing the development of syphilis, and will likely lead to further long term complications.

'Indeed, indeed. The Samurai. Yes, well. I'm not sure we should go quite so far. There are other Japanese traditions which I feel may be better suited to restoring the economy from, how can I put it, a "grass-roots" level? A return, maybe, to an agrarian economy? Agriculture, and indeed horticulture, have long been associated with your great nation. In fact, I must say I am impressed, Akira-san, not only with your collection of modern art, but also with your fine collection of cacti.' Bradley rose from his seat opposite Akira's desk and began to wander around the room, examining the plants. For a second, in defiance of all etiquette, he turned his back on his host and fumbled with the belt of his trousers. 'Tell me, do you cultivate them yourself?'

This man was known as the 'the Cactus' in Palembang. If you should run into him, you might remind him of this. As you see fit.

'Most certainly, Wallace, I do. It has been a passion all of my life. The species you see before you is *Lemaireocereus hystrix*.' Bradley inspected a repugnant-looking specimen, with tall, ribbed cylindrical stems and vicious spines. 'It's native to the arid areas of Cuba and Haiti.' He giggled before he continued. 'The locals call it the "Dildo Tree".'

When Wallace Bradley turned around, Akira was still laughing, head thrown back. His eyes had become indistinguishable from the other creased recesses with which his face was again covered, and as a consequence he did not see the sword until it's point entered his lower abdomen. By the time it had completed its journey to his sternum, he was still conscious, just, although the massive and free-flowing blood loss killed him shortly thereafter. He toppled from his posture-chair with scarcely a sound, and lay in a tiny, oozing heap on the sisal carpeting. Bradley withdrew the sword and laid it on Akira's desk. He then sat down, quite calmly, and removed two documents from his briefcase. One was a description of Akira's true identity, the other a photograph of his mother. *The* photograph. He placed them carefully on the desk next to the sword and left the room.

The office lady who greeted him outside bowed and accompanied him to the lift. She did not notice that the eminent professor was no longer limping. Bradley told her that Akira-san had become tired and wished to rest. He was not to be disturbed for another hour.

In truth, Bradley never really expected to get away with it. But then he did not really care either. He had originally considered trying to dress up the death as ritual *seppuku*, by a shamed man faced with the reality of his past and a lifelong deception, but he would have been tied up for days with the police and endless explanations. All he wanted to do was buy himself enough time to get to the airport and fly home. He knew they would catch up with him in the end, but if he could only see his mother, and tell her what he had done, that would be enough. He was humming to himself as he emerged from the lift, his head gloriously clear of the dark images of the past but filled with others. Pegasus! Pegasus, the horse which sprang from the blood of Medusa, had flown free! And Poseidon, her violator, was dead.

James Emerson was waiting for him as he emerged from the Yokosuka building.

'Professor Bradley. Bradley!' It took a few moments for Bradley to realize he was being addressed by a stranger on a Tokyo street.

'My name is James Emerson of the *Gazette*. I believe you knew my brother Hugh.'

He stopped and stared at Emerson.

'A St Mary's man, yes. I remember now. I see the family resemblance. A tragic story.'

'I have another story for you, Professor. It concerns the Pegasus Forum.'

'Oh, you gadfly, you probably think you know all about Pegasus by now, don't you? Well, I'm sure your public will find it an interesting fiction to go with their breakfast cereal or on the lavatory. Now, if you'll excuse me, I have a plane to catch.'

'Well the "fiction", as you call it, has an interesting postscript which I think you might be interested in. It concerns your son.' Bradley stopped walking away from Emerson and half turned back.

'The girl you discarded, Patsy O'Connor, has borne you a son, Professor. His name is Patrick. Would you care to see a picture of him?'

'Really, I have no time for the illusory fantasies of teenage undergraduates. Do you know she was trying to blackmail me? No doubt this fictitious child is the next step. How much does she want? What do newspapers pay for this sort of filth nowadays?'

'Oh the child is real, Professor. And yours. Look. There's a distinct family resemblance, although he doesn't really have your eyes.'

And Emerson thrust the photograph, the photograph he had asked Samuels to take and fax to him, in Bradley's face.

'But this cannot be! Look at the child! It's clearly not mine!'

'Oh, he's definitely yours. But I would say he has more than a look of his grandfather about the eyes, wouldn't you say?'

'What do you mean, man? Have you gone completely mad?'

'Oh, and another thing. I almost forgot to congratulate you.'

'Oh, you mean the Nobel Prize.'

'No. I mean for your birthday. It was yesterday, was it not? January the seventh, 1946. That makes you fifty-six. You carry it well, if I may say so.'

'Your researches are clearly not as thorough as they are reputed to be, Emerson. I was born in 1947, you fool. I'm fifty-five.'

'Professor Bradley. When your mother entered the United States in December 1945, in the care of Dr Bradley of the US Army, she was eight months pregnant. You were born in January 1946. They concealed it from you, and with good reason.'

'That cannot be, sir! My mother only met my father in October 1945! She cannot have been eight months pregnant. She was a sick woman.'

'Well, I'll think you'll find she met your father several years earlier than that.'

'Not possible! He was only sent out to the Far East after the surrender. He was a doctor, a psychiatrist by profession!'

'No, sir. Your father had no medical training. You see, he was a ship's captain.' Bradley was staring now. The drums began to beat in his temples again. 'Your father, Professor, is, or by now maybe was, Captain Kaifu Shimizu of the Japanese Navy. A man known to the world as Yoshimi Akira, Chairman of the Yokosuka Corporation. Did you enjoy meeting him?'

Bradley dropped the creased fax of the photograph he had clutched in his hand, and the flimsy paper was taken by the wind high over the skyscrapers of the Tokyo business district. It danced on the currents before fluttering back down to land in the moat surrounding the emperor's palace. The slanting eyes and straight, jet black hair of Patrick O'Connor stared out from the paper as it bobbed on the small waves before disappearing from sight under the Nijubashi Bridge.

CHAPTER 11

RESTORING THE CONFIDENCE OF THE WORLD'S FINANCIAL markets, repairing the mechanisms which the members of the Pegasus Forum had done so much to shatter, was a process, Emerson knew, which would take a long time. But the plan he had hatched with the help of Jake Samuels and Max Collins would at least give a helping hand, and the personal interventions of Byron Powell and Saul Krantz would add to it some credibility of its very own.

The morning of January the ninth began with the publication of a special edition of the *Gazette*. It was distributed for free all over the capital and it had been entirely written by Jake Samuels. In it was a complete and frank description of the activities of Wallace Bradley and the members of the Pegasus Forum. There were personal profiles of all the people involved, including photographs and family backgrounds taken from the files on Bradley's computer. There was a description of the various stages of their plan, from the initial forced insolvency of Pee Seuar Land and the Asian debacle it had prompted, through the massive currency sales of Sukon on behalf of Xenfin, and the nefarious activities of Morley Lafarge. Some of the details were not precise. Some of the gaps they had had to fill in, fabricate or imagine themselves, but that didn't matter. They presented it as fact. Many of the details they had got right though, thanks to the help of Cameron Dodds and Annie van Aalst.

Saul Krantz had put in a call to his new friend Byron Powell, who had passed the information on to the American Embassy in London concerning the whereabouts of a certain US citizen they, or the SEC, might want to talk to in connection with unauthorized dealing and the procurement of credit-lines on false pretences. When three men from the London-based detail of the CIA had burst into Dodds's apartment in the middle of the night, at around the same time that Wallace Bradley had been eviscerating Yoshimi Akira, they had discovered the couple, especially van Aalst, to be surprisingly compliant. Dodds had been a little indignant at his own rather rougher treatment, but they had both, at van Aalst's insistence, given the agents the information they had sought, and as they had been instructed, the agents had passed a copy of their statements to Samuels to reproduce in his own propaganda sheet . . .

Dodds had only really lost his temper once, when the CIA men had left him handcuffed to the bed to be picked up later by London's Serious Fraud Squad. Van Aalst they had taken with them to the embassy, where she was held on the express instructions of Byron Powell, before being whisked out of the country. She did not seem to mind.

By the end of the morning, the entire London market was talking about nothing else, and the articles Samuels had written had quickly been distributed for him all over the rest of the world by the newswires and television news services. Samuels had been right. This was 'The Emerson Bulletin' to beat all others.

All around the world, traders read of Scott Turner's arrest at Los Angeles airport on his way back to the Sudan, and Samuels added the fruits of his own warped imagination to the details of his interrogation by the FBI for supplying classified information to the public. Apart from the electric shock treatment, it turned out to be not too far from the truth after all.

They also read of the minor rôle played in the drama by Heinz-Josef von Lessing, and here Samuels had a field day. For he presented the German's participation as being the result of his father's Nazi involvement during the war, and that Bradley had sold Pegasus to him on the basis of its being a blow against Jewish control of the banks and the media. The initial sacrifice of Jakob Lichtblau and Bankhaus Löwen-Krugman had been his great pleasure. There were those on the creative team that day who thought that Samuels may have gone a little far in his invention in this particular case, and that he was almost condemning Lessing by remote control. But Samuels knew exactly what he was doing. The day after the article appeared Lessing's body was discovered in his Frankfurt apartment. The Mossad hit squad which had been despatched from Munich had slipped quietly out of the country for a few days until things had calmed down somewhat, but they need not have worried really. No one made too much of a fuss.

Nor was Johnnie Quaid spared. His personal beliefs as a communist fanatic striking an anti-capitalist blow were suitably embellished by Samuels to ensure that his future in Hong Kong would be sufficiently uncomfortable. It was simply a question of who got to him first. As it turned out, his political masters, amongst the more radical elements in Beijing, were just too late to spirit him out of the old Crown colony to parade him as a hero in Tiananmen Square. Charles Emerson, fresh back from New York, had beaten them to it. He had lunched the previous day in a small restaurant in Gerrard Street, the heart of London's Chinatown, where he owed a long-standing favour to the ageing proprietor. Quaid's home address was duly passed on to a Triad leader in Hong Kong, who saw to it that Quaid followed a similar route to his death as that taken voluntarily by P.L. Chumsai, the recipient of his letter bomb.

Morley Lafarge went straight from the orthopaedic ward of his Jakarta hospital into the custody of the local police following a tip-off from Tamana Wang and corroborative testimony from Moe and his fellow Batak Stompers. Despite earnest protestations from Mrs Lafarge through HM Ambassador in Jakarta, no official request was made by the Foreign and Commonwealth Office to secure his deportation to friendlier shores, but it was widely reported in the local press that his amply proportioned hindquarters were providing comfort and succour to the other inmates of the notorious Cipinang Prison block to which he was confined. (It would be three intolerable years before sufficient evidence was gathered by the Crown Prosecution Service to bring him home for trial for the murder of Hugh Emerson. Christopher Blake and Daniel Brookes appeared as principal witnesses for the prosecution, in exchange for which they traded the suspension on their own professional licences to practise.)

And slowly the markets began to show some signs of life.

Of course, exposing the truth would not have been enough alone. The implications of what had actually been achieved were condemnation enough of the fragility of the system, and many market commentators had been quick to point this out. What was reassuring, however, was that things were not quite as bad as everyone thought. Japan was not going to be downgraded, at least not to a single B, and Braxton Federal could be turned back into a viable concern.

But the vulnerability of the banks was still a major concern, especially in the Darwinian world of the free market, and the world's central banks had, it could not be forgotten, publicly stated that it was a question of survival of the fittest. That had been the outcome of what was still being talked about as the Cong Accord. But this was where James Emerson, and more particularly Max Collins stepped in to help.

As Yoshimi Akira had said, it was all a question of guiding perceptions. In the markets, perception *was* reality for as long as those perceptions were trusted, and for a limited period James Emerson proposed to control those perceptions. For between them, Samuels, Collins and Emerson were going to create their own version of 'reality'. To Collins it was like one big video game.

He had spent the time, whilst Emerson was away, gaining access to the servers which controlled the output of the major newswires: Reuters, Dow Jones, Bloomberg, and several others. He had gained entry to their networks and accorded himself all sorts of privileges. Most notably these included direct input to the newsfeeds, the actual text which would be flashed on to trading screens all over the dealing world. What Emerson, Collins and Samuels then spent the rest of the day doing was creating their own version of the news. For a while they were playing at being fate.

They did not want to overdo it, of course, and they stopped short at fabricating stock prices or exchange rates. That would have been too apparent, too readily contradicted by the prices visible on the exchanges around the world. And they had to restrain Collins, who was like a child in a sweetshop, from making spurious announcements about volcanic eruptions in Monte Carlo and plagues of locusts in Oslo. But they still had lots of fun, limited only by their own imaginations and guided by Emerson's market expertise.

They announced reports of putative cuts in interest rates, they made bogus releases of key economic data, they even reported on an alleged major oil find off the coast of Indonesia. With Bruce Phipps's blessing they put out stories regarding potential rating upgrades in the credit markets, news of a major release of gold reserves by the Russian Government, even a decision by OPEC to boost oil production in an attempt to damp down global inflation of commodity prices. None of it was true.

And the engineers at Reuters and the other news services had no idea where these reports were coming from. They knew *they* were not putting them out, but if not they, then who? The last thing they wanted to do was question the authenticity of reports being made on their screens all over the world. So the London bureau blamed the New York bureau and everyone else blamed Tokyo, but they did not shut the system down and the reports continued to appear. Good news, after good news, after good news.

And soon the market traders began to cotton on to the fact that this was a one-way street. The signs of life that had been in evidence on publication of the *Gazette*'s special edition and its revelations of the conspiracy began to blossom into full-blown bullish activity, and the stock and bond markets of the world began to rise together for the first time in several weeks. Credit spreads began to narrow, currencies in Asia strengthened and investors began to see light at the end of the tunnel.

This was all well and good, but the real problem had never been the weakness of the markets. The much more fundamental problem was a lack of confidence in the banking system and the concept of currency as a medium of exchange. This had been Bradley's major weapon, and it was this that had caused the rioting, the violence, the deaths all over the world. And this is where the clever idea suggested by Byron Powell in his meeting with Charles Emerson a few days earlier came into play.

Up until that point they had been dreaming up imaginary events which the markets would view as positive, and presenting them as reality via a trusted medium. What they really needed to do was to give the public the confidence to take its first, faltering steps on the road back to trusting the entire *system*, and what Powell had suggested they do was really quite scandalous, but beautiful in its ingenuity and simplicity. And this is what they did.

Over the course of that morning the finance ministers and central bank chiefs of all EU-member states 'made' a coordinated series of statements. They talked about the Cong Accord, and how they had perhaps been too hasty in advocating such a *laissez-faire* approach. They realized that, in the light of what had been happening, it was perhaps better to exert a light rein over the previously unrestrained free market, and henceforth it would be stated EU policy to step in to support any bank seen to be in trouble. Limited currency controls would be introduced between the Euro-zone and the rest of the world, and working parties set up to explore the possibility of returning to a new Gold Standard. The Governor of the Bank of England was quoted as saying that the three banks which had been forced to close their doors would be reopened as soon as practically possible, and that all their commitments would be guaranteed by the British Government. In short, as Max Collins had expressed it, they put 'virtual' words into the mouths of real people.

The television news services were astonished. Where were these statements being made? How had the newswires got hold of them? Why hadn't *they* been sent the press releases? But they swallowed their pride and reported them anyway. The traders in the dealing rooms all over the world were astonished at such a *volte-face* from the officials, astonished but delighted, and in time they began to buy the hell out of the bank stocks and the bond market.

There was, of course, nobody more astonished than the finance ministers and the central bank chiefs of the EU-member states, seeing themselves quoted by reporters on the television from speeches they had never made. But then everyone saw Byron Powell. He *was* on television. In the flesh. This was the agreement he had promised Charles Emerson during their meeting.

And in front of millions of viewers worldwide he, Byron Powell, the most powerful banker in the world and guardian of the global economy, declared himself surprised but cautiously optimistic at the coordinated statements coming out of Europe, and that he would be very happy to meet, at their earliest convenience, to renegotiate the Cong Accord in terms that were more appropriate to the current economic environment.

And then he made a very public gesture, which was no less effective than, if not quite as colourful as, that of Sir Peter Taverton a few days previously. He took a copy of the Cong Accord and tore it up on global television. 'Ladies and gentlemen. We are here to protect the value of our currency, and by extension the value of the savings of our people. Central bankers cannot always take popular measures, we cannot be dictated to by markets, but when I see the reaction of those markets to the statements coming out of Europe, it is clear to me that we have to explore a solution along those lines. Thank you.'

'James, man, pick up the phone. It's Jake for you.'

'Hi Jake. What do you think?'

'A masterstroke, James. Love it. I can't believe your father persuaded Powell to say that stuff.'

'Oh he didn't. It was Powell's own idea. Seemed to work pretty well though. Things seem to be straightening themselves out.'

'It'll take a while. But in the meantime on to the next thing, eh? No use dwelling on yesterday's news in this business. You're only as good as your next story, I always say. Anyhow, I've been put on to a story I want you to look into about . . .' Emerson hung up and thought back to Powell's idea. It was very clever, frighteningly simple and went to the heart of how finance operated these days. He smiled to himself.

As children he and Hugh had played similar games on their father. The script was almost identical. '*Dad, may we go to a party tonight? Simon's parents say he can go.*' Yes son. Then to Simon's parents: '*Dad, may I go to a party tonight? James's father says they can go.*' It only needed one to say yes, and the others would go along. Byron Powell had said yes. The others would fall in. In fact, they would soon be congratulating themselves on having had the foresight to make those statements in the first place.

When he had worked in banking it had been just the same. His clients always wanted to know what everyone else was doing so they could do it themselves. It did not really matter in the end what they did as long as they were not wildly out of line with everyone else.

It was all the same game, just a question of the stakes.

EPILOGUE

AS PROTOCOL DEMANDED, WHEN ANNIE VAN ALAST ARRIVED back in New York she was handed over by the CIA agent who had escorted her on the civil flight into the hands of the waiting FBI. The CIA man was surprised that the welcoming committee comprised no less than the Deputy-Director himself. He handed over his charge with a few last minute words of advice. 'You're in some kinda serious shit now, honey. You know who this guy is? I reckon you should breathe as much fresh air as you can before these guys throw away the key.'

'Don't worry about me.' She seemed cool, unconcerned. 'I guess I should've been expecting something like this,' and she climbed into the back of the waiting sedan.

She rode the entire journey into Manhattan in silence alongside the Deputy-Director of the FBI, the same man whom Byron Powell had phoned to tip off about the activity of Scott Turner during his conference with Charles Emerson. The car cruised finally into Liberty Street and pulled up outside the New York offices of the Federal Reserve.

Van Aalst's escort sprang from the car first and ran round to open her door. He then guided her inside the building and announced their arrival to the security guards at reception.

'She's all yours now,' the FBI man said, and handed her into their custody. Five minutes later she was sitting in a leather armchair in the private office of the world's most powerful banker. Byron Powell sat behind his desk and had not troubled himself to rise as she had been ushered in. The reflection of his desk lamp in his glasses was set at such an angle as to shield his eyes from direct scrutiny.

'Well, thank you for joining me so quickly, young lady. Drink?' Byron Powell was politeness itself.

'Better here than left to the mercy of those Brits. They suffered a lot more than we did over here. I'll have a vodka ginger ale.'

'Yes, well I was of course in a position to control the situation somewhat better than my colleagues in London.' Now he rose and walked to a cupboard in the panelled wall concealing a well-stocked drinks cabinet. He poured the drink personally, a generous measure. 'But I do think they'll get things back on track before long.'

'Yes. I'm sure you're right. Not like our friends in Tokyo.'

'Quite. There it will take some time. But again it will happen. No irreparable damage has been caused. The Pegasus Forum did not entirely succeed.'

'Thank God. But we did enough, don't you think?'

'Oh yes, Annie. You were quite remarkable. In fact I think you probably saved us a good five, if not ten years in terms of our bargaining position *vis-à-vis* Tokyo. They would have dug themselves into a similar hole in the fullness of time, I'm quite sure of that, but maybe we would not have been in such a strong position to exploit it then, who knows?'

'Well, after ten years of boom-time, corporate America is still pretty much fully loaded, isn't it, even after the recent problems?'

'Absolutely. That was the key, really. That was the reason I could afford to let your little games run. *We* could afford it, at least in the short run. I was prepared to allow you, and they could not. They've been pricing us out of business in our own back yard for twenty years, and we let 'em do it without getting a sniff of a look-in on their territory. When you approached me the opportunity was obvious.'

'But I guess you couldn't have been seen to be involved in anything like that yourself.'

'God no. Of course we've tried in the past. I'd like to say we had a hand in the bursting of the Japanese economic bubble ten years ago. But even that backfired. The yen devalued and our exporters lost out big. And don't forget, official means, even covert official means, take too long and Bradley was too good an opportunity to pass up. When you approached me it was like a dream come true. We had a perfect fall guy, a crazy stool pigeon who would do our work for us.'

'You did well with Turner too. Promoting him to Bank Supervision was a masterstroke.'

'Well I needed someone with me at Cong to put the case. I personally couldn't be seen to be pushing *too* hard, so I gave him his head for a while and he made a most convincing case.'

'But didn't the FBI cotton on? Didn't they question how you knew where he was when you called them to pick him up?'

'No, no. They were just glad of the arrest. But I needed the favour in the bank with them to secure *your* return to freedom.'

'Well thanks, Byron. And now comes the fun part.'

'Too damn right. Corporate America is going on a buying spree.'

'"Jeez, if Uncle Sam had any money left he could buy up Japan Inc. for the price of a Big Mac!"'

'You noticed that one, good.'

'A "highly placed" anonymous source at the US Federal Reserve? Gimme a break!'

'Thought you would. Hope it wasn't too obvious to the rest of the world! Just my little message to you. Let you know we were still on.'

'Who did you leak it to, as a matter of interest?'

'Oh, Hal Bramfield at the *Washington Post*. He and I go way back. Before Watergate even. He could hardly believe it when Charles Emerson approached him for information on Bradley. I'd had him check that information out when you and I first spoke. The main difficulty was getting him to wait as long as he did before giving Emerson the information he wanted.'

'So who's first on the shopping list?'

'Well, I've spoken to some of the guys in Detroit. I think one or two of them will be making a move early tomorrow. Toyota's the prize, and they'll slug it out amongst themselves who gets it, but whatever happens, the price'll be a joke. Then I think we'll see some activity in consumer electronics. Sony, maybe, or one of the other biggies will be under the Stars and Stripes before long. It'll be a reverse takeover, Annie, Uncle Sam riding into the Rising Sun, and not before time.'

'Well, all I can say is, glad to be of service, Chairman Powell. Now. About that banking licence . . .'

The doctors' mess at Aldate's Grange was a fine Georgian drawing room by most standards, very large, in keeping with the stature of the once splendid residence, and furnished accordingly. The languid pulse of an oak long-case clock in one corner seemed to slow the pace of life, and various overstuffed armchairs and sofas arranged around the space, strewn with a selection of well-thumbed, old periodicals, completed the image of the rural dentist's waiting-room or Agatha Christie stage-set. It was a relaxing setting in which the staff could unwind, and well out of earshot of any screaming, wailing or other such noises as might emanate from the less stable inmates.

But this evening it had been converted into a makeshift screening room for the benefit of the visitor. Heavy brocade curtains had been drawn across the three pairs of French windows which normally looked out across the lawns where the patients would take their afternoon air, and a large, old-fashioned 16 mm projector, all Bakelite and chrome, had been set up on a green baize card table in the middle of the room. A couple of slim volumes had been placed under the projector's front feet to achieve the desired elevation for projection on to the rudimentary screen, which was nothing more than an old white bedsheet stretched across a large wooden frame knocked together by the clinic's handyman, and which had been positioned on an antique mahogany easel borrowed for the evening from the art-therapy stockroom.

A tall man in a long white coat fussed over the projector with a small can of oil and a soft photographic-quality brush for cleaning the lens. As the double doors to the room opened, the man looked up and straightened to greet his guest.

'Professor Wasserman, what a tremendous pleasure. I am so grateful to you for taking the time to visit us personally. It is a great honour. How is the weather in Washington at this time of the year?'

'It is a hell of a lot colder than Oxfordshire, Doctor. I am very happy to be here. I felt I really had to deliver the film personally. It isn't every day the military lets us into their archives. I'm very much looking forward to seeing it.'

'You mean you haven't viewed it yet yourself?'

'Hell, no. That would have been criminal. It was only your persistence that led to this bit of history being released, and I must say, after your letters I've had a hankering to meet both you *and* the patients. Mother and son. Seems like an extraordinary case. You've had *her* here for what, twenty-five years?'

'Close to it. She came to us in seventy-seven. Before that she'd been passed around a bit. Both here and in Switzerland. Nobody could do much, I'm afraid.'

'And you personally have had sole care for how long?'

'Thirteen years.'

'And she has uttered no word to you or to any other member of staff since?'

'That is correct, Professor. Not even to her son, who used to visit every day.'

'He was the university guy, right?'

'Yes. A professor like yourself. Most highly regarded. Economist. As I said, he used to come every day. They would sit staring at each other. No words necessary, he used to say.'

'So what exactly triggered her condition?'

'The profound trauma she suffered, back in '62. The boy was only sixteen at the time, and away at school. He took it very badly. Nobody told him about the suicide. As far as he was concerned, his father was killed in a car crash. He effectively lost both parents that day.'

'But until then there had been no signs of any abnormal behaviour?'

'Absolutely none.'

'From neither of them?'

'Well, the father had a small record during the war. Minor run-ins with the Military Police. Dust-ups in the local brothels out east. At least, those are the instances we know of. There are probably more, but those sort of attacks tend to get hushed up. Looking back I suppose they were hints at what was to come. But nothing like what happened in '62. That was a particularly vicious attack.'

'So that was the first example of true psychopathic behaviour?'

'Quite so. Mrs Bradley was very badly damaged. And she has not spoken a word since. We didn't really know about PTSD at the time. If she'd had the correct treatment back then, maybe she wouldn't need to be still in here today. Anyhow, I am most curious to see the film. I hope it will shed some light, if only on the mindset of Bradley himself. We may be able to learn something which will help us in the treatment of the son. Her original medical notes from the time are missing, so we don't know precisely what happened to her during the war. I think Bradley had them and destroyed them.'

'All we really know is that in the camp she was well looked after by Shimizu.'

'The botanist.'

'That's right. He took her out of the camp at an early stage. Installed her in his own quarters. He was a sensitive man. Probably one of the first truly scientific homeopaths. Treated her with plant extracts.'

'From his beloved cacti.'

'Yes. He was quite an expert. Although he was lucky.'

'Why do you say that?'

'Well, the species he favoured was a large, erect plant known as *Lemaireocereus hystrix*. But he misinterpreted the name.'

'Go on.'

'Well he thought the Latin word *hystrix* referred to *hustera*, the Greek for uterus, the same root which gives us words like hysteria and hysterectomy. He thought it had been named because of its uterine healing properties, and he made creams and potions and even drinks from these plants. He made her use them and take them, thought it would keep her gynaecologically healthy.'

'But he was wrong?'

'Well, yes and no. You see, it turns out the alkaloids present in the cactus do have mild healing qualities, a bit like aloe vera or arnica. Did her no harm, and may have done her a bit of good. But not in the way he intended.'

'But the *hystrix* part. What's that all about?'

'Oh that. That's nothing to do with the uterus. It's actually Latin for porcupine. As I said. Shimizu got lucky. Good intentions and all that.'

The English doctor gestured to a file which lay open on the table next to them. A black and white photograph of a nurse in a starched white cap beamed out from the first page. 'But there was nothing like this rubbish. Not in her case. Our Dr Bradley was very creative, you know. He concocted the whole thing himself.'

'It continues to amaze me. The creativity of the psychotic mind. If only one could harness it and eliminate the violent side.'

The portly visitor balanced his briefcase on the arm of one the sofas and fiddled with the combination. He opened the case and pulled out a large round flat film can – old, gunmetal grey with the occasional dent and scratch – and handed it to his host, who examined it with interest. A faded and torn label on one side of the can told of its origins: *United States Psychological Warfare Team. G-2. Palembang. Dutch East Indies, 1945.* A tape was fastened around the seam of the two halves of the can and sealed with a lightweight wax tab, which bore the letters 'J.W.B. – 1947.'

'This has not seen the light of day for fifty years, Professor. It seems almost sacrilegious to break the silence now.'

'For God's sake, man. You were the one who spent the last five years lobbying for the release of this material. Don't get squeamish on me now. We have to see this. I have travelled thousands of miles to see this with you, and I will not be disappointed.'

'But look at the initials on the seal – J.W.B. – you realize who the last man on Earth to see this film was? Jason Bradley himself. I don't imagine he ever dreamed that this evidence would see the light of day again. At least while his wife was still alive. Maybe it shouldn't.'

'Jason Bradley buried this film in the archives with good reason. He couldn't afford for it to be found. Don't forget, he was a professional. One of our own profession, and a damned good psychiatrist to boot. I took the trouble of looking him up before I came over here. Before this little episode he had had a thriving practice in New York. Serious, mainstream therapy, diseases of the rich as somebody put it. The war put all that on hold of course, but he never went back to it. The Psychological Warfare Team was a natural fit for him, and he took to it immediately. But he dissimulated extremely well. Nobody in his unit had any idea just how sick a man he was. In his defence, I don't think anything in his training had prepared him for the things he saw in those camps. Or for meeting the lady you have sedated down the hall. He was obsessed by her. At least until '62.'

'But they were married for Christ's sake. Surely it was more than some psychotic fixation?'

'For her, of course. But as I said. He was extremely creative, and well-practised at deception. And he gave her a son.'

'Ideal therapy, really. Especially after the still-birth, and having to abandon the man she had loved.'

'Captain Shimizu. Or should I say Yoshimi Akira.'

'Indeed. Bradley was a doctor and a psychiatrist himself, don't forget. He knew how important it was for her to have a child. Blood relations were something she had never known. She was adopted, you see. A foundling. Abandoned on the hospital steps in Christchurch and brought up by an Australian couple living in New Zealand. We don't know who her real parents were, but judging by the O'Connor child's appearance, one of them was probably Maori. The father I guess. The mother probably couldn't bear the shame of it in those days, hence the abandonment.'

'And those genes waited a couple of generations before making themselves known.'

'Yes. A throwback. It's very rare. No sign of it at all in Charlotte Bradley or her son.'

'Well, we know whose genes *he* inherited.'

'But Charlotte remained a whore in her husband's eyes. Is that what you are saying?'

'Oh yes. And he must have loved it. That was his thing. When he saw what was going on in those camps, it was his dream, his crazy, sick, psychotic dream made real. The medical file found in his desk by the son after the suicide, that was all Jason Bradley's doing. He made it up. It was his fantasy. Oh, he had *seen* women in that state. He had examined them, and treated them. It makes my flesh creep to think how he must have enjoyed it. But Charlotte Bradley was never like that. She came back well fed, well nourished and very pregnant. She had been singled out for special treatment by Shimizu. It was Bradley who created that sordid past for her, because that is what he wanted her to have been through. That gave him his thrills. He just based it on some other cases he'd seen and would read it to himself like some kind of sick pornography.'

'So from what we know of his subsequent behaviour, he must also have been very distraught when she miscarried Shimizu's child.'

'Yes. He would have loved to have had the fruit of her imagined violation running around in his house. The child would have been a constant reminder of what he imagined had gone on. That is why he wanted another child so quickly afterwards. After Wallace was born, he even changed the boy's birth certificate so the dates matched. For him, Wallace *was* Shimizu's child. He even managed to fool that journalist, Emerson, over fifty years later. But he could not fool us. He was a doctor but he made a bad mistake, really. Too long a psychiatrist if you ask me.'

'What was it?'

'Well if the mother, Drabble, *had* been suffering the symptoms he describes in his report at the time, riddled with syphilis, and been delivered of the young Wallace shortly thereafter, there is no way the offspring could have avoided it. Congenital syphilis is a nasty thing to inherit from one's mother. The child would clearly have suffered some form of birth defect, some form of abnormality.'

'But he didn't.'

'No. I examined him last week. He's in perfect shape in that respect, apart from, of course, upstairs.'

'But what triggered the father's final frenzy?'

'I guess in the end, the fictional background of violence he had created for his wife was not enough for him. He needed the real thing, and that is what happened in the Summer of '62. He tried to make the script he had written become reality. *Exactly* what triggered that outburst we will never know.'

'Maybe the brothels he used to visit weren't enough for him any more?'

'Whatever. But he took it all out on his wife and then he committed suicide.'

'And when the sixteen-year-old son found the bogus file . . .'

'He jumped to the wrong conclusion. Who wouldn't have? It was very authentic looking.'

'And the son turned out to be just as sick as the real father.'

'Yes. It's definitely genetic. He created the Pegasus Forum. You remember, all that fuss in the financial markets a few months back. But that's another story.'

In another room along the corridor a man with bandaged hands sat holding a newspaper. His frown of concentration was intense, yet the scene would have been unremarkable but for the fact that the steel door to his outside world was securely locked, the room itself was in complete darkness and he had been staring at the same page of the newspaper for almost eighteen hours.

The fingers with which he grasped the paper were still relatively freshly snapped, the bones not yet knitting together as a result of the great force used by the burly Jamaican orderly to prise them from the throat of the elderly lady patient, in his care for almost fifteen years. The article at which the man stared was a small piece in the *Washington Post* describing the launch party for a new 'ethical' on-line bank based in South Carolina called TuLiP. The Chairman and Chief Executive of the new company was listed as one Anna Mieke van Aalst, and the President was Cameron L. Dodds.

The elaborate cocktail of chemicals oozed around the man's brain but they could not quieten the screams, the voices. The blood was pounding in his temples again.

Afterword

At the time of writing the world is looking anxiously at the markets.

Everyone's former darling the NASDAQ has lost more than sixty per cent of its value in the last twelve months (thirty in the last two) and the Japanese Government has just cut interest rates to zero as their economy implodes.

How timely, I hear you cry, and maybe even a touch callous and mercenary, to be rushing out a novel about market catastrophes!

Alas, and my agent and publisher will ruefully vouch for this, I cannot claim to have jumped on a bear bandwagon and bashed this out in the last three months while the markets crashed around us; nor can I lay claim, although I do not actually hear you crying this, to any great feats of foresight. Luck then? Well maybe not.

The fact is that the world is always looking anxiously at some market or other. It was doing when I started writing over three years ago, has done on numerous occasions since, and is again now. And I am sure it will regularly continue to do so, because the Free Market must have its dark side.

But in what sense are the markets 'free'? And is it a good thing? Even the shorter version of the Oxford English Dictionary has no less than twenty-nine definitions of the word, almost all of them enjoying positive connotations (a possible exception being 'free verse'). 'Free' things are good, are they not? Free love, free speech, free will, free votes, free gifts, free bus-passes, free houses, free-range. They smack of lovely things we admire, such as abundance, liberty, democracy, value, pleasure, even health. But I suspect the almost unconditional admiration for the 'free market' has been amassed by semantic association. Most of our markets are indeed free, but in a more ruthless, Darwinian sense, in the manner of wild animals – free to maul you and have you for lunch. And, as we are often told, lunch, especially the ten-year lunch we have been enjoying in the stock markets, is never free.

Need we always worry so? Markets will always go up in the long run, we are told by our independent financial advisers, and that has been true for a long time. But then again, to risk paraphrasing Keynes, in the long run we are *all* broke.

DS

London, March 2001